The Voice in Your Ear

The Voice in Your Ear

Steve Piscitelli

The Growth and Resilience Network®

Also by Steve Piscitelli

*Sharing Wisdom Across the Ages:
From Elementary School to Retirement*

Roxie Looks for Purpose Beyond the Biscuit

Community as a Safe Place to Land

*Stories about Teaching, Learning, and Resilience:
No Need to be an Island*

Choices for College Success, 1st, 2nd, & 3rd editions

*Study Skills: Do I Really Need This Stuff? 1st, 2nd, & 3rd
editions*

Engaging Activities for Student Success

*I Don't Need This Stuff! Or Do I?
A Study Skills and Time Management Book*

*Does Anyone Understand This Stuff? A Student Guide to
Organizing United States History, 1st, & 2nd editions*

DEDICATION

To all who struggle for inner peace, respect, and visibility.
May we find comfort in ourselves and with each other.

GRATITUDE

As with all my books, I benefited from a diverse group of people who reviewed my efforts and provided input. Their help proved invaluable. Any errors or shortcomings in this book fall on my shoulders.

Some read an early draft of the entire manuscript and gave me suggestions to improve various aspects of the story. They shared frank feedback about what they liked, what worked, and what did not connect with them.

Others helped with background information, a scene review, or cover design input.

Ann Pearson did the deep dive and provided a detailed manuscript critique. She helped me develop, clarify, and enhance elements of tone, character, and plot development.

Mike Shackelford, Roy Peak, and Tamara Colonna shared their thoughts about music's impact on the musician's life. They drew from decades of personal musical experiences. Billy Bowers helped me record my song *The Voice in Your Ear.* I appreciate their input and friendship.

My heartfelt gratitude goes to (in alphabetical order): Amy Judd, Ann Pearson, Barbara Coen, Billy Bowers, Eileen Crawford, Gary Bilderback, Kevin Brown, Kevin Gay, Jim November, Joe Cuseo, John Louis Meeks, Jr., Judy Coady, Laurie Piscitelli, Linda M. Lanier, Mike Shackelford, Roy Peak, Roz Hoffman, Sande Johnson, Shawn Eager, Tamara Colonna, Tim Deegan, and Vic Gaulillo.

1

"I don't want him fired, damn it! I want him dead!" The Senator pounded his oak conference table, and the coffee spewed from his visitors' cups.

"You don't mean that," Doyle Bartley stammered. "I mean. I mean that would be an extraordinarily bad thing to do. Kill someone. Extraordinarily bad. Extraordinarily." His thin-fingered hands shook as he raised his coffee cup to his pale, skinny lips. Halfway up, the coffee was sloshing out. Pat Turkle reached across the table and steadied his president's hand.

"Doyle, of course, Senator Wackenslong doesn't mean *that*."

"Really? I don't? So both of you want to spend the next 20 to 30 years in prison? Trust me. Neither one of you is built for doing time!" He mashed the unmute button on his office TV's remote and pointed toward the wall. "Look at this!"

A throng of inner-city residents had reached the gates of the proposed construction site. The protestors resembled the residents of so many other inner-city communities.

Multi-ethnic, underemployed, displaced by gentrification, and battling age-old discrimination and prejudice. They held protest signs proclaiming: "Stop Corporate Greed!" "You Are Killing Us!" "Invisible No More!" The crowd cheered as a dozen or so picketers stretched out on the ground in front of the smoke-belching heavy equipment revving up to begin the project.

Behind the gate stood a row of crumbling mid-century buildings. All had "CONDEMNED" signs taped to their doors. Most of the windows had been shattered by stones. The trash piled up along the street. Not long ago, this was a living, breathing community with two and three-story walk-ups and mom-and-pop businesses on their first floors. That was before the chain stores and online businesses began to suck the prosperity out of the neighborhood. Now, the area needed life support. Landlords sold the property to private investors and fled the area. The residents had no such option.

"We are residents of Marina Norte, Florida, just like the rich people. Just like the politicians." The leader of the protestors, a full-bodied African American woman with waist-long dreadlocks sported a rainbow-colored shirt with the words "Invisible No More!" as she yelled into a handheld megaphone.

"The so-called city leaders need to hear us *and* see us!"

The crowd chanted, "Invisible no more! Invisible no more! See us! Hear us! Invisible no more!"

The senator muted the TV and tossed the remote on the table. He paced a few steps before he sat down and pounded the conference table again.

"Invisible no more!" he yelled. "Does that sound familiar, gentlemen? Huh?"

"Incredibly, I have not heard that before, Senator," Bartley said as his eyes darted between Turkle and the senator.

"It comes, as I understand the story, from one of your professors," Wackenslong said with pursed lips and widening eyes. "Some group he sponsors to help...let me see if I can remember the academic drivel...*to help his marginalized students find their voice in society.*" He glared at the two men in suits at his table. "Does *that* ring a bell?"

Pat Turkle thought he saw a tear dribble down Bartley's cheek.

"That would be Professor Cole Fitzgerald," Turkle said. As the Director of Human Resources for Central City College he was well aware of the professor.

"Doyle, take a break. Go wash your face. When you come back the Senator will have caught his breath. We'll finish this and get to the performing arts center for our opening ceremony."

Wackenslong's eyes turned to a squint.

Bartley mumbled and excused himself. As Wackenslong readied his next volley, Turkle pushed slightly against the back of his chair. A strategy he learned in mindfulness training years ago was to lean away from the noise. At least, he tried to.

"What the hell is wrong with him?" Wackenslong asked pointing toward the bathroom door. "He's the president of the college but acts like a first-year student on his first date. Geez, has he no freaking balls?"

"He's fine. He's a thinker, Senator. He is still building his support base to accomplish our plans."

"Well, he needs to start *doing*." The senator said pointing toward the muted screen on the wall, "This is unacceptable. My family has a lot riding on this industrial park being created. Those people have nothing in their community. Nothing! This will bring them jobs—especially in the apparel warehouse. Our representatives had talked with, what we thought, were the de facto leaders of those, *those* people. Looks like your professor has riled them up. Damn it! Do something about this. Do something about him!" The senator clicked off the TV. "The college event starts in 90 minutes. I hope our president can act presidential and get things moving in the right direction."

Bartley entered the office wringing his hands as if he were still washing them in the restroom. "Pat, don't you think it's time to get to the convocation?" Bartley asked. Then he looked at the Senator like a student asking for a hall pass.

Turkle nodded his head and stood up. The senator remained seated and grim-faced. "Pat," he said, "we need to talk."

"Me, too?" Bartley asked hoping the answer would be no.

"You go. Pat and I will be there shortly."

"It will be an incredible event! Especially, when I introduce you, Senator. Extraordinarily incredible!" Bartley said as he quickly escaped through the office door. Wackenslong shook his head in disgust at the departing president.

"Pat. Do you remember when you and I first met?"

"No way I could forget. Homecoming basketball game. You heard Wendi was interested in one of the players and wanted to meet him."

Wackenslong's eyes drifted toward the photo on his desk of a young woman and small child smiling and snuggling together on a sofa. "More like I wanted to make sure you knew who was the man of the house already."

"Never any doubt."

"Never in my mind. But all Wendi talked about was 'The Young Turk'."

Turkle smiled as he lowered his head in remembrance of his college nickname. "The coach called me that. I wasn't fond of it, at first. But it caught on. I grew to like it. A long time ago. Don't much feel like that now." He rubbed his right knee. "God, I miss them," he said nodding toward the photo.

"Me, too, Pat." The senator cleared his throat and turned his stare back at Turkle. "You were The Young Turk because you took control of the game whether you were blocking a shot, scoring points, or cheering from the bench. Your teammates loved you for your tenacity, discipline, and commitment. And so did my Wendi."

They both sat silent for a moment before the Senator continued. "Pat, I was never the greatest father. I tried, but the family business took so much of my time. Wendi's mother, God rest her soul, did a great job stepping in when I wasn't available. Which was often. Then you entered our lives. I saw early on the bond you and my daughter had. And," the senator paused and cleared his throat again, "when she fought for her life, you never faltered, never left her side."

"We were one. The thought of *not* being by her side never entered my mind."

"I know. Then Bridgette dies. Again, you never wavered. I don't know how you managed to keep it together. Your teammates got it right. You are The Young Turk!" Wackenslong managed a smile.

"I was, then. Now, I have memories," Turkle said.

"You still are and you are about to build new memories. You never lost that discipline and commitment to a goal. That is why I believe in you, got Bartley to hire you, and know you are the guy we need now."

"That means a lot, Senator."

"I need you—we need you—to help Bartley get control of the ship. We don't need distractions. We need action. No prisoners. What was that saying you said your military dad told you?"

"Don't piss on someone when they have a gun to your head," Turkle said.

"You and Bartley have institutional power. Remind your president that's your *gun*. You both need to use it when anyone—especially loud-mouthed faculty—attempts to piss on our plans. Got it?"

"Yes, sir. I got it."

As Turkle got up from the table, he read an incoming text from his administrative assistant. The letter had been delivered. The ball was now in Professor Fitzgerald's court.

• • •

The protest crowd split in two. One remained at the gates creating a human shield against the trucks, payloaders, and workers ready to start demolition of the rundown seventy-five-year-old row houses standing in the way of an industrial park that would welcome one of the nation's largest online retailers. The other group marched on to the Marina Norte city hall about one mile up Main Street. Cole Fitzgerald walked behind the community leaders. Earlier that morning, Cole had delivered a few comments as the protestors gathered at their community headquarters.

While he was invited by one of the founders of the organizing group "Invisible No More," his participation had been challenged by others.

"How does a white man understand what our community experiences and needs?" was a question floating within the inner city leadership circle. "How does this help us?"

"He's here because he cares. He taught, listened to, and helped my son find direction. We need and can use his visibility to help us with our invisibility," the founder of the community-based group said.

The protestors marched past the homeless encamped on the sidewalk and in various abandoned lots. Every city block they walked by had two or three boarded-up businesses. About halfway between the construction site and city hall, they walked by Central City College, a forty-thousand-student multi-campus institution. Even though the box-like 1960s architecture of the urban campus lacked the pizazz of a larger state university, it had become a focal point for the inner city. About 85% of the student population was what the power structure referred to as the *minority population*. The community referred to themselves as *marginalized*. Ignored by the entrenched unless they needed cheap labor or votes, the residents experienced all imaginable economic, social, *and* political deprivations. While not as old as the surrounding buildings, the compact urban campus was beginning to show its age.

During the two decades Cole taught at CCC, he came to recognize the need for a student safe space to have conversations about race, gender, ethnicity, and disability. Cole learned, with the help of his students, that the various demographics and labels could not be separated. They intersected and created separate and distinct dynamics that the mostly white power structure couldn't even begin to understand. In most cases, they didn't care to understand and didn't try. Cole's so-called safe place was a corner of his cramped campus office where many conversations started. No one was quite sure why, but it acquired the name of *Ian's Corner.* The conversations often expanded to the courtyard, café, and classroom.

"Part of standing up to the power structure," Cole would tell his students, "is first, learning how to stand up for yourself." It was an uphill battle that he waged one student at a time. And one that he experienced himself.

As the protestors reached city hall, news cameras and microphones stood rigidly in front of the white marble steps. The crowd continued chanting "Invisible No More." The group's leaders ascended the stairs. Cole remained on the sidewalk with the rest of the crowd. It was neither his event nor his classroom. He marched to show support. One of the local news reporters thrust a microphone in Cole's face. "Excuse me, I was told you're a professor at Central City College. Why are *you* here today?"

"For my students and our community," said Cole looking directly at the reporter. "There is no Central City College without a community, without *this* community. We need our elected officials to understand they represent the entire community. We need more government to help our marginalized citizens, not less government to further enrich the elite."

"You tell 'em, Marco!" Cole looked to his left at a short woman in bright white horned-rimmed sunglasses. She held one of the "Invisible No More" signs. Cole shook his head and smiled as he said to himself, "Aunt Philomena."

The eager reporter then leaned toward the preacher standing next to Cole. "Sir, do you agree with the professor?"

As the preacher reached for the microphone, Cole looked at his watch and nodded to the march's organizer. Classes begin tomorrow. Today, to Cole's regret, the college had its annual convocation. A command performance he never enjoyed. He waved to the lady in the white sunglasses and discreetly made his way back to campus.

Once there, he picked up his campus mail. One of the envelopes, from the college Director of Human Resources office, had **URGENT** stamped in big red letters. At the top of the one-page letter, he saw the words, also in big red let-ters, **CEASE-AND-DESIST**.

> *Dear Professor Fitzgerald. With the full backing of the Central City College Leadership Team and Board of Trustees, I hereby relay the message that you are ordered to suspend your on-campus club, Ian's Corner, immediately. It has been found to violate the intersectionality edict recently issued by the state governor.*
>
> *Sincerely,*
> *Patrick Turkle, Ed.D.*
> *Director of Human Resources*
> *Central City College.*

• • •

2

What's it gonna be, Cole? Old complaints for a new semester? Maybe today you'll make a difference and they'll notice you? Time to move forward or end it.

The voice. The ever-present force that intruded upon his thoughts. Or did it create his thoughts? Would he—could he—silence it today?

He paused for a moment, shook his head, and then pulled on the glass door entering the three-story tiled auditorium lobby of the *Wackenslong Center for Performing Arts*. Located on the urban campus of Central City College, the center hosted concerts, plays, and guest speakers throughout the year. In recognition of a sizeable donation to the college's fine arts department and development fund, the center was named for the Wackenslong family when it was built and dedicated some twenty years ago.

"Hey, Cole! Over here!"

Professor Benny DiJohn leaned against a makeshift coffee table on the edge of the lobby. Raising a disposable cup above his round bald head, he waved to get Cole's attention. However, it was hard to miss Benny in his magenta linen sport jacket, starched white shirt, matching skinny jeans, and purple high-top sneakers. He stood in stark contrast to his approaching colleague who was dressed all in black: jeans, a mock tee, a sports jacket, and boots. His salt-and-pepper hair brushed his collar. With a look of resignation, Cole made his way through the crowd. These professors were not your pedantic academic stereotypes. Not in the way they dressed, taught, or interacted with the administration.

"Going to a funeral, Dr. Fitzgerald?" Benny asked with his ready smile. "You kind of have the urban-cowboy-meets-the-hippie-meets-the-mortician look."

"I'd be happier at a funeral. At least we wouldn't have to listen to the guest of honor." He nodded in appreciation as Benny handed him a cup of coffee. "Looks like the masses have come out of the woodwork for the coronation. Guess everyone wants to say they attended the regime's royal event. Ready to shake hands with the 'incredibly extraordinary' leader?" Cole mocked the meaningless phrase President Doyle Bartley often used. "And look at this piece of crap!" Cole handed the cease-and-desist order to Benny.

"Huh? What is it you're doing in *Ian's Corner*?" Benny shook the letter as he handed it back to Cole. "That makes it sound like you are about to engage in an act of war. Sons-of-biscuits!"

"To them, the mismanagers of this place, *Ian's Corner* is more like sedition. You know like, 'How dare they claim they are marginalized. We know what's best!' And it is not a club as he calls it. It's my office or the café or the courtyard. Any place we can talk and connect. Those morons have no idea about teaching, let alone authentic connections."

Cole shoved the envelope into his backpack. "I'll deal with the weasels. First, we gotta get through this pig and pony show."

"No telling what we'll hear or see," Benny said as he looked at the gathering flock, "but you're right. *Coronation* it is. The new king is about to be sworn in."

"And his congregants," Cole said as he moved his coffee cup hand toward the still-arriving crowd, "grovel to do his bidding. A new semester, but the same pomp and arrogance."

A chime sounded oddly reminiscent of the opera, and the assembled foyer mass moved as lemmings toward the auditorium doors. Off the cliff, they marched with a smile on their collective faces.

"And here comes the royal highnesses of the regime." Cole pointed to the stairs leading down from the restrooms. An attractive brunette with model-like features, meticulously attired in a baby blue bodycon dress with a matching cropped blazer made her way toward the foyer. She walked with confidence as she placed her six-inch stilettos toe-heel, toe-heel on each step accentuating her muscular calves.

"How in the hell does a 35-year-old with no teaching experience end up as the college's Vice President for Teaching and Learning?"

"She doesn't need to know about teaching. All she needs to do is know how to manage the message of the administration. Teaching would just get in her way. And I believe she knows how to control other things as well." Benny nodded his head as Vice President Darla Merlot descended the final step, waved coyly, and moved toward the man standing beside the doors to the auditorium seating area.

With a perpetual tan, shaggy blonde hair, chiseled facial features, and bleached teeth, Director of Human Resources Pat Turkle still looked like the athlete he had been in college 20-something years ago. Despite her towering heels, Merlot stood on her tiptoes to reach up and gently embrace the six-foot-six director. They blew socialite air kisses at each other's cheeks. Turkle opened the doors. He and Merlot positioned themselves to greet the faculty entering the event.

Merlot's major reason for being was to serve as the president's image maker and protector. For her, it was always about marketing the message, seldom about the educational implications those directives might have. An odd role given her title at Central City College.

"A shame isn't it?" Benny pondered as he looked at Turkle. "Such a hunk, but such a bastard. He's enough to make me want to swear off men."

Cole curled his lips into a smile.

The lights pulsated, indicating the meeting would start in ten minutes.

"The light flickers and the world dims. Shall we enter, my good man?" They slugged down their coffee, tossed the cups in the trashcan, and joined the crowd entering the doors.

"Good morning. Glad you could join us today, professors!" Turkle patted Benny on the shoulder and then extended his hand to Cole. "I'd like to get on your calendar, soon. Give my secretary a call, will you, Professor Fitzgerald?" Turkle's steel blue eyes bore into Cole as he held the handshake for a few more seconds as if reminding Cole who held the power.

Cole nodded. "Perhaps we can talk about intersectionality."

Turkle smiled as he turned to hand a program to the next person in line.

"*Get on your calendar?* Wow! Aren't you the important one around here? Hey, can I call your secretary and get on your calendar, Dr. Fitz?" Benny fluttered his eyes like an infatuated young adolescent.

"Bite me," Cole shook his head. "Why me? Why that weasel?" He pointed toward two empty seats in the back row, underneath the sound booth window.

"Morning, Cole." The Associate Vice President for Academic Affairs, Lori Craig tapped him on the shoulder. "You ready to make another dent in the educational universe this semester?"

Cole smiled and hugged her. "Good to see you." Authentic and principled, Lori's small stature belied her tenacity and determination for all things related to teaching and learning. Cole never figured out how she fit in with the college leadership team. Probably because, as the only African American to be seen in the presidential cabinet, she helped with the diversity count for the administration.

"Let's catch up soon. I have to get to my seat before the program begins. Call me and let's schedule a lunch." She smiled and walked toward the front of the auditorium stopping, smiling, and exchanging greetings along the way.

"At least," said Benny as they settled into their seats, "she brings the faculty perspective to the president's cabinet. I miss her as a teaching colleague. Maybe her climb up the ladder will help other real faculty get through the administrative barriers and double talk. Unlike Merlot over there." He looked toward the gathered administrators. "Once she got to the top, she kicked the ladder away."

"I miss Lori, too," Cole said. "And then there's that putz." He nodded his head toward a squat, middle-aged, absent-minded-looking man at the edge of the first row just behind the orchestra pit shaking hands with the dignitaries as they entered. Associate Vice President for Faculty Relations Richard Edwards wore his perpetual look of a lost child in an adult's world.

"Do you think he ever had an original thought?"

"Doubt it." Cole shook his head in disgust.

The house lights went black as multi-colored spotlights began to circulate on the closed stage curtain. A low drum roll came from the student band.

"Ladies and gentlemen. Staff and professors. Board members and community dignitaries. Please welcome Central City College's president, Dr......Doyle......Bartley......!" Each word drawn out as a wrestling match announcer would.

The curtains opened wide enough for the not-so-distinguishable president to strut to the front and center of the stage. He held up his lanky arms and threw back his head soaking in the applause. His thin pale fingers extended toward the balcony seats as if he were about to part the waters. The spotlight bounced off his thick-lensed, tortoiseshell glasses.

As the applause died down, the six-foot-two-inch bony-framed Bartley walked back and forth along the front of the stage as he spoke. Despite evidence to the contrary, Bartley saw himself as a gifted orator. He never used notes, never rehearsed before an event, and he had never met an adverb he didn't like. His curly red hair, hazel eyes, creased forehead, and unremarkable jawline with no discernible chin did not create an awe-inspiring image. There he stood or paced, ordinary in just about every way.

"You are incredibly extraordinary! Thank you for that extremely warm welcome. And thank you for coming today to authentically celebrate our college." Bartley smiled and scanned the audience as polite applause arose again.

Cole slouched a bit further in his chair. "The only thing that will be celebrated today is his raging ego. Nothing but weasels and ferrets."

"Hey, bud, why are you being so negative?" Benny leaned toward Cole, and with his index finger slowly circling alongside his temple, he looked toward Bartley and said, "Woo, woo! Pop goes the weasel!"

"It is hard to believe that I have been here two years already. You will kindly remember, that when I was humbly honored with the selection as your president, I told the Board that I did not want any ceremony at that time. Some of you, I know it's hard to believe, had doubts that I, coming from a for-profit college, could lead this incredible public institution. I hope I have won your confidence. It takes a year to get to know everyone. And another year to start making a difference. So, today, we celebrate our awesome journey. And since the Board has not fired me yet, I guess today is a good one for the official inauguration of my administration." The crowd laughed and Bartley applauded them. Or was he applauding himself? It was difficult to tell.

"A year to disembowel the faculty and another to get the Board under his thumb would be a better characterization." Cole looked at his watch.

"I have loved getting to know you and building my astonishing team." Bartley nodded his head toward the front row where his cabinet sat.

Pat Turkle sat ramrod straight with his hand massaging his right knee, a constant reminder of his athletic injury during his college days. Next to him was Vice President of Finance, Bradley Niblick. As usual, his left leg was bouncing up and down as if he were smashing grapes. At sixty-seven, Niblick was the oldest member of the presidential cabinet. Recently retired from the corporate ranks, he helped Bartley with his number one priority, revamping the college's antiquated financial accounting system.

To Niblick's right sat Lori Craig, Darla Merlot, and Senator Wackenslong. Behind them was the college's Board of Trustees.

"I want to thank Vice President Merlot for orchestrating this phenomenally magnificent event. And thank you to the local press for being here to celebrate what we do for the students in our community. Thank you for your wonderful service to our community." He held an arm out toward the back of the room where a roped-off area held a few camera crews.

"Interesting, that Teagan Cross is here. Doesn't he usually cover the governor's office and the state legislature?" Cole looked at a slouching reporter with his cameraman.

"Hey, maybe Bartley will announce he is running for governor and leaving the college!" Benny offered with a chuckle.

"We should be so lucky."

"I realize you have experienced terribly difficult financial times here. And that has impacted your paychecks. I commend you for going the past three years without a pay increase. And you continued, in those times, to provide the best education for our students. You are, in a word, incredibly extraordinary."

"Isn't that two words?" Benny whispered.

Cole shook his head with resignation. "He didn't mention the million-dollar contract the Board gave him. Plus a car allowance and an annuity fund. Wonder if that is, in a word, 'incredibly extraordinary'? Weasel."

Bartley continued, "I have learned from you. In tough times, we should pause, take a breath, and maybe even lay down for a power nap." He waited for the expected chuckle. He got few.

"Lie! Lie! Lie!" someone shouted from the back of the balcony. Bartley squinted, held up his hand to shield his eyes from the spotlight, and looked for the yeller. The crowd went quiet. The president decided to continue his stream of consciousness.

"And I know this is an extremely small gesture, but it is the beginning of what is to come as I show my appreciation for what our CCC employees do. Just before I stepped through those curtains, I signed a presidential order for each of you to receive a one-time special bonus of $250."

A small gasp went up from the audience. Cole couldn't discern if they were shocked at the parsimoniousness of the action or felt like the chosen ones.

"And, if we could, lights and a drum roll please," Bartley said looking at the orchestra conductor. The house went black and the colored lights again swirled on the black curtain. Bartley stepped to the center, arms raised over his head out toward the audience.

"I have a gift for every faculty member. Actually, three gifts." As he stepped aside, the curtains opened to reveal the spectacle of a floor-to-ceiling mountain of cardboard boxes. "By the end of the week, each faculty member will receive a shiny new high-speed laptop computer, an incredibly fast new tablet, and the latest model cell phone. With these devices, you will be better able to reach out and be accessible to our students. I could not have done this for our deserving faculty without the unselfish assistance from one of our city's greatest philanthropists—businessman and State Senator Wilbur Wackenslong. His family has long supported CCC, and this wonderfully spacious facility is one example of that incredible support. Truly incredibly extraordinary!"

He motioned to the slender gray-haired, white man sitting next to Merlot. Wackenslong stood, buttoned his tailored suit jacket, smiled, waved, and sat. "The good senator knows the hardships of inner-city residents—more of whom will be in your classrooms this semester thanks to our major initiative offering more financial aid. Times are difficult and that is why the Wackenslong family is building the industrial site downtown. For jobs and benefits. For our community."

Bartley turned and applauded the senator. The crowd followed with a polite golf clap.

"Wonder if Merlot gets her stilettoes from his apparel chain," Benny cracked.

"Geez, how much of the college's soul did Bartley sell to that powerbroker?"

"Hang in there, bud. Maybe we'll each get a car, too! Then we can do home tutoring for all of our students."

"I can't take any more of this. I'll see you back on campus." Cole made his way to the end of the row as the audience, some standing, applauded the weasel-in-chief.

Go ahead. Why wait? Get this over with now. Do it! Get the respect you deserve. Or end it!

As if a little person sat on his shoulder and whispered in his ear, the voice challenged, mostly doubted, and often demeaned. Today, Cole took the bait. He stopped in the aisle, turned away from the exit, threw his shoulders back, narrowed his eyes on Bartley, and charged toward the stage.

• • •

3

About time you stand up and confront the little weasel. No one else in this room has the courage. Do it or shut up!

"Excuse me! President Bartley. I have a question for you."

Bartley saw Cole approaching down the aisle and attempted to ignore his presence by moving to the other side of the stage.

"Dr. Bartley, this, this show," Cole pointed toward the boxes on stage, "is a distraction, isn't it?"

"Dr. Fitzgerald," Bartley rolled his shoulders backward, "we will have time for illuminating questions. If you will graciously and kindly wait for a few…."

"We are tired of waiting! We have waited for years for pay that at least brings professors out of the bottom tier for faculty in this state. We have waited for consideration about classroom resources. Consideration about our healthcare. Consideration for our clerical staff who make less per year than your various personal stipends. Consideration for us as human beings. And consideration for our students."

"Ah, Professor, you do know that we, me, and my wonderfully capable administrative team, have only been on this job for two years. And...."

"Stop it!" Cole's yell echoed throughout the silent room. "Stop blaming the previous administration. Stop it!" And turning toward the Board members, "You, you make policies about this college that affect everyone in this room. But you never set foot in a classroom. When was the last time you engaged a student in a conversation or walked the hallways of our campuses? But that doesn't keep you from rubber-stamping the piffle and flapdoodle that comes from this guy and his minions."

Cole paused, looked at the floor, and took a deep breath.

"And the students. What are we doing to help our first-generation college students on our campus? And what about those who have been bullied, taunted, beaten, and ignored."

"Professor, I must object to that innuendo. We have a robust—an extraordinarily robust—Student Affairs department." He looked toward the administrative seats to recognize the V.P. for Student Affairs but for the life of him, he could not remember who he was. Or was it a she? So, he just opened his arms as if to embrace his cabinet. "I think our students would be hard-pressed to find another institution that does so much for them."

"Do you ever listen to yourself?"

"Dr. Fitzgerald, this is not the place. You are out of order."

"With more respect than you show us, this is *the* place. In front of *the* people you were appointed to lead. So damn it! Lead the faculty and the students. You, Mr. President, you are out of order, and I fear for everyone in this room, you are way over your head."

Cole turned and looked at the audience. He raised his head to the balcony. "Are you happy with this state of affairs? Is this what you want? A measly couple of bucks and technology they should provide anyway? Is that the extent of our vision? You're OK with a daily diet of manipulative micro-management and an atmosphere of mistrust and disrespect? It's a microcosm of our larger society. Come on! Stand up for one another!"

Turkle looked at Edwards and motioned for him to do something. Edward's eyes just got wider and he shrugged his shoulders. As he got up to do God knows what, Cole spun around and took a few steps toward the Board. Edwards returned to the cover of his seat.

Cole stopped and took a moment to look each one in the eye. Pointing toward Bartley he said, "Since you have hired that poor excuse for a manager, we faculty have experienced a display of organizational power simply because it can be done. It has gone beyond the issue of faculty representation at the table for important educational issues. Narcissistic bullies, all of them. Some of you may have family members who are in education or are thinking of it. Please ask yourselves, would you want them treated in the manner that my colleagues have been treated? Would you?"

Cole turned and walked toward the exit. Hand claps could be heard up on the balcony and in the back of the room. Someone whistled and another shouted, "Go, Cole!" Bartley strained to see who yelled.

Before he left the auditorium, Cole turned and looked at Bartley. "Mr. President, I am, we are," he held out his stretched arms, "tired of being invisible!" He turned and exited the auditorium.

Wackenslong leaned into Turkle. "Who is that maniac?"

"*That* is Fitzgerald. Professor Cole Fitzgerald."

"That's *him?*"

"Yes, sir. A tenured de facto faculty leader who can create trouble for us."

"Well then, let's create trouble for *him* before he does for us!"

• • •

4

3AM the following day.
Are you going down this road again? Same tune.
Different song. Come on, Cole. Let it go. No one cares about
it or you!

It had become an unwelcome ritual. The hour of trepidation. When the voice awakened. In reality, though, the voice never went away. Mostly, it appeared at night but at times, like at yesterday's event, it tapped Cole on the shoulder during the day. It would then get quiet. It would move to the background. But it never, ever left. And it was taking a toll.

Cole sat on the living room sofa, rocking his body as the haunting ritual played out.

You don't like these corrupt and incompetent bastards.
Who cares? Not your colleagues. They are too busy caring
about themselves. Focus on your teaching.

"I can't take this any longer. First, you encourage me, and now this. Leave me alone! Why are you doing this?" He leaned back on the cushion and closed his eyes.

Sliding back into bed at 4:30 AM, he pulled the covers to his chin and fell into a deep sleep. The voice quiet—for now.

The day would begin in a few hours. There would be more voices of a different sort.

• • •

"Morning. Time for coffee or something else?"

Cole felt a light kiss on his shoulder and the cool touch of skin. The digital clock showed 7 AM. Heather nuzzled closer to him.

"I'd like nothing more than 'something else' but I've got to get to campus. First day of class. Can't be late."

"Ah, but you're the professor. Don't those students have to wait for you? What is it, 15 minutes for a PhD?" She hugged his arm.

"You're showing your age." Cole laughed, kissed her forehead, and slid out of bed.

Heather propped herself up on one arm and watched his firm naked butt as he slid into his slim-cut jeans. He walked to the kitchen where freshly brewed coffee awaited. Thankful for automatic gadgetry, Cole reached for the cups.

She rolled on her back, pulled the sheet up to her chin, and smiled. "Well, I know your students, especially the female students, will wait. They all love Dr. Fitz." She loved teasing Cole about the to-be-expected coed crushes. A beginning-of-semester ritual. He had the air of a cool academic. Which he was in her estimation.

"They couldn't care less. To them, I'm as old as their father and look like their grandfather."

"Pretty sexy granddad if you ask me," Heather wiggled her eyebrows up and down.

"Who's on the hot seat today? What unsuspecting poor souls will lose their sense of balance and self-importance as you help separate them from fact and fiction?" Cole sat on the side of the bed handing her a cup as she leaned against a pillow. He raised his cup to hers.

"No rough stuff for me or the guests. I can't play the ignorant third grader today. The producer lined up three students from your college. A star athlete, a computer genius, and a single mom. I think we're calling the segment 'Why College? Why Now? Why You?'"

"The exact questions I ask myself each time I sit in a meeting with the dark side of the college. Bartley and his crowd know how to suck the air right out of any room. You should have seen the carnival atmosphere they created for their coronation yesterday. Only those egomaniacs could take the ceremonial swearing-in of the college president and turn it into a made-for-TV eye-roller."

"Oh, I saw it on the evening news. Looks like you all got an early Christmas gift of technology." Heather took a sip. Dating Cole about as long as Bartley had been with CCC, she lived the daily drama of higher education. "Maybe, just maybe, it's a turn in the right direction for you and the students. Maybe."

"Don't get me started. After the letter I got yesterday about *Ian's Corner* and intersectionality, well they just raised the game to a new low level."

"I'd expect that from a politician running for office, not a director of human resources. Doesn't make sense."

"You didn't see who was sitting in the audience. Senator Wilbur Wackenslong. His family is involved with the technology gift and who knows what else. Remember, he wants that industrial site, as he said, to help our Marina Norte citizens. Guessing he did not like me at the protest and told Turkle to take care of me."

"Maybe you impressed him when you single-handedly stole the show from Bartley."

"I doubt that," Cole said. Tapping his cup to hers, "I'll need a lot more of this before I get to campus."

"You want a lot more of something else before you go, Dr. Fitz?"

They both laughed as Cole leaned in for a lingering kiss.

"As tempting as that is, I need to get home for a shower and feed Big Betsy." Cole slid on his loafers and finished buttoning his shirt.

"Mmmm. Big Betsy has all the fun. You sure you can't get to class a few minutes late?" A mock pout covered her full lips.

"I'll make it up to you tonight. It is our anniversary, after all."

"You remembered! I guess we can give Bartley credit for bringing us together. If the Board hadn't selected him for the appointment, and I hadn't been assigned to cover that meeting for the station, we might never have met."

He smiled at the reminiscence and walked back to the bed. "That's one Board meeting I am glad I attended." They kissed again.

With that, he tossed his backpack over his shoulder and picked up his guitar. "See you at *The Silver Fox?*"

"You don't think I'd miss *HTRB* do you? Couldn't think of a better way to celebrate. You be good to the president today, and I'll be good to you after the show tonight."

As the door to Heather's condominium closed, she drew her knees to her chest, pulled her brown hair over her shoulder, and said a silent prayer for the man in her life.

• • •

Cole entered his second-floor two-bedroom unit at the Skyview Condo Complex. What it lacked in spaciousness it made up for in convenience with its proximity to Heather's condo, campus, and *The Silver Fox.*

And it was a short drive to the beach where he could catch his breath. He found solace on the sand. He felt at peace whether walking, sitting, or watching the sunrise over the incoming waves. While Cole never took up surfing, he lived by the mantra attributed to John Severson the founder of *Surfer Magazine:*

> *In this crowded world, the surfer can still seek*
> *and find the perfect day, the perfect wave, and*
> *be alone with the surf and his thoughts....*

Unfortunately, today the perfect wave would have to wait. His thoughts led him to consider the posers and aggros—the imposters and bullies—of another sort at the college.

He tossed his keys to the table, leaned his guitar in the corner by the door, and squatted to stroke the purring feline that leaped from the kitchen counter to greet him.

"Morning, Big Betsy. Looks like you kept things in order around here last night."

He picked her up and nose-nuzzled her face. She purred and he smiled. "I needed you last night when my visitor came knocking."

He filled her bowl and sorted quickly through yesterday's mail. At least today there would be students to help ease the pain.

How long could he keep this up?

• • •

As Cole swiped his keycard and unlocked his office door, he heard his name called. "Excuse me, Professor Fitzgerald do you have a moment." A student from one of his previous semester's classes, with downcast eyes and a disheveled look, tentatively walked toward Cole.

Cole had gained a campus-wide reputation for being available for students who needed a shoulder or an ear for support. Over the years he began adding stories and little-known facts about marginalized groups to his classroom discussions. Cole wanted his students to know he heard them and wanted to provide a safe place for their questions and discussions. His classes filled each semester. The students saw him as one who would listen and advocate for them when no one else seemed to care. And they, in turn, many of them the first of their families to attend college, helped Cole understand their day-to-day struggles. He led impromptu discussion groups on campus about what Marina Norte needed that most people didn't know—or care—about.

Cole waved the student in and pointed to the seat in *Ian's Corner*. On the wall behind the chair was a faded black-and-white photo of Cole's brother, Ian. On the table next to the chair, a vase of carnations.

"Before you leave, please take one," Cole said nodding toward the flowers. "Keep it for yourself or give it to someone you care about." The men often hid the carnation in their backpacks but no one refused.

"What's on your mind?" Cole asked, and the conversation began.

This was why Cole did what he did. It would take more than an administrative letter for him to stop.

• • •

5

"Senator, shall I show your visitor in?" Wackenslong's secretary stood at his office door.

"Yes. Please, send him in." The senator closed a file folder, stood up, and stepped around his desk.

The secretary led Pat Turkle into the inner office and closed the door as she left. Turkle had no idea what to expect. The senator vacillated often between his many faces. A necessary talent for a successful and still-rising politician.

"Pat. Good morning." Wackenslong extended a hand and pointed to the conference table in the center of the room. "I got your favorites here. Black coffee and a blueberry bagel. Or was that only a meal for a struggling college kid?"

"Thanks, Senator. I still remember how Wendi and I met in the campus cafeteria every morning before class. That was about all we could afford." Turkle's laugh belied his sad eyes. All these years later, the memories and the heartbreak had not faded.

"You seem in a better mood today."

"Yeah, that. Sorry. But Bartley, damn it. When I orchestrated his appointment I was expecting someone with more chutzpah."

"He's got a lot on his plate."

"We all have a lot on our plates, Pat." The senator poured them each a cup of coffee. "Now, before Doyle arrives, tell me about the athletes. Anything new on that front?"

"I will approach Coach Gil in the next few days. Since the governor just signed the *Pay for the Name* legislation, there are a lot of questions about what, who, how, when, and why. I will have the answers they need to hear."

"Good. Good. Very good!"

And, I've reached out to Ricky Peroni," Cole continued. "He's on board."

"The agent who almost was yours?" the senator asked.

"Yeah. Until the injury," Cole tapped his right knee, "he was ready to represent me. But we stayed in touch over the years. And when Wendi and Bridgette passed Ricky became my rock. I'm not sure if I would have made it without him. Or you."

"We're a team." The senator raised his cup and returned to the conversation at hand. He never let sadness interfere with business.

"I've got the apparel company in the wings. With your help, we can move it to the front of the list for endorsements and branding the basketball team. Moved to the front, that is, quietly. We have to keep the family business out of the conversation. We do not want the evening news in on *that*."

"Understood."

"The company needs this. And it is why Doyle, unbeknownst to him, got the Board to approve your appointment as Director of Human Resources Director." Wackenslong winked.

"You mean, why you got Doyle to appoint me," Pat said.

"No matter. You have the chops to get this done. Doyle gets flustered if he goes off script. He doesn't adlib well. Like yesterday when the professor interrupted."

They let the words settle in the air and then the intercom buzzed. "Senator, Dr. Bartley is here."

"Send him in."

The Senator took a breath as Bartley scurried through the door like a student late for class.

"Good morning, Senator. Pat. Sorry, I'm late. The traffic was incredibly unbelievably bad this morning." He grabbed his usual seat across the table from Pat.

"That was a nice touch to have lined up the news team at yesterday's event," the Senator said. "Anytime we get a look-at-the-good-we-do piece on the six o'clock news is a winning day." The senator slid a coffee in front of the president and pointed to the bagels. "Doyle, I liked your staging of the boxes. Clever."

Bartley puffed his chest as if he were just recognized as the valedictorian of the graduating class. But just as fast, it deflated as if someone hit him in the gut.

"Now, gentlemen," the Senator said as he rolled his chair closer to the table. "Fitzgerald, the professor, what are you doing about him?" He cast his squint from one side of the table to the other.

"We're most certainly weighing our options, Senator," Bartley said as he wiggled his neck back and forth. "It was an incredibly rude thing he did. But other than maybe a reprimand, there isn't much we can do. Even the protest march, well, it was remarkably peaceful with all those people waving those signs."

"Don't give me that shit, Doyle. You heard him. On TV! TWICE! He condemned my family business at the protest during the morning. And then he made an ass of you, which was caught on the evening news. Quite a day, wouldn't you say!"

The Senator reached for the intercom on the desk behind him and pounded the button. "Betty, have my car brought to the front."

Turning back to Turkle and Bartley, "He is a huge problem waiting to happen. I've seen his type over the years. They start peacefully as you say. Then they become more emboldened as the spotlight shines brighter. He needs to be stopped now. Tell him he's messing with the wrong person!" Then looking at Turkle, "Mr. Director of Human Resources, what is your suggestion? Doyle says we can't do much. I say crucify the son-of-a-bitch. Why don't you break the tie."

Turkle placed his hands on the table, palms down, and tapped his fingers. "I say ignore him."

"Ignore him? That's your solution? As our president here might say, that sounds incredibly stupid."

Turkle held up his index finger and said, "If I may Senator. Let me explain."

What are you doing? The Senator wants action.

"Please do. Please explain why you want to avoid confronting this person who can create problems for us." The Senator sat back and crossed his arms over his chest.

"Senator, while Professor Fitzgerald might look like a self-composed and overly confident man, he is anything but that. He is starved for attention." Turkle paused.

"He wants to be seen. Being visible, using one of his words, is a status symbol for him that he constantly reaches for. He's insecure. The more attention we throw his way, the more he will step out and stand out."

Doyle raised his eyebrows and interrupted, "Senator, I think Pat may have a point here."

"Oh, you do? Explain it to me."

Bartley froze and Turkle continued. "Think back to what we saw on TV about the protest. *Invisible No More.* That's their plaintive plea. If we go after the professor, he gets the visibility he wants. We give him credibility. Which then gives him more of a public platform which then leads to more of a following." Turkle paused.

Bartley's eyes screamed, "Thank you, Pat!"

"I'm listening," the Senator said.

"When we say *ignore*, we don't mean *forget* or *pardon*. No, we keep an eye on him, and unbeknownst to him we will continue to shorten his leash. He'll continue to pull like an agitated dog. And we never let up."

"Yes, certainly," Bartley said as he leaned toward the center and pointed toward the Director. "I could not have said it any better than Pat. It is an extraordinarily out-of-the-box plan."

"I'll meet with him this week. I have an idea to get this moving. Lead him to think we are listening to him. But I'll need your help."

Wackenslong raised an eyebrow. "Keep it simple. This has to be a college thing."

"Intersectionality. I stretched the college's authority on that. But, knowing Cole, I hit a nerve. When we meet, I'll tell him I was able to pull a few strings and not only get *Ian's Corner* reinstated but also have secured an anonymous donation for his cause."

"I guess you want me to be that donor?"

"Not much. A thousand dollars or so for him to buy coffee for the students. Maybe an occasional lunch. It will catch his attention. It looks like a win in his eyes. You know, he'll think his convocation conniption made an impact." Turkle took a sip of coffee and then continued. "He'll like the attention we," Turkle pointed toward Bartley, "give him. He could help us in the community as well."

"Hope so. We don't need distractions. At least none that we don't create. Fortunately, the mayor and his team have been pulling some strings with the local pastors. Throwing a few bones to them for their neighborhoods. Looks like the demolition will start later this week at the site."

"Let Doyle and me talk about this," Turkle continued. "We'll handle him in a less public and messy way. And, in the end, he will be visible but not quite like he had imagined."

The secretary knocked on the office door. "Senator, your car is here."

Wackenslong stood up, buttoned his coat, and looked first at Bartley, then at Turkle. "OK. To use your wording, you are now on a short leash with this. Don't screw it up."

"We won't let you down," Turkle said.

You better not. You know his expectations. Be on your game.

Pat shook his head as the three conspirators walked out the door. The voice had a way of stating the obvious.

• • •

6

Later that same morning.
"Thank you, Aintin. I owe you again. And again. And again!"

"Suzy, dear. We're family. You're going to college. No one in our family even made it through high school." Aintin paused. Suzy knew she was probably wiping a tear. Sentimental, loveable, and dependable.

"Aintin, look I just arrived at the radio station. My advisor told me this would only be about fifteen minutes. And then I need to get to campus. It's the first day of classes and I'm scared to death."

"You gonna do great, dearie. And little Shauna and I will stay busy 'til you get home. She gonna help me prepare our Shepherd's Pie for dinner tonight."

"Not sure a four-year-old will be much help. But who knows? Gotta go. I'll call you when I'm going to campus."

Suzy pulled into a visitor parking space. She tugged the review mirror toward herself.

"Geez," she thought, "I'm glad this is radio and not TV." She pawed her milky white Irish skin and red hair. "Why did my advisor ever call me for this?"

A knock on her window startled her back to the present.

"Hey, Suzy. I thought maybe you'd like to walk in together. I'm Johnny Valentine."

Suzy cracked her driver's side window a sliver. "Ah. Um. Hi. How do you know my name?"

"You're here for the interview with Ms. Rivera, right?"

"Yes. And how did you know that?" She tugged at the end of her blouse sleeves.

Johnny's radiant smile looked like a starburst. "I am a student at CCC. My coach told me two other students would be here too. Gave me your name and, ah," Johnny reached into his nicely fitting blue jeans and pulled out a piece of paper. "Yeah, Kerwin. And I saw the CCC parking decal on your rear window. Kinda put one and one together."

Suzy cranked up the window, opened the door, and exhaled a sigh of relief, followed by a few shallow breaths. Johnny held the door for her. He was tall. Really tall with dark brown eyes and matching tousle-top brown hair that he had bunched up in a bun. He wore a CCC t-shirt with the word *BASKETBALL* across the front. It made a snug fit around his biceps. She could only imagine what his ripped abdomen must look like. Some would say he was a hunk. But self-conscious Suzy smiled and looked toward the station's front entrance.

The security guard buzzed them through the double glass doors, and they entered the lobby seating area. When the doors closed, the security guard signaled to a tiny Asian man with a shoulder bag sitting along the wall.

"Hi, I'm Kerwin. Guess you're the other two students?" He extended a thin hand that belied the energy in his voice and the vigor of his handshake. "I am so pumped about this. I hope we get a tour of the facility so I can see what kind of technology they use here. It's gotta be so cool!"

They followed the guard down a short, carpeted hallway with photos and plaques from the floor to the ceiling.

Over his shoulder, the guard explained, "Those are a few of the guests who have been on Heather Rivera's show. She has quite a reputation."

Johnny laughed and clapped his hands. "I know that guy! He's a stud athlete at State."

Kerwin pointed at a photo about halfway up the wall and midway down the hallway. "That's Bill Gates! Really? *The* Bill Gates was here?"

"About three or four years ago," the guard replied. "He was in town to speak at an IT convention. Heather reached out on a whim. He came in and was nicer than anyone could have imagined."

Suzy pulled on her ponytail. And again wondered, "What the hell am I doing here?"

Ahead they saw a sign that said, "On the Air." Behind the glass, a woman sat in front of a laptop and a microphone that hung from a big boom stand.

"That's Heather Rivera," the guard said pointing to a forty-something woman with reading glasses perched on her head. "She's finishing up with her first guest of the hour. Take a seat here. Someone will come to get you." He opened the door to a small room with a compact black cushioned sofa, three straight-backed chairs, a table, and forest green walls. "Help yourself to coffee, water, and snacks," he said pointing to the corner where a small refrigerator and a coffee pot sat. A basket with chips, cookies, and fresh fruit was on top of the refrigerator. The door quietly closed, and the three students giggled as they looked at each other.

Three first-year college students. They felt like royalty. Or at least two did. Suzy felt like an imposter.

"This ought to be interesting," she thought as she took a seat at the end of the sofa, crossed her legs, and clasped her hands.

• • •

"And you're on in 3…2…1."

The "On Air" light flashed and behind a sound-proofed window, the producer, a kindly-looking grandmother type in her 60s and with the preciseness of a drill sergeant, pointed at Heather.

"Good morning, and welcome back to *The Facts and Fiction Hour*. I'm Heather Rivera. Glad you can join us this morning. Remember you can reach out to me and our guests with your questions by phone, email, or social media where you can look for #TNBZ. With our guests and your questions, we want to move beyond the confusing words of corporate- and government-speak, as we search for a deeper understanding of community issues."

Heather had her phone, tablet, laptop, and microphone before her. Jill, the producer, stood about ten feet away in the sound room keeping track of the technical pieces of the show. Across the rectangular, brown wood table sat her guests. To the show's following, Heather was a voice of reason who raised difficult topics in a respectful yet pointed manner. She would never go for the headline. She asked probing questions, moving beyond clichés and sound bites. And she would metaphorically kick a guest in the butt if he or she attempted to obfuscate. Off air, she was known to greet more than one studio guest with a handshake and "Welcome to The No Bullshit Zone." Hence the sign above the door: "TNBZ!"

"Today we are blessed to have the future with us: Three students from Central City College. With the new semester beginning this week, they will share with us 'Why College? Why Now? Why You?'" As she spoke, Heather smiled at her three guests.

"So, let's get started. Johnny Valentine, Kerwin Lucas, and Suzy McDonald welcome to our show."

"Thank you, Ms. Rivera, for allowing us to be on the show." Of the three, Johnny appeared most self-assured. Not cocky but confident. His physical size and appearance set him apart from the other two. "Oh, I'm sorry," Johnny said. "Hope I didn't commit a foul. I'm just so excited to be here. Not many from my neighborhood get this kind of opportunity."

Kerwin nodded toward Johnny and said, "I get it. My pleasure, as well, Ms. Rivera." Slightly built, Black with Asian features, sporting a mohawk haircut and wide smile, he looked like he might have difficulty carrying Johnny's backpack. But what he lacked in physical prowess, Kerwin made up for with his academic abilities. Johnny would have had trouble carrying just one-quarter of Kerwin's academic load. A straight-A student with perfect attendance, Kerwin graduated as his high school's valedictorian.

Suzy nodded and looked toward the tabletop. Her ponytail accentuated her thin nose and smooth complexion. Her blue eyes had a hint of sadness to them. She could have been a homecoming queen, but something told Heather that was probably not part of her resume.

"Let's talk about why college, why now, why you? Johnny, as I understand it you are on a full athletic scholarship. And last year you had a stat-popping first season on the CCC basketball court. Aren't you among the national leaders in Triple Doubles? That means, listeners, Johnny V, as his teammates call him, had double digits in points scored, assists to teammates, and rebounds snagged under the basket. Your coach said you are the best player he's ever coached in his 30 years. Period." Heather leaned away from the microphone, her hazel eyes glistening as if she were the proud parent of this basketball hero.

"Wow! You do your homework, Ms. Rivera." Johnny rolled his chair closer to the table mic. "My dream, from a little boy, has been to play professional sports. I was fortunate to have great high school coaches and a supportive mom who have helped me keep my head screwed on straight and focused. The college offered me a way to develop on and off the court."

"Why Central City College? You had other scholarship offers. At six-foot-ten, you could play in any college conference."

"I wanted to stay close to my mother. She's a single mom; and works two jobs. My dad died in a car crash when I was five. She's always been there for me. I need to be here for her."

"I'm sorry to hear about your dad, Johnny. That had to be difficult. Sounds like Mom keeps you focused with hugs and expectations."

"Yes, ma'am. She does."

"You and your coach have had some interest—from NBA scouts. While that is typical at the larger schools, we aren't used to that kind of attention in our part of the world. With the new law, *Pay for the Name*, you might have the opportunity to get business endorsements and earn money for things like clothes with your name and image. I know it doesn't take effect for another six months, but I will ask you more about that in our second segment today."

Heather noticed that Suzy still had a downward gaze. She was fidgeting with her shirt sleeves pulling them toward her wrists. Palms closed and fingers holding on to the end of the cotton cuffs. Heather decided to give her more time to get comfortable.

"Kerwin, I understand in high school, you had been a three-time 1st Place finisher in the county's annual high school science fair. Can you tell us a little about that?"

"I'm a geek," he said, paused for effect, and then let out a laugh. "And proud of it. In high school, the teachers came to me with computer questions. More than one told me that I was more help to them than the school's full-time IT staff." He looked down and shook his head. "I don't know about that. I do know that it comes easy to me. Guess I got it from my mom and dad. She works as a software engineer, and he has his own website development business doing a lot of work for a community group in the inner city where he grew up. As an African American, he's seen first-hand the disparities in our community and he's helping young Black entrepreneurs get technological training."

Heather typed a note to herself, "*Ian's Corner?*"

"So why Central City College? You, too, could have gone to any of the bigger schools. Why here?"

"After my mom immigrated from Japan, Central City College gave her a break. She enrolled in an ESOL—that's English for Speakers of Other Languages—class and eventually got her IT certificate before going to State for her bachelor's degree. She now has a PhD. At CCC I can get a two-year degree and be ready for a job upon graduation. The college has an internship program with the local police's IT department. My ultimate goal is to land a job with an agency like NCIS. You know, work for Jethro or Pride."

Heather laughed at the reference to the popular television series. "So, will your choice be to work in DC, LA, or New Orleans?"

"I'll go to any of those. But I was thinking of Hawaii. And, by the way, I think you need some defragging."

Heather cocked her head and looked at Kerwin. "Excuse me?"

"That computer," his thin index finger pointed toward the laptop in front of her. "I noticed you've been frustrated with its slowness. And I see you keep getting a message, 'Not Responding.' It might need to have the hard drive defragmented to help it—and you—get a little more processing speed. Just saying."

"Well, ladies and gentlemen, this is a first for *The Facts and Fiction Hour*. I have had a live, on-set, computer evaluation and service call. Not sure I can afford this—but I'm taking you up on it, Kerwin."

"No charge, Ms. Rivera. Just give me a good word at the college…and with Jethro and Pride."

Laughing, Heather turned to the remaining student panelist.

"Suzy, when I asked the Student Affairs office for recommendations for this show, Ms. Robertson mentioned your name first. Sorry, Johnny and Kerwin, Suzy rose to the top on the recommendation list for this show."

"I love Ms. Robertson. When she visited my high school I felt an immediate connection with her." Suzy's shoulders relaxed and her fingers unclenched.

"What brings you to college? Johnny wants to be on ESPN highlights and Kerwin is going to track down cyber-criminals. How about you?"

"Don't know. Just know I want to do something where I can make a difference for me and my family. Maybe something with photography. I don't know. I live with my Aintin Cara. Aintin, ah, that's Irish for Aunt. Anyway, she has sacrificed a lot for me and my daughter. And has helped me appreciate my family roots. It's time I do something for her." With each sentence, and with Heather's encouraging smile, Suzy relaxed her muscles.

"That's cool, Suzy," Johnny said, "I feel the same for my mom."

Suzy softened. Heather could see her let out a breath and smile for the first time.

"How old is your daughter?" Heather asked.

"My Shauna just turned four years old. If it weren't for Aintin, I'm not sure where we'd be. Central City College is my chance to do good by my family." Heather sensed future hope that had been dashed by past reality.

"OK, listening audience," Heather leaned into her mic. "You know how it is, we have to pay the bills with a commercial or two. We'll be right back. Please send your questions in for our guests. They will be with us for one more segment and then they have to get to class. Talk to you in two."

The "On Air" sign darkened.

"Two minutes until we are back on, Heather," said the producer holding up two fingers. "I'll be right in with some water."

"You three are a breath of fresh air. If you are our future, we're in good hands." Heather was swiping through her tablet screen. "Lots of questions coming in from, it looks like, high school students and their parents. To them, you are role models."

Jill entered and placed a bottle of water in front of each student. She refilled Heather's coffee cup and then returned to her booth as she readjusted the gray bun on top of her head.

When Suzy unscrewed the bottle cap, her sleeves slid back a few inches. Heather noticed the fresh bruises. Their eyes briefly connected.

"And you're on in 3...2...1." The "On Air" light flashed on, and from behind a glass partition, the producer pointed at Heather.

"Welcome back to our session on 'Why College? Why Now? Why You?'"

And with that, Heather launched into the next segment and started taking phone calls for her three guests.

• • •

"That's a wrap, Heather," Jill said, "We need to get ready for our next guests."

Johnny, Kerwin, and Suzy stood and shook hands with Heather.

"Thank you so much for being with us today. Here's my card. Call me anytime you want to come back. You will increase my street cred."

As they headed to the door, Heather softly touched Suzy on the shoulder as the other two exited the room. Suzy stiffened.

"Hey, Suzy, you got my card. Call me if I can ever help you get settled in with college or anything else. If you need a job, let me know. We can always find something around the station for an inspiring young woman like yourself. You know, even radio needs a good photographer to market the station."

"Thank you, ma'am."

"Heather is fine, no need to be formal. I mean it. Call me anytime. You are fortunate to have someone like Ms. Robertson. Make sure you stay in contact with her as you get used to the college environment. And, if you get a chance, look for Professor Fitzgerald. He has a good reputation for helping students navigate college."

"Thank you, ah, Heather."

"If you ever want to go for a jog, let me know." Heather pointed to Suzy's well-worn running shoes.

"I run when I can but don't have much time. Was on my high school track team until, well, you know, Shauna came along."

"Well, you can be my pacer. I could use some young blood making me move faster."

Suzy smiled. "Yeah, I'd like that. Thanks again." She joined her fellow students in the hallway and out of the studio.

Heather leaned over her desk and wrote a note to herself.

· · ·

7

*L*ater that evening.

Cole stepped onto the stage, put his travel-worn guitar case down, leaned in, and flipped the "on" switch to his vintage Fender amp. The red glow and the buzz always brought a smile to his face. He turned and saw Joe the bartender with his arm extended.

"Figured you could use this. Your first week back to campus, right?"

Cole reached for the glass, rattled the ice cubes at the bottom, and took a sip. "Ah! Joe, you have no idea how good that tastes. I needed you at nine o'clock this morning. And ten...and eleven...." They both laughed. "Good news is that the students are in my class not the puzzle palace police. Those nimrods bewilder, confound, and obscure more effectively than a thousand irregular pieces of colored cardboard."

"Nice crowd building for the first set. Some of your college buds are at that back table. Never saw them in here before. Look a bit out of place in their fancy clothes. The guy gave me this." Joe placed a business card next to Cole's glass.

"Now why do you want to spoil a good Scotch with this?" Cole fingered the card.

*Patrick Turkle, PhD * Director of Human Resources * Central City College * Where Dreams Lead to Reality **

He turned and saw Turkle sitting in the back with Darla Merlot. By the looks of things, they had been there a while.

"The hits just keep coming, don't they, Joe?"

Turkle saw Cole and waved him over to the booth. Cole placed his empty glass on the bar and rolled his eyes toward Joe. "I will need another when I return."

"I'll have it on your stage stool. Now, go forth and mingle with your fanbase."

"Hi, Pat. Darla." Cole extended his hand as he approached the table. "Not sure I've ever seen you in here before."

"Scuttlebutt has it a hot band plays here. Darla and I thought we'd enjoy some good music after our long day."

Cole smiled, and on the inside, said, "Your long day? You have no idea." On the outside, "Glad you could come. Nice people, a comfortable place, and *HTRB*. What else could you want?"

Wait for it.

"That was quite the oratorical show at the swearing-in ceremony the other day." Turkle paused and waited for effect.

There it is!

"Had to be said."

"And that's why I want you," Turkle said still locking eyes. Just like he had done at the auditorium entrance.

"Excuse me?"

"Well, not in *that* way. I think I'm spoken for if you know what I mean." Turkle looked at Darla. "No, I got an offer for you. Can you sit for a moment?"

With that, Darla excused herself. "I'll let you two boys talk shop. I need to step outside and make a phone call."

Cole slid into the booth facing Turkle across the table.

Watch yourself. No, better watch him.

"You know, Cole, that President Bartley and I have been doing our darndest to turn this college around. I know from your speech that you don't believe this, but the last administration left us in a budgetary and enrollment mess." Turkle leaned forward as if sharing a top secret. "And there are problems in the faculty ranks. You know. The old timers, the tenured bastards. I mean the senior members who are so set in their ways they are holding us back." He sat back and continued, "Good leaders, like President Bartley, realize that they must step outside of the usual way of doing things and find innovative strategies. At times, those innovations may make some people uncomfortable."

Turkle paused and turned his drink around on the coaster, pushing back a stray hair off his forehead, he smiled at the professor.

"Cole—and we have been watching you—you're different. You get it. You know how to connect with the new generation of students. Faculty admire you because you have standards and integrity. They listen to you. And so do the students from what we hear."

What we hear? Hmm.

Turkle waved to the waitress. "Ginger ale, please."

"Too much alcohol at happy hour," Cole said, glad for the diversion from wherever this conversation was taking them.

"Something you don't know about me. I don't drink alcohol. It leads to fuzzy thinking. There's a lot you and most people don't know about me. I like it that way. Surprise factor if you know what I mean." The waitress placed the ginger ale in front of Turkle. "But you will have the opportunity to understand me and see that I care about this college—and what you care about. More than you think. That is if you take the offer I have for you."

Cole noticed Benny walk in and head to the stage.

"Listen, I know you need to get tuned up for your first set. Here's the short story. I don't want an answer now. I've set aside time for you to meet with me on Monday for lunch so we can discuss it more."

"It?"

"I'm offering you a newly created position at the college. You will be in charge of faculty development, and I will double your pay immediately. Well, not me, the Board has to approve it. But that is almost a rubber stamp. We need you to help us motivate this faculty, Cole." Turkle's gaze again bore a hole through Cole's soul. "And to sweeten the pot, I've pulled a few strings. Listen, I don't know much about *Ian's Corner*...."

"Just enough to put a dramatic stop to it—for no reason." Cole did his best to be civil, but his edge was obvious. "You know, or maybe you don't, that's just the name that I gave to the corner of my office where the visitor chair sits. It's not even a club. Just me with students for office hours or in the café for a coffee."

"Cole, we all have orders to follow. But like I was saying, I have been given the authority to lift that cease-and-desist order. And I have been able to secure a donation for you and your students. For coffee and lunch. Small, I know, but perhaps it will help you. I've already established an account for you at the campus café."

Cole sat back.

"I don't like drama," Turkle continued. "This new position is best for the faculty, students, and, most importantly, for you."

Dumbfounded, Cole said nothing. He stared across the table.

What the hell did he just offer you? You? Work for the Ferrets? Watch out. But then, he is going to double your salary. And help Ian's Corner. *Not bad. Maybe you should listen? Who are you kidding, Cole? They are going to destroy you one way or another.*

"The band's name, *HTRB*? What's that mean?" Darla asked slurring her words as she made her way back to the booth. She drank more than soda. "Let me guess. *Hate Those Rude Bastards*? Or *Hugging The Rugged Bachelors*?"

"No, but I'll keep those in mind if we ever rebrand ourselves," Cole said. "*Hit The Reset Button.* Something we all need to do to stay sane." Cole looked toward the stage as the last two members joined Benny. "But we are all bachelors now that you mention the Rugged Bachelor name. Billy B, the lead guitarist up there, is in a relationship but not married. Justin the drummer, divorced. And you know Benny. Math professor at the college. Not married either."

Turkle leaned closer to Cole. "I hear he likes the same team if you know what I mean."

"You'd have to ask him. I don't care much for what he does or whom he does it with, as long as he keeps our bottom together with his bass guitar."

Turkle slapped Cole on the hand, laughed, and sat back. "You think about that offer. We'll talk details later. And one more thing. You might not know it but the work you do to help those kids would work all over the place. You just have to market it better to get around the hot-button issue of intersectionality. You and I can work on that. The cease-and-desist is politics, you know that, Cole!"

"Unfortunately, it's more than politics. It's about people's lives."

Turkle brushed the comment aside and continued. "I have an idea—and a team in place—to bring this noble quest of yours to our inner city. Hell, weren't you at the protest rally? I thought I saw you on the news. I've already reached out to a few of the pastors and school principals. I'm telling you, Cole, we can make history in this city. CCC will be like no other college in this nation for the impact it will have now and into the future. Because of you. Now you and the band go and help us all hit the reset button. Rock this joint!"

In a fog, Cole stepped up on the stage and retrieved the drink Joe put on his stool.

"Hey, see you already partying with your best bud Turkle. You two debriefing your coronation speech?" Benny winked at Cole. "And *piffle*! Love that word. I want no piffle from you tonight, young man. Nor any *flapdoodle*!" He laughed as he set his vintage Rickenbacker bass guitar on the stand next to Cole's guitar. "You ain't thinking of becoming an administrator and going over to the dark side, are you?"

"Hell, Benny, if you were in my head, you'd know I live on the dark side. But you won't believe he just offered me a job in his office."

"Say what?" Benny looked toward Turkle and Merlot. Then back at his bandmate. Then it was his turn to sit down on a stool. "As my students say, OMG! Or should I say, OMFingG?"

"I ain't going nowhere. If you ever hear me even consider something like that, you have permission to slap the crap out of me. Hard."

"Oh, I'd love to spank you, Dr. Fitz. Hard." Benny batted his eyes in mock jest.

"You sound like Heather."

"And here she comes in the door as if on cue. Go get your hug and kiss, I'll get the mics tested and the instruments tuned. And will your new secretary schedule me for lunch with you?" Another howl of laughter from Benny.

"Knock it off. I gotta meet him on Monday. Here we are in the midst of a budget crisis with impending layoffs, and he creates this position and offers me a higher salary *and* money for *Ian's Corner*. Doesn't make sense."

"Woah! *Ian's Corner*. I thought…OK, you have a lot to explain during our first break tonight. But I guess you'll figure it out once you are officially sworn in as AFWD— Associate Ferret to the Weasel Director." Benny's face was red, tears rolling down his cheeks. He was holding his sides, howling.

"Glad you're amused."

Heather waved to Cole as she found a seat. Joe made sure there was a "Reserved" sign at her usual table. He approached with a glass of Pinot Noir.

"Evening Heather. I understand tonight's a special night. Wave when you need a refill."

As Cole approached, Joe slapped him a high five and returned to the bar.

Heather leaned into Cole's embrace and gave him a warm kiss. "I'm a lucky woman."

"I'm the lucky guy. Surprised I haven't scared you off yet."

"Never." A smile and another kiss. "Good day?"

"The students are *always* the best part of my day."

"Any blowback about your remarks at the swearing-in event?"

"No, not that I know. It's always possible. But then Turkle over there just offered me a job in admin with a higher salary."

Heather furrowed her brow. "That doesn't make sense. Does it?"

Cole shrugged his shoulders. "Not to me."

"Be careful with them." She kissed his cheek. "But since you're getting a promotion, that means I just get to reward you for good behavior." She raised her glass to him and took a sip.

"Looks like he's in a good mood," Heather said as they both looked at Benny still wiping tears from his eyes.

"Yeah, at my expense."

Cole rolled his eyes and chuckled at this turn of events. "Anyway, how did things go with the students on your show this morning?"

"Nice kids. One, the girl, I don't know, concerned me a bit. Noticed bruises on her wrists. Looks like we have a lot to talk about later. Go break a leg but not a string! You want to impress your new boss." She blew a kiss and held up her glass.

It had been two years since they started dating and Heather had always been there for him. One of the few positive constants in his life. He knew that. After a frustrating day on campus or when he returned to bed after battling the voice in his ear, she gave comfort. *Especially* after the voice.

"Hey, Joe. Don't forget me."

"Just wave, my good man."

Cole stepped to the microphone. "Good evening. Welcome to *The Silver Fox*. We're *HTRB*. Glad you can join us."

Justin counted down, the band rolled into their first song, and the joint jumped.

Heather, smiling and wiggling to the beat at her table, looked at the crowd. She loved to watch how the band connected with them from the first song. Heck, the first note. Cole needed this. His soul needed what music provided.

• • •

8

Friday morning.

Cole could feel the tension over the phone. Professor Dawson was livid.

"Can you believe it?" Dawson asked. "He did it without shame. As if it were no big deal. I don't even think he *knows*. Idiot! Or as he would no doubt say, 'an incredibly extraordinary idiot!'"

Each word Dawson pitched out with sharp acid.

"Professor, I shouldn't throw stones given my impromptu convocation interruption. But, maybe, in the grand scheme of things around this college, it *was* no big deal. And maybe you shouldn't have...."

"What?" Dawson asked. "No big deal. You call yourself a professor. Come on Fitzgerald, where are your standards?"

Cole bit his lip and held the phone a little further from his ear.

"I'm just saying we need to pick our battles."

Breathing heavily, Dawson continued his rant, ignoring Cole's placation attempts. Cole smiled and thought, "He means well." The word *blatherskite* came to mind.

"You heard me! Hell, the entire auditorium heard me when I yelled, 'Lie!'"

Cole tried not to laugh. Again, he attempted to bring his fellow professor in from the ledge. "Well, he didn't lie at *that* moment. He was not a liar."

"It has nothing to do with the truth. Bartley said. And I quote, 'We should pause, take a breath, and maybe even lay down for a power nap.' End quote. The moron."

Wait for it.

"One does not *lay* down," Dawson said, "One *lies* down." Lie! Lie! Lie!"

Dawson, or as some of the faculty referred to him, The Grammarian, was out of breath.

"Professor, at times, such things obscure the essential issues. Grammar is sacred to you. Each word, phrase, and sentence. But maybe you just need to—as the novelists say—murder your darlings for the higher good."

Dawson hung up the phone.

"Well, at least he brings a smile to my face," Cole said as he flipped the light switch, closed his office door, and walked to class.

• • •

Despite the inane chatter coming from the other side of campus, the endless committee meetings with minimal consequence, and well-meaning people like Professor Dawson tilting at windmills, Cole felt energized when he walked into his classroom. He loved and savored every moment working with his students. Helping them apply history to current events gave relevance to his life and, he hoped, to theirs. "If you cannot connect what we talk about in class to your life outside of class," Cole told his students at the beginning of each term, "then I failed you."

The students came in with dreams. Some were laser-focused, and others had no clue how to get where they wanted to go. The first-generation college students had few if any college role models in their families. Single parents predominated in his classes. Cole often wondered how they got out of bed to face the day. From past semesters, he understood they would have trouble adjusting to college. Still, they sat, ready to start this part of their journey. They had, he believed, more courage and chutzpah than he ever did.

Lately, he wished he could summon their energy. Each day became another hurdle for him. Despite his love for the classroom, he was tired. "Wish I had their inner push."

Stop whining!

Like the 27-year-old woman who enrolled in one of his classes a few semesters back and relied on the city bus for her transportation and her neighbors for childcare. She had five children by three different fathers. And here she was starting college.

That was something the voice often reminded him about in the hour of the wolf.

You don't have the oomph you once did. Time to do something and make a difference. Or remain invisible. Don't blame the college for your shortcomings.

"All right, young scholars, great class. Love your enthusiasm. You've finished one week. Only 14 more to go." He smiled at a student in the front row. She scrunched her nose. "Don't forget the quiz at the beginning of our next class. Stop by my office when you get a chance. It gets lonely sitting in there. I need you. Now give yourself a big hand for a great first week!" He raised his arms like the champions they were in his eyes. He clapped his hands. They groaned. Then they applauded.

"Kerwin Lucas, can you see me before you leave?"

The students filed out. Lots of chatter. Cole could introduce topics and start conversations that continued long after the class ended. The voice would try but it could not take that away from him.

"Yes, sir."

"I hear you're a radio talk show star."

Kerwin's face lit up. "You must've spoken to Ms. Rivera. She was so cool. My first interview ever on the air. She made it seem so natural."

"Well, talk on the street has it that you're the tech rock star on campus."

"I can find my way around a keyboard and hard drive."

"Well, how about a new laptop? Any chance you can help me with that?"

"New? And you have problems?"

"It's a whole new operating system. Not intuitive, at least not for me. I need a tutor."

"Glad to help, professor. When would you like to meet?"

The door to the classroom opened. A stocky man in his mid-sixties with a jowly face waddled in raised his chin toward Cole and stood there with palms upturned as if saying, "Got time? Now?" Dominic Panagrossa wanted to talk. And act. That was what union organizers do.

Cole held up a finger and turned back to Kerwin. "Would you have time Monday morning?"

"I've got a 10 o'clock class. Would 9 work for you?"

"Excellent. See you then." Panagrossa held the door open as Kerwin exited.

"A good first week in class, I assume," Panagrossa made his way to the front of the room, pulled out a chair, and motioned for Cole to grab a seat. "Not sure about your class, but I heard from my department that about 20-25% of the students on the enrollment list didn't show up. Didn't the idiots at the dog and pony show make a lot of noise about increased enrollment?"

"Yeah, come to think of it, I had a few more absences than usual for the beginning of a semester."

"Maybe it's just a sign of the times, I guess. But we have a bigger problem than student no-shows." He drew his chair closer to Cole. "We gotta talk about those morons in the puzzle palace. Not a bit of common sense among all of them. But you know who are bigger *mamalukes*? Our fellow professors! What's with them? You know the meeting I scheduled next week following the faculty meeting? Only three are coming. Three!" Dominic put his hands together as if he were praying for answers. "What the hell, Cole? Do these faculty got salami for eyes? I mean, look at you. The other day you hit that Bartley right in the scrotum. You nailed it. We *are* invisible. We gotta stand up for ourselves. And what did most of the faculty do? Clap for a measly 250 bucks. Stupid."

Dominic had a gruff demeanor. And that scared some people. But when Cole looked at him, he saw a teddy bear. Albeit a teddy bear who threw around Italian slang as a matter of course.

Unbelievably, this rough-around-the-edges guy had been on the administrative track. Early in Bartley's administration, Panagrossa had applied and been selected to be the faculty liaison for administration. But he talked too much. He never shied away from disagreeing with an administrative plan that was detrimental to the teaching and learning dynamics of the classroom. He saw himself as the faculty rep of reason in the administration building. That, however, did not sit well with Bartley and his minions.

"Bartley and his crowd have no idea what faculty do. I'll take it as my job to educate them," he told Cole when he began his administrative stint. He believed he could make a difference with the administration. What he did make were enemies. Quickly.

After just six weeks, Bartley sent him back to the faculty ranks. That was when the college was introduced to Richard Edwards, an AVP in training.

"Can you believe it? The idiot replaces me with that bonehead, what's his name? Dick Ed. Yeah, that's it, Dick Ed."

Once back in the teaching ranks, Dominic took it upon himself to raise the union charge. A competent science faculty member and an embittered foe of Bartley, he started to make good on his pledge to make the administration uncomfortable. But the problem was getting the faculty to coalesce. Some were oblivious as to why they should organize and others were downright confrontational with Dominic.

Cole smiled at his friend. "I think some of our colleagues, especially those not on tenure, are scared. The older ones, nearing retirement, feel what's the use. And the others, well, I don't get them either. How about I make a pitch for the union at our faculty meeting?"

"You're a *campione*, Cole." Dominic slapped his chubby leg and laughed. His belly rolled.

"You know, I curse Bartley every night. During Lent, I do a Novena where he gets food poisoning. God, forgive me." He made the sign of the cross and looked toward the ceiling. "They need to learn not to mess with faculty. When they screw with faculty, they hurt students. But that *mamaluke* has never done anything that hasn't helped himself. And now, he's best buds with that senator?" Panagrossa scrunched his nose. "We gotta stop him and his henchmen, Cole. How about we get a cup of coffee in the cafeteria and discuss some strategies? I think you're the only one who might hate those dimwits more than me."

"Well, I'm not sure I hate them," Cole said, "but I do see them as misguided." He thought about mentioning Turkle's offer and their lunch meeting but figured his colleague would have a heart attack if he heard that nugget.

"Misguided like a rogue rocket that'll blow this place up if we are not careful," he said as he leaned forward. "We need missile defense," he said while taping his finger on the desktop.

"I'll take a rain check on the coffee. I have a lunch appointment. Let's plan for next week."

Then they heard it.

Tap. Tap. Tap. "You-hoo! Marco? You in there?"

"Marco? Who the hell is Marco," Panagrossa asked looking toward the door.

Cole's lips pursed into a smile. "Aunt Philomena." He shook his head and said, "Come on in."

"Your Aunt Philomena is Marco?" Dominic squinted at Cole and then turned to the door. His eyes widened as the visitor entered.

"Professor Panagrossa, this is my Aunt Philomena. She's visiting me from Connecticut. I'm Marco, at least to her."

Dominic slowly pushed his ample body out of the chair and swiveled his head between Cole and Philomena. She placed a tinfoil-wrapped dish on the desk in front of Cole. Reaching up to his neck, Philomena pulled him down for a kiss on the cheek then backed away, smoothing out her blue shift. She smiled broadly at her nephew radiating pride at the man she had helped raise as a child.

"You work too hard, Marco. I thought you could use some of my pasta and *braciola* for a snack. I made a little extra in case you wanted to share it with any of your teacher friends. Or maybe even one of those *strunz* who run this building."

Dominic stood speechless.

She turned, pushed her white-framed glasses up on her nose, and stepped toward Dominic. "I'm Philomena. Nice to meet you." She extended her small but solid hand toward the still incredulous union activist. He enveloped it with his meaty mitt.

"Ah, nice to meet you, Philomena. I'm Dominic. Ah, Dominic Panagrossa. Nice to make your acquaintance." He held her hand for a brief moment as if he were an adolescent meeting the girl next door for the first time. He was smitten. "So, you know about the *strunz*?"

"Yeah, my Marco gets upset with their *merda*. Me, I placed a *maledizione* on them last night." She made the sign of the cross. Dominic looked to heaven and thanked the Lord for this Italian gift. "That's why I went to the protest the other day. Gotta stand up to the *strunz*.

"You were at the protest," Dominic said arching his eyebrows above his ever-widening eyes.

"Yeah. I was on the side waving a sign. Had to be done."

Then she turned to Cole. "Well, Marco, enjoy the food. I put a little extra spice in the marinara just for you." Aunt Philomena got on her tippytoes as he bent down to her four-foot-five-inch frame to hug her. "Do you know where I can get a good cup of espresso around here?" Then turning to Dominic and raising an eyebrow, "Do you?"

"Sure, Gambardella's. A few blocks from campus. Would you like me to take you there?"

"No. No. Dominic. That would be too much like a date. And we just met. How about I follow you there? And I buy my coffee. No date, remember." She waved her index finger back and forth. "But you seem like a gentleman. *Capisce?*"

Dominic stumbled to open the door. "Ah, Cole, we'll talk more later. Or is that Marco? I'm confused."

"It's his middle name from his mother's side—my side—of the family. The Italian side. The best side!"

Aunt Philomena waved back at Cole. Then looking at Dominic, "I'm ready for my espresso."

"Me, too."

"*Buono!* Who's better than us?"

The door shut and Cole looked under the tin foil. His mouth watered. "Yes, who is better than us?"

• • •

9

As Cole moved toward his office, he saw her sitting on the hallway floor, her back to the wall and head in her hands. He stopped in front of her.

"Young lady, can I help you?"

She looked up and used her blouse sleeves to wipe away the tears. "Thanks. I'm OK."

"Really? You're so 'OK' that you are crying on a floor in a hallway, by yourself?" Cole was attempting to lighten the mood, but he wasn't about to leave her alone. "Weren't you sitting in my class? Last row? Seat near the door? I think you came in late."

"Yeah, sorry about that. It's not been a good week. Not the way I wanted to start college." She stood and extended her hand. "My name is Suzy."

"Well, Suzy, how about you come to my office for a few minutes and see if we can sort through what's going on with you."

"I don't want to be a bother. I'll be OK."

"No bother. And truth be told, you're helping me get out of a lunch meeting."

They both smiled and walked to his office.

Exiting a classroom meeting down the hall, Darla Merlot watched the two enter Cole's office and heard his door close.

"Well, it's not fancy, but it is comfortable and there is always a chair waiting for my students to visit." Cole pointed to *Ian's Corner*.

"Who's that?" Suzy asked pointing at the photo.

"His name was Ian."

"He has a nice smile."

"Yes, he did," Cole thought.

"And the flowers? Carnations, are they?"

"Yes. Before you leave, please take one. One way to stop and appreciate the day."

Suzy plucked one, placed it to her nose, and smiled. "Thank you."

"You read all those books?" Suzy asked looking at the four shelves of paperback and hardbound texts. Cole wasn't sure if she was curious or attempting to avoid a deeper conversation.

"Yeah, I have. Some just a few chapters but most of them I have read from cover to cover."

Cole walked around his desk and deposited his backpack and his aunt's dish on a small, cluttered credenza behind him. Suzy saw him look at the flashing light on his desk phone.

"I can wait," she said.

"No. It can wait. Do you want to tell me what is going on?"

He offered her a box of tissues and an unopened bottle of water. She took a tissue and shook her head at the bottle.

"This is my first semester in college. You probably know that. But I'm already feeling out of my element. I'm not sure I can handle this. Guess I was crying because I felt like I would be letting my Aintin down if I failed college."

Cole sipped his water and waited to respond. He heard this every semester from students. Scared, they doubted themselves. They felt like imposters. And, if he were a betting man, he knew that each one of them had an unreasonable voice in their ears. He was all too familiar.

"Aintin? So you're Irish?"

"Yes," she smiled and softened a bit. "Aintin Cara is who we, my daughter Shauna and me, live with."

Another familiar scenario for Cole over the years.

"Suzy, I understand your hesitation. I do. And I know that doesn't make it any less scary or frightening for you. I hear it every semester. I know the fear is real. Can I share two things with you? Maybe they'll help you get through this initial fear."

Suzy looked at Cole and wondered what this professor could offer. How could he know what she felt? But his eyes were kind, his voice reassuring. She nodded.

"First, I can't speak for you," he said, "but I would venture to say that you have heard some chatter about why you need or don't need school. Some comes from people, perhaps, in your neighborhood. And the rest comes from a little voice of doubt inside you. Or, if it is like *my* voice, it's sitting right here." Cole pointed to his shoulder. "And it's whispering in your ear."

"More like a shout or a scream," Suzy offered.

Cole smiled. "So, you have heard the little person, haven't you? CCC has so many resources dedicated to your success and shushing that voice. You need to find them and use them. And I will help you."

Suzy smiled.

"And secondly, what is your dream? Why did you come to CCC? What are you curious about?"

"Interesting, I was on a radio show this week, and the host asked me the same question."

"*The Fact and Fiction Hour* with Ms. Rivera I bet."

"She spoke highly of you." Feeling a bit more comfortable she said, "I'll take that water if it is still available." Cole placed it in front of her. She opened it, took a sip, and continued. "I'm not sure what I want to do, but I am interested in photography. I like colors, textures, and the stories that photos can tell. No words are needed. Just the image. Simple, yet complex. A lot like my life." She tugged on her hair.

"That's the dream. At least, the seed for the dream. Now let's start fertilizing and nurturing it. You deserve it, Suzy."

He pulled a piece of paper from his desk drawer and handed it to Suzy with a pen.

"Suzy, write four words. *Now Is My Time.* Remember that each day brings you closer to your dream of being, let's say, a photographer but only if you continue to move toward it. I am here for you. Other professors are here for you. Ms. Robertson is here for you. You will soon learn that your classmates are here for you too."

Suzy wrote the words, looked at them, and sank back into her chair. Her stomach unclenched. "Thank you, Professor." She looked at what she had written and placed the paper in her backpack. "And I promise not to be late again to your class."

When she got up to leave, Cole pointed to her wrists and said, "Do you need to talk about that?"

She pulled her sleeves down. "Oh, that's nothing. Just me horse playing with my daughter that's all."

"From the look of those bruises, Shauna must have strong big hands. I'm going to the café for a coffee, why don't we stop by Ms. Robertson's office and …."

"No! I need to go, professor. Ah, thank you, again." Suzy grabbed her backpack and left the office.

Cole picked up his phone. "Hi, may I speak with Ms. Robertson, please?"

• • •

10

2:47 a.m. Monday.
***What are you thinking? You're not a union organizer.
Stay put! Keep your head down. Visibility brings problems.***

Cole paced in his living room taking short shallow
breaths.

***You can't hide from me. You're the poser. You want to
hide. But you don't want to be invisible. Make up your
mind! Who the hell are you?***

He brushed a tear from his pockmarked cheek.

Big Betsy leaned into his leg. He picked her up and held
her close to help slow his breathing. His eye caught the
photo on the wall and he smiled almost feeling the embrace
his mother was giving him. The camera caught her leaning in
and whispering in his ear. Aunt Philomena stood on his other
side, with a hand on his shoulder.

***She was always your speaker of fame. No matter what,
you stood tall in her eyes.***

• • •

Cole's cell phone alarm played the lead riff of Duane Eddy's "Rebel Rouser." He rolled over and stared at the ceiling.

He heard a faint tapping on the bedroom door.

"You-hoo! It's your favorite aunt in the whole wide world." Aunt Philomena opened the door with one hand and balanced a small tray with the other. Cole pulled the bedspread over his naked body.

"Oh, what are you hiding? I saw you before you saw you. Remember, I changed your diapers! When your mother had to work, I stepped in." She placed the tray on the nightstand. She opened her arms in a wide embrace that was almost as broad as her smile. Cole leaned in for a kiss. "Between the problems your mother had with your *stunad* father, and her issues both emotional and alcohol, I was your second mother."

She handed him a demitasse cup of espresso. "Here. Good things come in small packages. Just like me! And here, I made this last night while you were out playing your music."

She placed her signature dessert, a homemade cannoli, in Cole's hand.

"You keep this up and I might ask you to move in with me permanently." Cole bit into the crust and got a burst of ricotta and a hint of chocolate. He closed his eyes and let it melt in his mouth.

"Like every year since my Vincenzo passed, you got me for a month, Marco." She made the sign of the cross and bowed her head.

"And then, I need to get home to help the priest with the annual church fundraiser. I'm in charge of the refreshments this year." She sat down next to him pulled the second cup from the tray, and toasted her nephew.

"How did your date go with Dominic?"

"Remember, no date. I don't need any guy messing up my life with wild thoughts of ha-boo-do-gaga!"

Cole nearly spit out his espresso.

"But I did like Dominic. We had a good talk. He seems like a good man. He loves you. And from what he told me, those *strunz* who run that college need a castration." She sliced the air with her hand. "He said they been putting pressure on you. Is that right?"

His aunt was small but stood up to anyone. Even Uncle Vincenzo. In his day he was known to fracture a few laws. But even he backed down from Philomena.

"I'll be OK. Nothing for you to worry about."

As Philomena looked at her nephew, she saw his teenage self. Always trying to prove he was worthy, yet never receiving the respect he desperately needed, especially from his father. Philomena always tried to fill the gaps and encourage Cole.

"If I hear they mess with my Marco, they will have something to worry about." She squinted and pursed her lips. "You enjoy your cannoli. I got a few errands to run. And Dominic and I are going to dinner tonight. Don't wait up."

Cole shook his head and smiled as she gathered up the tray and kissed her nephew.

"Those *strunz* try anything, you call me. I'll let 'em know a thing or two."

• • •

Whether faculty taught on the urban campus as Cole did, or on the cross-town suburban campus, their cramped, weathered, and outdated offices and classrooms stood in stark contrast to the comfort and ostentatiousness of the administration building. While the faculty had mismatched hand-me-down office furnishings on threadbare carpet, the top administrators had opulent executive desks, ergonomic chairs, and wooden armoires sitting on large patterned plush wall-to-wall carpets.

Take President Doyle Bartley's office. Spanning half the 6th floor, its floor-to-ceiling windows offered stunning views of the downtown skyline and the river. One wall of windows scanned the central business district. Another looked down upon the city's poorest section where many of Central City College's urban campus students lived, where economic and social imbalances had been a way of life for generations. Problems that the college gave hope of addressing. At least in words and mission statements. From this suite, schemes were hatched, and people were called into account. Careers were made and lives were ruined.

"Well, did you get him on board?" Bartley looked across his desk.

"We were scheduled to meet, but he canceled." Turkle sat erect in the visitor's chair. The window glare from behind Bartley's head created a calculated challenge for any visitor. One reason why Bartley liked his desk where it was. Especially when the afternoon sun screamed through his blinds. Whoever sat in the visitor's chair had to contend with the strategic glare of the sun. While Bartley may have been a puppet of the Senator, he understood staging. Like the boxes at the convocation event.

"What do you mean *he* canceled? You're the Director of Human Resources! You let faculty tell you when they will meet with you? After that incredibly rude outburst of his, he's lucky to have a job. Apply pressure."

"He had a student in distress and had to deal with the situation then. Doyle, what am I supposed to do? Tell him to ignore the student? Don't worry, I'll sit down with him before the week's out. I already made the job offer to him," Turkle said. "But you know Cole, he's a faculty member through and through. He's not going to take that position. It's a long shot at best. That's why I sweetened the pot with the initiative for those down-and-out students he works with on and off campus."

"Keep leaning on him because we need him out of the faculty ranks incredibly soon. Faculty follow his lead. And now he's helping with the unionization talk. Find a way to apply huge pressure. Lots of incredibly big pressure."

"Don't worry about that. That dumb dago, Panagrossa, is the lead on that union. Remember when he was working with us for those few weeks? He's a nitwit. Couldn't lead a priest to communion."

"Isn't that why Fitzgerald is key to him and his movement? If the union gets in, that's just one more distraction for us and what we want to do going forward. They will feel empowered—more like enabled—and then what if they start asking questions and then find answers to questions we don't want them to find answers to and then what if they ask more questions and then...."

Turkle held up his hand and offered a kind smile. He was used to Bartley's stress-laced stream of consciousness. The president was good when events went according to plan—the script as the Senator referred to it—but the slightest deviation and he started to ramble and go into a torrent of what-ifs. Like he was a novelist looking for a new plotline.

"Maybe, maybe not. Remember what we told the senator? We ignore Cole. To a degree. Let him think we need him. Let the professors shoot off their mouths, tire themselves out, and start stabbing one another in the back." Turkle paused and then said, "And we have Darla."

Bartley's eyes exhibited his puzzled mind. "Darla? What's she got to do with this?"

"I've got an idea, Doyle. In short, while we make it seem like we are listening to him, Darla will slowly and deliberately build pressure. We offer the olive branch while she's loading the guns in the wings. Metaphorically, of course."

"Tell me more," Bartley said.

"We ignore the faculty, at least publicly. We throw a few crumbs and keep moving with our plan. You do know that probably 40% of the faculty will never vote for the union. Never. Even if they get lucky with a pro-union vote, it will take them years to gain traction. They will continue to bicker and dicker within their ranks. We can stonewall. We can obfuscate. We got lawyers. They have office hours. We can create a hell for them they never imagined! *That* is the kind of distraction I would love to have."

Bartley sat back. Behind Turkle's smile lived the mind of an arch-conspirator. Turkle did not like to lose. To anyone.

"We can't foul this up, Pat. If we do it's more than just our jobs here at Central City College. We can't foul this up."

His secretary buzzed in. "Dr. Bartley, Senator Wilbur Wackenslong is here to see you. Shall I tell him to wait?"

"No. No. Escort him in right now." Bartley stood and grabbed his suit coat from the back of his chair.

Turkle stood. "Guess I oughta be leaving."

"No, I wish you'd stay," came the answer from the doorway.

Turkle turned and faced the nattily dressed senator. His fake smile plastered on his face as he turned to the secretary. "Thank you, ma'am, for your kindness. You have a nice day." She closed the oak door on her way out. Wackenslong made his way to Bartley's desk.

"I want both of you here. Tell me what you have accomplished and how we're getting closer to our respective goals. What in the hell have you and the Young Turk here done? What movement can you tell me about?"

Turkle winced.

Remember he knows more about you than anyone at this college. Don't cross him!

Bartley waved his arm toward the conference table in the middle of his office. "Would you like some coffee, Senator?"

"No! I'd like answers, Doyle."

"Just so happens, Pat and I were talking about it. And it's incredibly complicated."

"Complicated? Talking about it? Listen to me. You two have titles, but I have the institutional control here. The Board does what I say. You have your jobs because of me."

"And you know for that I am incredibly grateful," Bartley interjected, hoping to soothe the senator "But, you also know, that I do good work. I mean, isn't that why you helped me get this position? Because I helped you when you needed assistance?"

Wackenslong's eyes narrowed. True enough, Bartley had used his influence so that his former for-profit school awarded the apparel contract to the Wackenslong family company. Every student in the nursing, dental hygienist, and radiology programs bought their uniforms from the family line. The senator did not like being reminded of the past business partnership.

He leaned in and over Bartley's desk, pounded a fist on the oak top, and glowered at Bartley. "Don't give me a history lesson, you little bastard! Follow the plan. I don't have time to do your job and mine, too."

He backed away from the desk, straightened out his suit jacket, smoothed his hair with his hands, and took a deep breath. "Let's simplify. Answer this for me. Has the college enrollment increased?"

Bartley started sorting through the files on his desk. "Well, yes, I have the figures here someplace."

"Forget the figures for now. Just answer me, has the enrollment increased?"

"Yes, it has. By 25%."

"OK! That's good! You've been able to bring more students in by offering more financial aid, correct? That's a yes or no answer."

"Yes, we have."

"Another plus! You see, you are reaching out to the disadvantaged. Isn't that what that pain-in-the-ass professor—the one you want to ignore—does for his poor students? We are helping them make ends meet. Good." His condescension trumped his sarcasm. "And have you been helping your star athletes understand the new *Pay for the Name* law concerning endorsements?"

Turkle interjected, "We are both on a steep learning curve with that one as it just came from the governor's desk. But, yes, we will sit with the coaching staff and the athletes themselves. I am working on that."

Turning to the Director, Wackenslong said, "Oh, you are? It's nice to hear that you're doing your homework." And then raising his voice, "Because I don't know what the hell you are up to out there?" Wackenslong waved his arm toward the window view of downtown. "For a smart guy, you're pretty stupid, Mr. Young Turk! If you and your buddy here don't produce the goods, you'll be lucky to get a custodian's job. *After* you get out of prison."

Silence.

"We've had a tiny little hiccup with the faculty and that's causing a tiny little bump in the road and distracting us momentarily," Bartley said, attempting to gain some semblance of control of the situation before him. "The faculty have been speaking about unionizing. We need to figure out the best way to handle that. We don't want it to interfere with our goals, goals that you know are incredibly extraordinary. Pat and I have a plan. Trust us. We will deliver magnificently for you, Senator."

"You mean like that professor who kicked your ass in front of the entire college? The one who said he refused to be invisible? The one who marched in protest against my company and family? For that, you have a plan?"

Again, silence.

Wackenslong buttoned his suit jacket.

"You two better get it together and fast. With all the good stuff happening—as you just attested to—get some of your people in front of the press. Start driving the story. Damn it all! Let the community know we have a Goddamn story! Doyle, call me by the end of the week with an update. And it better be a good one. I want answers, action, and accountability. I'm getting tired of putting lipstick on this pig."

Turkle and Bartley stood and watched Wackenslong leave the room. They exhaled and returned to their seats.

• • •

11

*L*ater that afternoon.

"Hey, Professor Fitzgerald, can I speak with you?"

On his way to the first faculty meeting of the semester, Cole would stop for anyone or anything to delay his arrival. He looked back and saw Kerwin trotting down the hall.

"Thanks, Professor. I need a favor."

"Already looking for a homework extension?"

"No, nothing like that. I was wondering if you could write a recommendation for me. I've put in for a work-study job over at the administration building. Ms. Rivera called Mr. Niblick about me."

"I don't know, Kerwin. If you ever get the job, I might lose you as my personal tech tutor and guru. Since you showed me how to navigate that new computer and tablet I haven't had a single problem. You're a genius!"

"That's perfect! Write that and send it to Mr. Niblick. I hear there are several applicants and I need to stand out."

"Hey, Cole, we're getting started in a minute down here." Benny was heading into the conference room and waving. "What's a faculty meeting without Dr. Fitz?"

Cole rolled his eyes and turned back to Kerwin. "I'd be happy to do that for you. I'll get it to Mr. Niblick in the morning."

"Thanks, Professor. You rock."

Cole watched Kerwin head down the hall to catch up with a few classmates.

Remember when you were like that? When you had a bounce in your step and had little to no trepidation to reach out for guidance.

Cole was conflicted. No way he wanted an administrative position. But, then, the thought of getting administrative support for *Ian's Corner* pulled at him. Should he forget what he wanted and focus on what his students needed? Or maybe, the two were related.

"Hey, professor, you lost?"

Cole turned back toward the conference room and there stood Lori Craig. When he started at CCC, she was teaching first-year orientation classes. They came to know each other on the various committees they served. She became a mentor.

Cole appreciated Lori's bullshit detector. Unlike most administrators and middle management, she came to the table each time ready for a considered conversation. She listened and asked hard, yet well-thought-out, questions about the various nuances of an issue. She trusted people to do the right thing.

Soon after Lori entered the administrative ranks, however, she learned that her blind trust was a questionable quality.

She never forgot the former assistant to the college vice president. He had assured her in a private meeting that he was on board with her proposal for a new course focused on critical thinking. "Lori, that is a wonderful proposal. I love how you have thrown your heart and soul into this proposal. I look forward to your presentation at the next Curriculum Review Committee," said the AVP, who was also the chair of that group.

When Lori got to the meeting, he eviscerated her with leading questions and dismissive comments about how such a course would punish people with unpopular opinions. He set her up to promote his political ideology.

Lori was not prepared for the aggressive and, ironically, non-critical thinking approach of the AVP. She stopped him one time when she asked, "So, did you just ask me a question or give me an answer?"

In the end, Lori's proposal was rejected. As she walked to her office, she promised herself, "I will always follow my heart. And from this point forward, I will always watch my back." It became her motto.

Cole did what he could to stay in touch, but with her promotion to Associate Vice President for Academic Affairs, their paths didn't cross much.

"Ah, AVP Craig. The flicker of light from the dark side of the campus."

"You need to cut that dark side stuff out. There are a lot of good people in the administration." She smiled as they gave each other a friendly, gentle hug.

"Yeah, and bank robbers are only trying to redistribute the wealth. You, my friend, are one of the few good people—I mean great people—that Bartley has yet to run off. What brings you to the meeting? You plan on coming back to the teaching ranks."

"You know I would love to teach one course, but the powers-that-be don't think that would be a good idea. Especially with the union organization gaining traction. Between you and me, they're circling the wagons. Today, I'm here to welcome the faculty back. Dr. Edwards is already in the room. He wants to pass on well wishes, too."

"Ah, too bad, ol' Dick Ed is not passing on." Cole held the door open. Lori raised an eyebrow in mock disapproval, lowered her head, and stifled a laugh as she entered the room.

Cole found his usual seat in the back of the room. Like their students in class, faculty members sat in the same place for every meeting. Some for years. Another unquestioned routine. He patted Benny on the shoulder as he slid into the seat.

Looking around the room, Cole smiled to himself. While his colleagues often complained about students being digitally distracted, most of the faculty swiped through a tablet or madly texted from their phones. Many were just putting in face time at these required meetings. They seldom spoke and spent more brain power watching the clock than participating in the discussion. And then there were the personalities that stood out. Like Dr. Eulonia Polonia.

She always had an opinion—the correct one all the time according to her. And when she was confronted or challenged, everything became a personal affront. Cole understood the best he could, but she was tough to get to know. She maintained her professional distance from faculty while staying close to her mission in the classroom. A tough instructor, she always received high evaluations from her students. With closely cropped hair, dark-hued skirts and blouses, and a perpetual scowl, she had a no-nonsense approach to her career.

Central City College hired her a few years after Cole came aboard. One of the few African American professors at that time, she kept her head down and did her job, while earning one PhD in economics and a second in statistics along the way. Quiet and analytical, she gained a reputation over the years as a colleague who did her homework when serving on committees. She never accepted what the administration or faculty proposed without asking questions. Each year she became more confrontational with the administration, always challenging their numbers, budget, and enrollment statistics. Rumor had it that the administration referred to her as Eulonia Bolonia. Ideological as she could be, Cole recognized her as a valuable faculty resource.

And there was her favorite saying, "There're elephants in those string beans!" Whatever that meant. Cole believed she was a brilliant personality behind a mask of crazy. Eccentric yet vigilant.

"Good afternoon, colleagues. Glad you could join us. Welcome back for another semester. I trust your first week went well and your second one is off to a wonderful start." The dean called the meeting to order. Dressed, as usual, in a tailored suit with a starched shirt and a yellow handkerchief in his coat breast pocket, the dean stood as a stark contrast to his more casual faculty charges. He fingered his finely coifed black goatee and smiled. The room quieted down, and most put down their digital devices and turned toward their dean. Except for Eulonia. She continued to read the morning newspaper—the print edition—spread out on the table in front of her.

"First on our agenda, I'd like to welcome our AVP for Faculty Relations, Dr. Edwards, and AVP for Academic Affairs, Dr. Craig."

Lori stood and waved. "I just wanted to come and say hello. Especially to the new faculty. Welcome to Central City College. A great place with students who need you. I miss my days in the classroom and, yes, even these faculty meetings. Many of us go a long way back." She smiled at Cole. "I am in awe of what you do for our students and your colleagues. Thank you. And please know you can call on me if I can ever be of assistance to you or your students."

The faculty applauded.

Professor Dawson, The Grammarian, raised his hand. "Excuse me. A suggestion. Do you *want* to say it or *will* you say it?"

Lori looked at the professor and then the dean and back to the professor. "I'm sorry. Can you repeat that? I didn't follow you."

"You said, 'I would like to' say such and such. The proper way—and most economical way sentence structure-wise is to simply say, 'I say' such and such."

The room was silent.

Remembering their phone call, Cole thought to himself, "He is a blatherskite."

The dean broke the awkward silence. "Now, please welcome Dr. Edwards."

A polite golf clap with no enthusiasm came from a few professors.

"There're elephants in those string beans!" Eulonia whispered to herself as she turned to the Metro section of the paper.

"Woo, Woo! Pop goes the weasel!" Benny leaned in toward Cole. "I'd say he looks like an aluminum siding salesman but that would insult all those dedicated people."

"I am so happy to be here today. Truth be told, there is no other place I'd rather be. Love your energy," Edwards said looking out at the mostly somber and pained faces.

And he continued for 15 unemotional and soul-sucking minutes. Mostly about how the administration was doing all it could to help the faculty with a pay increase.

"You may not see a raise, but you know that Drs. Bartley, Merlot, and Turkle all treasure your work. You have to believe they do not want faculty cuts. We need you. Just remember, your job is to teach and ours is to lead. Don't you worry about what we do. We have your backs during these tough times. And there you have it. I need to get back to my office.

Have a great semester." With that, he left the meeting. Lori stood, waved, and exited behind her colleague.

"Weasel," Cole muttered. "Yeah, they have our backs with one hand while the other holds a knife. Backstabbing ferrets."

Eulonia picked up the paper, ceremoniously folded it in half, and continued reading.

Dominic Panagrossa spoke out from his seat in the rear of the room. "And that *mamaluke* is an outstanding example of why we need to unionize. Come to our meeting after we complete this dog and pony show. It will be your opportunity to speak up for ourselves and be heard."

Eulonia harrumphed.

"OK! Now that our guests have left, I thought we'd have a little fun." The dean stepped from behind the lectern holding a stuffed squirrel. "When I toss it to you, give us a bit of bright news. Anything you choose. Let's start with," his eyes looked around the room. He thought about starting with low-hanging fruit—the typically positive people in the room—but decided to take a chance and go big. "Eulonia! Catch!"

Eulonia did not look up from her newspaper as the squirrel landed beside her arm on the table.

Thwack!

She glanced at it and shook her head.

"We've got a problem, Dean," Eulonia said, now reading the newspaper's obituary section. The room went silent as the dean attempted to regroup with the brightest response he could muster. "Yes, but we are starting with something positive!" He swallowed and mentally kicked his own keester.

She meticulously folded the paper, pushed it to the side, and looked the dean in the eye.

"OK. I'm sorry. I am *positive* we have a problem. Let me state that another way, the administration of this college has a problem, and because of that, this campus—our campus—has a problem."

The dean stepped back behind the lectern and grabbed each side with white knuckles. With a sigh and a constricting throat, he could only manage, "Care to share, Professor?"

"For the last three years, we have had three women in charge of our Student Services Division on this campus. The Associate Dean of the Division, her Administrative Assistant, and the Coordinating Advisor. It took a long time for that to happen. Three females at the top of a department at this college. As you know the Associate Dean has retired and the college hired someone to replace her."

"That is correct. What is the problem? Should we have left the position vacant?"

"No. The problem is the new AD is a *male*." The word spewed out of her mouth as if it were a bad clam.

"Correct again. And the recommendation came to President Bartley by way of the faculty search committee that screened applicants."

"Big deal. A *male* was hired." The same sour look on her face as if she got another bad mollusk. "Now, once he comes aboard, he will need to collaborate with two women. That is not ideal at all."

"I don't follow you."

"Of course, you wouldn't. You're a *male*." More gut-wrenching cherrystones. "The feel, the chemistry, the collaboration the former female triumvirate had is lost. As soon as the male enters, well, you might as well forget collaboration. The *male* will spoil the stew."

Crickets.

An awkward silence fell over the gathered faculty. The Dean looked at the squirrel still sitting next to Eulonia's arm. Not much help.

"You hypocrite. You *female* hypocrite." On the other side of the room, The Grammarian stood and faced Eulonia. He had the appearance of an all-you-can-eat buffet. His bright dyed green hair had the disheveled look of a salad bar that had been picked through by one too many customers. His pockmarked face looked like a mixture of peas, carrots, and corn. Cognitively sharp, he always stood ready to challenge his colleagues and administrators about issues grammatical or not.

"You, have the gall to say that our new person, just because he is a male, will 'spoil the stew.' What kind of stew are you brewing? I'll tell you what kind, *ideological female stew.*"

Eulonia waved him off, opened her paper, and continued to read. She pushed the squirrel to the floor.

"Consider this," the professor said. "Think back if you can in that ideologically trapped mind of yours. Think back to when the retiring AD came aboard. At that time, the admin assistant and the coordinator were males. I remember when her appointment was announced you applauded. Well, you still read your newspaper, but you did applaud."

That drew a muffled chuckle from most of the faculty.

"Can you imagine what *you* would have said if anyone in this room objected with the reasoning that, let's see, let me see if I can quote you here, "Now, once *she* comes aboard, *she* will need to collaborate with two men. The feel, the chemistry, and the collaboration the former male triumvirate had is lost. As soon as the *female* enters, well, you might as well forget collaboration. The *female* will spoil the stew."

Eulonia harrumphed, shifted in her seat, and turned the page to the Help Wanted section.

Panagrossa, the union organizer, shook his head and thought to himself, "They will argue with one another but not stand up to the real hypocrites. We're screwed."

The dean looked at his squirrel on the floor.

Faculty began talking across one another.

Welcome to the semester.

• • •

12

The good news: More than three people stayed for the union organization meeting. As he had promised Dominic, Cole encouraged his colleagues to remain for a collegial conversation about faculty organization.

The not-so-good news: Only about half of the faculty remained. But it was the best turnout yet for one of Dominic's meetings. Even Dawson the Grammarian was sitting in the back of the room. Cole wasn't sure if he was pro-union or just there to judge sentence structure. Eulonia attended, as well. Everyone knew she was not a strident supporter of the union. She questioned its true motives. Cole knew regardless of her opinion about unionization, she would do her due diligence. Dominic would do well to bring her into the discussion.

But Cole was not sure if Eulonia was in the room because of the meeting or if she had not finished reading her paper. She had turned to the Police Reports page.

The attendance of Professor Cliff Singer and Professor Savannah O'Rourke surprised Cole. Neither could be accused of being union organizers, boat rockers, or agitators by any stretch of the imagination.

Cliff sat there with his legs crossed so tightly one would think he'd pop a scrotal sack. Hunched over in his chair, with his right hand rubbing his temple he looked as if he had a perpetual migraine headache. A non-tenured professor of computer science, Cliff always seemed like he needed antacids.

Savannah was an anomaly. Well-dressed, toned, and sophisticated-looking, she gave an air of uber confidence. Once she opened her mouth, the real persona shone through. Timid, unsure, and ready to avoid a confrontation at all costs.

"Do you really think this thing, the union is wise?" she asked Cole as he grabbed a seat next to her. "I mean, ah, I don't know. Just look. Look at this, this room. More than half the faculty is not here. How do we challenge the administration this way? We'd be better, I mean, safer if we just worked with them. President Bartley wants what is best for the school. Right?"

"This is pathetic," Dominic said as he started the meeting. "Where is everyone? You telling me our colleagues like what is going on here with those *mamalukes* in charge? We'll criticize each other in our faculty meetings, but we won't stand up to the bullies who mismanage this place. I don't get it."

"I'm not sure they *like* it," Benny said from the middle of the room. "It's more that they look for the path of least resistance."

"They don't wise up, they'll be looking for the path to the unemployment office. Those poor excuses for managers are going to start cutting faculty. Bad for the students and bad for those of us *lucky* enough to remain."

Cliff untied one hand from his self-imposed body wrap and sought recognition from Dominic.

"What you got for us, Cliff?"

"I think they, Bartley, and the Board, have us by the throats. We have no power to challenge them outright. They can make life very tough for us. And those of us without tenure, well, we'd be risking everything to challenge them with a union. Why don't we attempt to work from within the current structure to effect change? Do we have to be so confrontational?"

Dominic's eyes widened as he inhaled. Cole stepped in.

"Cliff, I hear you. And Dominic hears you. All of us who have been here for decades hear you. Working from within is what we have tried with every past administration. And each semester it gets worse, not better. We get more students added to the rolls. We go one more semester without a pay raise. And each time we work from within, they see it as a weakness and take more. We, all of the faculty," Cole looked around the room as he spoke, "need to take a harder look. Yes, half the faculty is not here but half is. We start with that for this crusade. Like the students we serve, the CCC faculty need to find their voice and use it. Loudly."

"But," Savannah interjected as expected, "they are willing to change. I just know it." She rubbed her chin and cheeks, compulsive behaviors that increased in intensity as her anxiety peaked. "Take this morning, today, before my first class. Dr. Edwards called me and my colleague." She nodded toward the ever-tightening Cliff. "Did you know that President Bartley, is so committed to faculty development, that he has created a new teacher training initiative? With the 25% increase in student enrollment, we need to find novel ways to connect with all of these new students, many of them first-gen. He told me himself. We'd work under Dr. Edward's guidance for the training of faculty."

"We? Work under? Who are *we*? What?" Dominic asked.

"Me and Cliff, as the co-chairs of the newly formed Teaching Initiative Team. President Bartley is so committed to this that he has given us each a stipend above our salary. And we get to plan meaningful training events for faculty. You know like for online teaching and, well, you know.

Every eye turned toward Savannah. Cliff was becoming a tighter ball of protoplasm.

"Teaching Initiative Team?" Benny asked no one in particular, "T.I.T.?"

"What? Teacher training? What are we seals? Dogs? You said *yes* to that?" Dominic scrunched up his face as he leaned forward in his chair. "How? Why? They care nothing about us. *Train* is right. They want to *train* us to do what they say on command. We have to stop them."

"But you got them, ah, wrong," Savannah said. "Listen to me, all of you." She turned to the gathered faculty and stood. "Can't we just get along with the administration? Why waste time fighting? They understand us. Really. They want us to do well, our students to do well. Dr. Bartley and Dr. Merlot told me themselves this morning. They fully supported me coming to this meeting and speaking, like um, a liaison with the administration."

A few heads nodded in agreement. Cole saw this as a make-or-break moment. He stood.

"Savannah, I commend you for your abilities and desires to seek collaboration. And Cliff, the administration needs your critical thinking abilities. Unfortunately, you cannot have collegiality with people who do not value you as a colleague. I know you mean well. If you accept that assignment, you stand the risk of undercutting faculty strength, what little we might have. And the stipend. You've been around long enough to know how this works. We sell our collective souls for a few hundred bucks." He paused for effect. "No one knows this but Benny. Pat Turkle offered me a new position reporting directly to him. AVP for Faculty Development."

A gasp rose from the faculty. Eulonia put down her newspaper.

"I *have* not and *will* not accept that position. I am faculty. You are faculty. This is about our calling. We need to be with one another going forward. Cliff, they need you, but you don't need that assignment. Didn't you just get your cybercrimes article published in a leading journal? That's fantastic—and *you* did it. Not Bartley, not Turkle, not Edwards, or Merlot. You, Professor Clifford Singer. And we are proud you are with us."

"But I'm afraid we already accepted," Savannah said.

Silence. Except for the sound of what was probably Cliff's second testicle being scrunched further into his stomach.

"I'm at a loss for words. We need to unite but you help divide us!" Dominic dismissively pointed at the two and continued, "I don't get it. And I'm not surprised. You have hurt the faculty, but we will not be defeated by you. I pity you."

Then turning to the rest of the faculty in the room, Dominic asked, "What do we have to lose? Administration respect? Hell! They disrespect us already. We have to stick together. Don't you see that Bartley and his team are trying to divide us, and we are letting them? If we stick together, we can make a difference for the faculty. But we have to stand up and speak. Often and loudly! We gotta do something and make our voices heard by the entire college and the public at large. If we don't, Cole is correct. Just like our students, we continue to be disrespected and ignored. We will be invisible. Forever."

"That might be difficult," Benny said pointing toward his tablet. "Vice President Merlot just sent out a directive to all faculty." He tapped on the screen and read, "Per order of the Central City College President, effective immediately, no college employee will be allowed to speak to the press, write a letter to the newspaper editor, or otherwise make any public comments about college business including speaking at Board meetings unless their comments and/or appearance have been vetted and approved by the office of the Vice President."

"Hell, Benny," Dominic said, "they've had that policy or similar for as long as I can remember. They resurrect it when they want to scare the weak-kneed amongst us." He squinted at the two new T.I.T. leaders. "And they continue to marginalize us because we give them the permission to do that by our inaction!"

And then Eulonia spoke. "There're elephants in those string beans."

"Would you care to explain, Professor?" Dominic asked with a bit of impatience. "We need answers and I'm not sure how your elephants and string beans, whatever that means, help us get to those answers."

"One thing does not fit with the other. One thing takes attention away from what is happening," Eulonia said with a clipped tone. "The word *marginalized*. That's a problem." Eulonia's pursed lips highlighted the disdain in her eyes.

The Grammarian jumped in. "Marginalized. It means...."

Eulonia raised her hand. "Stop! You? You're going to tell me what it means to be *marginalized*? What the hell?"

"Professor Polonia. I don't think Professor Dawson means to diminish what you have experienced," Cole said. "He's seeing what we see with our students. What I see in *Ian's Corner*. What I heard at the industrial site protest this week."

"Professor Fitzgerald. Again, stop it. You," she waved her hand at Cole and Dominic, "have co-opted the word like it is some sociological paper you're presenting. Marginalization. You diminish the truly marginalized people. You mean well,

I'm sure. But I'm afraid what the truly marginalized see and feel is, and I hate to say it, white saviorism. Pure and simple. What do you know about marginalization and the intersection of demographics? How would you know what we go through daily?"

"Are you saying that me and my family before me, as Italians, never experienced prejudice and discrimination?" Dominic's eyes lit up and his nostrils flared. "So, what, now we have to engage in comparatory suffering before we can use certain words. I'd say to you, 'Stop it!'"

"Eulonia, I understand marginalization. As a member of the LGBTQIA community, I have lived it and still live it. The concept is not the purview of race." Benny used a measured, calm, yet forceful tone.

Eulonia bowed her head and took a breath. "What I am saying is too often the good intentions are not perceived as such by the community you attempt to work with. Too often labels are tossed around without thought. Benny, what is it *you* want?"

"To be seen. To be recognized. To be respected for what I do and who I am as a human being."

"And that is what my community wants," Eulonia said. "We want to be seen not *saved*. We want to be part of the conversation. Not diminished with pablum. If you don't truly *see* the people in front of you, how can you ever expect to build a lasting and meaningful relationship?"

• • •

Later that evening.

The waiter poured a glass of Chianti for Philomena and one for Dominic. "Your antipasto will be ready in a few minutes."

"Make sure to tell Chief Carl I want the deluxe version tonight," Dominic said.

"Yes, Professor Panagrossa."

Dominic raised his glass. "To you, Philomena. Where have you been all my life?"

Philomena clinked glasses, "Who's better than us?"

They sipped and then shared an awkward few moments. Philomena broke the silence.

"Dominic. Thank you for this," she said pointing at the wine. "This is buono. And so are you. But I must make something clear."

Dominic shifted in his chair, again feeling like that adolescent with the girl next door.

"I believe you and me are about the same age, give or take a decade. We've seen a few things. Been with a few people. Done a few things. And if you are like most of the men I have met along the journey, you are, how should I say this, thinking of a way to use your sausage."

Dominic's eyes grew wide.

"I don't want you getting any ideas that you and me are going to be doing any, ah, you know." She arched her eyebrows. "And I know you know what I mean. Capisce?"

Dominic froze.

"You see, Dominic, my body has gotten to the point where let me see...um." She paused and took a sip of the Chianti. Dominic wasn't sure if he should ask for the check.

"But," Philomena said, "then again," she paused, raised her glass, and an eyebrow.

Dominic moved his head from side to side, raised his glass, and said, "To you. There's no one better than you. Except maybe your nephew Cole. God, I love that guy! He has *coglioni!* Um, excuse me, Philomena, for being so rude."

Philomena leaned across the table. "I'm glad you see that. I knew you were a smart one! But," she grabbed the red crushed pepper shaker, "I fear he's losing his spice. He puts on a good show. The *strunz* are wearing him down. What are you doing to help him?" She sat back, lowered her head, and stared at Dominic. He motioned to the waiter for more chianti.

"I'm organizing, or at least I'm trying to organize a faculty union. Cole gets it. But most don't. It's not easy."

"Those *strunz*. We gotta hit 'em and hit 'em hard. Right in their *coglioni!*"

"We?"

"*Si!* Cole might think I'm just making sauce and braciola, but I always listen. I got an idea for you. Let's call it foreplay." She raised her glass with a wink.

"*A salute!*"

• • •

13

11 PM the same night.

Music has a way of making things right. Or maybe it helps block the bad. At the least, it puts distance between the musicians and what they want to forget. Eventually, though, the music stops and reality re-enters.

"Thank you for coming out to *The Silver Fox* tonight. Remember Joe, your bartender, and the wait staff. And don't forget the band. Half of us are teachers and need the tip money." Cole hit the stage lights button with his foot. The crowd whistled and applauded. Joe turned up the house music.

"I needed that tonight, Benny. Why don't we quit CCC and take the band on the road? We can play in a different town every night." Cole placed the guitar in his gig bag and zipped it shut.

"Not sure either of us has that stamina anymore. And why would we want to leave all the fun here at Central City College?"

"Not sure how much more of this I can take. I just want to teach, play music, and see Heather. That's pretty simple.

But Bartley and his, as Dominic calls them, *mamalukes* are killing me."

Benny wiped down his bass and slid it into his case. "Cole, the faculty needs your voice of reason. They see you as a leader. And obviously, Turkle does too, or else why would he offer you that job? And he did that after your convocation performance. He offers to reward you, not promise to punish you? Think about that."

"The job that I will not accept. I wouldn't want to follow me. Yeah, I speak up about stuff and maybe that's become a distraction. Faculty want me because they don't want to put their necks out there. Other than Dominic and a few others like yourself, who else takes a stand?"

"And that's caught Turkle's and Bartley's attention. Maybe that's why they want you out of the faculty. If so, they miscalculated."

"And they will be pissed. Make no mistake about that. Turkle will just give me that shit-eating grin he has when he is about to swoop in on prey. No matter how much I want it to be, it will never be over."

"Hey, can a gal get attention here? Any chance I can go home with the guitar player?" Heather walked on stage, hugged Benny, and then kissed Cole. "You guys were smoking tonight. What got into you?"

"Just letting go of a tiring day," said Benny. "You should have seen your man. He knows how to keep the heat on the bad guys." He started rolling up the cords scattered about the stage. "You two go get reacquainted; the guys and I will finish packing up."

"Hmm," she whispered in Cole's ear. "Sounds like you might need to talk. I'm a good listener."

"Let me finish packing up. Then let's go to Nico's Diner for something to eat. And maybe we can talk about dessert after that." Cole gazed into Heather's eyes. She was a tether for him in so many tempests. But even she was not aware of all the demons he was confronting. He didn't know where or how to begin. Maybe over a cup of coffee.

"Oh, remember that girl who was on my show last week? You told me she's one of your students. She came in with a man toward the end of your last set. Looked upset." Heather looked around the room. "There she is right there. Near the end of the bar."

"Suzy? She was in my office last week. Found her crying in the hallway."

At that moment, Suzy and Cole's eyes locked. He waved her over to the bandstand. She wrapped her arms tightly around her torso and walked toward the stage looking tentatively over her shoulder and then down at her feet as she put them quickly one in front of the other

"Hi, Professor." She looked at Cole, then glanced again over her shoulder.

"You remember Heather from the radio show, don't you?"

Suzy nodded.

"Nice to see you again, Suzy. Are you OK?"

"Yeah, I'm fine. Just a little tired. Here with a, um, a friend. He went to the restroom."

Just then a muscular white man, in his late twenties, wearing a ball cap backward with the lettering *Piss on Ya!* walked up. "Thought I told you to wait for me by the door? I don't have time to wait on your stupid ass."

"Ned, this is one of my professors. I was saying hi."

"Who gives a shit!" He grabbed her wrist and yanked her toward the door. Suzy stumbled and fell to a knee. "Dumb bitch. Get up." And he pulled her up.

"Hey, buddy, ease up. What the hell you doing?" Cole moved toward Suzy with his hand extended.

"None of your business, teach! Leave us alone." Ned pulled within an inch of Cole's nose.

"Suzy, how about we give you a ride home?" Heather asked.

"How about you all mind your business? Got that, ass wipe?" Ned pushed Cole who stumbled to the stage. As Suzy moved toward Cole to help him up, she felt the sharp sting of a slap across her cheek. "I said leave him be, and let's move!" Ned pulled Suzy toward the door.

Quicker than one of Cole's guitar licks, Ned's eyes bulged, and his head snapped back. He grabbed at his neck, or more specifically he attempted to loosen the guitar cord wound around his throat. Benny, holding the other end of the cord, reeled him in like a fish.

"Don't you want to apologize to the professor you just pushed for no good reason? And the young lady your sorry self just assaulted?"

"Go to hell you wally-eyed queer bastard."

Benny smiled. "As you wish, my good man!" And faster than Bartley could've said "incredibly extraordinary," Ned was face down on the floor, and the guitar cord wrapped from his neck, around his wrists, and tied around his legs that Benny had bent upward like an awkward yoga position. He leaned close to Ned's ear and whispered.

"Now, you're probably having difficulty breathing. As your legs get tired and you try to lower them, that cord will get tighter around your neck. It's going to get worse unless I loosen that cord. Glad to do that. But you need to apologize, you little freaking weasel. Or I can just say 'Piss on Ya' and walk away."

Ned gagged and coughed, and said, "I apologize." His eyes blinked. "Ok. All right. I apologize."

Benny untied him and then scrunched his nose. "You know, Mr. Piss on Ya, you smell like someone pissed on you. Or did you just shit your pants? You stink. Go home and take a bath."

Ned got off the floor and looked at Suzy. "I'll be waiting in the car." And he stormed toward the door rubbing his neck.

"I'm sorry, Professor. He just had a bad day. Are you OK?"

"Me? Are you OK? You're not going home with him?"

"It'll be ok."

"Suzy, you can't go with him. It's not safe," Heather walked Suzy to the side of the stage.

"He's having a tough day. I'll be ok."

"Tough day? He slapped you, pushed Professor Fitzgerald to the floor, and had to be physically brought to the floor by Benny. He's crazy!"

"You don't know him like I do. I'm one of the few people who he'll listen to."

"Oh. He listens by beating you?" Heather asked with widening eyes. "Joe," she yelled toward the bar, "did you call the police?"

"No! Don't do that. Please." Suzy grabbed Heather's arm and tearfully looked at Joe. "Ned's an idiot, I know. But he's my Shauna's daddy. And, he's on probation. You call the police, he's gone. Please don't."

"Yeah, call the police." Ned reappeared and pointed at Benny, "That one there assaulted me. All these people they saw it."

"Ned, what in the world are you doing? You called me to come pick you up. So, let's get out of here, now." Suzy touched Ned's arm. He brushed her away as he glared at Benny from a distance.

"Big shot band guy needs to pay for what he did to me."

"And who pays for your bail when you end up back in jail," Suzy said. "I don't have that money and neither do you." Her pleading eyes looked at Joe as he approached. Putting both of his hands on Ned's shoulders, he turned him toward the door. "You forget what happened here, and I don't call the cops on *you*. We have witnesses to *your* assault and battery. Don't be a jerk. Got it?"

"Ok. Ok. Leave me alone. I'm leaving." He looked at Suzy. "I'll be outside." Rubbing the back of his reddened neck, Ned stalked out the door. Suzy walked out the door, close behind.

"Benny, where in the world did you learn that move? Are you some kind of martial arts master?" Heather asked. "Never saw that coming."

"And neither did Mr. Stinky Pants. Something I learned spending summers on my grandfather's farm." Benny said. "Maybe I should use that move at the next Board meeting."

Looking toward the door, the three of them stood quietly. The face in the dark rear booth smiled to himself.

• • •

14

The aroma caught Heather's attention. She stopped as soon as she stepped through the front door, closed her eyes, took in a deep breath, held it, and exhaled. She smiled.

"Wonderful. Simply wonderful," she said as Cole closed the door. "Aunt Philomena?"

"About time you meet my favorite aunt."

They hugged and Cole led Heather toward the spicey bouquet of sauce, meat, garlic, and onions.

As they entered the kitchen, there she stood. All four feet five inches of her faced the pot as she stirred. She turned and thrust a wooden spoon toward Heather.

"Heather! He can't stop talking about you. Here. Here. Give this a taste. Let me know what you think."

Heather leaned into the spoon. "Hmm. Heavenly." She stepped back and said, "It is so nice to meet Cole's favorite aunt." Heather leaned down and gave her a warm hug. "And, Cole is right. You do know how to greet a guest."

"Guest nothing, you're his BFF. He told me himself. You're staying tonight and tomorrow morning I'll make us an egg scramble with peppers, mushrooms, and pepperoni!" She turned back toward the stove, scooped out a piece of meat, and placed it on a plate.

"This is an old family recipe. There's one other ingredient that brings it all together." She motioned for Heather to sit. "Cole, get your lady a glass of wine to complement her braciola!"

Heather bit in and closed her eyes as she slowly chewed and savored each second the seasoned beef melted in her mouth. "Oh my. Succulent." She took another bite.

"When Marco was a child, I helped his mother with the cooking. She had a lot to deal with." Cole returned and handed Heather a glass of wine.

"Marco, you remember how you, Ian, and your mother came to my house for holiday dinners? Where was your father?"

"Drinking and gambling."

"And do you remember how your mother made macaroni every Sunday, pork chops on Monday, leftover macaroni on Tuesday, and veal parmigiana on Wednesday?"

"And we ordered pizza from Vici's on Thursday and had fish on Friday," Cole said as he sat down.

"And Saturday?"

"You always brought your braciola to serve with my mother's spaghetti," Cole said. "That's why we have it tonight. Remembering the past."

"Sounds like a weekly menu for a five-star restaurant," Heather said as she took another bite. "I'm glad the band had this Saturday night off. Who'd want to miss this?"

"With few exceptions, it was always the same. It gave my sister focus and Marco and Ian positive consistency."

"And, my favorite Aunt would always say the same words right before dinner, 'Who's better than us?' She never let us get down on ourselves."

"God love my sister, she was a great cook. Marco's father, a kook!" Philomena looked at Cole, her eyes warmer than the sauté pan. "But enough of that. We have food to eat!"

Philomena placed another piece of braciola on Heather's dish, one for Cole, and one for her. She raised her glass of wine and said, "Who's better than us? No one!"

• • •

3:14 a.m. Sunday.

Cole rocked back and forth on the couch.

You have to shut up and keep your head down. You know these guys don't play fair. You are no match for them. Big shot you think you are. They'll chew you up and spit you out, tell more lies, and cover it up.

"Stop it! You're not helping. You told me to do it. Stop it!"

I'm the only one who is helping you. I'm your protector. No one else is there for you. No one!

"Cole." Heather walked in from the bedroom rubbing her sleepy eyes. She wore an *HTRB* tie-dyed t-shirt that hung to her knees, and her hair was up. "Cole, what is it? Who are you talking to?"

Cole looked at her. He just shook his head. She hurt just seeing the anguish in his eyes. Walking to the kitchen, she poured a glass of water, handed it to Cole, and sat beside him holding his hand. After a few minutes of painful silence, Cole looked at her.

"I'm spent. I can't do it any longer. I have nothing left."

She gently rubbed the back of his hand. "Talk to me, Cole."

Cole jumped up from the sofa, both hands holding his ears as if to shut out the outside world. Or was it the inside world? "I can't do this any longer. Stop it!"

"You're frightening me. What is it? Let me in. Let me help." Heather stood but had no idea what to do or what to say. This was not the man who used to go to the grocery store for his elderly neighbor just because it would bring a smile to her face. And it was not the same practical joker who helped his band members laugh when they needed to blow off steam. She didn't know this person and she was scared.

Pulling his fingers down his forehead, over his eyes, and onto his mouth, Cole stared across the room, at nothing in particular. Maybe if he didn't move, the voice would not see him. Then he felt something on his leg. Something soft. He looked down and saw Big Betsy rubbing between his legs. His mind drifted back to the present as he heard the soft purr. He bent over and picked up his feline companion. His face softened as he hugged her to his body. And then the tears came. He sat in a chair and sobbed. Heather walked to him, said nothing, and gently touched his shoulders.

"It's empty, Heather. Empty."

"What?"

"The bucket. My bucket."

She remained quiet still touching his shoulders.

"The bucket that holds all my dreams and energy. The bucket that feeds my purpose. It's leaking. I keep filling it by doing more, saying more, pushing back more, and staying busy more. And the holes get bigger and leak faster. My arms can't keep up; can't fill it any longer. I'm tired. Time to quit."

Heather never knew Cole to be a quitter. She wasn't sure what it was he was thinking of quitting. Her mind drifted to darker interpretations. She shuttered and brought her attention back to the man she loved.

"Who are you talking to? I mean, when I came in, you were having a conversation. Who is with you?"

He shook his head again, searching for an answer that would make sense. He found no option but the truth.

"The voice."

"The voice?"

"The voice in my ear. The voice that never shuts up, that always questions, doubts, and diminishes everything I do. I'm never good enough or do the right things. And it is getting louder."

"Your conscience? Self-doubt? You know we all do that from time to time."

"I don't know. But what I do know is that it won't let me sleep. It's always with me. Sometimes it's a whisper. Sometimes bolder. It sounds like it wants to protect me but then, the next thing I know, it's nothing more than a ball and chain. I'm tired, Heather. Exhausted." He sank back into the chair.

"Maybe it was what happened with Suzy and that guy at the bar the other night. Maybe all that has you worked up. It frightened the crap out of me."

"No doubt. But it wasn't just that. The voice has been with me for a long, long time."

He sat down, lowered his head, and took a breath. "Guess it's part of the Fitzgerald DNA. My mother would walk the house at all hours of the night. At times I'd get up to check on her. She'd be talking. To someone or something else that was not visible. Her voice in her ear, I guess. It took its toll on her as it is me. It's getting louder. And I'm doubting my ability to maintain a grip."

"Can you take a sick day tomorrow? I know you don't like to do that, but if you don't take care of yourself how in the world are you going to take care of anyone else."

"That's the problem." Cole stood and his voice raised. Big Betsy jumped to the table. "I'm tired of taking care of people, especially people who don't want to do it for themselves. And I'm spent fighting the pricks of the world."

"And they never seem to go away, do they? But what you do is important, Cole. You help your students to fight for themselves. You give me the strength to nail those idiots to the wall when they attempt to lie to me on the show. But, again, what can I do to help *you*? I want to see you happy again. Maybe we can go to the beach tomorrow. Have lunch. Just you and me. No weasels allowed." She smiled softly.

"I'd love that. Unfortunately, I've got a meeting I canceled once. I have to meet with Turkle and Bartley. They want me to reconsider my refusal to work with them."

Good luck with that, Mr. Invisible. Those pricks are going to eat you alive.

The guest bedroom door gently closed. Aunt Philomena walked slowly and climbed back into bed.

"For my sister. For Marco. I gotta stop these *strunz!*" She made the sign of the cross, pulled the quilt to her chin, and with narrowed eyes looked to the ceiling.

• • •

15

"President Bartley, Professor Fitzgerald is here to see you. Shall I escort him in?"

"Thank you, Betty. Give me a moment to finish up something." Bartley turned to Turkle. "Well, do we play good cop-bad cop? How do you want to handle this?"

Turkle poured himself a cup of coffee, walked to the conference table, and sat at the opposite end from the president.

"I'm thinking we do good cop, good cop. Let him think we are here for him, and that we'll bring together all the college's resources to help him get through this." Turkle held his cup in a mock toast and said, "Remember, we want him to think we have ignored his protest march and convocation conniption. Darla will keep the pressure on him."

"Glad you were in that bar last night and saw the fight." Bartley placed his elbows on the table. "Did he hit the guy?"

"We won't mention that I was there. No, it was his buddy Benny, the gay professor in the math department. I'll give Cole enough detail so he knows we know what happened. And that Benny could find himself without a job and in jail."

Turkle's eyes narrowed. "Cole is fiercely loyal to his colleagues and friends. This will catch his attention."

Bartley hit the intercom button. "Betty, please send in Professor Fitzgerald."

The oak door opened.

"Cole, so good to see you. I'm glad you could reschedule for us." Bartley rose and walked around the table to greet him with his limp handshake. "I hear you had a student emergency the other day. Thank you for your incredibly extraordinary service to our students. That's why we need you. Betty, please get the professor something to drink. Coffee? Water?"

"Water will be fine." Bartley directed Cole to the chair on the side of the table. There he sat, between the weasel-in-chief and his ferret. The secretary handed him a bottle of water and closed the door as she left the office.

Orchestrated silence.

Cole turned his gaze toward Bartley. "Listen, Pat and I spoke earlier this week about the new position. I appreciate that you think I'm the person for the job, but I'm not. I don't have that skill set. And I'm just not interested. I'm a teacher. That's what I want to do, teach."

"Well, Cole, you would still be teaching. Your students would be the faculty. Who better to help your colleagues develop their professional skills than you, a master teacher? Too many of them have been pulling out the same yellowed and tired notes and lectures for more than twenty years. Extraordinarily bad, very bad. And I think Pat mentioned we can phenomenally help with your safe place program for the marginalized students."

"And don't forget we'll help you spread your good work deeper into the community," Turkle said. "We have the resources to make that happen."

"And you could help save your colleagues from the inevitable."

"Inevitable. What is inevitable, Dr. Bartley?"

Bartley paused and looked toward Turkle who picked up the conversation and sidestepped the question. "Cole, we know you are a leader. Faculty look up to you. They listen to you. As we hear it, they are following you on this ill-fated union scheme."

"President Bartley, if I may," Cole started.

"Doyle, please. Call me Doyle." Bartley interrupted with his thin smile.

"Um," Cole paused just slightly, "you're mixing two different things here. The faculty unionizing has nothing to do with teaching methodology and everything to do with dignity. We're looking for a modicum of respect. This isn't some far-left liberal group of academics. We want a long-awaited pay raise, improvement in conditions, and a seat at the table—your table—so they can have a say in how this college moves forward."

Pat leaned forward, pointed at him, and said, "Cole, that is exactly what Doyle and I are offering. You, as a faculty representative, get a seat at the table. You don't need a union to do that. We can give it to you and it will be a lot less messy."

"Messy?"

"Cole," Turkle continued, "pardon me, but most of your colleagues could not find their way out of an elevator. They argue about arcane issues no one cares about. And the important stuff they let slide. Hell, I'm not sure they even know what the important stuff is." Holding his thumb and index finger about an inch apart, he continued. "Some are *this close* to losing their positions. And that is inevitable if they don't alter their direction. You, Professor Cole Fitzgerald, can change that inevitability."

I told you they would eat your dumb ass for lunch.

Cole closed his eyes.

You are way over your head. What the hell are you doing here? Protect yourself.

"And then there are the complaints we've received about, how should I say this, unprofessional behavior." Bartley slid a file folder on the table toward Cole. "My secretary found this in an envelope on her desk this morning when she arrived."

Cole opened the folder.

"Isn't that Professor Benny DiJohn? I hear he is a great math teacher. Since when did he start beating up students in bars? Look at those photos, Cole. He's got a goddamn cord around that guy's neck."

"Not sure where you got these photos, but did you get the whole picture of what happened? Benny was protecting a female student who that lowlife slapped across the face. And he, the lowlife slapper, pushed me to the ground. I think the police might call that battery."

"That's another problem here, Cole," Turkle said. "That girl, Suzy McDonald, right? As you said, she's a student. Of yours, I believe."

"So."

"She's underage and in a bar that you were in. You were talking with her. How does that look to the community? 'Professor partying with underage coed!'"

"What the hell are you talking about? She came in on her own—or maybe was forced there by that lowlife." Cole could feel his neck tightening and turning red.

"Easy, Cole." Bartley took the lead at this point. "We're just saying people talk even when there is nothing to talk about. People like Teagan Cross like nothing more than a breaking news alert on the evening local bad hour about the moral decay of faculty. Take Suzy. She's been to your office, right?"

"Of course, she's one of my students. Students come to my office all the time. The administration requires office hours!"

"And when she entered your office, it was reported to me, that you closed the door so no one could see you."

"What? What do you mean by 'reported to you'? She's a student, I found sitting on the hallway floor crying." Cole bit his lip, took a short breath, and continued. "She needed to talk in private. I noticed bruises on her wrists and offered to take her to student services. She refused and left. I then called Ms. Robertson and told her about it."

"Cole, we understand that. I'm just trying to show you how little things become distractions. Someone saw you close the door and thought it inappropriate. I got an email about it. That's where damage control needs to come in."

"Damn, you! I wasn't partying with a student. I wasn't doing anything in the office other than helping a student find herself and her reason for being at this college. And trying to get her to a counselor. I didn't even know she was at the restaurant until we were packing up to leave. That guy—"

"That *student*," Turkle interjected.

"That drunk, aggressive guy manhandled Suzy." Cole slammed his hand on the desk. The coffee cups and water bottle jumped.

Bartley saw an opening, "Easy. Easy. We don't want any harm to come to you or Professor DiJohn. But these kinds of stories can create incredible legs of their own. And right or wrong both the press and community want to believe what they want to believe. You help us and we help your friend. You see, Cole, we can have an incredibly extraordinary team with you onboard."

"I'm done." Cole stood up. "I don't know what you are up to but I'm not on your incredibly extraordinary team." Cole walked around the table and toward the door.

"Cole, you leave this room now, and you *will be* done. I promise." Turkle had stood and was in front of Cole blocking his way. "Listen, Doyle and I both believe you. That guy," he pointed to the photos on the table, "is a two-bit hoodlum. No question. We can make this go away for everyone. I know this is a lot to throw at you. But know we are on your side. We are. It doesn't have to be this way."

Cole walked around him and exited the room.

Turkle watched the door close. He turned to look at his boss.

Bartley nodded and asked, "I guess we do it?"

Turkle pulled his cell phone from his inner jacket pocket and hit a speed dial number.

"It's time. Meet me in the usual place tonight." He disconnected the call and looked at Bartley. "And I have an idea for the upcoming Board meeting. I need you to add an agenda item."

The office door opened. "Ah, Dr. Bartley," Betty said as she entered looking back over her shoulder. "This was left for you." She placed an aluminum foil-wrapped dish on the table. A little lady with a big smile and white glasses asked me to give this to you."

"Little lady?"

"Never saw her before. And, oh, she also left this note." Betty handed Bartley an invitation-sized envelope.

Bartley looked at Turkle as he opened the card and read it aloud.

"Enjoy the braciola! And remember, someone is always watching the *strunz!*"

• • •

16

Joe slid a fresh Scotch down to Cole's seat at the end of the bar.

"Either you had a tough day or want to be good and lubed for the set tonight. Hope Heather will be here to drive you home."

"Yes, yes, and I'm not sure."

Cole could not get the meeting out of his mind. He muttered, "Weasels and ferrets" a few times and absent-mindedly looked at the ice as he swirled the glass in his hand. "'I'm done.' Done with what?"

Don't you recognize a threat when you hear it?

"Evening, Benny," Joe yelled looking toward the front door, "Want the usual?"

"Hold the beer for now. I'm feeling like a Pina Colada with a rum floater. Yeah, that'll do it." Benny placed his bass on the stage, pulled up the stool next to Cole, and slapped him on the back.

"Hope your day was better than mine. Classes were great but I got stuck in a committee meeting. Did I need to know how much scantrons cost and the procedure for getting tests duplicated? I do all my testing online."

"Anyone from administration contact you?"

"The puzzle palace? Me? I'm not sure they know my full name let alone where or what I teach." Joe placed the drink in front of Benny.

"Oh, they know you. And all about your takedown of the idiot who pushed me and slapped the girl."

Benny took a sip and nodded his approval to Joe. "How in the world do they know about that? Not like it made the papers or anything. Was Turkle here again last night?"

"Don't know how. Just know they do and have photos."

"OK, so what? We got plenty of witnesses as to what happened. The guy was lucky we didn't call the police on him and have his smelly ass locked up." Benny moved the swizzle stick around in his drink. "Remember, Heather asked Joe to call the cops but your student intervened and they both left. What's the big deal?"

"He's a student at the college, according to Bartley and Turkle. I had to meet with them today to talk about it and their job offer."

"The college's president and Director of HR think they know about a bar fight, and they call a professor who had nothing to do with it to answer questions. Huh?"

"Short story, bud, they are using you to get to me. Let me rephrase that." He took a sip of Scotch. "They're trying to use you to try to get to me. I walked out on them."

"Back up. 'Get to me.' Again, huh?"

"According to the dynamic duo, while you violently pinned a student to the floor, I was talking to and partying with an underage student in a drinking establishment. They are threatening to take that to the Board and make us examples of the out-of-control faculty, and worse, unless...." Cole paused, took another drink, and bit his lower lip, "Weasels!"

"Unless what? They got nothing."

"They want me to take that shitass position in Turkle's office. They said, 'We are on your side.' You want them on your team?" Cole looked down at the drink in his hand. "When I said no and walked out Turkle said if I didn't accept the offer I would be done."

Benny stirred his drink. "Hey, Joe! Love the drink. Ever think of going to the islands to work?" Then he turned toward his friend and said, "Must have to do with the union. They are running scared. I'm not. Let 'em come after me. I'll pop that weasel and his ferret good. I'll tell them to bite me. They might like it. Hell, they probably would."

• • •

His car rolled to a stop in the darkened parking lot. He reached for his phone and sent a text, "I'm here."

Except for an occasional car on the road, it was quiet and deserted. Just like the empty storefronts that had been struggling to stay afloat in the latest economic recession. But then, in this part of the city there always seemed to be an economic recession. It was dying and the people with it.

He saw him step out of the shadow of one of the buildings and walk toward the passenger side of the car. Turkle fingered the unlock button and the man with the ball cap got in. Quiet. Apprehensive. Like Turkle had hoped.

"You ever take a bath?" Turkle scrunched his nose and then continued. "Ned, I hope you've had a speech class by now because we need you. And need you to be convincing. Short story, you need to prepare to talk to some important people.."

His eyes grew wide. "What? Who?"

"Here." He handed him a piece of paper. "This is all you have to say. Your homework is to learn it—by heart. And be convincing. I'll let you know when and where."

"I can't—"

Turkle grabbed Ned's shirt collar and pulled him nose to nose. "No, you *can* and you will! You don't and our deal is done, and your probation officer gets a phone call. Don't mess with me. You have no idea who you are dealing with! Got it?"

Ned pulled away. "Yeah, yeah. I got it. I just didn't figure on talking to any stuffed shirts." He rubbed the back of his neck and broke his gaze with Turkle. "Hell, you know I don't even go to class regular. This wasn't part of the original deal."

"No, it wasn't. But we all have to be flexible." Turkle paused. "You know how this works. You do what I ask you to do, and I take care of you. You don't, and you're screwed. Simple, huh?"

Ned nodded and reached into his pocket. "Here. You wanted these." He handed Turkle a baggie of pills. "See, I do what you say. Geez."

Turkle put the pills in his inside suit jacket pocket and flipped the door lock. Ned jumped out. Turkle drove away.

• • •

17

As he rode the mirror-walled elevator to the fourth-floor Board Room, he hummed the Kristofferson tune, "Why Me Lord?" With the Bartley regime, no one ever knew what would happen next; but something always did, and it was usually bad. Cole had heard nothing from Bartley or Turkle about speaking at this meeting until he got the invitation from the Board chair the day before yesterday. Odd.

The bell chimed, the doors opened, and Cole drew a deep breath.

"Hey, professor! How ya doin'?" Johnny Valentine waved from the middle of the lobby outside the Board Room. Other players from the basketball team surrounded him.

As Cole made his way through the clusters of talking heads, he thought the crowd large for a monthly Board meeting.

He finally reached Johnny and extended his hand.

"Hey, Johnny V," Cole hugged his former student's neck. "How many NBA scouts knocked on your door today? Remember us when you make the big show."

"Aw, Dr. Fitzgerald, stop it." Johnny was an athletic star with an authentic humble streak. "What brings you here?"

"The Board Chair asked me to say a couple of words about student success strategies."

"That must be why all these folks are here," Johnny said as he nodded toward the lobby full of people. "They heard you were the guest speaker today."

"Yeah, right," Cole said rolling his eyes. "Didn't expect to see you here. Slow day at the gym?"

"Award or something. Coach just told us to be here. It's funny, Professor. They cut our budget to the point that we have to maintain the gym ourselves. Now that we've won a district title, they want to parade us out and make a fuss over how much they care."

Pretty astute for a 19-year-old. While he wasn't the class scholar, Johnny had impressed Cole with his work ethic and ability to connect with fellow students. He respected others, and others respected him.

"I'll cheer for you when you're recognized," Cole said as he slapped Johnny on the back. "If I ever grow up Johnny, I want to be just like you."

"Oh no, Professor. The secret is not to grow up, or so I've been told," Johnny said with a wink and a smile.

Cole made his way to the other side of the room where he spied Benny reviewing the day's agenda.

"Benny, you here to give a budget-balancing lesson?"

"I'm a math professor, not a magician. These guys use more illusions than David Copperfield. It's mystifying to me.

No, I was asked to be here because the department just got a grant award. Turkey Turkle called me himself."

"Have you heard anything from them or anyone about the bar fight?" Cole asked as he looked around the near-capacity room.

"Nothing. Like it never happened."

At that moment, the lights flickered, indicating the meeting would start in ten minutes.

"Even the board meeting is a show. You'd think we're at the damn theater," Cole said, "Time to move in, or else we might miss the opening act."

"Don't look now, pal, but here comes the producer himself."

Cole turned and saw Doyle Bartley walking toward him with a broad smile.

"Professor Fitzgerald, I'm so glad you could make it!" The president extended his thin fingers and shook Cole's hand. Bartley's eyes darted around the room like a thief looking for an escape. Between his slightly stooped shoulders and the growing bags under his eyes, the president looked tired.

Still holding Cole's hand with his wet grip, Bartley drew closer. "You know, Cole, we've had our differences, but we agree on more things than you realize."

Cole seriously doubted it unless Bartley also thought he should be castrated.

"Hell," Bartley continued, "I was coincidentally the same as you when I was in the faculty ranks. We need incredible people like you to keep the juices flowing. You've got passion, Cole, and I like that!"

"Well, like Jefferson said, 'A little rebellion, every now and then, is good for the soul.'"

Bartley laughed, slapped Cole on the shoulder, and made his way to the next group of people.

"Didn't know you two were buds," Benny grunted.

"Bad enough I have to be here. Did I need a shot of him, too?"

"Think of it like an enema," offered Benny, "You don't like it when it's happening, but it feels so good when it's over. And you're about to get the second stick up your ass right now." Benny motioned with his head as they got closer to Turkle's post at the door.

"Howdy, Professors. We must be living right to have both of you here at the same time. Here's the agenda, Cole. I see your bandmate is already studying it. Enjoy the meeting. Benny, especially nice to see you."

"Didn't know you two were buds," Cole whispered as they walked into the Board room.

"Bite me! You might like it." Benny stopped and looked from side to side.

"Look at this place. It's packed with every kook, crank, and buffoon in this building. What did Bartley do, open the cages for a couple of hours?"

As they made their way into the main area of the oak-paneled Board room, they took in the assembled group. All of the president's cabinet was in attendance; not unusual, but surprising to see such a show of force for a mundane meeting. Benny and Cole waved to Dick Ed who stood conspicuously in the far corner of the room. He responded with a nod and pulled at his ill-fitting necktie as if he were imitating Rodney Dangerfield.

"That guy is about as significant as a flea fart at a big truck rally. I don't understand it." Benny shook his head.

Cole motioned to a couple of chairs toward the back of the room, and the two professors settled in for the show as the gavel sounded. The Board members had taken their places to either side of Bartley on the platform behind their oak bench. They looked like a court of judges as they smiled imperiously from their perch three feet above everyone in the audience.

Three oversized crystal chandeliers hung from the mirrored ceiling. The well-cushioned red chairs sat upon matching plush red carpet. It could have doubled as a 70s disco club. However, the newly installed multi-media production and sound booth rivaled any of the television stations in the city.

"Always looks like a mid-century bordello in here," Benny said.

Bartley led the pledge to the flag and then began a politically self-serving speech touting the "incredibly extraordinary" enrollment numbers. As Cole looked around the room in boredom, he noticed a late arrival.

"Yo, Benny, take a look. Teagan Cross from Channel 13."

"That's strange. Bartley typically keeps those folks far away from campus." Benny paused a moment as if to refocus his eyes. "There's Heather. What's she doing here?"

Cole looked at Heather, shrugged his shoulders, and turned up his palms with a "what gives?" look.

She held up her microphone and recorder and mouthed, "I was told to come here" as she pointed toward the floor for emphasis.

They were snapped back to attention when Bartley mentioned Cole's name.

"—and we are fortunate to have one of the shining examples of the faculty with us today. Professor Cole Fitzgerald has agreed to share some insights on student success strategies. As one of the long-time faculty members at this college, we look to him for leadership. Professor, would you please step up to the podium?"

Cole made his way to the microphone and placed a note card on the lectern.

"Ladies and gentlemen of the Board, Mr. President, thank you. I'm not sure what I can offer, but I have put together a couple of thoughts on—"

A commotion in the rear of the room, on the opposite side from where Cole stood and Benny sat, interrupted the presentation. Cole could only hear muffled voices but he turned as the crowd began to move aside for a latecomer. It was then that he noticed a familiar face. The loudmouth that Benny cable-tied at the bar walked toward the front of the room.

Using his well-defined arms and emanating his trademark fecal smell, people moved from his path as he made his way to the podium where Cole stood. Like the night at *The Silver Fox*, he was dressed in jeans and boots, but today he sported a button-down collared shirt and no ball cap.

Bartley looked at Turkle sitting in the first row of the audience and gave a subtle nod and an almost imperceptible smile. The Chair banged the gavel.

"Excuse me. Professor Fitzgerald has the floor. We would appreciate respect for his presentation."

"Excuse me!" yelled the smelly visitor in a tone that caught everyone's attention. "I, for once, would like some respect, too!"

The Chair hammered the gavel again. "Young man, you'll have a chance to speak, but we have procedures here. Fill out a card, and you'll be able to...."

"No! I will speak now. Or is this not the correct forum to speak of Professor DiJohn's dirty little secret?"

The crowd buzzed. Teagan Cross and his cameraman went into action. Heather stood transfixed. Cole looked at Benny.

"Weasels," Benny muttered to no one in particular.

Cole moved to the side as a hand reached for the podium microphone. "My name is Ned Spano. I'm a student here at Central City College. Why are you letting this man speak to you about student success? He is a fraud and a deviate. And he is protecting that man there." Ned turned, looked, and pointed directly at Benny.

"Young man, you are out of order!" cried the Board Chair as she banged the gavel twice. Cross moved toward the front of the room with his microphone extended and the cameraman following him.

"I'm out of order? He's out of order!" Spano's extended hand still pointing at Benny, as he turned to look at the Board

Chair. "Unless hogtying and beating a student in a bar is a new form of physical education exercise here at the college."

Transfixed, the hushed crowd looked at Benny, who stared directly at Spano.

"Yeah, that's right. That is what that professor did to me." The word professor rolled off his tongue as if he were about to gag on it. "For no good reason. I was trying to get my child's mother—another student here at your college—out of that bar. But that guy and his buddy right here wouldn't let me." He sneered at Cole. "I guess drinking with students must be a new internship program!"

Looking back at Benny, "And besides beating students, did you know that so-called teacher is queer as they come."

The Chair banged her gavel again. "Sir, you are out of order." The gavel came down harder.

Spano continued with his rehearsed script. "I'm in his class, and when I went to his office, he shut the door and tried to proposition me. I don't know but I think he was high on something. Slime!"

"That's it! Son-of-a-Bitch!" Benny jumped up. "Madam Chair, this man is lying. He might be on my roster, but I've never seen him in class or my office. I doubt he even knows where either is. The first time I ever saw him was the night he assaulted both a young woman and Professor Fitzgerald. Damn right, I took him down! I'd do it again." He glared at Ned.

Clearly beside herself, the Board Chair leaned toward Bartley and whispered in his ear. Bartley nodded. She banged the gavel again. "The Board will take a short recess. Young man, Mr. Spano, I would like to speak with you. Please see me at the side door over there. Security, can you escort Mr. Spano for me?"

The Board members exited along with Spano. Bartley and Turkle followed. Darla Merlot had been sitting in the front row next to Turkle and instantaneously appeared at Benny's chair. Cole was not far behind.

"Benny, the press is in the room. Say nothing and let the college—me—handle this for you. I know you have to be innocent of those charges the student tossed your way. As I speak to Cross and Rivera," she nodded toward them, "I advise you and Cole to remain right here." Merlot pivoted on her stilettoes and moved toward the other side of the room.

"Damn, Turkle! He delivered on his threat. Benny, I'm sorry you're getting dragged into this bullshit."

Benny took a deep breath and shook his head. "Not your fault. They want to play hardball. I'm ready."

"Ladies and gentlemen," an announcement came over the loudspeaker, "our Board meeting will resume in one hour. Professors Fitzgerald and DiJohn please come to the president's office."

• • •

"Cole, over here." Heather waved from a seat in the lobby.

He made his way through the still assembled mass, many of them on their phones relaying the events. A few pointed at Cole.

"Cole, are you OK? Where's Benny? Is he OK?"

"He's as OK as he can be given this shitstorm. I just got done hearing how Bartley and Turkle are here for us. Merlot is getting Benny's side of this. Heather, it's Turkle. When I refused his offer, he told me I would be done. He's doing what he can to take Benny and me down and intimidate the faculty. Damn him." Cole bit his lip. "And, what in the world brought you to this spectacle today?"

"Late this morning the producer told me to come here. It appears your Darla Merlot said it would be a good news day for the station. She mentioned that Johnny V and the basketball team would be getting a special award."

"A total setup."

"Ya think?" Heather said raising her left eyebrow. "Let me see what I can find out." She looked into his eyes and whispered, "I love you. We'll get through this."

• • •

18

People deal with stress in various ways. Cole turned to music and the beach. No matter what happened during the day, regardless of what the inhabitants of the puzzle palace yammered about, as soon as he strapped on his guitar or walked on the sand, he entered an alternative universe. He left the idiots and posers behind and found solace.

For Benny, the ocean, also, provided respite. He always found peace in the textures and colors of the morning sky. The motion of the ocean separated him from the landlocked weasels and ferrets. The fish didn't care about his sexual orientation. The soaring seagulls and pelicans became metaphors for his dreams taking flight. A passing pod of dolphins symbolized his yearning for close connections. The rising sun, God's promise that another day meant renewed hope.

A Saturday morning ritual found Benny pulling his kayak into the surf, sliding into the seat and gliding toward the horizon. The sound of his paddle cutting through the water soothed his soul.

Peace. Escape. Renewal.

Given the most recent Board meeting, Benny needed the solitude. That was why he almost called Cliff to cancel this morning. Cliff, the perpetually balled up, paranoid, second-guessing, second-year professor reminded Benny of his younger self. When he came to CCC he, too, was fearful. Who would befriend him? Who would sabotage him? Who would he become? Cliff needed direction and attention. When Benny learned of their mutual love for kayaking, he reached out. The ocean served as an impenetrable refuge for an hour or two. In many ways, mentoring Cliff helped Benny's soul as much as it did the fledgling teacher.

"Hey, Benny, you sure you want me along today? So much has happened in the last few days. I mean do you need time for yourself? I'm here for you if you need me, but if you need alone time, I understand." Cliff and Benny held their kayaks as the incoming tide lapped at their feet.

"What? You don't want to be with me when I need you most," Benny cracked as he looked at the massive expanse of water before them.

"No, no. I'm here for you. Really. I didn't mean I didn't want to help you. You've always been there for me."

Benny held up his hand and smiled. "Relax. I know. And watching you grow into your role at the college has made me glad. Couldn't think of a better person to share this sunrise with today. How about we start paddling?"

They walked into the surf, jumped into their boats, and paddled with measured strokes toward the horizon. Once beyond the incoming breakers, they turned their kayaks parallel to the shore and headed southward. This was their typical journey. Go against the current for thirty minutes or so, then turn northward and have the water's flow help push them back to where they began. Like life, the current is sometimes with you and at other times not.

On their southward paddle, they passed weathered beach bungalows that had survived decades of tropical storms and hurricanes. Interspersed with the old structures stood a few new high-rise condominiums. Classic cedar-shingled one-story homes dwarfed by concrete behemoths with little personality. And then it would come in sight. Just past the last building was a pristine nature preserve that extended two miles down the coastline. As usual, they turned their kayaks toward the shore and just floated. The rising sun behind them cast a warm glow on the palm, pine, and cedar trees on shore. A time and place to reflect.

On this day, the calming beauty took on more meaning than usual.

"Benny, how are you holding up? That meeting. That guy. I mean, I didn't see that coming. I still can't believe it. Do you need to talk about it? I understand if you don't. But—"

"No, I didn't see it coming either. But that's one of the things I learned over the years. If all we had to do was teach, it'd be as smooth as this paddle today."

The water lapped softly against their kayaks.

"We get to help our students plant and fertilize seeds for their future. Unfortunately, we have people running the asylum who have no clue about teaching. They spew toxins that kill the seedlings. And when they can't get their way, their adolescent side comes out. Childish, vindictive, and worse. Calling them adolescent is an insult to the teenagers of the world."

A pod of dolphins swam within ten feet of Benny's bow.

"Those dolphins there," Benny pointed with the end of his paddle, "they travel as a team. We—the faculty—could learn from them. Stay together for support. Instead, we end up weakening each other for a few measly bucks or some meaningless award."

Cliff stopped paddling and lay the paddle across his lap. He leaned back in his seat and closed his eyes. Benny back-paddled and came alongside Cliff, grabbed the side of his kayak, and let the silence be. Just the water and an occasional squawking gull. After a few moments, Benny spoke.

"Cliff, you cannot let it bother you. If you do, it will eat you up. Yeah, Turkle and Bartley have put pressure on me and Cole. It's all about the union. We'll work it out. Consider it another lesson you can add to your beginning teacher portfolio. It's OK."

"No. It's not OK. Benny, I don't have the courage you and Cole have. I'm married. We have a five-year-old daughter. I need this job. And I like it! I can't rock the boat like you and the older tenured faculty can."

"And I don't expect you to rock any boats. Just observe and learn. And develop into the best teacher CCC has ever seen. You have already been published in a significant journal. Do you understand how tough that is to do? You'll be fine. Hell, you already are better than fine."

Cliff shook his head. "I don't feel fine. I don't. What was it Cole said? He would not be invisible any longer? Hell, I want nothing *but* to be invisible. It's how I was raised as a Black kid in a White world. Don't get noticed. If spoken to, be brief and polite. Comply. Blend as much as possible. Don't stand out. Do my job, be good at it, and keep my head lowered.

"My mother's constant refrain made it difficult for me to take risks in life. When she sent me out to play, she always said, 'Don't break your glasses.' For me, that became short-hand for so many things my mind obsessed about. While it made me responsible for my spectacles, the overthinking ended up creating its own spectacle. And it still does."

"Caution is an admirable virtue, Cliff. I'm glad your mother helped you see that."

Cliff paused and tightened the safety strap holding his glasses onto his head. "However, when it becomes the guiding force, one ends up focusing on surviving rather than thriving. 'Don't break your glasses' allowed me to focus on what was near and valuable at the expense of not seeing what was a little further down the road and maybe more valuable. By keeping my glasses safe, perhaps in the long run I ended up becoming more myopic."

"But again," Benny said, "the article. Isn't your name on that article? That's visibility. People take notice of your work because you stand out from and above the mediocrity that many of our colleagues have fallen victim to over the years. You set high standards for yourself, your students, and your colleagues."

"Eulonia."

"Eulonia?" Benny tilted his head.

"Eulonia pushed me to do that article. Well, no, she pushed me to publish that article. It's hard to say no to Eulonia." Cliff cracked a small smile. "I'm fortunate to know her."

He unclipped his water bottle from the seat hook. He stared at it and then turned to Benny. "You know when Savannah and I took the appointment to the Teaching Initiative Team, it didn't play well with the union organizers. It's like they think we want to hurt faculty. We don't." Benny could see Cliff's agitation by the tightening grip on his water bottle. He attempted to lighten the air.

"Guess they got you by the T.I.T."

Cliff looked at him like he had gone daft. "Huh?"

"T.I.T. You know, the abbreviation for…well, never mind. Yeah, I know you felt pressured to join Turkle. He's good at that."

"Hell, I had no idea what was happening around me. I thought, at first, it was a great honor for the Director of Human Resources to reach out to me. Little did I know he is now setting me up."

"What do you mean?"

"When he's not asking me questions about you, Cole, and the union talks, he has me doing something for some overseas bank account to help international students get scholarship money to CCC. Seemingly innocuous but now given what happened at the Board meeting I'm uncomfortable.

How can I trust them? I think they're planning something. I don't know what, but, frankly, I'm scared. If I don't do what they say, I'm toast."

As he spoke, Cliff's body posture was taking on that balled-up look. If he could, Benny was sure he would have crossed his legs tight for comfort. Or just fallen over the side and sunk into the murky depths. Benny felt sorry for Cliff, someone who could easily become more collateral damage as Turkle escalated the stakes. All because of the union? Maybe something else was at play. But what? He looked back at Cliff and smiled.

"Tell you what, we'll worry about the puzzle palace inhabitants once we get back to shore. Right now, my friend, I challenge you to a race. The last one back to shore buys breakfast and the first round of mimosas! And make sure as you go by those big-ass condos that you look sharp for their surveillance cameras and fancy telescopes. Let 'em know we mean business! I'm thinking I might stop and throw them a moon."

"Benny!" Cliff said with a sheepish grin.

With that, Benny pushed off Cliff's kayak and began digging his paddle into the water. While they could never be sure about what lurked unseen, Benny knew, if nothing else, they better keep paddling.

• • •

19

Early afternoon, the same day. On a two-lane county road in central Florida.

Don't feel guilty, Pat. You didn't take her from her home. You helped her find her forever home. That's love. You are an important man doing important things for important people.

Turkle drove on as the sun peaked in and out of the clouds.

• • •

"I am pleased with her adjustment. As you know, moving into a community like ours can be traumatic for many. But Mrs. Turkle has fit right in with the other residents. She has made a lot of friends in her first month here at Timber Estates." The residential supervisor, Mrs. Hobart, stood and walked around the desk. "Do you need me to show you to her apartment? I know she will be happy to see you. She always talks about you. You're with Central City College, is that correct?"

Turkle stood. "Yes, been there for going on two years. And I am relieved that she has fit in, as you say. This—this move—was a difficult decision. I still wonder whether I did the right thing for her. But I had concerns about her being alone."

The supervisor could see the hurt in his eyes. She'd heard this often from family members who hadn't come to grips with relocating a loved one for what may be the last time.

"Dr. Turkle, I understand. At first, your mother had, what should I say? Expected difficulties," Mrs. Hobart pulled a file from the side of her desk.

"Memory issues?"

"Possibly. Or maybe it was just getting used to her new surroundings. The dining room manager reported that he had to walk your mom back to her apartment several nights. After the second week though, no problems that I know of. She is navigating the hallways and elevator. There is one problem, though. Her car." The supervisor paged through the file folder.

"My apologies, I meant to move it to my house. No sense having it here when she doesn't drive it."

"Well, she does. Or at least, tried to drive it."

Turkle's eyebrows raised. He remembered the conversation with his mother during his last visit. She promised not to drive anymore.

"Last week, the front desk manager got a phone call from your mother. She was in her car and lost in our parking garage. It seems instead of exiting, she drove the wrong way on the ramps and ended up on the top level. She got flustered. But the good news is she called us, and there were no damages or injuries. I know this is delicate, but have you considered taking her keys?"

Turkle bit the inside of his left cheek and moved his pursed lips to the right side of his face. "I'll do that today."

"This move was an adjustment for you as well as her," Mrs. Hobart continued. "The doctor has said, according to her clinical dementia rating, she continues to remain a mild case. However, over time it will advance." She paused as this was always a difficult conversation for family members. With a somber face, Turkle nodded and stood to leave the office.

"The staff watches this closely," Mrs. Hobart said. "We'll be ready to move her to the memory care part of the property as soon as needed."

Turkle chose this place for that reason. He had done his research. While the most expensive facility in this part of the state, it had the highest rating for health and well-being. He hoped to visit at least once or twice a month but even that would be difficult given what was about to come down at the college.

"Thank you. My heart hurts that I had to do this. I'm glad she is here with you and your staff. You know, she told me she had become a bit forgetful. I hoped it was just momentary lapses. I should have known. I underestimated."

Like when you found $5,000 stashed in her underwear drawer. Was that a momentary lapse or did she think that was the new bank?

"You did what you could when you could," said Ms. Hobart. "Give yourself credit. You knew something was off and you did something about it."

He left the supervisor's office, found the elevator, and hit the button for the third floor.

As he stepped from the elevator, he noted the apartment numbers on the directional sign and proceeded to the left. The facility was clean and the staff friendly, but he felt like he was walking down the hallway of one of the many nameless hotels he'd stayed in during his career. No energy. He took a deep breath and knocked on #302.

"Come in. It's open."

He entered and saw her sitting in a chair looking out at the manmade lake in the center of the complex.

"Not a bad view, Mom."

She swiveled the chair around, stood with the help of her cane, and smiled. "Come here, Patrick. Let me look at you."

It was like looking into a mirror. He had always been the spitting image of his mother. He got her good looks and height. Her gray hair was tied in a ponytail that hung to her waist and her turtle necklace stood out as the top two buttons of her silk blouse were open. As expected, her pants and shoes completed the tasteful outfit.

"You look wonderful," he said as he gave her a heartfelt hug. She returned it. As the hug lingered, he saw the photo of his dad on the end table. The last one taken. He was in his naval uniform. Right before the training exercise that took his life. Pat was in high school. As an only child, he quickly assumed the role of protector for his mother. And it allowed him to prove that his father was wrong about him.

That's the guy you are still trying to measure up to. You never were good enough, strong enough, man enough for him.

She held him at arm's length. "Yeah, not bad for an old lady. But I'll tell you what. I'm not as old as the people in this place. Damn if they complain a lot. And when they don't complain, they sit and think of what to complain about next." She laughed. "Bunch of fuddy duddies!"

"If anyone will put them straight, you will." His mother was strong and not given to self-pity.

"Hell, I can't waste time with them. I've decided to help with a community food bank. You know, kind of management stuff for them. They have an office in our social area downstairs and I get to use some of my old skills. I might have a cane, but you better not get in my way." She wiggled the cane toward him. This time he laughed. God, he loved this woman. She waved him to the couch with lace doilies on the arms as she lowered back into her chair.

"Mom, I do miss you. I'm sorry you can't live with me. With all the hours I have to put in at the college and in town, well, I felt terrible that you were always alone. I wasn't much company."

"You know I understand, Patrick. I'm fine here. Really! I have made a few friends and we even have happy hour every day. Of course, we start at 3 p.m. so no one falls asleep." She looked at the clock on the wall. "Which by the way, I would love for you to join us for that. The women will love you! We're having mimosas on the lobby terrace today. And you are now my date. Let me freshen up. I'll be with you in two minutes." She put her cane out to raise herself from the chair.

"Mom, wait. We need to talk first."

"What you don't want to be my date?" She cocked her head and squinted at him. "They told you, didn't they?"

"About the trouble in the parking garage last week."

"Oh, those snitches," she said with a forced smile. "It's a confusing place to park and exit."

"And you don't need to drive. That's one of the great things about this place. Timber Estates provides bus transportation into town if you need to grocery shop or go to the pharmacy."

"Oh, fiddle-faddle. That bus is for old people. Get off that bus in town and you're marked as feeble."

"I can make arrangements with one of the local ride-share companies so you can go solo, like the rock star you are." Both laughed. Turkle held her hand. "Mom, you know we've talked about this before. Your memory is not what it used to be. And, well, you shouldn't be driving anymore."

"Oh, fiddle-faddle! I know how to drive. Now, I might forget where I put my keys but once I find them, I sure know what they're for!"

Turkle needed to change the conversation. He spied the sixty-inch flat-screen TV in the corner of the living room. "Have you been watching much TV?"

"Patrick, that was so thoughtful of you to buy that for me. I watch it all the time. My favorite shows, the news, and sometimes a basketball game."

He remembered the last two times he visited. She couldn't grasp how to use the TV remote.

"Tell you what. I gotta go to the bathroom. While I'm gone, turn on your favorite show. I'd like to watch a little with you." He handed her the remote and then walked to the bathroom.

"Make sure you pick up the seat, young man."

She stared at the remote. Other than the "ON" button, she was flummoxed. She drew a deep breath when she heard the toilet flush, put the remote down, and walked toward her son as he returned.

"I have a better idea than TV watching. That's for old folks anyway. Didn't I tell you it's mimosa happy hour? See, I do remember things!" She winked at him. "Let's go downstairs and all the ladies can fantasize about you being with them."

"Mom." Turkle put on his best embarrassed look.

"Let me go to the bathroom." As she walked away she yelled over her shoulder, "I hope you picked up *and* lowered the toilet seat, young man!"

When he heard the door close, Turkle entered her bedroom, found her purse and the car keys. He placed the keys in his pocket and returned to the TV room.

As she exited the bathroom, Turkle's phone buzzed. A text from Wackenslong.

"Damn it," he muttered.

"You say something, dear?"

"Just that I can't wait to get one of those mimosas. What is taking you so long? Do I need to start complaining like your neighbors?"

"You do and you're grounded, young man!"

• • •

4:30 p.m.

Cole, you're better than this. You can't let them do this to Benny.

Cole poured two fingers of 12-year-old Scotch and drank it. It had become a habit. A drink or two, then a nap, and then off to *The Silver Fox* for the music. He hoped the voice would be drowned. But it always came back.

Listen, Cole, you got to do something. Stand up to Bartley and Turkle. Don't let them run over you like Daddy did to your brother, Ian.

"Damn it all! Don't you know that I hurt? My friend— my colleague, my bandmate—is being dragged through the mud, falsely accused. Those pricks just want to get at me. No matter how they do it. So, shut up!" He threw the empty glass at the wall.

It's not always about you.

Walking over to the other side of the room, he picked up his guitar, sat on a kitchen-counter stool, and noodled an old Dick Dale song. Music, his first drug of choice, provided space where he could run unencumbered from the noise in his head. And the old surfing music brought him back to his younger days on the beach. He remembered listening to the reverb and tremolo-drenched guitar licks as he drifted off to sleep. That life of baggies, music, beach picnics, volleyball, and friendship seemed like someone else's life.

He thought back to one of his early guitar mentors who said that music will always be there to mend, heal, and connect to one's soul.

As Cole fingered the fretboard, words attached themselves to the notes.

> "You can run
> You cannot hide
> You better be ready for a long, long ride
> I know you can hear…that voice in your ear."

He placed the guitar against the counter and poured another drink.

A text chirped. "Please report to my office on Monday @ 2 pm. Thank you. Darla."

• • •

5:00 p.m.

"Mr. Wackenslong, President Bartley is here." The secretary hung up the phone and directed the president to a waiting room chair. "Mr. Wackenslong will be one minute. Coffee?"

Bartley declined and continued standing as he looked at the framed photos on the wall. Everyone was either a high-powered local political figure, a well-heeled society type, or a sports celebrity. And with each person stood a smiling and backslapping Wilbur Wackenslong. A three-term state senator, he met many people who had helped him move up the ladder from Marina Norte's mayor to the state legislature. His next stop was anyone's guess. Governor? US Congress? Bartley knew that the senator never did anything without calculation.

"Doyle. We're glad you could come on such short notice. And on a Saturday as well." Wackenslong held the door to his office open.

"We?" Bartley thought it was just going to be him and Wackenslong.

If the waiting area was like a museum, Bartley always felt he entered a time warp when he visited Wackenslong's inner office. The dark wood paneling made it seem as though he'd been transported back to the 1960s. Lots of political paraphernalia. Buttons, banners, and a yard sign declaring "Wilbur Wackenslong—A Man Who Gets Things Done!" hung from the wall behind the desk. Bartley knew well the oak conference table in the middle of the room where deals were developed, alliances forged, and enemies identified. That's where Bartley saw him.

"President Bartley, I assume you know Ned Spano. One of your students at CCC."

Spano remained seated and stuck out his hand toward Bartley. "You were the guy up on the platform at the college with all those suits and skirts around you."

Bartley scrunched up his nose as he returned the handshake. The smell of farts wafted his way from the guest. The heavy cologne added to the odiferous cacophony. "Ah, yes. I guess, ah, you are referring to the Board meeting this week."

Bartley shook hands, looked at Wackenslong quizzically, pushed up his round tortoiseshell glasses, and sat across from Spano. Under the table, the president wiped his hand up and down on his pant leg. The senator sat at the head of the table.

"I hope you've recovered from the incident at the bar earlier this month," Bartley said. "That was an incredibly extraordinary story you told us that day."

"It was no *incident*. That professor *assaulted* me. One of your professors, Mr. President. And I'm a student. I wanna know what you're going to do about it. You know I can hold you responsible, too."

Bartley was lost. Why was Spano threatening him? Why was he here?

"President Bartley and I cannot convey how sorry we are for this unfortunate incident, Mr. Spano."

"Assault." Spano corrected.

"We thought you were ameliorated by Dr. Turkle for your troubles."

"Amelia tated?" Spano attempted to sound out the word. "What the hell you talking about?"

"Sorry," Wackenslong continued. "Didn't Dr. Turkle compensate you for your troubles?"

"He said he would see to it that I would get money to help me pay a few bills. You know I got a kid. That cost money."

"Did Dr. Turkle make good on his promise?"

"Well, yeah. But it ain't enough. I want more."

"More?"

"More money."

Bartley looked as though he just walked into a cockfight, and was about to be thrown into the ring. He didn't even know what to say or where to go with the conversation. This was all news to him. Turkle had just said he would "take care of things."

Wackenslong walked to his desk and retrieved a file folder. As he walked toward Spano's chair he read his notes. "Mr. Spano, according to what my people have told me, you make quite a bit of money as a…businessman. You seem to have clients all around town. Wasn't that the reason you were in *The Silver Fox* the night of the incident?" Wackenslong had the air of a man you did not play with. Ever.

"The assault. And that's none of your business what I do for my business, dickhead!"

Slam!

Spano's head bounced off the conference table. Wackenslong held a fist full of his hair. Benny might have been quick with his guitar cord, but Wackenslong pounced quicker than a lion on a wildebeest.

Wackenslong, within an inch of his guest's blooded nose, stared at him. "President Bartley, I'm considering what we should do next. Should I cut off his balls for being so rude to you?" With that, he slammed Spano's head into the table, again. Bartley crossed his legs as his glasses slipped down to the end of his nose.

"What do you think I should do with you, you no good miserable two-bit drug dealer? I know people who can make you go away without a trace. But I don't want to do that and have your kid never see Daddy again. And that pretty mother of your baby. What's her name, Suzy? Yeah, that's it. I'd hate to see anything happen to her."

He threw Spano against the back of the chair. "I know more about you than you know about you."

"I don't want no trouble. I just need money, that's all. Why you getting so bent out of shape?"

"You want to do a head bounce once again, numbnuts?"

"No." Spano crossed his arms in front of his face.

"What?"

"No, sir."

"That's a good drug dealer. Now, I'll tell you what you're going to do. President Bartley and I have important matters to discuss. You will wait to hear from one of my people. You want more money. We'll see. But it will depend on what you do for us."

"What else do I gotta do?"

Wackenslong held his finger to his lips. "Shh. You're starting to piss me off again. You go do whatever you do out there. You don't mention this meeting to anyone. You never met me. That way you will stay healthy. Got it?"

"Yeah." Spano rubbed the blood away with his coat jacket sleeve. "Can I use your bathroom to clean up?"

"Sure, the one down the hall. Just don't jerk off while you're in there."

Spano pushed his chair back, picked up his ball cap from the floor, and quickly walked to the door.

"Remember," Wackenslong called after him, "someone will be in touch, and you better be ready. Be a good boy. Remember, you never know who is watching you."

Spano waved his acknowledgment over his head as he left the office holding his other hand to his bleeding nose.

Wackenslong pulled a can of air freshener from his closet shelf and spritzed. He looked at Bartley, laughed, and said, "We have a few things to discuss about your athletes."

Bartley tugged at his collar.

• • •

20

"**I** love it! Absolutely love it!" Darla's eyes sparkled and her smile widened as she held the phone to her ear with her left hand and admired her right wrist. "It fits, sparkles, and stands out. I could not have asked for a more fitting gift."

She rotated her arm to see how the diamond tennis bracelet caught the light at various angles. She smiled.

"Just a token, Darla, of what's to come. Wear it well. And I'll see you tonight around 8. I've gotta run to a meeting. Keep working your magic with Cole." Turkle disconnected and Darla sat back still looking at her wrist.

This is great! You know those people at the club hold you in contempt. You'll stand out! If only the old neighborhood could see you now.

Darla snapped a selfie and immediately posted it to her social media feed. Despite outward appearances, she silently confronted her own I'm-not-good-enough story. She equated respect with standing out. She, too, would not be invisible.

You know how to make them take notice! The club doesn't know how lucky it is to have you. Nor do the people around this place.

Merlot looked around her 6th-floor administrative office. A heartbeat away from the president. She covered her city-view windows with ceiling-to-floor semi-sheer gold drapes providing the display of elegance she sought in furnishings, clothes, and accouterments. The view didn't matter as much as the exhibition.

A knock on the office door brought her back. "Dr. Merlot, your two o'clock is here."

"Thank you. Good. Please show Dr. Fitzgerald in."

As Cole entered, Darla stepped from behind her walnut L-shaped executive desk and walked with her braceleted arm extended in greeting.

"Good afternoon! Thanks for coming on such short notice, Cole. You don't know how much I appreciate you. Please have a seat." She pointed to the chair in front of her desk. As Cole sat down, he noticed the photos and memorabilia on the shelves behind her desk and on the wall by the entrance to her private bathroom. All sports photos. Nothing that seemed like family portraits.

"Still play?" Cole asked nodding toward the framed tennis photos.

"Kind of. More like I play at it now." She pulled down one of the photos. "I had the good fortune to be recruited to college on a tennis scholarship. Our team made it to the NCAA Women's Tennis Championship finals my senior year. Now," she continued as she pointed to a few other frames, "I mostly play weekends at the Marina Norte Country Club. I hold my own. Have you ever played sports?"

"Played football in high school." Ian's face flashed in his mind. "Now, music is my muse."

"Ah, that's right. *HTRB*. Have you rebranded it yet?" she asked grinning and thinking back to her comments in *The Silver Fox*. "Though, I still love the name. You're clever, Professor."

She kept her eyes on the photos drawing out the seconds of silence before she sat behind her desk, swiveled her chair, reached for a file on the left side of the desk, and slid it in front of her. As Merlot cast a look of concern toward Cole, the steady ticking of the oak-encased clock in the far corner of the room broke the silence.

"I know this has been hard on you with Professor DiJohn and all that's happening. He seems like such a nice man. I can't believe he did what our student Mr. Spano said he did. I'm hoping you can help us."

"Benny did not do what Mr. Spano alleges. And, while Mr. Spano has been on class rolls, I can't find a professor who has seen him in class. This whole thing looks like a shakedown."

Are you listening to yourself? Benny did hogtie the guy. In a public place. With witnesses.

"I wish you were correct, Cole. I do. But I got a call this morning. The Marina Norte Sheriff's Office is about to launch a full investigation into assault and sexual advances. By a professor on a student. It's serious for everyone."

"Pat said he could make this go away. Said he'd get the best lawyer. Benny is being set up and the college is letting it happen? And you said 'everyone.' Who is 'everyone'? It appears Benny is the only one getting screwed."

"It goes deeper than Benny. This is a mark on CCC, the faculty, and, of course, the poor student involved." Darla flipped through the papers in the file. "Mr. Spano has provided details."

"Then I'll talk to the Sheriff and the press. I have details, too!" Cole stood and looked down at Darla. "And there are other witnesses—public witnesses. This will not hold up in court."

"Cole, do you think Benny wants this to go to court? Even if he were to be found innocent, you know how the public forms its own opinions. This would have devastating consequences for his career, and his life. We need you to help Benny see that he is in a no-win situation."

"That's why he needs the representation Pat spoke of. And Benny needs it now."

"I thought you'd understand this as long as you've been around teaching. The college has an attorney—to represent the college. Her job is to stand up for the college first. I'm afraid Benny will need to get his own attorney. And as for you going to the sheriff's office or the press. You might remember I sent out a message to all faulty a few days ago. No speaking about college matters unless cleared through this office. Due to the ongoing investigation by the college, you are not allowed to speak about it."

"You can't do this. We have the right to speak our minds."

"Cole, I'm on your side. Same with Benny. But my hands are tied. This directive came from our Board. I guess you could get an attorney as well if you want to pursue that."

Again, they have handed your ass to you. Cole, get out of here before you lose your head as well. You are, once again, no match for these people. Over. Your. Head.

"I want to speak to Turkle. Now!"

"Dr. Turkle. And I'll see what I can do. He's at the athletic complex for the remainder of the day. I'll ask him to call you at his earliest convenience."

Cole stared into Darla's eyes. She did not flinch. He turned and left the room.

Darla reached for her cell phone. "OK. We're at the next level. Fitzgerald just left my office."

"How did he take the news?"

"He only sees rage. Not sure what he will do. He might be going to find Pat."

"That's perfect. Stop by my office on your way to the club tonight. I have something for you."

Darla smiled and jingled her bracelet.

• • •

21

Anger comes in various forms. At times triggered by an outside force. Other times, it might be a child-like temper tantrum set off by a selfish desire. Whatever the source, venom drives the outburst. Perhaps a voice in the ear pushes the person forward. Cole felt like a child lying face down on the floor, kicking and screaming, wanting someone to listen, to be reasonable. Another slight. One more disrespect tossed in his face.

You deserve respect. Act now or be invisible for the rest of your sorry life.

Cole stopped his car in front of the gym. Turkle's BMW convertible sat in a "Reserved" spot in the front row. Cole took a deep breath. His anger had not subsided. As he walked toward the gym he felt his body tighten and his pulse rate increase as his fists clenched and unclenched. Merlot correctly pegged his emotion. Rage had taken anger's place. He swung the outside door to the building open and it slammed against the wall.

Once inside the lobby, he could hear basketballs bouncing and players calling out to one another. "Practice in

Session" was posted on the door. The security guard waved him in.

"Hey, Doc. Here to give the kids some tips?"

Cole waved and walked into the gym, stopped courtside, and looked around.

"Hey, Professor! You come to coach us today?" Johnny V was at the top of the key, ball in hand. He tossed it to Cole.

"Where's Coach Gil?" He squeezed the ball between his hands.

Johnny V turned toward the opposite side of the court and pointed. "He's talking over there."

Cole bounced the ball as he walked cross court ignoring the players zigging and zagging toward the basket. With each step, he bounced the ball with more force. The noise in the gym faded into the background. His patience spent, he moved toward his target.

There's the bastard!

Coach Gil and Turkle stood face-to-face in conversation and didn't notice Cole's approach.

"You! Turkle!" Cole yelled, his voice carrying above the voices of the players. "You!" He continued his march forward not quite sure what he was about to do. Until he did it.

He threw the ball as hard as he could right at Turkle's head. Turkle and the coach turned and saw the raging professor and the flying ball. Calling on their athletic abilities, they both leaned to the side and the ball slammed into the wooden bleacher seats behind them. It bounced back and rolled toward center court, where Johnny V palmed it with one hand and looked at the adults in the room.

"You! How could you let that happen? You disgrace. You two-faced bastard!" Cole's voice had risen to a level as if he were belting out the hook of a song. His volume caught the attention of the rest of the players as they focused on the far corner and the yelling professor. The gym went quiet. The coach saw Turkle to his right and a screaming Cole approaching quickly from the left.

"Whoa! Cole, what the heck are you doing?" The coach stepped between the two as if forming a pick for a game-winning shot. "Cole. Timeout!" The coach grabbed him. The team circled them, looking, not believing what they were seeing.

"You tell that no good excuse for a human being he needs to take a timeout!"

Turkle straightened his jacket and shirt collar and walked toward Cole and the coach. He stared at Cole. And smiled. That shit-eaten grin that Cole had come to know and despise. The look that said, "Game on, mother!"

He doesn't know who he's messing with.

"Not sure what you are doing, Professor. But whatever it is, do you think this is how to behave in front of our students? All witnesses, by the way, to you throwing a ball at me with intent to do harm. Assault on a college administrator. Might even be a battery charge. Cole, how about I ask, what are you doing?" Turkle looked at the coach, "Let him go."

Turkle looked at the ball players. "Hey, Johnny. Jonny Valentine. Would you please call the security guard to step inside, please?"

"Do we need to do that, Pat?" the coach asked. "Let's go to my office and take a breath. Do you want this to get out?"

"Thank you, coach, but Dr. Fitzgerald has committed a foul. I'm calling homecourt advantage. He is part of something bigger than you know and I don't want you involved with any of this more than as a witness. At the least, we need documentation." Then looking at Cole he said, "You wanted visibility. Guess you just got it."

• • •

An hour later, Turkle stopped in Bartley's office to bring him up-to-date on Cole's tirade in the gym.

"He actually threw a basketball at your head? What the hell, Pat?" Bartley paced in front of his desk. "This is getting incredibly ugly. Not sure how this works out for anyone."

"Cole just gave us a gift. Think about it, Doyle. The MNSO is investigating one faculty member for assaulting a student, another just assaulted a college administrator, a union that, as I see it, will drive a deeper divide between the faculty, and the Board directive shutting down interviews between faculty and the press. The entire faculty looks dysfunctional in the public's eyes. And it's up to us to keep that as the main theme."

"How does that help us gain students or build a reputation in the community? An out-of-control faculty is really to our advantage? Unimaginably difficult to see." Turkle let Bartley ruminate. He knew the president had limited capacity for the nebulous and even less desire for a public brawl with the teaching side of the house.

"It helps us because we have the tentative faculty and the anti-union faculty desperate for leadership. This is your opportunity to step into the vacuum and play peacekeeper. Throw them a few scraps and they will think you have invited them to a banquet. First, start with a meeting you call to address all faculty. Present an ultimatum—with a kind face and reassuring tone."

Bartley slowed his pacing. His hands were still behind his back as he looked toward the floor. "You could be right. This new incident with Cole may keep the faculty from asking uncomfortably probing questions."

"I know I'm right. You think about it tonight. I'll bring you my plan tomorrow. Go home and have a nice dinner with your wife."

They shook hands and Turkle headed for the elevator. He sent a text to Darla. "Look forward to seeing you at the Club tonight."

A return text with a smiley face and heart immediately pinged his phone.

• • •

Darla knocked on the slightly ajar office door. The secretary had already left for the evening. "Anyone home."

"Come in."

He heard her stilettos tap through the door and into his office. Dressed in her black form-fitting sleeveless minidress, she looked delicious. He stood and walked around his desk.

"So glad you could stop by. And that bracelet accents your outfit well. Nice fashion decision. Here," Wackenslong said as he handed her a bourbon on the rocks. "You remember the first pair of stilettos?"

"Yes, sir. Almost broke my neck! But heck, I was a mere twenty-five-year-old intern working a mayoral campaign." She clinked his glass and took a sip.

"That campaign started a lot of things in action," he said. "I was fortunate to meet you."

"Thank you, Senator. And I was blessed as well. I hope I did well for you today."

"Yes, you did, Darla. Between your conversation with Cole and also getting a spot on the Heather Rivera show, you did very well. Keep the heat on. Just like we discussed."

"Yes, sir. And Dr. Edwards will appear with me on the Rivera show as well."

"You go to the top of the class, young lady."

Wackenslong held up his glass, they toasted and drank. He pulled her close. They kissed.

• • •

22

The following morning found Cole sitting on the beach, facing the rising sun. A brief time away from the drama of life. No conversation. No disagreements. Just the ocean swells rising and falling. The occasional ripples of a dolphin, tarpon, or from a boat in the distance. Solitude. Except today his mind drifted back 30 years. As he gazed out at the horizon, he thought of his brother.

Ian found himself drawn to the plight of the bullied and downtrodden. How much of that was because of their mother's mental, emotional, and alcohol issues or his father's bullying attitude toward Ian, Cole was not sure. Cole, the athletic stud in high school, stood mute on the family's sidelines.

Ian didn't. The more his father demeaned him, the more Ian pushed back and the more he came to understand he needed to stand up and be heard. A gay pride flag stood in Ian's bedroom. It was one of many symbols of the oppressed Ian had gathered in his search for community justice. Was Ian gay? Cole had no idea. They never discussed it. While Ian engaged in difficult conversations, young Cole did what he could to avoid such interactions.

Their dad saw Ian's predilection for the underlings in society to be "sissy stuff." One night at dinner, Ian proudly slid across the table an essay on which he received an A: "Are We Really the Greatest Country in the World?" Ian posed a careful statistical study that showed where the greatest countries stood regarding healthcare, education, crime, incarceration, free press, diversity, equity, inclusion, and other variables.

His dad sneered and flicked the paper back. "Yes, we are! And if you question that you deserve to have your ass beat." Ian answered with stats. His father spewed vitriol. His mother asked if anyone would like another meatball. Cole asked to be excused.

How Ian coped with his father's aggressive behavior was beyond Cole's understanding. Perhaps the counselor his mother arranged for him to see helped. Maybe the medication. Again, since Cole avoided familial confrontation, he didn't know. Until it was too late.

A tarpon broke the surface of the water and brought Cole back to the present. "I failed Ian and my mother. I stood by and did nothing," he quietly said to himself. He drifted back to that terrible night when his world changed. Forever.

Three weeks after the essay incident, Cole heard a blood-curdling shriek from Ian's bedroom. He ran and found his mother holding Ian and sobbing. Ian was dead. A drug overdose. While Ian appeared to have everything under control, he needed medication to help him deal with anxiety. From what Cole remembers, the medical examiner's report said Ian was mixing various drugs. The kid who wanted to make a difference, died attempting to cope. He wanted to stand out behind the scenes. Whereas Cole the football star attempted to live a life of standing out in front of his classmates.

Cole changed the night Ian died. Or at least the beginning of his mental and emotional transition was tied to that night. He turned down the football scholarship he got to State. Instead, he enrolled in Central City College. The flag ended up in his room. His father ended up divorcing his mother. She continued making meatballs, drinking, and doing what she could to avoid dealing with her inner demons until she died. Ian and his mother lost to their inner voices.

Was history repeating itself?

Cole kicked the sand, turned, and walked toward his car and the waiting day.

• • •

"Good morning. Welcome to 'First-Cup-Free-Day'." With a yawn, the barista pushed back the security gate that separated the CCC Café from the lobby. "Coffee is ready for you." He pointed toward the island in the middle of the food service area. "I think it's fresh. But I could be wrong." He smiled and winked.

Suzy filled her thermal cup to the rim, made her way to a corner booth, and opened her backpack. Aintin Clara had the late shift at the diner today and this allowed Suzy to get to school early and catch up on reading for her 8 o'clock class.

"Balancing everything is becoming harder and harder," she said to herself as she opened a book and took a sip of coffee. "Yuck," she said as she looked into her thermal mug. "The barista was wrong. This coffee was fresh three days ago!"

"Looks like today's coffee is no better than yesterday's." Suzy looked up and saw Ms. Robertson standing at the end of the booth.

"Well, it's better than what I make at home." Suzy managed a smile as she squirmed to find comfort.

"I heard you're a radio star. Even mentioned my name," Ms. Robertson said. "Do you have a moment to talk?"

She knows. The Professor said something.

"Well, I, ah, I'm studying for a quiz. I could come to your office sometime this week."

Ms. Robertson slid in and sat opposite Suzy. "That's why you are going to do well this semester. You are diligent and disciplined. I sensed that the first time we met."

"Thank you, but I always feel behind."

Be truthful. You feel like an imposter!

"And you are doing something about it," Ms. Robertson said as she pointed toward Suzy's books. "Professor Fitzgerald also thinks you have talent. He said that you know that…"

"Now is my time." Suzy finished the sentence and took another sip.

"And," Ms. Robertson said, "now is our time to talk. Or at least to begin talking. Professor Fitzgerald said he wanted us to speak the other day. But you refused. What's going on?"

"I was a mess. Crying in the hall when he saw me. I was questioning why I came to CCC. I'm not college material."

"I wasn't 'college material' as you say, either. Flunked four out of five classes my first semester and was placed on academic probation," Ms. Robertson said as she emptied a packet of sweetener in her coffee.

"No way."

"You bet. Scared the beeswax out of me. With the help of a few professors, I got my mind refocused and started to climb out of the hole I had put myself into. Professors like Fitzgerald. They care and can make a difference."

She paused, stirred her coffee, and let the words settle on Suzy before she continued.

"He told me he saw bruises on your wrist."

"It's nothing. I wish he hadn't said anything," Suzy said holding her hands below the table.

"He had to. It's the law. Even if it's nothing, as you say, he is obligated to report it. Do you want to talk?"

"Not really. I'm OK." Suzy avoided eye contact with Ms. Robertson.

"Suzy, are you or your daughter in danger? I can call Protective Services to help you if that is what you need?"

"No!" Suzy shouted with a panicked look. "No, not them."

Suzy reflected on when her parents were either in jail, prison, or rehab. Invariably, a member from P.S. would begin an investigation into child neglect. Thank God for her Aintin. She saved her and Shauna.

"Ms. Robertson, it's nothing really. Listen, my daughter's daddy can be a handful at times. We don't live together but I still care about him. He's having a difficult time in his life. On probation. He's working off and on. When he can he gives me money for Shauna. Not much but it helps me. We need his help."

"And do you need him abusing you?"

"It's not like that."

"So, the bruises were caused by someone else?" Ms. Robetson asked.

"No, no. He did it but, I asked for it."

"You asked to be abused?"

Suzy slid her book into her backpack and picked up her coffee. "I need to get to class, ma'am. I appreciate your concern. But there is nothing to worry about. I have it under control."

"Before you go, please take this with you." Ms. Robertson wrote a number on the back of her business card and handed it to Suzy. "Call me any time you decide you need to talk. Or stop by my office. You know where it is. And the number on the back of the card is the Domestic Abuse Hotline."

Suzy placed the card in her jeans pocket, pushed herself out of the booth, and walked toward the lobby.

• • •

"Professor, do you have a moment?"

Eulonia looked up from the stack of essays in front of her. "Sure, Professor. Have a seat. I was hoping you'd stop by." Cole placed his backpack on the floor and folded himself into the visitor's chair, feeling like a student during office hours.

"I need your guidance," Cole said, "and I need your understanding. I appreciated you speaking your mind at the union meeting."

"It needed to be said."

"I know we have different backgrounds, experiences, and obstacles," Cole said.

"And opportunities," Eulonia added.

"And opportunities, yes. But white saviorism. That stung. All I'm trying to do is what's best for my students and the marginalized community they come from."

Eulonia reached for her cup of tea and pursed her lips. "That's the problem."

Cole could feel his neck tingle and his cheeks redden.

Control your ego. This woman has something to share. You're not the only teacher in the room.

"Well, two problems, really," Eulonia said. "First, from what I have observed and heard from students and colleagues, your heart is in the right place. You want to help. But what makes you think that you know what's best for the Black, Indigenous, and People of Color in our community?"

This is what students feel like when you put them on the spot. You always think they can learn from you. Your turn to learn.

"From classroom discussions and office visits," Cole said.

"So, an academic discussion in a seventy-five-minute class—or over a semester—has led you to believe you know what's best for your students, their families, and their neighbors."

Eulonia let the words settle over the office. They had a bite to them but she wasn't meanspirited. She continued, "You mean well but—"

"Doesn't that count for something? I'm doing something. Reaching out. Letting them know they're not alone." Cole's voice, while not a yell, had risen in tone.

"Sure it does. You care yet you don't understand. You come from a perspective of 'I'm here to help you' but what do you know, what have you experienced from their shoes, front porches, or kitchen tables?"

Cole sat back. "You said there were two problems. What else am I doing wrong." He braced himself for the next exchange.

"Marginalization. Not the word itself but your use of it."

"Am I forbidden to use the word?" he said with a hint of defensiveness. "As I removed the blinders, I became humbled by what I didn't know and, also, about what I wanted to do. When I look at my students and, yes, the marginalized community our CCC serves, I see that they want to be seen and heard just like you and I want to. As I listened to their stories, I came to understand, as best I could, what they experienced on the margins of our community. On the edges of life."

"The word marginalization," Elonia said. "It's tossed around so much by people who know the academic definition but not what it means to be a person of color on the fringes of survival. That's white saviorism. What makes you think you understand that?"

"Ian started that transformation for me. My students have continued it."

"Tell me about Ian's Corner. I've heard that he was your brother. I'm guessing he's deceased."

"Yes. About thirty years ago. Drug overdose. It took our family by surprise but it shouldn't have. Ian was my younger brother. I was seen as the high school football stud." His self-description left Cole with a tinge of disgust for himself. "Ian reached out to students who didn't fit in. He stood up to bullies. He helped people be respected."

"Sounds like a decent young man."

"Yeah. He *was*. You see, Eulonia, all those years ago I was part of the problem that I am helping, or at least I think I'm helping, to identify, address, and fight along with my students. Back then, and perhaps even now, I assumed a lot of things about a lot of people I didn't understand. I took the easy way out. Jumped to conclusions. Though I never acted on those conclusions."

Cole paused. Eulonia saw his eyes well up.

"If I may, Cole, at times when we fail to take direct action, we actually *do* act. Our inability to confront an ill allows that ill to continue. I know, I have done that myself in the past. I'm not proud of it and I won't do it again."

"I can tell you I don't see myself as a savior. More days than not, I feel like I need a protector to survive. You've given me a lot to think about. Thank you." Again, Cole paused, at a loss for words. "I need time to catch my breath and then I would like to talk with you again about this. Maybe a cup of coffee or tea," he said pointing at her cup.

"I'd like that," Eulonia said. "From what I can see, you've been under quite a bit of pressure from the administration."

Cole sunk back into his chair, exhaled, and then leaned forward placing his folded hands on Eulonia's desk. "And that's something else I need your help with."

"You got my interest. If I can, I will. How?"

"Well, I'm not sure whether to start with the Sheriff's Office investigation, the college gag order, or the basketball I threw at Turkle's head."

• • •

23

From the moment his mother gave him a used gut string box guitar, music spoke to Cole. That his mother found the inexpensive and banged-up guitar at a neighborhood flea market mattered little. As he fingered his first chords Cole entered a space where time stopped and everything but the music disappeared. Almost out-of-body-like, the space embraced him in joy and peace. No future and no past. Just the moment. In later years, the stage became the space that allowed him to be who he was. His territory; his domain.

But, now, even that safe haven seemed to be in jeopardy.

"Joe, when you get a moment." Cole held up his empty glass from the end of the bar.

"And pour me a cold pint of your house brew while you're at it," Benny added as he slid his guitar case onto the stage, walked to the bar, and stood next to Cole. "Ah! That's a brewer's pour, Joe. You are a master!"

"A few years of practice and a lot of spilled beer along the way." Joe placed fresh coasters under their drinks and moved toward a new customer at the other end of the bar.

"From the look on your face, I'm guessing you've heard the latest from the puzzle palace weasels." Benny took a sip of beer.

"I had an agonizing meeting listening to Merlot's corporate bullshit. This has ratcheted to a level I didn't anticipate. The sheriff's office and the publicity are bad enough, but the college's prohibition about speaking to the press keeps us off the radar. And you have to find and pay for your legal representation because, after all, according to Turkle's mouthpiece the college attorney isn't *your* attorney; she's the *college's* attorney!"

"Yeah, she's his mouthpiece and I can only imagine what piece that mouth has been servicing." Benny laughed and drank his beer. "Cole, I'm used to this. I'll admit this is a deeper fecal deposit than usual, but accusations and innuendo are nothing new. Being locked out of my classroom, though? Well, I didn't expect that. And it pisses me off."

"What?"

"Oh yeah, Turkle's mouthpiece didn't share that juicy nugget with you? As of today, I am not allowed on campus. I cannot communicate with my students. She told me it was just a 'precaution' until this all 'blows over.' Dip wads."

"But you haven't been arrested, have you?" Cole asked.

"No. Yet to be determined if charges will be pressed. Still, I can't be in the classroom, and that hurts my soul." Benny looked at the beer in his hand, placed it on the bar, and closed his eyes.

Cole swiveled his stool to face Benny. "Well, I might join you with an assault charge." Benny's head turned toward

Cole. "I went after Turkle. Threw a basketball at his head. Had to be restrained by Coach Gil. God only knows where that'll end up."

"Did you hit him? I hope he pooped his fancy tight pants."

"No. But the ball made a racket bouncing around the gym. And the players witnessed it." Cole shook his head and sipped his Scotch. "I shouldn't have done it. But with your situation, the union, the pressures on campus and, well, I'm tired, angry, and not thinking straight."

"We're both under a lot of pressure, bud. Anger is understandable. I am concerned for both of us."

"Me, too. Me, too."

"What do you say we put this aside for the next few hours? We've got our music. That stage, as you have said, is our domain. Period."

Cole wished he had the ability, like Benny, to compartmentalize the crud. Or at least, not to rage about stuff he couldn't control.

"And," Benny continued, "these sons-of-bitches have inspired me to write a new song. Key of E. Straight forward with a groove and an edge. Straight-out blues. Just what we need. God knows I need it."

Benny paused looked toward the stage, back at Cole, and then continued. "It might look like I'm just brushing aside what those assholes do. But I'm not. I can't. I bounce back and forth between being pissed off and scared. And, I'm tired, too, Cole. Tired of being on alert because of my lifestyle or who I hang with."

Cole looked at Benny as his words settled.

See. It's not always about you.

"But you, the guys," Benny pointed toward Justin and Billy B, "and the music help me cope. Come on, follow me. We'll do my song as our soundcheck."

Benny pushed himself from the stool and stepped onto the stage. Cole followed, battling the memories of the day, the voice, and what Benny shared. He looked like a man being dragged to a proctology exam. As he strapped on his guitar he muttered, "Shut the hell up." The drummer looked at him with a quizzical look.

"Not you Justin."

"I hear that same voice each day. Thank God for music and drums," Justin said as he continued to tune his snare drum. "I just beat it quiet with my sticks!"

"Hey, guys this is a new one for us," Benny said as he tuned his bass. "Follow me. And as for that voice, Justin, we all know that when we're playing music—bad day and all—it lifts the weight from our shoulders. As if nothing else in the world matters except the now. Let's do it, boys."

Benny did a few riffs so the guys could hear the rhythm and chord progression. "And Cole, in honor of the puzzle palace patrons I call this one 'Weasels and Ferrets'." With that came the downbeat, Benny sang, and the guys joined in. You would have thought it was a regular in their repertoire.

Weasels and ferrets
Moles and slugs
Liars and cheats
Felons and thugs
Ain't got no morals
Ain't got no merit
Ain't got no honor
Call 'em weasels and ferrets.

A woman who remained at the bar long after happy hour ended, turned toward the band and raised her glass. "You sing it, Benny!" She waved to Joe for a refill. "Sounds like they wrote that song about my boss."

"Could be anybody's boss," Joe replied.

Yeah, they talk a good story
Smile in your face
When you walk away
They'll steal your space.
Spit you out
Use you up
Tell you lies
And cover, cover it up.
They say, "Believe in me, 'cause I'm your man."
But if you challenge them
It'll hit the fan.
There is no code among these thieves
Guess we'll wait
'til another one leaves.

Cole smiled to himself, "If only one of them left it would be a start." He looked at his bandmate and winked. Benny nodded as he delivered the next verse. The song was his catharsis.

> *To them it's a game*
> *To you a big mess.*
> *Everyone's pain*
> *Is their success.*
> *Here's a crank*
> *And there's a kook*
> *That they're so evil*
> *Well, it ain't no fluke.*

As they belted out verse after verse, their edge became more prominent. Cole joined in on the harmonies. Each time the words *weasel* or *ferret* were sung, Justin made sure to give an extra kick on his bass drum.

The gathering crowd erupted with applause and whistles.

"Thank you! Thank you very much!" Benny said wiping the sweat from his face. "Guess we all know our share of weasels and ferrets, don't we? Give us a sec to retune, and *HTRB* will kick off the night and help you reset your collective buttons."

Benny smiled and looked at the band. "When they screw with you, you gotta screw 'em right back. Harder."

"My, my. Love it when you play with an edge," Heather smiled and walked toward the stage.

"Good to see you, Heather. We need you tonight. Been a rough day on several levels," Benny said.

"Let me guess. Has something to do with weasels and ferrets." She raised her eyebrows. "It so happens, that I have two of those weasels on tomorrow morning's show. Darla Merlot and Richard Edwards. Merlot called to set it up. I have an idea that I want to float by you two. We'll talk after your show."

She leaned in and gave Cole a kiss and a reassuring hug.

• • •

Sometimes the music does not create the state a musician hopes for. The harmonic angels go silent. The notes and lyrics cannot drown out the head noise. It didn't happen often but this was one of those nights. Cole was spent. And Benny wasn't far behind.

As he zipped up his guitar case and grabbed his gig bag, Cole took a deep breath. "Sorry guys. Not sure I pulled my weight tonight."

"You did fine," Billy B said, "we've all been there."

"The voice just won't shut up at times, will it?" Justin pushed his drums to the edge of the stage for the loadout.

"Shut up? I wish it would just stop yelling." Cole stepped off the stage as if every muscle in his body ached. He moved listlessly toward Heather's table.

"Hey, I know you wanted to talk with Benny and me. I can't. I'm beat and going home."

"OK. Let me say goodbye to Benny, and I'll be ready." She placed her purse strap over her shoulder and stood.

"Not tonight, Heather. I need to be alone." Cole's eyes were beyond sad, his shoulders slouched, and it looked like he hadn't slept in days. Heather saw anguish and desperation. But she no longer knew what to do or say. His moods, more and more frequently, swung from hopeful to hopeless to somewhere in between.

She touched his arm. "Cole, let me be with you. You don't have to talk. But when you want to I'll be there."

"No, not tonight. I don't even want to be with me. But I'm stuck with me. I need to sort things out."

Like the night she found him talking to the voice in the living room, Heather feared for Cole. Was the voice just self-doubt? She experienced that like so many other people. Sometimes that inner chatter could be fear of a challenge. But given the little she had learned about Cole's family, she felt like Cole's inner voice was more sinister.

"Cole," Heather whispered in his ear as she hugged him, "I'm here for you. But you have to let me in. When you suffer, I suffer. We suffer."

"Don't worry about me. You know once I get back to the condo Big Betsy takes care of me. And there's always my aunt's braciola." He managed a weak smile and kissed her cheek. He turned toward the stage, waved goodnight to the band, and walked through the door to his car as Benny approached the table.

"Benny, I'm worried for him. A lot. He's turning away when he needs connections. Until he can deal with what's inside, he'll have a difficult time handling what's outside. He's tired. I get it. But he can't do this alone. I'm frustrated."

"He's trying to help me. So, I need to help him," Benny said.

"Well, I got an idea and it starts with my show tomorrow with Merlot and Edwards. Got a few minutes to talk?"

"Sure. And I want to update you with some of the college issues that you might want to toss toward Merlot and Dick Ed."

• • •

Cole placed his guitar in the corner of the living room, dropped his gig bag to the floor, and walked to the kitchen where he pulled the bottle of Scotch from the cabinet. He held it at arm's length for a moment as if reconsidering his choice. But then said, "I need your help, Mr. Scotch Maltman."

So, you sort things out with more alcohol? You can run but you cannot hide.

Cole poured three fingers, dropped in an ice cube, and sat at the kitchen counter. Big Betsy jumped up and rubbed against his arms. Cole saw a note leaning against the saltshaker.

Marco. Dominic and I are having dinner at Gambardella's. Eggplant parmigiana on the stove. Buono!

A tear rolled down Cole's cheek. Followed by another until he sobbed.

"I'm lost. I'm useless to me, to everyone around me." He hugged Big Betsy to his chest.

So, what are we going to do? End it? Don't see how you can continue like this. Sometimes it doesn't work out and you just have to admit it and give up. You did what you could.

Cole wiped his cheeks with a napkin and took a long drink from his glass.

You've been trying for years—your entire life—to fit in while standing out. And you wonder why you're tired. Poser comes to mind.

"What do you want from me? You're just like everyone else. Criticizing without helping. Demeaning for no good. It's like I'm a child again."

A few more cubes clunked into the glass. Big Betsy purred. Another three fingers.

Avoider! Rather than confront, you postpone. Yeah, go ahead. Have another drink rather than deal with your fears!

"No! Damn, you!" Cole pounded the counter. Big Betsy's eyes grew wide and she jumped to the floor.

Cole's phone chimed. He saw Heather's name. He rejected the call, slugged back his drink, and poured another. He picked up Big Betsy and walked to the sofa.

You better be ready for a long, long ride. I know you can hear that voice in your ear.

Grabbing the remote, he flipped through the channels, settling on a Yankee's game. They were in the later innings of their game and behind.

Just like Cole.

• • •

24

The flexible class schedule had long been a benefit of college teaching. Cole's seniority in the department allowed him to schedule mid-morning and early afternoon classes. This helped accommodate his nights with the band and his morning beach walks. In all his years, he never missed a class or started one late. Punctuality was as important to him as keeping the beat with the band.

That's why today was odd.

Bang. Bang. Bang.

"Cole, you in there?"

No answer.

Bang. Bang. Bang.

"Cole!"

Benny looked at his cell phone. Another text from Heather. "You find him yet? I'm on in five minutes."

He moved the front door flowerpot, grabbed the key under it, and opened the door slowly.

"Cole! Good morning, Cole! You in here?"

The TV droned as he walked toward the living room. To his right, he saw an empty bottle of Scotch on the counter next to a laptop. Big Betsy jumped up on the counter to greet him.

"Hey, Big Betsy, where's your person?" She leaned into his stroke on her haunches. Benny walked around the counter and saw Cole lying motionless on the sofa.

"Cole. You OK?"

Nothing.

"That's how I found him when I got home last night." Aunt Philomena entered from the kitchen, a dishtowel in one hand, and a spatula in the other. "I put a blanket over him and he hasn't moved. Didn't eat the eggplant parmigiana either." She pointed toward the stovetop. She held out her hand, "I'm Aunt Philomena. Who are you? The neighborhood burglar?"

"*The* Aunt Philomena?" Benny said with a wide smile. "I'm Benny, his teaching colleague and bandmate. We missed him on campus today."

"He ain't doing too much teaching or playing today. I worry about him." She walked to the sofa, leaned over the coffee table, and walloped it with the spatula.

Bang!

Cole sat straight up. His face had the confused look of someone being pulled out into the ocean by a rip current.

"Marco, I told you, that night when Heather was here, this has to stop." She leaned toward her nephew with the look of a mother tired of a child who continued to disobey. "You're pushing away Heather. And now, your fan club president here," she waved the spatula toward Benny, "tells me you missed class today."

Benny backed away hoping not to be hit by a stray piece of eggplant.

"This can't go on, Marco. Don't be a *strunz* like your father." She turned toward Benny and said, "I'll get the food. You're in charge of getting him to the table." She marched toward the stove mumbling to herself.

Cole placed his feet on the carpet and rubbed his head. "Well, Benny, guess you met my Aunt Philomena."

"Wow! That's all I can say. I wouldn't want to piss her off. Like you have." Benny moved closer to Cole. "What the hell is going on? I know things are rough on us, but you need to take care of yourself. We need you in this fight with the administration."

"Am I dreaming or did you take advantage of me last night?"

"You should be so lucky," Benny said, "but don't change the subject. You missed your class this morning. Cliff called me looking for you."

Cole rolled his neck. "Probably just as well. Not sure if I would have been much good today. Who are you texting?" Cole said as he stood and walked toward the coffee maker.

"Heather. She's worried about you. As was Cliff. As am I." Benny hit send and looked at Cole. "Got an extra cup of coffee for your favorite bass player? And how about telling me what's going on? You scared the crap out of us last night. Remember, you and I can withstand anything those weasels and ferrets throw our way."

"You two need to take care of those *strunz* now!" Philomena turned from the stove. "They need a good *sculacciata*! I put 'em right across my knee." She made believe she was spanking the weasels and ferrets with her spatula. "They learn to leave my Marco alone. *Mamalukes!*" She turned back to the stove and reached up to the frying pan. Then, turned again to look at Cole. "You need food and a good *sculacciata*, too! And I'm not kidding."

"We'll keep that in mind," Benny said stifling a chuckle.

Cole handed Benny a cup of coffee and slid the sugar his way.

"I know. I'm tired and lost, Benny. Hell, I'm that and more. Now I got a hangover." He half smiled and rubbed his head.

"Not sure how much a 12-year-old can help you, especially when morning rolls around," Benny said looking at the empty bottle.

Cole winced at the Scotch reference. He widened his eyes as if that would quickly restart his brain.

"While I'm here why don't we listen to Heather's interview with Merlot and Dick Ed?"

Cole woke up his laptop and clicked the bookmarked live stream link for *The Facts and Fiction Hour*. He turned up his speaker and sat at the counter, head in his hands.

"Good morning, and welcome to *The Facts and Fiction Hour*. I'm Heather Rivera. Glad you can join us. Remember, you can reach out to me and our guests with your questions by phone, email, or social media where you can look for *#TNBZ*." Heather launched into her opening.

Cole looked at Benny. "Did you two get to talk last night?"

"Yep. This ought to be interesting."

They both sat back, coffee in hand, and listened. Aunt Philomena slid a plate in front of each of them.

"*Mangiare!*" She climbed up on the stool next to Cole, wiping the steam from her glasses. "These more of the *strunz*? My God, they're everywhere!" She clutched her crucifix necklace and shook her head. They listened as Heather made the introductions.

"Today we have two of Central City College's top administrators with us. Dr. Darla Merlot, Vice President for Teaching and Learning, and with her is Dr. Richard Edwards, Associate Vice President for Faculty Relations." Heather stifled a giggle as she looked across the table at Dick Ed. "I am glad that you reached out and offered to join us today."

"We are grateful that you've made time to speak with us today." Merlot smiled, crossed her legs, rested one stiletto heel on the studio carpet, and flexed her other foot as if getting ready for a match at the club.

"Likewise," Edwards mumbled as he sat with his usual forced smile. His arms resting on the table, hands clasped, back erect. Heather thought she saw beads of sweat gathering on his forehead.

"Heather, you're a role model in this community. You don't know it, but what you do each day behind that microphone spurs us to have conversations that we need to have. Sometimes those conversations are uncomfortable. Yet they're needed."

"Thank you, Dr. Merlot. I appreciate that. Are *we* about to have an uncomfortable conversation?"

Merlot laughed. "Not that I'm aware of, but we'll never shy away from the tough questions."

Edwards, still with a forced smile, shifted his weight in his chair and tightened his clenched hands as Merlot continued.

"Our community needs us, CCC, to do that. You know that we serve students from all over the region, but more recently we've been holding ourselves accountable to the neighborhoods around our urban campus. Those students, typically, lack college role models and the financial resources to attend our campus. We're here today hoping you can help us spread the word that our professors and advisors are waiting for them. They'll help them discover their passions and curiosity."

Merlot continued spouting the administrative refrain about increased enrollment, new college majors, and available financial aid. She also threw a bone at any athletes or their parents who may have been listening. "And the new law, *Pay for the Name*, that the governor signed allowing athletes to benefit financially from endorsements has been a long time coming. Thankfully, our own Senator Wilbur Wackenslong ushered that bill through the legislature in the last term. Within six months, our athletes will be able to cash in for themselves and their families."

"If you could name one thing that has led to all this positive trajectory, what would it be?" Heather asked.

Almost as if he'd rehearsed, Edwards jumped into the conversation. "President Doyle Bartley without a doubt. He has done an amazing job. He is a leader. And there you have it."

The awkward pause gave Heather the opening she'd been waiting for. "Speaking of uncomfortable conversations, tell me, Dr. Edwards, about no-shows. Tell me why, as my research has found, 25% of the students on CCC's class rolls have been no-shows. As in, they have not attended any classes this term. And why are they getting federal financial aid? Sounds like the college is receiving money for people who don't exist. How's that possible? Tell me where I got this wrong." Heather shuffled through some papers in front of her and then returned her gaze to Edwards.

Silence.

"Looks like you did a good job of bringing Heather up to speed last night, Benny. You get an A. Maybe Dick Ed needs your help, too."

"What's wrong with that *mamaluke*? Philomena sliced a piece of eggplant and, holding the fork backward pushed it in her mouth. She shook her head. "*Stunad!*"

"There's no helping that moron." Benny reached for the pot of coffee.

"Oh, I can try to answer that, Heather." Merlot leaned into the microphone. "I don't think Dr. Edwards or myself are the ones who can speak to the issues of student success and attendance. That would be our Associate Vice President for Student Success. But let me give it a shot. My best guestimate is we're still at the beginning of the semester. Many of our students struggle to find childcare and transportation. As the first in their family to attend college, they have to navigate a new set of expectations and obligations. While it's difficult for them, I am confident the no-show stat you quoted, if it's accurate, will decrease considerably soon. Our advisors and staff are reaching out to them."

"Sounds like the college, on one hand, is going full throttle to help those who've been labeled as marginalized people in our community. Yet, I have information that your Director of Human Resources will not allow professors to create safe places on campus for those very same students. Something about violating state law. Can you explain?"

Merlot pursed her lips. "You'd have to ask the Director. As you said, he made that call."

Dick Ed looked like he'd been lowered into a snake pit.

"You know, I got an idea of how to deal with them. Dominic and I talked about it last night." Philomena poked at a sauteed potato slice.

Cole and Benny looked at each other as Philomena passed the platter to Benny and motioned for him to take another helping.

Heather moved another paper to the top of her pile of notes. "I have it from a reputable source that one of your professors is being framed for a non-existent assault on a non-existent student. I've done some digging and it appears that his accuser, a supposed CCC student, but in reality a high school dropout, is one of those students—one of the 25%— getting financial aid. How is he a student at CCC? And I understand the Marina Norte Sheriff's Office is looking into this fraudulent assault allegation. Is that true Dr. Edwards?"

Edwards' ashen face and wide eyes spoke volumes without saying a word. But God love him Heather thought, as he tried to offer something.

"Well, ah, if the sheriff's office is investigating anything, wouldn't you need to ask them about it? I would think so. And there you have it."

"I'm not sure what I *have*, Dr. Edwards, other than the facts." Heather held her paper up. "And you said 'if' the sheriff's office is investigating. Don't you know if that is happening or not? You're one of the top administrators at CCC."

"What I think Dr. Edwards is attempting to say is that you will have to talk to the Marina Norte Sheriff's Office about your allegation. That is something we cannot comment on." Merlot's stare bore into Heather's eyes.

"We have a few minutes left. Again, we're here at *The Facts and Fiction Hour*. Thank you, audience, for joining us today and our guests for being with us in the studio. Drs. Merlot and Edwards, before we end this, it's been a badly kept secret that Senator Wilbur Wackenslong will be running for governor this year. His family's business gave your faculty laptops, tablets, and cell phones. In what way is his philanthropy to the college connected to that upcoming campaign? And since he is the so-called education candidate and the accountability candidate, how do you think he feels about these financial aid questions and the MNSO's investigation?"

Edwards coughed.

Merlot rattled her tennis bracelet and repeated her noncommittal committal script. "We at CCC are grateful for any community gifts that will help us further our mission to help the students reach for their dreams and aspirations. I cannot speak for Senator Wackenslong or his family. All

I know is they, the entire family, have been friends of the college and supporters of our community for decades. We thank them for their gifts. Just like I'm sure you would do for those who donate to your station. Again, you must ask Senator Wackenslong for further input."

The producer counted down with her fingers to the commercial break.

"Thank you again for joining us today, Drs. Merlot and Edwards. Listeners, don't go away; we'll be right back on the other side of the commercial as today we start our analysis of the upcoming statewide elections."

Heather removed her headphones, stood, and extended her hand to Merlot. "Thank you, I'd love to get you back so we can continue having the uncomfortable conversations you know are so important to our community."

"Don't you date Professor Fitzgerald?" Merlot asked attempting to throw Heather off her rhythm.

"Don't you date the Director of Human Resources?" Heather held Merlot's stare.

Edwards adjusted his tie as if loosening a noose.

• • •

25

"**M**y father used to smoke Lucky Strike cigarettes. Their slogan was 'LSMFT—Lucky Strike Means Fine Tobacco.' Do you know what LSMFT means when it comes to Rivera's so-called news hour? 'Lame Stream Media Fakes Truth!'"

Wackenslong had Heather's producer on the phone within two minutes of the episode's end. "You call that a news show? Rivera's a hack! And you're worse for letting her get away with that sort of lopsided reporting!"

"Well, Senator, Heather is rated Number 1 in her spot," the producer said. "She's noted for asking hard questions. And sometimes those questions might be difficult for the guests. But it's in the name of getting to the truth of the matter at hand."

Wackenslong paced around his office conference table. "Truth? Are you kidding me? Truth? Do you know that she—your 'Number 1 in her spot'—is sleeping with a professor at CCC?"

"Respectfully, Senator, we don't ask Heather about her off-air calendar or relationships. Would you like to share yours?"

"You better damn well care about what she does in her *airtime*! A CCC student could do better than that."

"And we would welcome the opportunity to have a student intern learn from her. Heather would be quite the mentor. As we heard this morning from the guests, the college has experienced a spike in enrollment. I'm sure there are future radio personalities in the incoming class. Unless they're casualties of the 25% no-show statistic." The producer held the phone away from her ear waiting for the expected senatorial fury.

"You are messing with the wrong person! I can make things difficult for your station."

"Senator, that sounds like a threat. I'm sure you didn't mean it in that way."

"I don't make threats. I watch out for my constituents."

"Great! So do we. Anything else I can help you with today, Senator? I believe Heather has given you a standing invitation to appear on the show. Are you interested in—"

Click.

"Hey, Heather," the producer said hitting the intercom button to the studio. "Senator Wackenslong just called to say thank you for the piece with Merlot and Edwards." She winked and laughed.

"I can only imagine," Heather said as she readied herself for the next segment.

• • •

Wackenslong grabbed his suitcoat from his office closet.

"Bitches and bastards!"

"Excuse me, Senator?" His secretary said, walking into his office.

"No, no. Not you."

"Sir, the mayor called. He's running late with a news conference. He'll meet you at the club for lunch at 1:00."

"Damn press is getting on my nerves." He poked his arms through his coat as if punching at one of the news corps.

"I had your car brought to the front door by the garage attendant. Shall I have him return it to its spot?" She dangled the keys from her hand.

"No need. I have a few calls to make and I can do that from the car. I'll be back in the morning." He snatched the keys from her hands. As he walked toward the door, he stopped and turned.

"Do me a favor. Call the Heather Rivera show and ask for the producer. Tell her I accept the invitation to be on the *Facts and Fiction Hour*. ASAP!"

"Yes, Senator."

As soon as Wackenslong hopped into his car, he hit speed dial.

"Hello, Senator. Nice surprise. What can I do for you?"

"Did you listen to that shitshow on the radio this morning? Darla held her own with that bitch. More than I can say for your man Edwards. What in the world is wrong with him? No umph. He sounded like he was reading from a script. How in the hell did he ever get his position?"

"He's a dutiful staff member. He does what we tell him to do when we tell him to do it," Turkle said. "What he lacks in spontaneity and pizazz, he makes up for in loyalty."

"Well, keep him away from the press. He's as useless as mail-in ballots without a post office."

"What can I do for you, Senator?"

"We go after both of those professors—the queer one and his buddy. We nail both to the wall for assault. Get that low-life Spano in gear. We need to make a big splash and keep the press looking at the left hand while our right hand takes care of business."

"Yes, sir. Got it."

"Let the community know what the college is doing! Highlight the college's achievements. The enrollment spike makes for a simple talking point. Keep it basic. Simple arithmetic. Dismiss the talk of no-shows as the cost of doing business with first-generation students, and then move to how we are helping the financially disadvantaged get to college. Maybe a photo op or two with some of those students. Keep the ball moving. Bring in the *Pay for the Name* law. Again, right-hand-left-hand strategy. Not that hard."

"Yes, sir."

"Emphasize that good leaders take calculated risks. At times, innovations may make some people uncomfortable. That doesn't mean anything wrong or illegal has occurred."

"Anything else, Senator?"

Click.

Turkle looked at the phone, shook his head, and punched in a number.

"Meet me tonight. Same time. Same place. You have a job to do."

Turkle hung up just as his computer sounded an incoming message. "A deposit has been received." He smiled and hit speed dial on his cell phone.

"Professor Singer, I want to commend you on your good work. I knew this would be a great fit for you. How about we have lunch tomorrow and talk about our next project?"

Cliff tightened into a ball.

● ● ●

Wackenslong threw his keys to the Country Club valet.

"Afternoon, Senator," the doorman said as he pulled the door open.

"Thank you." Wackenslong threw back his shoulders, smoothed back the hair on the side of his head, and buttoned his suit jacket. His rapid pace broadcasted his impatience.

The maître d' smiled as the senator approached. "Nice to see you, Senator. The mayor has not arrived yet, but your other guest has. Let me show you to the private dining room."

He led the way through the crowded dining room to a quiet room overlooking the 18th-hole water hazard. "The waiter will be with you shortly." He left and closed the doors behind him. Wackenslong smiled and walked to the table.

"You were wonderful today. That bitch Rivera didn't know who she was up against. Glad you could make this lunch. I need your help with the mayor."

"No problems with Rivera. Two-bit-local-wannabe-big-shot-talk-show host. Don't worry, I'm no novice."

"And keep the heat on Fitzgerald."

"Not a problem, Senator." Merlot smiled and pulled a folder from her oversized leather tote bag. "As for the mayor, I've already laid the groundwork for our kickoff rally. He's on board to serve as the host that night. As instructed, he has contacted names on his last campaign's donor list. We've already seen an uptick in donations. This quarter will be our biggest yet." Merlot spoke with the confidence of a seasoned campaigner. She knew how to please the men who thought they were in charge.

"Looks like you've earned your bodycon today. The best thing I ever did was to get the Board to appoint you as V.P." Wackenslong leaned in and kissed Merlot on the lips.

• • •

26

Cole pulled into a space in the faculty parking lot. He kept his hands on the steering wheel, bowed his head, and closed his eyes.

Maybe today you'll make a difference.

On his way to his office, Cole stepped into the Student Affairs Office and peeked into Ms. Robertson's office. She was talking with a student but gave Cole a smile and a wave. The two had developed and delivered a few workshops over the years for their colleagues. On more than one occasion Cole had walked a distressed student to her office for immediate intervention. Like he tried with Suzy the day he found her crying in the hallway. Robertson proved time and again that she was a rock of stability for students and Cole.

"Good morning, Professor. I briefly talked with your student. More to come."

Cole thanked her, exited the counseling suite, and walked the length of the lobby toward the security officer sitting at a small wooden table checking identification as students, faculty, and visitors entered the first floor. This was a new security measure that CCC had incorporated during the final year of the previous administration. Due to an uptick in violent incidents around the nation on college campuses, there were heightened safety concerns. Cole, though, wasn't sure how secure the security was on his campus. There were numerous entrances into and out of the building that the in-house officers only checked on their hourly rounds.

"Morning, Sergeant. How are those night classes going for you?"

"All is good, professor! Hey, I just checked a student in who is here to see you. Should be outside your office by the time you get there. Bright-eyed, bushy-tailed, and ready to learn," the officer said.

"Or, ready to challenge a grade." Cole smiled, moved through the checkpoint, and climbed the staircase to the second floor where most of the classrooms and professors' offices were located.

He made a quick detour to the faculty lounge to place his lunch in the already-overstuffed refrigerator. To call it a *lounge* was a bit generous. More like an oversized broom closet with poor lighting, worse ventilation, and a hint of mold in the air.

"Morning, Savannah. How are you doing with the Teaching Initiative Team?" She sat at one of the two small tables in the room, her face buried in her laptop.

"Morning, Cole, ah, Professor, I mean Dr. Fitzgerald. Fine. Trying to find my way. We're planning an online teaching strategy workshop. And a few other things. You know, well."

"We have a union meeting tomorrow afternoon. I hope you can make it. You have a lot to offer this faculty. Especially the younger ones. They need your guidance. You are a respected colleague, Professor O'Rourke."

She briefly softened with the compliment and then tightened again, remembering herself. "Ah, yes. No. We, I and Professor Singer, have a meeting with Dr. Turkle. Won't be able to make it. I appreciate the compliment. And Cole," she hesitated as if she would not finish, then continued. "I'm seeking normalcy and peace. I'm not the one to be storming the walls. You're much better at that. Not me. You know."

What she referenced as normalcy and peace, Dominic the union organizer attacked as negligence. Cole felt sorry for Savannah. Such a talent in the classroom. A brilliant mind. But no self-confidence.

Sounds and looks just like you. Knotted up with self-doubts that are slowly eating away her insides. What the hell?

"Professor, that is why we need you. A lot of faculty are scared and intimidated by union talk. So they lower their heads and keep to themselves," Cole said to his reticent colleague. "They hear the same few faculty speak up. After a while, they tune us out. They see you as a voice of reason. If you speak up, it will catch attention."

Professor O'Rourke smiled. "Thank you for that vote of confidence. I'm not sure I, um, agree. Have a nice day." She turned back to her laptop.

As Cole made his way down the carpeted hallway to his office, he could hear discussions from the classrooms and in offices. Some professors were on the phone. Others conferring with students. Tardy students quietly ducked in classroom doors. Others sat on the floor checking their phones or reading their textbooks for upcoming quizzes.

This was, by and large, his daytime family. He felt comfortable. Perhaps that had become the problem. He was going through predictable motions, almost like a script. Maybe he'd become complacent as well.

He turned the corner near the end of the hall. His was the last office on the right, #234, next to the rear staircase, and the furthest office from the lobby. A former dean had assigned it to him after a building renovation. Benny suggested it was her way of isolating him. Probably so, Cole thought. And the window in the hallway, right outside his door, had a view of the puzzle palace. The first thing he saw as he approached his office.

"Morning Professor!"

"Hey, Kerwin. Morning to you. Good to see you as always. Come on in." Cole unlocked his door with the swipe card that hung from the lanyard around his neck. In a nod to modernization and upgraded security, Bartley had removed all the old keylocks and replaced them with a keyless entry system.

"Grab a seat, Kerwin." Cole wedged the door stop to hold the door open.

"Professor? Do you mind if we keep the door closed?"

Remember what Turkle said, "Someone saw you close the door and thought it inappropriate...That's where damage control needs to come in."

"Not at all, Kerwin." Cole closed the door and made his way around his desk as Kerwin took the visitor's chair in the corner. A few carnations remained in the vase on the credenza. "Everything OK with you?"

Go ahead. Ignore me. But you know I'm on your side.

"Oh, yeah. I'm fine. My classes are great. Love my schedule." He placed his backpack on the floor and pulled out a folder. "I need your advice about something with my work assignment. Well, more like something I stumbled on in Mr. Niblick's office."

He slid his chair closer and placed the folder on Cole's desk.

"I've been helping with backing up student information. You know basic stuff like addresses, phone numbers, majors, and the like. Most of it is coded and protected due to governmental privacy regulations. But the way the office is set up, there are computers with student advising information and other computers with financial aid information all in the same open area. If someone knew what they were looking for, well, they could easily see it from the display screens. Does seem a bit lax considering confidentiality laws. But what do I know, I'm a student; they're the professionals."

Cole bit on his inner cheek.

"As you may have noticed, I'm an inquisitive type," Kerwin continued, "so, I decided to conduct a curiosity test.

I wanted to see what I would find if I typed in my name. And look what I found."

Kerwin opened the folder and handed Cole a letter. "I discovered four interesting things."

"Kerwin, I thought you were an IT major. I heard you were going to work for NCIS." They both laughed remembering his comment on Heather's show. "I didn't know you changed your major to Logistics. Why the move?"

"That's the first interesting thing I found. I haven't changed my major. I haven't spoken to anyone about changing my major. And, I'm not even considering changing my major. But there is a letter, over Mr. Niblick's signature congratulating me for changing my major."

"When did you get this letter? I see it's dated one week after the start of classes."

"That's the second interesting thing. I never got the letter. Nor did my parents. I printed that when I found it in the digital backups."

Cole thought that while this was odd, it could be explained as some sort of clerical error. Strange but something that could be fixed by an advisor in Student Affairs.

"Not sure why that would happen, Kerwin. But then I've never worked in Student Affairs. Have you spoken with your advisor about this? There might be an explanation."

"I did speak with Ms. Robertson and she confirmed that my major is still IT. No change. No request for a change."

"So, it's just an error?" Cole asked.

"That leads me to interesting thing number three." He handed Cole another paper. Again, it was on college letterhead and over Niblick's signature.

"Congratulations, Kerwin! That's a sizeable financial aid award. I'd heard that our college foundation has been working to get more money for our students to help lighten their financial load. Your mom and dad must be proud." Not sure what was amiss, Cole laid the letter on the desk in front of Kerwin.

"Professor, I have never received a nickel of financial aid. My parents make too much money. I've been applying for some scholarships sponsored by local community groups—but nothing from the college. I never even completed an application. We knew from the get-go that financial aid would be a no-go. And," Kerwin continued as he sat back in his chair, "we never got this letter either."

Cole leaned forward and looked at both letters.

"Does anyone know you have these copies, Kerwin?"

"No, Professor. I don't want to get in any trouble. I like my job in Mr. Niblick's office. I wasn't sure who I could speak to. So, here I am. I haven't even told my parents about this."

"May I hold on to these for a day or two? I have a friend who might be able to shed some light."

"Sure. And there's one more thing." Kerwin reached inside his puffer vest and produced a silver USB drive. He gently placed it on Cole's desk as if he feared it would explode.

"I was finishing up my shift yesterday and packing up to go to my 1:00 p.m. biology lab. I was kinda procrastinating as we were going to dissect fetal pigs. Not high on my to-do list. Anyway, when I reached under my desk for my backpack, I saw that," he pointed to the USB, "lying on the floor. I picked it up and looked around the office but everyone was either at lunch or in the VP's office for a meeting."

Kerwin slumped back in his chair, took a deep breath, blinked his eyes, and continued.

"My curiosity got the best of me again. I plugged it into the computer. And well up came an entire spreadsheet of names, addresses, and dollar amounts. My name was on it, too. With a dollar amount matching the figure the letter I showed you said I received for financial aid."

"Money you never received, right?"

"Correct. I printed one page." He pulled it from his backpack and handed it to Cole.

Cole leaned forward, a little more interested. "May I hold on to the USB, too?"

"Please. I don't want it. I'm not sure what any of this means but it's way above my pay grade." He grabbed his backpack. "I need to get to class. That's all I have. Do you need anything from me?"

"No. Go to class and have fun with the pig. And ask lots of questions. Oh, take a carnation with you. Give it to your mom."

"Thanks, Professor. She'll appreciate it."

Kerwin tucked the flower in the water bottle holder on the side of his backpack, kicked the door stop in place, and left the office.

"Odd," Cole thought to himself, "the college claims to be doling out more financial aid, while at the same time, the no-show rate is unusually high. This letter says Kerwin got aid, but he didn't receive aid or the money." He sat back in his chair. "And then there is a list of people with dollar signs attached to their names and addresses."

Cole dialed the AVP for Student Success.

"Dr. Craig's office."

"Is Dr. Craig in? This is Professor Fitzgerald."

"No, she's in a meeting. I'll let her know you called, Professor."

Cole hung up and looked at the two letters and the spreadsheet page again. He fingered the USB drive. A major field of study changed and financial aid was awarded. Two things that did not happen, at least to the student named in the letters. And the spreadsheet. He reached for the phone again. He got voicemail and left a message. "Hello, Eulonia. Call me when you can."

• • •

27

Cole grabbed his backpack, locked the office door, and headed for the mailroom where he picked up his and Benny's mail. He had a few errands to run before Heather came to his condo for dinner. His aunt was preparing her to die for clams and linguine. As he was sorting through the mail on his way to his car, he heard his name.

"Hey, Cole." Lori Craig, with an armful of file folders, made her way up the hallway. "Wait up. I'll walk you out."

Cole held the door from the lobby to the courtyard.

"My secretary texted me that you called. Anything we can talk about now?"

"It's pretty deep," Cole said as he stopped under a palm tree. "Do you have any time tomorrow? Late morning or early afternoon?"

"Sure, I can make that work," Lori said as she rebalanced the folders. "I'll check my calendar and get back to you."

"OK. Let me ask you one thing now that a student brought up." Cole looked from side to side and continued. "Do you know anything about students' majors being changed without their knowledge?"

Lori tilted her head and squinted her eyes. "Nope. That's a new one for me. Do you think it was an error? I guess that could happen with the increased enrollment."

"How about financial aid? Is it possible for students to get that if they haven't applied for it?"

"You got my interest. What's going on?"

"Not sure," Cole said. "And, Lori, please keep this between us. Call me when you look at your calendar."

On his way home, Cole stopped to pick up Big Betsy from the groomers, and two bouquets of flowers.

• • •

By the time Heather arrived, Aunt Philomena had set the table. Cole uncorked a bottle of wine and caught up with Benny on a quick phone call. He answered Heather's knock with a glass of Pinot Noir and a tired smile.

"Not a bad way to greet your woman, Professor."

"You-hoo! Heather! Good to see you." Aunt Philomena, dressed in her *Kiss the Cook* apron, waved with her sauce spoon. "I hope you like clams."

"Love them!"

"Buono. How about you two sip a drink? I'll call you when it's time to eat."

Cole and Heather moved to the sofa. "We have a lot to unpack," she said.

Heather shared the in-studio dynamics of the Merlot-Edwards on-air conversation and the follow-up tirade that Wackenslong subjected her producer to after the broadcast.

"I think we caught the senator off-guard with an open invitation to appear on the show to discuss the technology he gifted to the faculty," Heather said as she toasted Cole. "His secretary called to accept or rather, as my producer relayed, demand a spot on my show. For the conniver he is, I'm surprised he took my bait."

Big Betsy jumped onto Cole's lap possibly to show off her new coif but more likely to have her haunches scratched. She loved that. Heather reached over to extend a little loving under the cat's chin.

"Remember, she's not a chinny-chin-chin fan."

"Oh my! I forgot. Once again, my man comes to my rescue."

"Well, I didn't want you to sue me. Like I thought the condo custodian would last week. When he reached out to stroke her chin, he brought back a bloodied hand. Almost lost a chunk of his nose, too."

Big Betsy purred as if to say, "A girl knows what a girl likes." She licked her paw.

Aunt Philomena ambled in with two huge platters. On one, antipasti. The other, a steaming bowl of linguine topped with red sauce and cherry stone clams. She placed them in the center of the table.

"And just for our chef," Cole said as he turned up the Bluetooth speaker, "a little Dean Martin."

"When the moon hits your eye like a big pizza pie, that's Amore!" Aunt Philomena let loose. "Wish I had met Dino back in the day. We would have been quite a couple!"

Cole and Heather moved to the table to eat and continue the conversation. Wine for the ladies. Cole switched to Scotch.

"Love the flowers," Heather said as she leaned in toward the freshly cut tulips in the center of the table. "My favorite."

"That's why I got them. Favorite flowers for my favorite person." He raised his glass and they toasted. "But I have something to confess." He placed his drink beside his dinner plate, and with a somber look, he stared straight into Heather's eyes. "There's another woman who got some flowers, too. It's time I tell you about her."

Heather cocked her head and squinted her eyes. "Do we need to talk?" She gave a glance toward Philomena.

Cole reached across the table, touched her hand, and said, "Her name is Fran. I've been seeing her for about a year off and on. Recently, more on than off."

Aunt Philomena put down her fork.

Cole paused. "And she's 93 years old. Lives next door."

Heather laughed and tossed her napkin at him. "You cad!"

"Marco!" Aunt Phil had a big grin.

"She has more energy than I do," Cole said with a laugh. "Once or twice a week I'll run an errand for her or pick up some flowers just because."

For a brief moment, Heather saw the old Cole. The man who did for others, who smiled, and who had a sense of humor. "When you speak of Fran, it brightens your face. That's good to see. I've missed that."

"Me too." He bit on his lower lip and then continued. "Now for the not-so-cheerful stuff from the daily drama at the college."

As Cole recounted Kerwin's discovery, Heather noted to herself that Cole's mood was turning darker with each recollection and sip of his drink. His sentences became shorter and more abrupt. She looked as he poured his third drink since sitting for dinner.

Aunt Philomena excused herself. "I gotta call Dominic. I trust you two won't try anything while I'm out of the room." She untied her apron, walked to her bedroom, and closed the door. And then quietly opened it a crack.

"Four fingers tonight?" Heather asked, looking at the increased amount of liquor in his glass.

"I need the distraction." He became quiet. She let him be and just looked at him not quite knowing what to say.

"Is this," she pointed to the liquor, "wise? Is this helping?"

Cole shook his head. "I don't know, Heather. But it is one way for me to silence the voice. Or at least try to."

Heather paused, took a breath, and reached for Cole's hand.

"Speaking of... have you considered counseling? Someone you can talk to."

"I talk to you."

"I mean a professional. Someone who can help you sort this stuff out. I'm concerned about you, your drinking, and your mood swings. I'm not seeing the Cole Fitzgerald that I love very often these days."

"I'm not sure any of you have ever seen the real Cole Fitzgerald. Not sure I know him either. Remember that night you were here and you found me talking to it? To the voice? It's been relentless."

"Cole, that's why a counselor might help."

"No! I'm not crazy! I'm frustrated and tired. Very. Tired. Listen, I drink because it's the only way for me to remain sane." He looked at the drink in his hand. "I know this is not the best way to cope but I'll get through this. Listen," Cole said with a deep breath. "I appreciate you more than anyone or anything. If ever there was one, you're my soulmate. Maybe a good night's sleep will help. But please don't talk shrinks and counselors. That's not helpful. It didn't work for my mother. It killed Ian." He finished his drink.

Ain't no way around it. Come on confront me. You can't have peace if you don't understand me. Ain't no way around me!

Heather pushed her chair back, walked around the table, and kissed him.

"I love you, Cole Fitzgerald. But I am at a loss, and I'm frustrated. You need help that I cannot provide. Aunt Philomena can't provide it. You keep pushing us away." She reached over and touched his hand. "You need help. Please get it. Tell Aunt Philomena I said thank you. I'll call you when I get home." She got up and left.

Aunt Philomena closed her bedroom door and punched a number on her phone. "Dominic? We need to talk. We do it tomorrow. *Capisce?*"

•   •   •

Just before midnight.

Unlike a few hours ago when the halls were jammed with the clattering noise of students, an eerie silence existed as nighttime descended on the CCC campus. Spano, for all his Board meeting bluster, had never set foot inside any college, so he had no comparison. All he was sure of was that he did not want to bump into the security guard. But that didn't seem likely as he was asleep at his desk when Spano snuck up the hall and into the back stairwell. Now it was time to find the room.

He fumbled around in his jeans pocket. First the front, then the rear, and then the little key pocket on the side.

"Damn it all, I left it in the car. Let me see it was '2'-something. Three digits. Not too hard to find. I'll remember it when I see it."

His soft-soled shoes made their way past one office, then another. "That's it!" He pulled a card from his back pocket, swiped the door, and heard a click. He slid in, shut the door, and removed a small plastic baggie from his back pocket.

"Let's see. Hmm. Where should I—." He smiled and reached up behind the top shelf of books. Gently he pushed the baggie behind some books.

"Have fun in class tomorrow, Professor. Or wherever else you may wind up. You swishy bastard. May you get hog-tied in prison."

Spano left the office and exited down the rear stairwell.

• • •

28

Squeak!
"You-"
Squeak!
"—hoo!"
Squeak!

A student leaned in and said, "Remove your thumb from the button. Move your arm a little further from your mouth." He guided her arm a few inches from her mouth. "No need to kiss the microphone."

"Thank you. I feel like such a *stunad* at times."

"Ma'am?"

"You know, a *stupid* person." She winked and grabbed the young man's hand. "You stand right here. I might need you again."

Behind the woman with the microphone stood seventy-five to one hundred students in a semi-circle, three deep, in the courtyard of the administration building. Johnny V emerged from the crowd and stood beside Aunt Philomena.

A TV 13 news van pulled up and out stepped Teagan Cross. From the visitor parking lot, Heather approached the crowd.

"Excuse me, I'm Heather Rivera from the *TNBZ* radio show. Can you tell me why you're here?" She held her microphone as she tapped a student on the back. It was Kerwin.

"Ms. Rivera! Hey, good to see you. I heard about this rally from students in the café this morning. Johnny V, you remember him from when we visited your show? Well, he helped to organize this." Kerwin looked at the crowd as more students joined in. Some carrying signs. "From what I can see most of these students either have had Professor Fitzgerald or Professor DiJohn or both."

"And why are they—and you—here?"

"Something to do with Professor DiJohn being unable to teach and Dr. Fitzgerald being accused of intersectionality. Whatever in the world that's about. Mostly, because it seemed like the right thing to do."

Aunt Philomena bent backward, looked up at Johnny V, and handed him the megaphone. "Do what we talked about earlier. I'm gonna stand over there out of the way."

As Teagan Cross and his cameraman got into position, Heather made her way forward and saw Aunt Philomena moving toward the back of the crowd. Out of the camera's view.

"We, the students of CCC, need some answers," Johnny V said as he looked at his fellow students. They applauded as Johnny V continued to speak to them as Heather followed Cole's aunt to the side of the courtyard.

"Aunt Philomena! What on earth? Does Cole know you're here?"

"Not sure. I didn't say anything. He has enough going on. I thought this could help."

"Help?" Heather raised her eyebrows, then lowered them. "How?"

"I told you and Marco that Dominic and I had an idea. Here it is. If Marco can't speak to the press, the students can. And it got you here? And the hunk of salami over there, too." She pointed at Cross who was making his way toward Johnny V with his cameraman in tow.

"But the students." Heather looked around the court-yard. "How did you get the students here?"

"Dominic told me another professor helped. Someone named Eulonia. I think that's her name. She introduced me to the students so we could practice. Whatever and whoever, it worked."

"Practice? What in the world did you practice with these students?" Heather could only imagine.

"Listen," Aunt Phil said and pointed toward the students as Johnny V yelled into the megaphone, "Who's better than us?"

The students yelled back, "No one!"

They went back and forth as they did when cheering on Johnny V and his team during a game.

"Now," Aunt Philomena said, "watch this."

Heather turned toward the students. Cross's camera person focused. The students were now arm-in-arm chanting "Who's better than us?" and answering, "No one!" They waved signs.

"Cute," Heather said, "but what's with the alphabet soup?" She pointed to the waving signs. Some said, "Let our teachers teach!" A couple proclaimed, "Invisible No More!" invoking the demonstration and protest at the Wackenslong downtown construction site. Others, though, just had one letter.

"I see an 'R.' There's a 'T' over there." Heather pointed to the middle of the crowd. "And there's a 'Z.'" Her eyes grew wide and she looked at Aunt Philomena who stood there with the proud smile of a matriarch looking at her family. She winked at Heather.

The signs spelled *STRUNZ!*

Philomena pointed toward the administration building. "Heather, you know what they are doing to this school, students, and teachers. I'm doing nothing." She held up her hands as if backing away. "Just glad to see the younger generation taking a stand. Go speak to them. But before you go," she leaned into Heather's ear. "It's time you and me need to have our rally with Marco. He needs help. And we are going to make sure he gets it. I got another idea."

• • •

29

"Good morning, Professor. Do you have a moment?" The dean stepped into Cole's office.

"Sure thing. What's up, Dean?"

"This is Detective MacEachern from the Marina Norte Sheriff's Office. And this is his dog, Roxie. She's a drug-sniffing dog."

Other than seeing one or two at the airport, this was his first face-to-face encounter with a drug-sniffing dog. Roxie wore a Marina Norte Sheriff's Office vest. A black lab mix, she followed Detective MacEachern's every move and voice signal. When she looked at Cole, she bore into his soul with her full brown eyes.

"Nice looking pup you got there," Cole said transfixed by Roxie's stare and her snaggle-toothed look. The all-business detective nodded. "Yeah." He scratched Roxie's ear as she leaned into his leg.

"I'd like to ask you a few questions about your colleague, Dr. DiJohn, if I may."

Cole hoped he didn't exhibit a facial expression that would give away the knot in his stomach. Roxie watched him.

"Well, no, I don't mind. But faculty are under orders from the administration here that we cannot talk to any non-college person about college matters without clearance. Have you spoken with VP Merlot?"

"He has," the dean interjected, "and she contacted me saying anyone the detective wishes to speak to is fine with her, and she hopes everyone will be forthcoming."

Forthcoming? Watch yourself. Don't be a hero.

"The sheriff's office has been investigating the allegations one of your CCC students has brought against Professor DiJohn for assault." The detective referred to a pad with handwritten notes.

"I believe you're referring to the *incident* involving a person who *claims* to be a student but has never attended a class." Cole squinted at Roxie.

"Be that as it may, there are also accusations about drugs. I understand that you and DiJohn play music together." He flipped a few pages of his pad. "*The HTRB Band*. Have you ever known the professor to engage in drug activity?"

"This isn't the '60s, detective. Playing music doesn't equal drug use."

Roxie seemed to smile as her teeth flashed beneath her stuck upper lip.

"Is that a *yes* or a *no*, Professor?"

"It's an emphatic no. Benny DiJohn is the most upstanding person I've had the pleasure to work with on campus and on stage. The man has integrity. Someone's—for God knows what reason—attempting to smear his good name. Did you find drugs in his office? I'm guessing you didn't. Just like you won't find them in my office. We're teachers and musicians. Not drug users."

"We're just doing our job. With integrity. Just like you say DiJohn does."

"That's *Professor* DiJohn."

"And as for your office," MacEachern said, "we know you don't. Roxie would have sniffed them out by now." He reached down and scratched her head.

"Have you ever known or seen the Professor lose his temper like that night in the club?"

"Again, in the club, Professor DiJohn *stopped* an assault from escalating. Not only does he not lose his temper, he is known as the faculty member most likely to calm a tense situation with a bit of wit or sarcasm." Cole paused and shook his head.

"How do you characterize his reputation with other faculty members? Do they feel about him like you do?"

"I can't speak for others, Detective." Cole let out a short breath. "Listen, Detective, I have nothing but respect for my colleague. Like all close friends, we disagree from time to time but we always do what we think is right and compassionate. I trust Benny. He is not a cage fighter, drug user, or whatever other miscreant label his accusers wish to use."

MacEachern closed his pad, tucked it in his pocket, and turned to the dean. "I think we have what we need here. We can go. Come, Roxie."

Cole got up and watched them leave. He shut his door and sat down to compose himself when his phone rang. It was Lori Craig.

• • •

One hour later.

Cole had just returned to his office following a coffee meeting with Lori Craig. He brought her up to speed on his attempts to piece together Kerwin's findings, student absences, increased financial aid, and the administration's strong-arm tactics against him and Benny. And Roxie's visit.

Lori said she would do some discrete digging and agreed to keep Cole in the loop on whatever she found. No email exchanges. No voicemail or text messages. No digital footprints.

Cole sat at his desk attempting to make sense of everything when his phone rang. He saw the caller's name on the screen and took a deep breath.

"Good afternoon, Professor DiJohn. Thank you for checking in with your favorite acolyte." Cole wasn't sure how he'd break the news about the detective and dog.

"Good day, Dr. Fitz. When it comes to acolytes, I think your Aunt Philomena has more than most movie stars. Did you see that student protest on the evening news? I thought I saw her standing off to the side like she was a quiet passerby."

"Oh, yeah. We both watched it with a glass of wine in our hands. She and Dominic created the scheme. Basically, the puzzle palace patrons said faculty can't speak to the press. Nothing about the students speaking to the press."

"Priceless, Cole. She's priceless."

"I can only imagine how it played out with Bartley and his tribe."

"They can bite me! Those students gave us all a great George Orwell reminder, 'If liberty means anything at all, it means the right to tell people what they do not want to hear.'"

"And there is a lot they don't want to hear, Benny."

"Oh, and by the way. Speaking of devotees, you know that pile of mail you dropped off for me? Well, there were several—what should I call them? Fan letters? Let me read one of the more touching lines." Cole could hear Benny reach across his table and slide the letters toward him.

"Here ya go, Cole. A drumroll please for my top fan club submission!

'The cops are on to you, you dope-sniffing, cock sucking, lazy professor.'

"Can you believe that low-life?" Benny asked. "Why, I'm not lazy!"

Cole didn't laugh. His concern rose with each day and each new grenade that the Bartley-Turkle team lobbed their way. Benny sensed his unease.

"Cole, like I told you, I'm not new to this type of garbage. I never 'accept' it, and I *never* let it dictate my day. I understand the situation is serious. And getting more so."

"Did you know there was a drug-sniffing dog and a detective in my office today? Asking me questions about you."

"A what with whom?"

"Yeah, a freaking dog looking for drugs. In your office."

Silence.

"Whoa," Benny said, "I didn't see that coming. Geez, Louise. What the hell?"

"Yeah."

Benny sat back in his chair. "Well, that catches my attention. A drug-sniffing dog? He would be hard-pressed to find so much as a bottle of aspirin. It's hard to have hope when it seems to be trumped each day by a new alternative reality."

"She."

"She?"

"The dog is a she. Roxie."

"Roxie? See even the ladies know I'm not a drug user!"

Then came a knock on Cole's office door.

• • •

30

"Hold on, Benny. Come in."

The door opened, Cole smiled and said, "Benny, you won't believe who just walked in. Your kayak paddling buddy, Professor Cliff Singer."

Cliff smiled and pushed his black horn-rimmed eye-glasses up his nose. Cole pointed Cliff to the chair in Ian's Corner. "Benny, you and I can finish our conversation later." Both of them knew not to talk about the police, dogs, and drugs around Cliff. "Let me put this on speaker so you can say hello."

"Hey, Cliff, what you doing hanging around rabble like Fitzgerald? Slow day on campus? Or are you recruiting him for the administration's T.I.T.?" Sophomoric as it sounded, Benny howled at the acronym.

"I'm not sure I could ever talk him into that, could I, Cole?" Cliff said knowing the answer but hoping for a different response. Cole shook his head no as Cliff continued.

"I'm glad I can talk to both of you now. I'm in a bit of a quandary. I spent all morning in the administration building.

Like most days, Dr. Turkle has me working on more than the Teaching Initiative Team. He has Savannah doing most of that. He's got me doing computer work with an organization in Belize. Something about an international higher education consortium that's raising funds to help international students get enrolled in US colleges. From the sound of things, there are some major donors involved. High-powered people."

Cole could sense Benny was looking at his phone just as strangely as Cole was looking at Cliff. Cole thought of Kerwin's USB discovery.

Benny's voice came through the speaker. "What exactly are you doing, Cliff? Are you doing development work, like raising funds? Counseling students? What?"

"No. That's the crazy thing. What I'm doing—at least what I think I'm doing—is somehow related to students, enrollment, visas, and the like. I've been helping establish connections between The Bank of Belize and donors here so that they can easily get money into one location for uncomplicated international student access."

Silence.

And then a knock on the door.

"Benny, stay there." Cole looked at the door and said, "Come in."

The door opened and Cliff's eyes got wider than the Marina Norte River. In walked the dean, Detective MacEachern, and Roxie.

Roxie sat beside her partner and faced Cole with her De Niro look and those piercing brown eyes.

"What else can I help you with?" Cole asked

MacEachern looked at Cliff. "Sir, are you Clifford Singer, Professor of Computer Sciences, Office #254?"

"Ah, yes. Yes, sir."

"Please stand, Professor. You are under arrest."

"What?" Cliff and Cole said at the same time. "For what?" added Cole.

"For criminal drug possession. You have the right to remain silent." As the detective read the Miranda Rights, Cliff began crying. He looked to Cole for help.

"Dean! You know that couldn't be possible. Cliff? Come on!" Cole felt his already tenuous grip on reality slipping. First, Benny. Now, Cliff.

When and for what will they come for you?

"Cole," the dean shrugged and turned his palms upward. "When we left your office earlier today, Roxie stopped in front of Professor Singer's office, placed her nose at the bottom of the door, and started scratching at it. They entered and found the contraband."

The detective held what appeared to be a sandwich-sized plastic baggie. "Professor, we found these pills on the shelf behind your desk. There was a trace on the floor near the door. That's what alerted Roxie and gave us probable cause."

"Impossible," Cliff said. "I wouldn't know where to get drugs legal or illegal. I don't even take prescription drugs. There's a mistake." His breathing was rapid, his words clipped.

"Sorry, Cliff. Nothing the college can do at this point. The detective has to take you to the jail for questioning and possible booking." Then looking at Cole, "I'll contact Human Resources about this. I'll call Ms. Singer, also."

As the detective took Cliff away students watched. Cliff sobbed. The dean stood next to Cole as they watched the spectacle unfold. "I'm as devastated as you. Let me see what I can find out." The dean walked to his office.

"Benny, did you hear that? All of that?"

At the same time, they both said, "Turkle!"

"Benny, I'll get back to you as soon as I learn something. Anything. Poor bastard. What in the world?" He disconnected from Benny and immediately called Turkle's private line.

Turkle smiled when he saw Cole's name populate on the phone's caller ID. "Finally coming to his senses," he thought as he answered.

"What the hell are you doing? Cliff Singer? You hired him. Now you get him arrested?"

"Cliff's been arrested? For what?" Turkle's voice raised an octave with each question.

"It appears illegal drugs were found in his office by the drug-sniffing dog you and your team sicced on him!"

"I have no idea what you are talking about. I need, we need Cliff. He's doing a great job with the Teaching Initiative Team. This makes no sense."

"Shit! Nothing makes sense anymore. And now Cliff's in jail with a charge that will kill him professionally and personally. Damn it all!"

Turkle let the silence hang for a moment. "Professor, I'll have to get with the college attorney before I can comment further on this."

"Yeah. Sure. Whatever." Cole disconnected, grabbed his backpack, and headed out the door, dialing Benny at the same time.

Turkle hit speed dial. "What did you do?"

"I planted the drugs just like we agreed. Why you got your panties in a wad?"

"Because you, you dipshit two-bit drug dealer put them in the wrong office!"

Silence.

"No, I didn't. Put them in Office #254 just like you said."

"Did you even bother checking the name on the door?"

"No need. I had the number. The card you gave me opened the door. So, I went in and did it."

"No indeed. The card you had was a master card for all the offices on that floor. The office you were supposed to enter was #274. You got the wrong office, Spano."

• • •

31

Cole knocked on the door. Benny stood to his side.

"Not sure what we can do or say that'll help." Benny shook his head as Cole gently tapped the door knocker again. Neither had the words.

The door cracked open.

"Debbie, it's us. Cole and Benny."

Dressed in sweatpants, a t-shirt, and running shoes, she looked the antithesis of Cliff's insecure academic demeanor. Cliff told Benny on one kayak paddle, "Where I like the solitude of the ocean, Debbie draws energy from a throng of runners in a 15K race through the neighborhoods of Marina Norte. She loves the adrenaline rush."

Today, she looked as if she had just lost a race. She held a tissue in one hand while the other grasped that of their five-year-old daughter, Marie. Stepping aside, she held the door open for her visitors.

In the entryway, a picture collage of the family sat proudly on a small table. Strewn about the living room were Marie's toys.

"That's quite a doll house," Benny said pointing to the middle of the room.

"Cliff built that for her. You know how meticulous he is. You would've thought it was to be inspected by a city building official." She had a slight smile with the remembrance but it quickly disappeared as she turned back toward her visitors.

Cole hugged her. Benny placed a hand on her shoulder. Marie tugged on her hand, "Mama, why are you sad?" Marie dropped Debbie's hand and hugged her mother's leg. Her eyes grew wide looking at the strangers.

"Mama's OK. These two men, Mr. Cole and Mr. Benny, work with Daddy." Marie pushed her head into Debbie's thigh.

Benny squatted to be at eye level with Marie. "I am glad to meet you, Marie. Your daddy is always talking about you. Did you know he has pictures of you on his desk at school? He has one of that, too." Benny pointed toward the doll house. "It's prettier than the picture. And almost as pretty as you!"

Marie smiled. "Daddy built it," she said and relaxed her grip a bit on her mother's leg but did not let go. "Just for me."

"Tell you what, sweetie," Debbie said, "can you go into your doll house while I talk with Mr. Cole and Mr. Benny? Isn't it teatime for your dollies? Maybe you can set up a place for our guests to have some tea."

Marie squeezed her mother's leg a bit tighter. "I don't wanna, Mommy."

Debbie rubbed Marie's head. "Baby, can you do mommy a big favor? You put dolly in her carriage and then we can take her for a walk. Just you, me, and dolly. How about that?"

Marie smiled and ran to the other room. "OK, Mommy."

"What's happening? I briefly talked to Cliff. As you might guess, he's an emotional wreck." Debbie wiped away a tear. "I'm doing what I can to keep it together for Marie. Barely."

"We don't have much more to offer either. Cole and I are going to get Cliff out on bail now."

"Is there anything we can do for you or Marie?" Cole asked.

"Just bring my husband home."

• • •

Benny and Cole saw Cliff approaching. He, along with a correctional officer, stopped at the property desk behind an iron gate. Cliff signed a piece of paper, tucked his wallet in one pocket, his cell phone in another, and held his belt. A loud buzz sounded as the officer pushed the gate open. He'd only been in jail for a couple of hours, but Cliff looked as though he'd served hard time for years. As he walked toward his colleagues, with his shirt hanging over his pant waist, and his shoes untied, Cole's heart sank.

"Cliff. How are you doing? Benny and I are going to take you home."

Cliff just looked at them. First at Cole. Then Benny. He was sweating and trembling. No words. He saw a restroom, rushed in, and as the door closed, they could hear Cliff puking.

"Damn it all, Cole," Benny said looking at the restroom door. He held out his arms as he took in the jail lobby. "This is because of a union, or you didn't want to become an administrator? Because I'm gay? Bullshit!"

"I am doubting that more and more. I have ideas," Cole said, "but right now, I'm worried about Cliff. You know how he teeters on the edge of panic most of the time. I don't even want to think where this might send him."

The restroom door opened. Cliff had tucked in his shirt, put on his belt, tied his shoes, and washed his face. He rubbed his red eyes.

"Do you think we can get a bottle of water or soda? Something? My mouth is dirt dry." Cliff licked his lips as if searching for a hint of moisture.

Cole retrieved water from the hall vending machine. Other than Cliff slurping the water, they walked to the car in silence. Cliff took exaggerated deep breaths, held them, and then exhaled. Benny slid into the front passenger seat and let Cliff have the backseat to himself.

"Thank you," Cliff whispered. And then a bit louder, "Can anyone tell me what happened? I was led through the halls in handcuffs—in front of students and colleagues. I did nothing wrong. Did everything that Dr. Turkle asked. And my wife and kid. Oh my God." He lowered his head and rubbed his temples with both hands.

"Cliff. We stopped by your house on the way here. Debbie and Marie are waiting for you."

Benny turned toward the backseat. "We saw Marie's doll house. That is quite the mansion you built." Cliff briefly smiled and then closed his eyes and bowed his head.

"As for what happened, I'm at a loss. I talked with Turkle." Cliff looked at Cole expectantly. "He told me he knew nothing of this and would look into it immediately. Said don't worry, he'll take care of it."

"Don't worry?" With trembling hands, Cliff took another sip. Some water dribbled onto his chin. He rubbed his forehead back and forth. "Benny, you remember when I told you how I grew up to be invisible?"

"Yeah, Cliff, I do. That's a hell of a way to grow up."

"I did everything I could to stay under the radar and make no missteps. I know to most people I seem a neurotic mess. You don't go through life denying yourself and end up 'normal.' After years of putting on masks and taking them off, you forget who you were—and who you are. I did all I knew to do and I got arrested. Arrested! And for something I didn't do. Bottom line, I've complied, but it looks like that wasn't enough."

The words "you don't go through life denying yourself and end up normal" resonated with Cole—and the voice.

Haven't I been telling you that?

"Cliff, your phone, I think it's buzzing."

Cliff pulled it out of his pocket. "It's Debbie." He punched the button. "Hey."

Benny and Cole spoke quietly up front.

Cole's hands dug into the steering wheel as he stared at the road. Benny's phone chirped.

"Great, just what I need," he pointed at the incoming text. "I am summoned to meet with Ms. Stilettos in the morning. This *is* getting to me. I'm about ready to hog-tie the lot of 'em." He looked out the window as they merged onto the highway. He tightened his fist and lightly tapped it against the side of the door. "They have no morals. How in the hell do you fight that?"

Cole's phone rang. "Professor, this is Kerwin. Can you talk?"

"Sure. Is everything OK?"

"Yeah, I'm good. But I did another of my curiosity tests today. Are you familiar with something called a BEC, Business Email Compromise? Short story, it's a scam that can be used to either steal or transfer money. I came across what I think is a BEC, or something close to that. All the emails I saw had the same initials, PTM, in the signature lines. It's somehow connected to the country of Belize."

"Belize?" Cole leaned toward Benny. "Didn't Cliff mention Belize earlier back in my office?"

"I think so."

"Kerwin, have you mentioned this to Mr. Niblick?"

"No."

"Let me get back to you." He ended the call. Something else, Cole thought, to share with Lori and Eulonia. Another piece to the puzzle.

In the backseat, Cliff finished his conversation with his wife and leaned back in his seat.

"She's a strong woman," Cole said.

"Stronger than I've ever been or ever will be. The TV stations have all been knocking on the door for interviews. I heard little Marie crying in the background. And, she had one other visitor. Dr. Turkle. He just left."

"Turkle came to your house to talk to your wife?" Benny turned and looked at Cliff.

"Yeah. Debbie said no sooner than you two left, he was knocking on the door. Told her he'll do whatever it takes to exonerate me. Neither of us should worry. Said he'll keep us both up-to-date. And one odd thing my wife passed along. He tried to connect with Marie."

"What do you mean?" Cole looked at Cliff in the rear-view mirror.

"Well, when Dr. Turkle first walked in the door, Marie was, like we've seen her do with strangers, standing behind Debbie and holding her leg for dear life. She can be very tentative."

Benny and Cole looked at each other as if to ask, "Wonder where she got that from?"

"And then Dr. Turkle squatted to her eye level and smiled. He talked to her about the doll she was holding. He said he knew a little girl just like her a long time ago who liked dollies, too. She handed it to him and said the doll's name. It was not what Debbie expected."

A text message popped up on Cliff's phone. He held his phone toward the front seat. "Great. Dr. Turkle wants me in his office tomorrow afternoon."

Cliff leaned over and hugged his knees tightly to his chest.

• • •

32

"So glad to see you." Turkle squeezed Cliff's hand and stared into his eyes. "I'm devastated that all this happened to you. Please come in. Let me get you some water."

The office had the feel of a sports shrine. Trophies, photos, and a few signed basketballs.

"That one," Turkle said as he pointed to a team photo, "was taken the night we won the high school district championship." He handed a bottle of water to Cliff. "It led to that photo. That's me signing my letter of intent for college."

"That must be your mother looking over your shoulder."

"Yes, it is." Turkle smiled at the photo. "She was always my best cheerleader. The next best was that man there. Ricky Peroni. Sports agent."

"You had an agent in college?"

"No, not really. He was a family friend but he and my mom talked about him representing me. You might get to meet him someday. We still stay in touch. We became close friends. He's a fan of CCC hoops."

"Did you sign with him?" The small talk made Cliff uncomfortable, but he didn't know what else to do or say.

"No, I didn't." Turkle pointed to a photo of him being carried off the court on a stretcher. "Had a hell of a mashup under the bucket. Came down with the rebound but fell over my opponent. Ended up with a shattered kneecap. Ended my career and any hope of signing with an agent. Back then you either played or you didn't. There were no hopes for endorsements like the athletes have today."

Turkle popped a pill in his mouth and washed it down with a gulp of water. "Still need these things," pointing to the pill bottle, "to ease the pain now and then. In college, the world seemed to be ours." He picked up a photo of a cheerleader and him standing courtside under the basket. "But things happen we can never foresee."

He lingered with the photo then replaced the frame on the credenza. Looking directly at Cliff, Turkle said, "Even today—especially today—things happen. We don't plan on them but we have to move forward with determination. Ricky, the agent, reminded me years ago that real friends step up when you need them most. Cliff, I'm here for you."

He pointed to the conference table. Cliff sat while Turkle continued.

"I hate that moment of my life," Turkle said pointing to himself being carried off the basketball court. "But I make sure I look at that photo every day as a reminder to take nothing for granted—and let no one ever stand in my way. No one. Ever."

He tucked the pills in his coat pocket and looked at himself on the stretcher. His eyes had a somber look before they focused on Cliff.

"I know you got the letter about having no student contact until the case has been resolved. Don't worry about that. It's just procedure. Keep a low profile and keep working on our initiative. There's no reason your career has to end."

Cliff felt like he would faint. He hoped he wouldn't puke.

"But my students. My job. My family." Cliff couldn't put together a full sentence.

Turkle turned and slapped him on the back. "I got an idea. Let's get out and grab some fresh air. Come on, let's go for a ride."

They got off the elevator at the parking level. "Cliff, I'm sorry this happened to you. It wasn't supposed to happen that way."

"Not supposed to happen that way? I'm not sure what that means, Dr. Turkle. You mean something else was to happen to me?"

"No. Definitely not. Remember that photo of me on the stretcher? When I took the floor that night, that was not the way the game was supposed to end for me." Turkle pointed toward the first row of cars. "When I said 'it' I meant that your involvement with me and the Teaching Initiative Team was supposed to be a time of professional growth and personal exhilaration for you. It wasn't supposed to cause all this trouble."

Turkle squeezed his fob, the car lights flashed and the front doors unlocked. As they secured their seatbelts, Turkle ratcheted the conversation.

"I never thought the union organizers would stoop so low as to do this to you. Mind you, I have no direct evidence.

But their pettiness and desire to ostracize faculty who won't jump on their little socialist bandwagon concern me."

Cliff was dumbfounded. "You think my colleagues would set me up like that? I mean I could see the cold shoulder in the hallway or maybe even berating me in a meeting, but to set me up with a drug bust, threaten my career, and ruin my family? For a union vote?"

"Stranger things have happened. I promise you that as long as we continue our working relationship, nothing will happen to you. They play hardball with you; they better be ready to play hardball with me. And they—whomever they are—do *not* want to do that."

Cliff rubbed his right temple and closed his eyes. His stomach rumbled.

Turkle steered the car through the inner city. Abandoned buildings interspersed between storefronts, tenements, and day laborers on the corner looking for work.

"Cliff, this is where many of our urban campus students come from. It's a tough area. Economically poor. Lacking appropriate health care and housing. Generational poverty."

Cliff, although from a Black middle-class background, heard stories from his parents about family members in neighborhoods like these. They faced daily survival challenges. He didn't need Turkle to remind him of the obvious.

A young Black boy caught Cliff's eyes as Turkle stopped at a traffic light. The boy held the hand of a little girl waiting to cross the street. Both were about the age of his daughter. He could not imagine her crossing a city street without him or Debbie.

"Cliff, these people, our students from these neighborhoods, need people like you. They need your skills and role modeling. They need someone to give a damn!" Turkle pounded the steering wheel as he saw his young self in his mind's eye. Living with a single mom in a tough area just hoping someone would give a damn.

Yeah, you remember the sacrifices your mom made for you. You've come a long way. People don't understand what you endured.

"It would be a shame, Cliff, if we lost you. A shame for the college, the students, you, your wife, and your daughter—Marie. They need you with them."

Cliff squirmed and pulled at the seatbelt harness. He did what he could to keep his breathing calm. "Am I being fired? I didn't do anything."

"We know you didn't. We have the best attorney in town to figure this out for us." Again, Turkle didn't mention that "us" referred to the college, not to Cliff. "And, I'm confident we can make all this go away. Here's what I suggest you consider."

Turkle had looped back to the faculty parking lot, stopped, and turned to Cliff.

"We need you, through your position on the Teaching Initiative Team, to get faculty more interested in training than in organizing. We need you to sell the faculty on how we all benefit when we focus on teaching and learning. Especially the young faculty like yourself. The old ones want a union because they fear change. They are avoiders, Cliff.

Rather than deal with what is in front of their faces, they sidestep and hold on to the past. You, my friend, can be their ticket to paradise. Without you and your younger colleagues leading the way, well, it's a road to hell."

"Hell?"

"All the talk about unionization. It just protects the weak and older faculty. It will hurt young up-and-comers like you. They might not show it, but they fear you. Your ambition. Your intelligence. Your skill set. You get it, Cliff. They don't."

"But Cole and Benny have been mentors to me. Good people who have helped me adjust to the demands of teaching. Same with Professor Polonia."

"And they are good people," Turkle replied, slightly shifting gears in his approach. "At times, they can get overzealous and misguided. That's what got Benny into the mess he's in. And the IT work you've done for me with the educational consortium in Belize for our international students; well, I can't trust any of the yahoos in Niblick's office with that work. I won't forget what you've done and neither will those students and their families. You have the chance to make a mark on a lot of lives. You're the ace in my pocket, Cliff."

"Shit!" Cliff thought to himself as he scrunched his knees together.

"The grey sedan with the 'Family on Board' sign. Here it is." Turkle pulled up behind Cliff's car.

"How'd you know that?" Cliff asked.

"I make it my business to know about my business partners."

"You mean college colleagues, don't you?"

Turkle smiled and hit the unlock button for the passenger door.

As Cliff exited the car, Turkle said, "Cliff, you and our team can and will do great things for this community. This is your big chance. You need to help some of your colleagues understand that it's not in their best interests to piss on someone when that someone has a gun to their head."

Turkle drove away. Cliff walked to the side of his car and leaned on the door with his two shaking hands. His shirt was wet with perspiration and his breath heavy.

"What the hell am I to do now?" he said. "God damn it!"

Turkle headed to the CCC Gym and his appointment with Coach Gil. As he drove, he rubbed his knee, popped another pill, and tuned into a national sports radio talk show. Today's topic examined the pros and cons of student-athlete endorsements. The time had come for Turkle to advance his plan to the next level.

• • •

33

Bouncing balls. The squeak of the players' sneakers. The smell of sweat. Plays being called and passes thrown.

Turkle stopped at the courtside, just inside the lower level door from the locker room. He saw Johnny V slam dunk the ball at the opposite end of the court and then make his way back to defend his basket. He had impressive speed and agility for his size. As Johnny set up for the approaching play, Turkle said to himself, "Watch the lane. Watch the lane."

Just then, as if he heard the warning, Johnny stepped to his side. The opposing player stopped, jumped, and put up a one-hand set shot toward the basket.

Smack!

Johnny sent the ball flying cross-court into the stands.

Turkle smile. "Yeah. He's good."

Coach Gil called time, the players took a knee, and the assistants brought water.

"You teach Johnny V to do that, Coach?" Turkle extended his hand.

"I just stay out of his way. The kid's a natural. Just like you were back in the day."

"Yeah. Back in the day," Turkle smiled. "The kid's got a few inches on me. And good knees. And he has you as a coach. Wish I could've played for you rather than against you. Your team always challenged us."

"And your team always kicked our fannies up and down the court!" They both laughed and slapped each other on the shoulders.

Turkle's first year playing collegiate ball coincided with Coach Gil's introduction as an assistant coach for a rival team in the same regional division. The coach stood out as a relentless competitor. He'd pace the sidelines yelling out instructions and encouragement. Combined with his thick mustache cascading on either side of his chin, chiseled body, and command of the game, he made an imposing opponent. He developed a reputation as an old-school straight-as-an-arrow coach. No funny stuff on his team.

Today, the mustache, though white, remained as thick as his southern accent. A few extra pounds could be seen at the beltline, but he could more than hold his own in the weight room and on the court.

"Coach, thanks for giving me a few minutes. Is this still a good time to talk?"

"Sure." The coach yelled to the players. "All right, do ten laps around the court and then head to the showers. We have a strategy meeting in thirty minutes. I'll see you in the locker room." He turned to Turkle and pointed toward the bleachers.

"I've been thinking," the coach said as they sat, "what happened to the professor, Fitzgerald? The one who threw the ball at you."

"All good. He's a respected teacher but misguided on a few issues—like how to run a college. And he's one of the faculty banging the drum for a union. It all comes with the territory."

"Anything going to happen to him?"

"Coach, you don't want me to give away my plays do you?"

They both laughed and the coach said, "He never would've made my team with a weak arm like that. You, on the other hand, still have quick reflexes."

"And so do your players, especially Johnny V. He's one of those players who will benefit when the *Pay for the Name* law takes effect."

"Six months from now as I understand it. I'm not a big fan, Pat. Old school, you know, is where you get a chance to play, get some scholarship money, go to class, commit to the team, and graduate. Then you get into professional sports if you have the skills." Coach looked out at the basketball court and shook his head. "This seems complicated and ready-made for problems."

"And" Turkle interjected, "you know the college and your program stand to earn money that you'd never see in a traditional annual budget."

"Yeah, I do. That's one reason I'm willing to listen."

"Coach, I know we're a small town here at Central. And we won't see the large contracts that the major colleges see.

You know, some of those big-time college coaches have made millions on these endorsement deals."

"I could only wish," the coach shook his head.

"I've got an angle." Turkle turned to directly face the coach who raised his eyebrows. Turkle responded to his look, "A legal angle, of course. Well, maybe we stretch interpretation a bit, but it's all on the up and up. As you say, we really can't do anything for six months. But we can set our strategy and be ahead of the game when the law goes into effect. Our legal department will be involved."

"Go on." Coach stroked his mustache and squinted as he listened.

"I have an agent and a major brand interested in getting in on the ground floor with the endorsement of Johnny Valentine. Being a small-town stud, he presents an attractive storyline. Coach, these people can help Johnny and the entire CCC basketball program. The companies make money by selling CCC uniforms, hats, jackets, and shirts. Things like that. We buy equipment from them, as well. Let me set up a meeting. You, me, the agent, and the company rep." Turkle paused to let the coach absorb the information, and then he continued his pitch.

"Your program benefits with payments. Think of them as royalties, like what authors get for selling books. And now the bonus is that the student-athletes, who put the team on the radar, also will get something. They earn money from things like shirts, sneakers, and bobbleheads. The school gets publicity. You then have a better chance of recruiting more

Johnny Vs. That leads to championships and more money for you and your staff."

Coach leaned back and stretched his arms against the bleacher bench behind him and looked at the court, the scoreboard, and the door leading to the locker room.

"We sure could use some money to modernize this gym. It hasn't had a facelift in more than two decades. It's showing its age. But I still don't get it. Why CCC? Yeah, I understand the attraction to Johnny V, but how does this one athlete, in one sport, in one relatively small-time school help an apparel company or justify an agent's time? I don't get that, Pat."

"Coach, I can't argue that at all. Trust me, though, these people are big-time. They see a bigger picture than you and I can envision. Think about the times when one of your plays unfolded on the court; the other team had no idea it was coming and you scored. Or what about those occasional times the other team pulls that on you? What we think we see is not always what will unfold."

The Coach, looking at the court as if he saw the plays Turkle had described, nodded his head.

"And the endorsement angle could get those funds you need for your facility, Coach. Let me set up the meeting. You come and listen to what they have to offer you, your team, and CCC. Bring your assistants if you'd like to get their feedback. The worst that happens is you lose thirty minutes of your time."

Coach sat up and placed his arms on his legs as he looked at the floor. He took a breath and said, "Do it. But tell these people I don't want to be sold to—I want to be educated. If I feel like I'm being sold a used car, I'll walk out."

"Deal!"

"And one more thing I'd like you to consider," Turkle pushed a little further. "I've got an anonymous donor willing to fund class compensation time for your team."

Coach Gil's eyebrows raised and then he squinted. "You mean, pay my players for going to class?"

"It's legal coach."

"But they already get scholarship money."

"True but it's hard to work, play ball, and go to class. And you know these young men, many of them, come from poor households. This is just another way to help the players and their families. Think of it this way: playing sports becomes their work—like an internship. I'll get you more information the next time we meet."

Coach continued to look at Turkle. Other than on the court, he wasn't one to play games, especially when his players were involved. "You have more angles than a geometry teacher, Pat."

Turkle laughed, stood, and extended his hand. "Thanks for making time coach. You know how much I respect your input and collaboration."

The coach departed for the locker room to meet with his players. Turkle pulled out his phone and punched in a number as he walked to his car.

"OK. The meeting is set up, Ricky. Time for the next deposit. You know the account."

• • •

"Hey, Johnny. Over here." Standing by his car, Turkle waved as the team exited the gym, their strategy meeting complete for the day.

"Yes, sir. Dr. Turkle?

"Very good. You pay attention on and off the court."

"A habit my mom instilled in me early on. Always remember someone's name. Sign of respect."

"Smart mom. I'd like to meet her someday and thank her for you. And I'd like for both of you never to want for anything ever again."

Johnny cocked his head. "What do you mean?"

"I'm sure you've heard about the *Pay for the Name* law that allows athletes like you to get money from sporting goods companies by endorsing their products."

"Yeah, I heard but that's for the Bulldogs and Gators of the world. Not someone like me or CCC."

"Johnny, it's for someone *exactly* like you. Maybe we can set up a time when I can talk with you and your mom about this."

Turkle's phone rang, and he felt the dread before the caller finished speaking. "Dr. Turkle? This is Mrs. Hobart at Timber Estates. Your mother has injured herself, and we had to take her to the hospital."

• • •

34

Poor does not mean dirty. It doesn't indicate a personal or familial dereliction of responsibilities, nor does it point to bankruptcy of virtue.

Poor co-exists with struggle. It may be pitied by those with more comfort or ridiculed and patronized by those who need to step on someone to feel a bit taller.

Suzy didn't need pity or ridicule. As she cleared an area on the scuffed kitchen table to do her homework, she knew the formidable challenges that stood in her way were due to actions of her own as well as circumstances beyond her control. She hadn't asked for a drug-addicted mother or an incarcerated father. Her mother died from an overdose when Suzy was three. Her father was serving a 20-year sentence for drug trafficking. Just like everyone, she didn't choose her birth family.

She also knew she created some of those odds with ill-advised decisions. Like believing that sex equaled love. Seeking to create a new family to replace her nonexistent one. Getting pregnant at 15 created more life lessons she had to confront. For the rest of her life.

As she opened her textbook and class notebook, she looked at her daughter sitting on the floor in between the mismatched sofa bed and side chair with a fistful of crayons.

"Look, Mama," Shauna said holding up a brightly colored drawing of the sun, grass, and a bench. "I drew your picture." She pointed to a photo held to the refrigerator door by a rainbow magnet. Suzy snapped it on one of their walks to the park.

"Wow! That's beautiful, Sweetie. It's better than my photo. You're the best four-year-old artist I've ever known."

Suzy wanted Shauna to know the encouragement that she never did.

Her mother's older sister, Aintin Cara was the only real mother Suzy ever knew. They'd lived in fifteen different apartments. Cara served tables at a small restaurant near the college. She persuaded her manager to hire Suzy part-time. The two of them pooled their minimal tips and even more stingy shift pay to move into this tight but tidy one-bedroom, second-floor apartment on the edges of the core city. They couldn't afford to move out of the area, but Aintin did what she could with each move to get them closer to the better side of town. "Better" in their case meant "safer."

"Mama's going to do some schoolwork. Why don't you draw one more picture before you go night-night?"

Shauna giggled, pulled another piece of notebook paper toward her, and began her new masterpiece.

Bang! Bang! Bang!

"Open up, Suzy!"

Shauna looked at the door, eyes wide. She dropped her crayon and ran to Suzy's side.

"Open up. I don't have all night."

Suzy forced a smile for Shauna and tousled her hair. "It's OK. He'll just be here for a minute."

She took a deep breath and opened the door with the security chain still in place. "Ned, please be quiet. You're scaring Shauna. And me."

"I can go away and take my money with me." He reached into his pocket and squeezed a roll of cash in between his thumb and index finger. "Don't I come through for you and my daughter? Every time I can, I do."

Suzy looked at the money. While not a lot, it did help her and her aunt make ends meet. She stared into Ned's eyes. Why did she continue to let this man into her life? Yes, he was the biological father of Shauna but not much more. She flashed back to before Shauna was born. Ned attracted her with his sense of self-confidence. In the early days of their relationship, he was rough around the edges for sure, but Suzy sensed something deeper. She saw a man from the same dysfunctional family structure she grew up with. They had commonalities. And she thought he was the answer to her self-confidence issues.

Unfortunately, that didn't work. She continued to feel like an imposter while Ned had drifted into the drug world. When he was stoned, like tonight, that was not the Ned she first met. She kept hoping for a return to those early days but little by little she understood that would never happen. She now felt like she was the one who needed to help Ned.

Unlatching the security chain, Suzy held the door for him to enter. "He still smells like a truck stop bathroom," she thought to herself as she closed the door and followed him to the kitchen. Shauna had a firm grasp on her hand.

Between work and school, Suzy hadn't seen Ned Spano since that night at *The Silver Fox* when Benny threw him to the floor. She counted her blessings and wished it had been longer. Trouble seemed to follow close behind him.

"That's the greeting you give to your baby's daddy?" Spano wore a sarcastic smile, pulled Suzy toward him, and kissed her. She pushed away and looked down toward Shauna.

"Mama needs you to do something for Aintin, OK?"

Shauna looked up at Suzy and then at Ned.

"Can you start a drawing for Aintin? I will help you." As she was talking, Suzy led Shauna back to her self-made artist circle. She leaned over, kissed Shauna, and whispered, "Mama needs your help, OK? I'll just be over there by the table. You can still see me. And I can see you." Suzy hugged her daughter and walked toward Ned. She looked back at Shauna and winked at her.

"What's the problem?" Ned asked. "Just showing our daughter that Daddy loves Mama."

"What do you want, Ned?" Suzy didn't offer him a seat. She wanted him to leave as soon as possible. Leave the room and her life. For good.

"You and I have a date coming up."

"A date?" Suzy pulled back and scrunched her face. "We don't have a date. I have shifts at the diner, homework, and Shauna." Suzy looked over at her daughter and smiled.

"Hell with that! This is more important. And anyway, it ain't a real date. You gonna lie about it." Spano narrowed his eyes and moved closer to Suzy. His breath reeked of alcohol. His clothes smelled of marijuana. "Not sure when. I'll call when I need you. All you have to do is tell people who might call you asking if you were with me on a certain night, that we were here having a family night."

"Who is going to call me, Ned? And why would they ask me about you?"

"Could be the police. Maybe someone from your goody-two-shoes college. Maybe nobody. I'll tell you when to be ready."

"I'm not lying to the police for you."

"Oh, you *will* do that. Don't get cute. This means money for me, and that means money for you and Shauna. Save that look of yours for your pissant professors. " He reached down and twisted her wrist with a smile.

"Ouch," Suzy whispered with her tight lips. She did not want to frighten Shauna. "OK," she said shaking from his grasp. She just wanted him to leave.

"That's a good girl. You don't want me to hit you in front of our precious daughter, do you?" He put his hand behind her head, held her, put his lips to hers, and forced his tongue into her mouth.

"You do good for me, and I'll place something else in your body. Be a good girl and no one gets hurt." He looked toward Shauna, back at Suzy, and reached into his pocket. "Here's the money. See, I keep my promises. You keep yours for when I call you." He turned and left the apartment.

Suzy stood there momentarily, then reached to double bolt and chain the door. She turned and walked back to the table.

"Mama, why are you crying?"

"It's nothing, Sweetie. I'm fine. We'll be fine. Are you going to draw Aintin that picture now?" Suzy wiped her cheek, got on one knee, and hugged Shauna.

"Mama, he scares me." Shauna buried her head in Suzy's chest.

"Me, too," Suzy said to herself.

"I tell you what, Shauna, would you let me work with you on a drawing?"

Shauna looked up into Suzy's eyes and nodded her head.

"OK. Go get the crayons ready for us."

Shauna ran to her space and began placing crayons in front of her. Suzy composed herself and reached into her backpack. She placed the roll of money from Ned in a zippered pocket and then pulled out two business cards.

"Heather Rivera. Radio Personality. *The Fact and Fiction Hour.*"

She entered the number into her phone and hit "Save Contact."

Suzy did the same for Ms. Robertson.

• • •

35

The stands of pine trees blurred as his headlights sped by. No one shared the road with Turkle as he neared the rural hospital. His tie hung loose after a long day. He popped a pill and washed it down with the caffeine drink he had been sipping since the gas station. Like he told Cole that night in the *Silver Fox*, he didn't drink alcohol. But caffeine and pills had become his go-to. Sleep was difficult. Too many visitations from his voice about things in the past that could never be fixed or undone.

This was the third time this month his mother had fallen. He didn't know what to expect as he pulled into a visitor parking spot in front of the emergency room entrance.

The unit secretary directed Turkle to Room 101. "She's been sedated for comfort. I'll let her nurse know you're here."

Turkle made his way down the narrow linoleum hallway. He could hear the quiet beeping of machines as he passed rooms. In one room, a nurse was handing medication to a patient. A certified nursing assistant in the next room helped another to the bathroom. When he reached his mother's room, he eased open the door and stepped into the dimly lit room. Turkle could see his mother lying still. He stopped and stared at her chest. When he saw it rise and fall, he exhaled and approached.

"Hello." Soft as it was, the greeting startled Turkle. In a chair in the shadows sat Mrs. Hobart. She stood and extended her hand. "I hope you don't mind that I stayed with your mother until you arrived."

He looked at his mother and then at Mrs. Hobart. "Not at all. Thank you for caring and, well, being here for her." He approached the bed and gazed at his sleeping mother. A fresh bandage wrapped around her skull. "What happened?"

"As you know, she's had a few minor mishaps over the last few weeks. Each time she's fallen she's been able to use her medical alert necklace to get help. This time was more serious and, I shudder to think, could have been deadly. She fell in her kitchen and hit her head on the counter. Thank God it happened just as the aid was bringing dinner into her apartment. Her quick thinking got an ambulance to the building and your mother to the hospital. I've been told she'll be fine, physically. A little sore but no brain injury or broken bones. She's a tough one."

"Yes, she is. Thank you again, Mrs. Hobart, for being here. I'll be staying with her tonight." He looked toward the vinyl-covered couch underneath the window that overlooked the parking lot. He looked back at his mother.

You did make a good decision for your mother. She depends on you as much as you need her.

"One more thing, Dr. Turkle." Mrs. Hobart motioned him toward the door. "Her behavior has gotten, I hate to say, a bit more peculiar."

"Memory issues again?"

"Yes, some. She's having increased difficulty explaining herself." Mrs. Hobart searched for gentle words. "Like the other night when she called the dining room asking for her red slob."

Turkle cocked his head.

"We finally determined she wanted a tomato on her salad."

He looked at his mother. She looked serene but he knew her mind was anything but.

"And there have been other incidents, that, when taken alone, aren't big. But when viewed in total may speak to her overall wellbeing." Mrs. Hobart looked at Mrs. Turkle and back at her son. "She pretty much has forgotten everyone's name. She just says 'Hey, fella!' to men and women. With a smile, of course. One day, God love her, she brought a new cocktail to her mimosa happy hour group. She was so proud. She said she experimented with bottles from her kitchen cabinet. It was undrinkable."

"Time for memory care?" Turkle asked knowing the answer.

"Let's talk in the morning."

Mrs. Hobart exited the room. Turkle poured himself a cup of water from the plastic pitcher on his mother's night-stand and sat in the recliner beside her bed.

She deserves so much better than this.

"You just said this was a good decision!" Turkle muttered.

Defensive? Just saying what you're thinking. Or are you thinking what I'm saying?

"Did the best I could with what I was given. I had a lot to deal with." Turkle rubbed his neck. He closed his eyes and flashed back to another hospital room two decades ago. He saw himself leaning over a young child in a hospital bed. He holds her hand as tears stream from his face.

"I did the best I could. You try to deal with that knife to the heart!"

The scene pixilated in his mind's eye to a funeral. Two caskets. One for his wife and the other for his daughter. He sees the graveside preacher say some words Turkle cannot remember. Friends approach a sobbing Turkle saying life isn't fair. And neither is death. The two women in his life had been taken within days of each other by a highly contagious strain of the flu. First, he loses his athletic career, then his wife and daughter.

It's tough. But, you know, being there at death isn't the same as being there for them in life.

"Shut the hell up!"

"Patrick, please don't talk like that," his mother said opening her eyes and tilting her head toward her son. "And who are you talking to anyway?"

"Mom, how are you?" He stood and covered her hand and kissed her forehead. "I got here as soon as I could. How're you feeling?"

"I'm OK," she managed through the drug-induced haze. "Takes more than a countertop to break this ol' noggin. Still wish you hadn't come all this way in the dark. You could have come in the morning."

"I'm here for you, Mom. I know in the past I haven't been. But I am now. I'll be here when you wake up in the morning. We can have coffee together. OK?"

"Well, I'd rather have mimosas, if you can arrange it. Or I can make you one of my new favorite drinks," she said weakly as she drifted back to sleep.

"I'll see what I can do, Mom. I'll see what I can do."

The night nurse introduced herself and while she checked his mother's vital signs brought Turkle up to date on his mother's condition. She excused herself and returned a few minutes later and placed two sheets, a pillow, a wash-cloth, and a towel on the couch for him.

"Let me or the aid know if we can do anything for you. We'll be on duty until the change of shift at 8."

Turkle stood by his mother's side, kissed her on the fore-head, and told her he loved her. Stepping a few feet back to the couch, he slid off his shoes and stretched out on the couch. His phone buzzed with a text. It was Bartley.

"Need you in my office bright and early. Important."

Turkle punched in his reply. "My mother's in the hospi-tal. Will be staying with her a few days. I'll call you in AM"

"Sorry about your mother. Not a good time to be away. Pressure coming down on us."

"I'll take care of it like I always do." Turkle sent the message and turned off his phone.

As he tried to drift to sleep, his mind took him back to the gravesides of Wendi and their daughter, Bridgette. He remembered the dark emotional hole he fell into. Alcohol, drugs, and near suicide.

You were lucky your father-in-law and Ricky stepped in when they did. Those two and your mother saved you from you.

Turkle looked over at his mother. He remembered how her hugs, words, and tenderness helped him through those turbulent waters. The Senator, in his gruff way, understood more than anyone else what Turkle was trying to deal with. Along with the agent, Ricky Peroni, they intervened and got Turkle the professional help he needed to survive. All three believed in him more than he ever believed in himself.

Pat Turkle would never forget or disappoint any of them.

• • •

36

"I'll buy the professor's coffee." Benny walked up behind Cole in the campus café line. "And anyway, I'm a better tipper. He's a bit cheap if you know what I mean." Benny leaned toward the cashier with an exaggerated wink.

"You're chipper for first thing in the morning. Excited about your meeting with Merlot?"

"Yeah about as excited as I am to sit through a faculty meeting. In fact, I'd much rather sit through a faculty meeting. I think."

"Benny, be careful with her," Cole said as they moved away from the cashier's line. "Bartley and his crew are up to something. I met briefly with Eulonia. A few of the pieces seem to be fitting together. We think."

"Eulonia?"

"Yeah. She's helping me connect the dots. They could be using you and me as a distraction for whatever they are up to. While we can't prove anything at this point, Eulonia and I are developing, let's call 'em, some talking points."

"And Cliff," Benny asked, "is he a distraction, too?"

"Don't know. We'll talk more later. Again, be careful with Merlot."

They bumped to-go cups in a toast and parted ways. Cole to his office for his scheduled office hours. Benny across campus to the puzzle palace.

• • •

As he rode the elevator to Merlot's office, Benny sang to himself, "Weasels and ferrets, moles and slugs, liars and cheats, felons and thugs." He smiled as the door chimed and opened on the 6th floor. He checked in with the secretary who led him into the vice president's office.

"Professor! Good to see you. Thanks for agreeing to my request for a meeting."

"More like an order, wasn't it?" He sat in the chair in front of her desk.

"Benny," Merlot said with the fake sincerity of a blind date gone wrong, "this isn't going as I'd hoped. The MNSO continues its investigation. Our attorney hopes she'll find nothing and drop all charges. But who knows?"

"You mean *your* attorney, don't you? The college, unless I've missed something, has done nothing for me."

"Not totally accurate. You're still employed, getting your benefits, and your paycheck."

Benny stared at her. Yes, that was true, but at what cost in the long run he wondered.

Merlot walked back to her chair, sat, and leaned over the desk. With her tennis bracelet arm on top of the other and resting on the desktop, she continued, "We realize it's been difficult for you to not be able to work with your students on campus or online. But, given all that's going down, we think it's the best strategy. Going forward, it would be best, as well, if you didn't contact any faculty members."

"That's not going to happen. Cole and I play in a band together. You know that!" Benny wanted to say, "And neither you nor the douchebags who mis-mismanage this place are going to tell me what to do with my off time." Benny thought of Cole's admonition and bit the inside of his cheek.

Merlot took in a breath and sat back, giving the impression of evaluating what he just said. Benny had responded as she had hoped. She drove the knife a bit deeper.

"First, I would watch out for Cole. I know you're friends, but he's losing control. You probably heard he threw a basketball at Dr. Turkle. Our legal team is investigating what should happen there. And second, listen, Benny, we are here for you. Really. But you seem to get deeper and deeper into this and you don't look good. You continue to diminish your standing with outsiders looking in." Merlot waved her arm toward the window as if to indicate the entire community was watching this show unfold. "And, going forward, it might help if you could tone it down a bit. You know what I mean?"

"No, I don't. Could you explain it to me?" Again, he wanted to say, "You know, like I were a lost administrator attempting to find my way to a classroom. Show me the error of my ways, Madam Vice President." But he held it in, though that was getting more difficult to do.

"You know that your sexual orientation is your business and you know the college has a strong anti-discrimination policy. We are, after all, a forward-thinking institution. That being said, it might play better out there," she again waved her arm toward the imaginary community audience, "if you acted less colorful."

"Oh, OK. Will that be coming to me from the Director of Human Resources Department?"

"Benny, you're killing yourself. Slow professional suicide."

He looked at her. His ears felt as if they were on fire. His neck muscles throbbed.

"Well, listening to you, I've little to stand on. So how 'bout I just stand and leave you to whatever your plan may be." He stood and continued, "And while you're at it, maybe you want to stay away from TTV."

Merlot looked confused.

"Yeah, you know, Turkle the Vagitarian. Doesn't look good to the people out there." He mocked her arm wave toward the window.

He walked out the door.

She called Turkle.

• • •

Cole, unlike many of his colleagues, enjoyed office hours. He found it the best way to connect with many of his students on a personal level. For many, like Suzy, he helped them visualize and then start moving toward their dreams. The course outlines established the larger context for each of his classes. But his connection to his students, well, that was the dance he liked.

On the first day of the semester, he gave each student a piece of paper that he said was as important as their syllabus. Maybe more so. He titled it *The Seven Core Values.* Cole posted a copy in his office to remind his students and himself.

- Surround ourselves with respectful **RELATIONSHIPS** that will help us grow as people and as a community.
- Discover and use **RESOURCES** to increase chances for progress, growth, learning, and connections.
- Evaluate experiences for their **RELEVANCE** for growth and community.
- Give voice to our **RAINBOWS**—our dreams and aspirations—and act to move toward them.
- Remain curious and set aside time for **REFLECTION** about what we do, why we do it, and adjustments we may need to make.
- Act with **RESPONSIBILITY** toward others, our planet, and ourselves.
- Pay attention and foster self-care and **RESILIENCE**.

As he looked at the list on his wall, he thought that too many of them had been lost in his life. Could he ever get them back on track?

He turned on his computer and was about to check his voicemail when he heard it.

"No! No, no, and no!" came the mournful moan from an office down the hall.

"Cliff?" Cole closed his laptop and made his way to his colleague's office. He found Cliff, with one hand rubbing his forehead and the other banging aimlessly at his computer keys.

"What's going on? Lose your grade book?" Cole slid into the weathered chair in front of Cliff's desk.

"No. This can't be happening. Why me? Why now?"

"Cliff?"

"You know how I get a little anxious at times," Cliff said.

Cole raised his eyebrows. "Well, yeah. You're known to jump out on the ledge every so often. But lately, I don't blame you. You got a lot on your plate."

"I think I'll need to jump *off* that ledge now," Cliff said, tightening his crossed legs even more. "You know Vice President Turkle has been on me to do IT work for him. And-." He stopped and banged the keyboard again. "You know I don't want to do it. He creeps me out. But he keeps pressuring me. So, I wrote a draft email practicing being my forceful self with him."

Cole raised his eyebrows again, "Your forceful self?" Cliff's idea of *forcefulness* was—well, Cole didn't know since he never saw the *forceful* Cliff.

"I wrote a frank email explaining why I could not—and would not—do this work for him. I sent it to myself to make the whole practice feel authentic." Cliff shut his laptop and looked across the desk at his colleague. "I told him how I had boundaries that he needed to respect and how this project seemed to blur the lines of ethics. It was a great email. I hit 'Send' and waited for it to come to me. I wanted to open it and see how it felt to look at this email in the Inbox. That's when I saw what I did."

"I'm guessing you sent it to yourself and..."

"And to Turkle. His name was in the 'TO' box. I missed it somehow. And now he has that email."

Cole let out a low whistle. "Well, did you cuss, accuse him of anything, insult him?"

"Not exactly. But I did mention I had ethical considerations." Cliff opened his laptop as if expecting to see that he hadn't done what he had. But there it was. The email meant for his eyes so that he could see the impact of forceful Cliff was now in the Inbox of Pat Turkle.

"No, no, no, no! What do I do now?"

"Um, yeah, that'll catch his attention." Cole was searching for calming words to help Cliff prepare for the expected tempest. "You were your *forceful self*. Turkle won't like it but maybe—"

The phone rang next to Cliff's arm. The name on the phone showed the incoming call was from Turkle.

"It's him. Damn it all." He hit the speaker button. "This is Professor Singer," Cliff managed with halting speech.

"Cliff," Turkle said, "I got your email."

"Director, I'm sorry. I'm going through so much that I'm not thinking straight. I'm scared for me and my family."

"I've told you, Professor, we're a team."

Cole shook his head with disgust as Cliff rubbed his.

"Didn't I tell you how much I approved of your work? We need each other. And remember, why would anyone piss on me or you when I'm holding a gun to their head? My secretary will contact you with a time you and I will meet for lunch."

Turkle disconnected.

Cliff looked more dazed than the day Cole and Benny bailed out of jail. He stared at Cole and said, "I don't see a way out of this. I'm screwed!"

• • •

"Good morning, Professor," Kerwin knocked on the open door. "Still a good time to meet?"

"Hey, good morning. Yes, please, come on in. You have a reservation for one in the seat of honor. You said you found something else?" Cole walked around his desk and closed the door.

Kerwin opened his shoulder bag and retrieved an envelope.

"After I found that entry about me receiving financial aid that I'm not receiving, I started digging a little further. I mentioned BECs to you the other day. Know about them?"

"Other than the acronym stands for Business Email Compromise schemes, but you told me that. Educate me."

"They exist in various formats. You might've received one of the thousands of BEC phishing emails that clog our inboxes. You know, looking for account numbers or other personal information. Well, as I started digging more into the financial aid issue, I noticed my college email address listed on another piece of correspondence addressed to me. Look at this."

Kerwin showed Cole an email, from the college's financial aid office, informing him that $2,500 had been deposited to his student account at the school.

"And you haven't received it yet?" Cole asked still a bit perplexed.

"And I never will. Remember I told you I'm not eligible. And here's the kicker. Look at my email address—the first part of it before the @ symbol."

Kerwin pointed to "kerwyn.lucas."

"My email address begins with "kerwin.lucas" an "i" not a "y." I'm still searching, but it looks like the money is not even going through the college but going offshore to an account in Belize. And another thing. I keep seeing, I think I might have told you, the initials PTM."

"PTM?

"Yes, sir."

Cole would need more coffee to get his head around all the moving parts here. An off-shore account. In a country that Cliff had mentioned in connection with his work for

Turkle. Apparent financial aid fraud. Sheriff's office investigation. Cliff. Benny. PTM.

Watch your ass. Watch your aging white ass. You're next!

A knock on the door. "Come in," Cole yelled as Kerwin returned the paper to his bag.

Professor Polonia entered the office.

"Professor Fitzgerald. Shall I come back?" She looked at Kerwin.

"Ah, no ma'am. I'm leaving. Chair's all yours."

"Thank you, young man. Would you mind closing the door on your way out?"

Cole stood to welcome Eulonia. Still, a ways to go, but they were gradually beginning to understand each other.

"Cole, I've been thinking about what you told me about financial aid letters and the change of major notifications. And then there are the issues of the no-shows on our rolls. There are elephants in these string beans."

For the next 15 minutes, she detailed how she had been doing her research about the increased number of no-shows on professors' class rolls. She confirmed they mirrored the increased number of financial aid recipients.

Handing Cole a piece of paper, she said, "I've found that either many of the names do not exist or are eerily similar to the names you *will* find of real people—actual students. Whoever is doing it, they're good. The names never appear on the same roll with the same professor. No, they appear across disciplines, buried in amongst other names. Look at this," she said pointing to one entry. "You see the name, Suzy McDonald?"

"Yeah, I have her in my 10:00 class," Cole said.

"Yeah. I have her in my afternoon class. Now, look at this." Eulonia placed another enrollment form next to the first one. "This is from the sculpture class at our cross-town campus. See the spelling? Susie MacDonald."

Cole held both forms. "Whoa!" he said. "I've got information that financial aid notices are being emailed to the students supposedly getting the aid. Some of the email addresses are, as you might say, eerily similar to real people—actual students. One changed letter in the student's name and—"

"And the student never gets the notice but the money goes somewhere," Eulonia finished Cole's sentence.

Cole looked again at Eulonia's evidence, looked into her eyes, and said, "I have to agree with you. There *are* elephants in those string beans."

Eulonia smiled. "Yes. There. Are."

• • •

37

An outsider can oftentimes see things about another person that the person cannot. The view from the outside does not have to contend with the commentary from the inside.

Debbie understood her husband's family rearing. She remembered her parents giving the same "remain respectful and vigilant" speech she and her siblings grew up with. An unfortunate right-of-passage, this practice placed watching one's back far above following one's heart. But since Cliff returned from jail, he looked like someone who had had his heart ripped from him.

Cliff cared about what he did and for whom he did it. Like the time he bought Marie that doll house that stood in the living room. Cliff obsessed about the exact spot to erect it, how to position it in that spot, and how to stage the interior. Once Marie was playing with her dolls in the new house, Cliff smiled and went on to his next project.

He enjoyed developing demonstrations and lessons for his students. Rather than straightforward lectures, he developed hands-on brainteasers to engage his classes. Unlike many professors, Cliff loved grading projects and papers, and providing feedback. When his students improved, Cliff felt he did, too.

All that seemed like another lifetime for someone else. He paced from room to room. He picked at his food and ate little. Last night, he didn't sleep. And worst of all, he couldn't teach. Today, with a vacant stare, he sat on the backyard deck.

"Cliff, what can I do?" Debbie asked as she sat in the deck chair next to him. "How can I help?"

Cliff drew a deep breath and held it for a moment. He exhaled and shook his head. "I don't know. I just don't know. I've been arrested for something I didn't do—would never do. This will be with me the rest of my life."

"And I will be with you the rest of your life. And so will Marie. I'm scared and worried, too. But we will get through this. You have great friends who will help you."

"And, they took away my soul. I'm a teacher. I want to be with my students. But now, according to this letter," he pointed to a letter near his coffee cup, "I am not allowed on campus any longer. The only one I am allowed to speak with is Dr. Turkle. And he's scaring the shit out of me." He looked at his wife, his eyes welling with tears. "Debbie, I don't feel hopeful. My life has been taken from me."

She hurt just looking at him. Her stomach turned thinking of the turmoil he was enduring. She felt helpless and scared about his state of mind.

"Never lose hope. We have each other." She went to the kitchen and came back with a fresh cup of coffee and handed it to him. "Have you been in touch with Benny or Cole today?"

"No."

"Call Benny. He's having a tough time too, from what you've told me. I'm sure he'd love to hear from you, and it might help your mood. Maybe you can set up a kayak paddle for a little exercise and guy talk." She touched his shoulder and handed him his phone. "Give him a call. Now." Debbie leaned over and kissed him. "We'll get through this. I have hope in you and us. Please call Benny." She retreated to the house.

Cliff stared at the phone for a moment and called Benny's number.

"Hello, you reached Benny DiJohn, bass player and suspended teacher. Please leave a message. BEEP!"

Cliff was about to hang up when he heard a hearty laugh. It wasn't a message, it was Benny being Benny. "Gotcha, didn't I, Cliff?"

Cliff smiled and shook his head. "I love you. How can you be so calm during all that's going on? I mean how do you do it?"

"Oh, you think I'm calm. You ought to feel my stomach. God knows you don't want to be in the bathroom with me. My insides are doing more cartwheels than the basketball cheerleaders."

"Benny." Cliff felt his pulse slow down. Benny could make him laugh. He had an uncanny way to help Cliff take notice of where he was and, more importantly, who he was.

"Debbie suggested that we go for a kayak paddle. What do you say? She might be right. It could help me. Not sure how much fun I'd be for you, though. And Turkle told me to stay away from faculty as well."

"Good by me. Merlot thinks I shouldn't associate with faculty, either. Might not look good she said. You know what I say, buddy? Screw Merlot. Screw Turkle. You ain't keeping me from my man Cliff. Let them sow chaos and fear. We'll not be harvesting with them."

For the first time in weeks, Cliff let out a loud laugh. Debbie peeked in from the kitchen and smiled. "Benny, I want to be like you when I grow up."

"Two things, kid, that I've heard around campus. You gotta set your goals higher than that. And never grow up." It was Benny's turn to laugh. "OK, I'll meet you on the beach tomorrow twenty minutes before sunrise. And Cliff," Benny said with a more serious tone, "remember together we can work this out for you, for me, for our colleagues, for our students, and your family. Bartley and his crew will have a day of reckoning. I promise you that. You have a lot to live for. I'm glad I'm your friend. See you on the beach."

"Thanks, Benny. I needed that."

"So did I. Thanks for calling. Hey look, I gotta go. I think I heard a delivery truck. I'm expecting a shipment from my wine of the month club. Don't want any porch thieves to get it."

Cliff put his phone on the table, took a sip of coffee, and for the first time in days, he smiled.

Benny smiled as well when he found the package sitting against the wall beside the front door. "Ah, come to Papa." He leaned over and reached with his left hand to move the package toward him.

BOOM!

•   •   •

38

"And you're on in 3…2…1."

The "On Air" light flashed and from behind the glass partition, the producer pointed at Heather.

"Welcome back for more *Facts and Fiction*. I'm Heather Rivera. Glad you can join us this morning. Our next guest needs little in the way of introduction. His family has generational ties to our community. They've built a successful shoe and apparel business with franchises throughout the Southeast. And in his spare time, he serves us as our state senator. Wilbur Wackenslong, thank you for taking the time to be with us today."

"Thank you, Heather." Wackenslong rolled his chair closer to the table. "Always a pleasure to help share facts and debunk fiction."

After tossing a few softball questions to the senator about his business and philanthropy in the city, Heather pitched her first changeup.

"Let me get to a question I asked two guests last week, Dr. Darla Merlot and Dr. Richard Edwards, two administrators with Central City College. They had difficulty answering it. I'm sure you can. Pretty straightforward really. As you said earlier, we look for facts over fiction." Heather paused for effect while the senator held her stare with a contemptuous smile. "At the beginning of this academic semester at CCC, in the name of your family's company, you provided a new laptop, tablet, and cell phone to every faculty member. That's impressive. Why did you do it? Is it connected to your expected gubernatorial campaign?"

"I see you've read the editorial pages and what they speculate about my political future."

"The *Marina Norte Gazette* has followed your career for years. Are you saying they got this wrong?"

"I'd never say the *Gazette* got anything wrong. Not our local newspaper. No fake news ever on those pages." His eyes gave away the lack of sincerity in his laugh. "It would be premature for me to say anything now other than my team and I are evaluating. We want what is best for this state. I have no grand plans to go beyond state senator. I love serving our area. But one never knows if one will be called to a higher duty."

A non-committal committal.

Wackenslong continued. "The donation to faculty just shows my respect for CCC and education in general. It's an extension of my family's community commitment. And, as you know, I did spend two years as the chair of the legislative committee studying higher ed. Not that difficult to understand."

Time for Heather's fastball. "And your community commitment has been particularly strong with Central. It's no secret that you've been instrumental in securing appointments for every member on the college's Board of Trustees. And you pushed to get Dr. Doyle Bartley appointed as president. Why and how did that come about?"

"That's right. I'm proud of what Dr. Bartley has accomplished since his arrival. You do know, Heather, that he inherited quite a mess from the outgoing college administration. From enrollment decline to deteriorating infrastructure to disgruntled and underpaid faculty, Dr. Bartley and his cabinet have had their hands full."

"But that's what I don't get. Why him out of all the candidates the Board could have hired? He had never led a school larger than 7,500 students. CCC has nearly 40,000. And he was at a for-profit school. A novice from a much smaller school with a different culture than a public college. Explain that to me."

"Heather, when was the last time you chose a campus president, or for that matter when have you been involved in deciding who will lead your station?" Wackenslong paused for only a split second as he had no intention of letting her respond. "Sometimes a college needs to step outside of the box of picking the stereotypical leader. Yes, we could have offered the position to an applicant from a top-tier university. But if anyone took time to look at the applicants, you'd see Bartley was a clear choice. He's in the middle of what will continue to be an illustrious career. He has time to build

CCC. We didn't, that is, the Board didn't want someone who would use the college as their last stop before a Florida retirement. We needed someone committed to the job. That was Dr. Doyle Bartley. Hands down. Again, the legislative time I committed to studying the needs and challenges of the colleges and universities in our state introduced me to leaders like Doyle Bartley."

"And if I may," Wackenslong continued, "under his leadership, the college enrollment has spiked by, I believe, 25% this semester." Wackenslong figured Heather already had an enrollment question in her quiver, so he decided to sling the arrow first and put the conversation on his terms. "Dr. Bartley's team," the Senator said, "has given the most financial aid in the history of CCC. I'd say we look like geniuses for hiring, as you say, a *novice* from a much smaller school." Wackenslong's legislative career taught him how to stand his ground, swing hard, and stay on message.

Heather was about to ask a follow-up question when Wackenslong held up his hand.

"If I may before you move to your next question. Earlier you asked about my expected entrance into the governor's race. Let's say I did become a candidate. I can tell you this, I'd be running on a strong education platform as well as the need for increased accountability by all state officials. The state of education is at a crossroads. We need to reimagine the mission of higher education. Unfortunately, many times we end up with people who lack imagination, fire, and creativity. Bartley and his assembled team represent a younger, smarter, and more creative generation. We need that. Our community deserves that."

"Did Bartley's hiring, have anything to do with him choosing Patrick Turkle as his Director of Human Resources?" Heather asked.

"That's a Dr. Bartley decision. The president gets to choose whomever he wants for his cabinet. With Board approval of course."

"Interesting. My research shows that Turkle and Bartley never had any professional contact before CCC. Never worked together and from what I can see, never collaborated on a project."

"You'll have to ask Dr. Turkle and Dr. Bartley," Wackenslong interjected with a slightly irritated tone.

"They had no prior contact but Dr. Turkle is brought on board to act as the gatekeeper for hiring, firing, and training. He controls new faculty orientation and chairs the committee that reviews all recommended terminations. That's a lot of power for one man. Did the Board's selection of him have anything to do with the fact that Dr. Turkle was married to your daughter?"

Silence. Stone cold silence.

"What was in his background that moved him to the front of the list?"

"Dr. Turkle went through a thorough vetting process."

"And there are family connections to you."

"Which have absolutely no bearing on his position. Is this really what you want to talk about? Genealogy?"

"OK. Let's talk about something you brought up. You said enrollment is up considerably at the college this semester. About 25%."

Wackenslong smiled at the question. "Because of Dr. Bartley and his team. Again, not bad for a novice coming in from a much smaller school with a different culture." The comment rolled off Wackenslong's tongue with the disdain he had in his heart for the host.

"But class attendance has dropped by at least 25%. Odd coincidence? Enrollment is up by 25% but attendance is down by 25%?" Heather held up both hands mimicking a balancing scale. "Not sure about you, Senator, but I wouldn't want any of my investments to go up by 25% and drop by 25% at the same time."

"Well, that would be better than continually losing money in that investment. Let's suppose for a moment, your figures are accurate. Which I doubt. But if they are, for the first time in the last five years, this college has not lost enrollment. Staying the same is better than losing ground."

Heather's patience and the segment's time were expiring. The producer had just announced through her headset that she had less than two minutes remaining until the commercial break. She had to get Wackenslong now. She doubted he would come back to her show.

"Talk to us about the case the college is pursuing against Professor Benny DiJohn."

"Not familiar with it."

"Really? It's been in the news. Short story: He came to the aid of a young woman who was assaulted. Now, the college and the MNSO have been investigating the professor for an alleged assault."

"Ah, yes. Now I remember. I believe Professor DiJohn was in a bar. The woman was an underage student in that bar. The man in question was the underaged woman's baby's father. Your professor choked that man. Who, as I remember, is also a student at the school." Wackenslong wore a self-satisfied smirk. "But as with any potential criminal charges, I'd have to defer to our fine Marina Norte Sheriff's Office."

Heather was about to rebut the rebuttal when the producer entered the booth and gave her a note.

"Oh, my God!" Heather said. "Breaking news just in. Professor Benny DiJohn, the man we have been discussing, has been rushed to City Hospital. It appears a package bomb exploded at his home."

She glared at Wackenslong who sat back in his chair with a confused look. "Oh my God, that, that is terrible," the Senator said. "We have to find the reprobate who did this! Unbelievable."

As the producer went to a commercial break, Heather stared at Wackenslong.

• • •

Later that morning.

An urgent email arrived in everyone's inbox at the college.

To: All Central City College Employees

From: The Central City College Board of Trustees

Subject: Emergency Board of Trustees meeting on Thursday at 1:00 PM.

Message: Please do your best to clear your calendars and attend this meeting.

• • •

39

The phone in his coat pocket sounded one buzz after another. Each with a different emergency. Somebody else's imperative. He let the messages pile up and focused on his number one priority.

"Patrick, should you be answering those messages?" Turkle's mother was propped up in her bed. All things considered, she spent a restful first night back at home.

"They can wait," he said as he entered the bedroom with a tray. "The most important thing right now is your morning tea and an egg that I poached especially for you, madam." He placed the tray on the overbed table and kissed her on the forehead."

"I'm a blessed person to have you in my life."

"That would be my line. Water?" Turkle held up a pitcher. She nodded and he poured.

"You would have been a good father. You were a good father." She started to cry.

"I know. And you would have been a wonderful grandmother. But it wasn't to be. It is what it is, Mom." Turkle fought back tears of his own.

"Mrs. Hobart and Timber Estates have been wonderful, haven't they? They've done so much, right down to this table that fits across my bed so nicely. They think of everything."

"Your home care nurse will be here in a few minutes." Turkle looked at his watch. "She just texted me from the lobby. I spoke with her on the phone yesterday and brought her up to speed about your situation. I need to get back to the college to put out a few fires. I'll check in with you. I hate to go but—."

"No buts, Patrick. You've done more than any mother could ask for. I guess I did do something right when I raised you." She reached out and held his hand. "I'm sorry I put you through all this. Not sure why I fell. It won't happen again."

"It might be time to talk about moving you to the other side of the complex."

"Thanks, but no thanks. I stumbled in my kitchen. No need to shuttle me off to the bad side of town." She smiled but the words carried weight and contempt with them.

"You've 'stumbled' three times." Turkle used air quotes. "We need to talk. No arguments from you right now. Or I'll take that delicious poached egg and eat it myself."

The doorbell rang. "That's the nurse. You eat and chill."

Over the next 30 minutes, the three of them discussed a care plan. "The good news, Mrs. Turkle, you're a strong woman, and the doctor's prognosis is for a speedy recovery. You won't need me long," the nurse said. "Maybe a week or two."

"The good news is," Turkle quipped from the back of the room, "that she has a strong head. There was more damage to the kitchen counter." The nurse laughed. His mother raised an eyebrow.

Turkle hugged his mother, thanked the nurse, and left. As he rode the elevator, he flipped through the text messages from Bartley, Wackenslong, Merlot, and Heather. And then there were the voicemails to listen to.

"Heather Rivera? Probably wants some inside scoop on the Benny bombing. I'll let Darla handle that one." As he walked to the car, he began returning the other calls and texts.

• • •

An hour later, Turkle pulled his BMW into the gym parking lot. He finished up a text he started at the last traffic light and exited the car.

"Hey, Dr. Turkle. I like your Beamer. Wouldn't mind having one myself." Johnny V was leaving the gym with a few other team players. Turkle walked toward him.

"Hey, Johnny. Hope you guys had a good practice."

"Coach killed us today."

"Good for the Coach!" Turkle said. "And I have a bit of trivia for you. Did you know the car there," he pointed toward his BMW, "is not called a Beamer? It's called a Bimmer. Beamer refers to the BMW motorcycles which came before the cars. Thought you'd like to know that before you go out and buy one." They laughed and Turkle asked to speak with Johnny alone for a moment.

"Remember when we talked last week about the endorsements? Well someday soon, a Bimmer can be yours. Mark my words. Now go enjoy this beautiful day with your teammates."

Turkle watched them walk away, laughing and high-fiving one another. He missed those days. A lot.

"Pat."

Turkle turned and waved to two men walking toward him. "Glad you could make it," he said as he shook their hands. "You remember why you're here? I've billed this as a workshop. A session for the Coach and his assistants to learn all they need to know about the new *Pay for the Name* law. Ostensibly, you're not here representing your companies. You are serving as mentors for the process. Got it? My colleague will be in there as well."

"We understand and we both appreciate you reaching out to us. After all, we do have history," the taller and more athletic of the two said.

"Yes, we do, Ricky." He and Turkle held each other's gaze for a moment and smiled. "Let's go. They're waiting."

As Turkle led them toward the gym, he reminded them about Johnny Valentine's skills as well as Coach Gil's no-nonsense old-school view of the world. "Don't piss Coach off. Leave that to me if need be."

He opened the door to the gym and they saw Coach and his assistants in folding chairs in a circle courtside. Sitting with them was Darla Merlot. Turkle and his two guests entered the circle.

Following introductions, Turkle got to the heart of the session.

"I need to remind all of us," Turkle said, "this is just educational, like a workshop. These two representatives," he pointed to each in turn, "one a sports agent and one a representative of an apparel company, are here to make sure you understand how the new *Pay for the Name* law works. Vice President Merlot is here to make sure we stay within the letter of the new law. She'll keep us honest. The bottom line is that you'll soon be inundated with calls and visits from sports agents who want to represent CCC athletes like, say, Johnny V. You will have apparel companies approaching you to have your athletes represent their brand. In all instances, your program will benefit from money earned and, more importantly, exposure to the broader public. That helps your recruiting. That helps your team. That all helps CCC. A win-win-win situation."

As Turkle promised Coach, the meeting lasted 30 minutes. Questions were raised and answered. Everybody shook hands. Ricky and the apparel company representative left their business cards before they walked out the door.

"Coach, thank you for allowing us to talk to you and your assistants today." Turkle remained behind as the others departed the gym. "As I mentioned, this can be quite the windfall for everyone involved."

Coach Gil scratched his head. "Pat, I understand the law. What I still don't get is why they," he pointed toward the two men leaving the gym with Merlot, "are interested in us. We're small potatoes."

"Plain and simple, Coach, they want Johnny V. He's the face of the team. They know all about his stats from last year. They want to sign him now."

"OK. If that's correct, then won't other agents be on his doorstep? And wouldn't that potentially raise Johnny V's value? You know supply and demand." Coach may have been old-school but he understood basic economics. He could do math just like Turkle.

"True. But that's where you can help Johnny V and his mom. Johnny V will do anything for her, and she for him. I know she works a few jobs. They have a challenging life that can become more manageable. And soon. If they can sign Johnny V now, the pot will be sweetened for you and CCC as this will be the first signing in the state. That is big."

"Pat. I can't do that. The law doesn't take effect for another six months. Sounds like we are starting to tread beyond ethical limits. That's not how I work. And aren't you a little too close for comfort with both of those entities? Especially with the sports agent, Peroni. Doesn't pass the smell test."

Turkle paused. While he had hoped for a different response, he expected Coach's stance.

"Coach, the college needs this. Yes, this is your school, your program. You built it but the times have changed." Turkle paused. Not seeing the Coach softening, he continued. "And I would think you need this as well. I believe your contract will be coming up for review by the Board in the next few months."

"Don't go there, Pat."

"Not going anywhere, Coach. Just saying contracts have a way of being enhanced or ended."

"Are you threatening me?"

"All I'm saying is don't piss on someone when they have a gun to your head."

Coach stepped toe-to-toe, nose-to-nose, and glared at Turkle. "You won't be able to piss on anyone if my gun shoots you in the balls. Don't mess with my players! I'm telling you, Pat, you and your business associates are not welcome in my gymnasium."

With that, the coach walked to his office in the locker room.

When Turkle got to his car, his two friends from the meeting were waiting for him.

"Where's Darla?" asked Turkle.

The agent pointed toward the just-closing security gate. "Said she had a meeting."

The three of them began to debrief what had happened and what needed to happen going forward.

Across the road and just outside the security gate, a camera focused on the three men.

• • •

40

2:30 a.m. the next morning.

You're lucky it wasn't you. Next time it will be!

Cole opened his eyes and then shut them tight.

You can run. You cannot hide. How many times do I have to say that?

The voice and dry mouth.

Cole kicked the covers off, rolled out of bed, and stumbled to the bathroom to rinse his mouth. Scotch tasted better going down than it did three hours later. He looked in the mirror. Droopy eyelids half covering his sad eyes, and a face that had forgotten how to smile. "I can't keep this up," he said to himself. "Just leave me alone."

You ain't paying attention. Benny. Cliff. You make up the triumvirate. No wonder your anxiety level is high. Watch your back!

He checked his phone on the nightstand. One message from Heather saying she loved him and would see him in the morning at the hospital. She signed off with, "Get some sleep tonight."

Fat chance of that happening.

•   •   •

Heather approached Cole who sat in the Progressive Care Unit's waiting room. His elbows on his knees and his head in his hands.

"This might help." She handed him a cup. "How are you doing?

Cole nodded his appreciation, took the cup, and recoiled at the smell. "Better taste than aroma I hope?" He took a sip and shuddered.

"Have you been in to see him?"

"Stuck my head in but the nurses and doctors were having their morning meeting with him. He looked at me and stuck out his tongue."

"How he keeps that sense of humor amazes me. Maybe he can give us both a few lessons." Heather leaned in and hugged Cole.

Cole was about to speak when the Charge Nurse interrupted them.

"Professor DiJohn said he would be glad to see you now. Actually," she leaned into Cole and Heather, "he told me to say he couldn't wait to see her. You, he wasn't too sure about." Heather and the nurse laughed. Cole shook his head as they got up and walked into the room.

"I understand you're the midnight comic. Are you thinking of quitting the band to do stand-up?" Cole asked as he and Heather took a seat on the padded bench under the window.

Benny held up his gauzed-wrapped left hand. "Well, with this mitt I don't think I'll be able to play any recognizable guitar chords. But, hey, it's not as bad as you look, Cole. Have you been sleeping in your car, son? You look terrible."

"So glad I came to see him," Cole said as he turned to Heather. She fought back a laugh.

"The good news," Benny said with a darker tone looking at the wrapping on his hand, "is that I still have a hand. However, according to the doctor, the metal bomb fragments caused nerve damage. The extent is not known yet. It looks like it could be months before I can use it for anything, let alone a bass guitar." Benny adjusted his butt in the bed. "This sucks. A freaking bomb on my porch. This does scare me." Cole and Heather sat quietly. This was not the Benny they knew and loved.

"I don't understand this. Is all this for union activity or to get Cole in their administrative cabinet? This doesn't make sense." Heather said.

"Like I've said," Benny hit the bed control button to lift his head, "this has nothing to do with the union any longer. I'm sure of that. And Cole, I love you brother, but not everything is about you, or Heather, or even me. Something else is at work here."

"Any ideas as to who would do this?" Heather asked pointing at his hand. "I mean, this is no prank. This is deadly. Did you hear I got word of the incident when I was on the air?"

"*Assault.* Not an *incident.*" Benny smiled at the turn of words remembering what Spano told the Board.

"Yes, the assault. And Senator Wackenslong was my guest at the time."

"Sorry, you had to endure Senator Wack-his-slong. And, yes, I have a few suspects that rise to the top of the list."

"I'm not sure if this connects to your situation or not," Heather added, "but I got a phone call after the episode with Wackenslong. The caller was cryptic. Would not identify herself. Said she had information about financial irregularities at CCC. Hung up before she gave more information."

"Sounding more and more like we have a Deep Throat." Benny wiggled to get comfortable in the bed. "Any idea who the caller was?"

"No. But she was odd. Keep saying something about elephants and string beans."

Cole and Benny looked at each other. "Eulonia!"

"Eulonia?" Heather asked.

"Yeah, one of our professors. Eccentric and smart. She has found some information about the enrollment numbers," Cole said. "She and I have been sharing information we both have uncovered about the no-shows, the financial aid, and the off-shore account."

"Off-shore account?" Heather asked.

"I first got a hint of that from a student. Benny, remember when I got that call the day we bailed Cliff out?" Benny nodded his head. "A student for God's sake!" Cole continued. "And Cliff shared the same information. Anyway, Eulonia and are trying to see how these pieces fit together?"

"Benny, do you think Turkle had a part in the package landing on your porch?" Heather asked.

"He's in the top three."

"Bartley?"

"He's too stupid to think of this—at least not on his own. You know that guy is just one brain cell smarter than Dick Ed. No, not him. I'd put the Senator in the top three. But my number one suspect is my hog-tied friend from *The Silver Fox* incident."

"You mean *assault*." Cole raised an eyebrow. "What makes you suspect him?"

"He's another, as Panagrossa and your aunt would say, *mamaluke*. A *stunad!* Surprised he didn't blow himself up. The detective investigating the case said it was the worst homemade bomb he'd seen in his 20 years on the force. While this isn't good, I was lucky." He held up his taped fist. "My guess is either Turkle or his controller, the Senator, forced Spano to do it."

"What's the sheriff's office say?" Heather poured Benny a cup of water.

"They're still gathering and analyzing fingerprints and video camera surveillance from the neighbors' homes and my doorbell video cam. One cop asked me if I thought it was a jilted lover. I looked at him, winked, and asked, 'What do you think, handsome?'"

"Yeah, you need to do comedy for sure," Cole said as he stood. "I don't know how you do it, Benny. You're constantly battered. Yet, you fight on each day."

Benny was about to give another off-the-cuff cutesy remark, but he couldn't. He was spent. "What are my options?"

"Look the other way. Fly under the radar. Live your life but avoid them," Cole said.

Benny shook his head. "*Them*," he said, "are all around. I tried the under-the-radar method for a while. You know what I discovered? As I constantly avoided them, I was avoiding myself. How the hell can I live with myself knowing others are going through the same or worse?" He paused and moved his bandaged hand.

"The Jamaicans have a saying, 'One-one Koko full basket'—'Take it one day by one day.' Look at the LGBTQAI+ community. They're fighting. And at times, it's deadly. How can I *not* say something? Or do something? Cole, you keep flying under the radar you're going to end up hitting a mountain with such force it will kill you. It not only avoids the problem it creates more problems for you and the people around you. I'd rather not create collateral damage. Unless it's to the bastards who deserve it!" Benny pursed his lips.

Cole looked at himself in the mirror over the hospital room's sink.

"Can we do anything for you, Benny?" Heather asked.

"Well, I could use a ride home when they release me. Should be the day after tomorrow. A little tough to drive with this useless hand."

"I'll pick you up."

They turned toward the door where Cliff stood stooped-shouldered, hands thrust into his pockets. He looked worse than Cole.

"Cliff! Come in here and talk to me. About time someone helped me get rid of these two."

Cliff shuffled in and nodded to Heather and Cole. Benny made a slight move of his head toward the door for their benefit. He wanted to talk with Cliff.

"Heather and I are going to leave you two ocean kayakers to talk about your next paddle. Maybe someday you'll take up a real watersport like surfing."

Cliff did not lift his gaze from the floor as Heather and Cole left the room.

"How you doing, Benny? Why did this happen to you? I'm next aren't I, Benny? They're going to kill me. I know it. And this," he pointed to Benny's hand, "This…this…what are we in a mob film? I don't know if I can go on." Cliff clasped his hands together rubbing his thumbs back and forth.

Benny let Cliff dump his emotions. He didn't interrupt. Finally, Cliff took a breath.

"Cliff, I wish I had answers. More than anyone I need answers. And, like you, I'm concerned."

"Concerned? Benny this is beyond being concerned. This is now life and death."

"Like you, I'm disturbed," Benny continued. "The sheriff's office is on it. I think this turn of events will help with my case. I'm now the victim of an assault—a real assault. It'll work out, Cliff. We'll be on the water in no time. Trust me."

"I'm not like you. I don't like this. It's too much." Cliff turned and walked toward the door, rubbing the side of his head.

"Cliff, wait a minute. Look at me."

Cliff turned, pushed his glasses up his nose, and raised his head toward his mentor.

"I want you to think of kayaking in the ocean. Have you ever flipped your kayak when coming into shore? You know, a wave gets you and tosses you?"

"Yeah, sure. Plenty of times."

"Then why do you ride the waves knowing you're going to more than likely flip? Why not just roll out of the kayak, swim in, and let the kayak float and flip to shore? It could be safer."

"But not near as much fun," Cliff said with a tentative smile.

"Exactly. There's the adrenaline rush you get when you are on the crest and riding in. But to ride the crest, you have to find the right wave. At times you get tossed. It comes with the sport. And it comes with life. Right now, I'm looking for the right wave. I'll find it. You will too. I have confidence in you."

Cliff stood silent for a moment. He removed his glasses and rubbed the bridge of his nose. "Benny, I wish I were more like you. I really do." He turned and walked to the door.

Benny yelled out, "I'll see you the day after tomorrow. You're my ride to the next wave!"

Cliff nodded, waved his hand over his head as he shuffled to the door, and disappeared down the hospital hallway.

• • •

As they approached the lobby exit the automatic doors swung open. Sirens blared as first responders made their way to the Emergency Department with the latest casualties from the streets. Heather and Cole handed their tickets to the valets and sat on a curbside bench.

"Cole, too many things don't add up. Or maybe I should say, too many things are beginning to add up. This is the stuff of an Evanovich novel. The only thing we're missing is a murder."

"And we almost had that," Cole said. "We almost had that." He let go of a long exhale. Heather held his hand.

The valets pulled their cars up. Heather hugged Cole. "We'll figure it out. You take some time to just be still in your mind."

Cole looked at the woman he loved and thought, "She has no idea. Easier said than done."

Cole drove toward his condo thinking a bike ride might help him catch his breath. Heather made her way to Nico's Diner. Suzy McDonald had called and asked to meet with her. Heather wasn't sure why.

• • •

41

"Excuse me, Professor Polonia?" Suzy stood at the opened office door. "Do you have a moment?"

Eulonia looked up from the pile of essays in front of her. "Yes, Ms. McDonald, what can I do for you?"

"Well, nothing. I, well, I have something for you if I may come in?"

Eulonia pointed to the chair in front of the desk, placed her red pen on the stack of papers, and removed her reading glasses. A small smile creased her lips. "It's not often I get something other than a request for a homework extension."

Suzy reached into her backpack and pulled out an envelope. "Professor, one of my hobbies is photography. I'm just learning. And all I have is my phone for photos. Anyway, there's something you say every so often in class about elephants and string beans."

Eulonia smiled and nodded.

"Well, when my daughter and I were at the zoo the other day I thought of you when I saw this." She handed Eulonia a close-up shot of an elephant.

"Thank you, Ms. McDonald. I do appreciate this. I'm going to frame and hang it in this office. Right over there." She pointed to a spot above her diplomas. "It will add character to the wall."

Suzy smiled, placed her backpack over her shoulder, and headed for the door. She turned, smiled, and said, "I'll see what I can do about finding string beans."

Eulonia gave a small sincere laugh and asked, "Do you have a minute? I have a photography question."

"Sure. But I'm not much of a photographer," Suzy said with her usual self-deprecation.

"Better than me, that's for sure. I'm doing a little field research and wonder if you can help me. Maybe take a few photos for me?"

"OK. Where are you doing the research?"

"In the city cemetery."

• • •

Suzy arrived at Nico's first and was relieved when the booth in the back was unoccupied. She felt like all eyes were watching her. Walking to the booth, Suzy wrapped both arms around her torso tight as if the squeeze would make her invisible to any of the customers.

"Just a coffee for me. I'm waiting on a friend." Suzy pushed the menus the server left to the end of the table. No appetite today.

The server delivered the coffee.

Who is going to believe that you know what you say you know?

Her stomach churned and her head ached.

What about Shauna and Aintin? Ever think of them?

Heather walked in and Suzy tentatively raised her arm, almost like a student who wants to get the professor's attention but is fearful of what to do if she does get called.

That woman has confidence because she has it together.

"Hi, Suzy. Thanks for getting a table." Heather smiled and glided her frame into the booth as the waitress appeared. "I'll have the same," she said pointing to Suzy's coffee cup.

"I'm sorry to bother you, Ms. Rivera. But I wasn't sure who to call or if I should even call anyone."

"No, I'm glad you did. And remember, it's Heather, and I'm glad you kept my card and reached out. Are you OK?"

Suzy scanned the room as if expecting an unwelcome visitor. She pawed at her neck. Her discomfort was palpable so Heather attempted to melt the tension and reached into her backpack as the waitress delivered a cup of coffee.

"Here, this is for you." Heather slid a hand-sized single-shot camera across the table. "You still interested in photography?"

"Yes, I am. I use this from time to time," she said picking up her phone, "Saving my tip money to buy a real camera."

"Well, save your tip money for Shauna. Here's your camera. At least a beginner's version."

"Ma'am? I can't take this. It's nice of you but I can't." She moved the camera back toward Heather who held up her hands.

"Listen, I have ulterior motives," she said with a wink and a grin. "See this camera is an old one from the studio. No one uses it. My producer found it buried in the back of a desk drawer." Heather held up a slip of paper. "The day you were in the studio with Johnny V and Kerwin, I wrote this note to myself." She held it up: *Camera for Suzy!*

"You had mentioned your interest in photography. I want you to practice with it. Take photos of what catches your attention. In the community, around campus, and at home. Any place. All I ask is that you share a few with me so I can show them to the station manager. I'd like to see about getting you a part-time job with us."

Like the day in Professor Fitzgerald's office, Suzy wondered how she could be so fortunate to meet Heather.

Wow. You are blessed. You don't meet many people like this, Suzy.

Suzy smiled and thought how nice it was to have an encouraging word from her inner critic. And she totally agreed.

"Thank you, Heather." She held the camera as if it were a fine piece of art, carefully examining it, and then placing it in her backpack. "Ironic," she thought, "just an hour ago, one of my professors asked me to help her with some photographs. Hmm."

"You know," Heather said, "I remember that you like to run. We both have our running shoes on, how about we get fresh air and go for a jog in the park?"

"Oh, no. No. This is better. In the back."

Heather sat back and let Suzy breathe. She motioned to the server for a refill. "Suzy, I also remember how you spoke of Shauna when we first met. She's lucky to have such a loving mother and aunt."

"I do my best. It's hard. Most people don't understand."

"I do. I grew up with a single mom. Dad left us when I was two years old. Mom worked two jobs and expected me to be on board to help her. That consisted of me always checking in with her as soon as I got home from school, doing my homework immediately, and starting dinner. Mom and I ate together, talked, and listened. And she encouraged me to follow my dreams. She taught me that bullies will take advantage of anyone they believe is weak." She took a sip of coffee and let the words sink in for Suzy. "While we're all vulnerable at some level, that's not a weakness. When I see the bullies, something goes off in my head. I have to take them down. Of course, I can't use my fists, so I use my radio platform to serve the community. I don't want to hear BS. I want the unvarnished truth. And then I hope for a real conversation."

Suzy exhaled and moved closer to the table. "I wish I had your courage. I do my best for Shauna. But at times I feel outnumbered."

"When you were on my show, I remember you mentioning one of your counselors. Ms. Robertson, I think. Have you spoken to her?"

"Well, funny you mention that. I have an appointment with her later this afternoon." Suzy tugged on her ear and took a sip of coffee.

"Suzy, are you OK? I mean, are you safe? You sounded troubled when you called."

Suzy had her hands clasped on the table behind her cup. Her elbows close to her sides. She looked from left and right and then leaned forward toward Heather.

"I assume you know what happened to Professor DiJohn. The bombing and all."

"Dr. Fitzgerald and I just came from visiting him at the hospital. Looks like he'll be released from the hospital in a day or two and have a full recovery, though that will take some time. I shudder when I think of what could've happened."

"I'm glad the professor is OK."

Heather took another slow sip.

"Ms., ah, Heather. I think I know who did that to Dr. DiJohn. The bombing, I mean." Suzy looked around the diner.

"Suzy, would you rather we go someplace else? I could come to your home or we could go for a walk and talk."

"No. Too much of a chance he'd see us."

"He?"

"The bomber. I have a thought about who planted that bomb on Professor DiJohn's front porch."

"Excuse me? How, Suzy, do you know that?"

"I got a phone message and a request the day of the bombing. I can't prove it but I'm pretty sure."

• • •

Heather knew Cole needed time away from all of this drama with Benny and with the college administration, but she didn't know where else to turn. She sat in her car and had second thoughts about disturbing him. Should she go to the police about Suzy's revelation? Probably not, this would be considered hearsay and it would put Suzy in the public eye. The threat was too great. She turned off the car, walked to Cole's front door, and knocked. Cole answered the door leaning on crutches.

"What on God's green earth happened to you?" Heather said as Cole hobbled to the side so she could enter.

"A bike ride." Cole shook his head in disgust.

"I just left you a few hours ago. What kind of bike riding did you do? Cliff diving?"

Cole shook his head part in disbelief and part in irritation with himself. He pointed to the sofa where they could sit.

"I went for a bike ride to clear my head. Instead of clearing it, I almost busted it."

"Did you break your leg?" She kissed him. "And where's your aunt?"

"No. Nothing serious. Twisted my ankle, banged my knee, and bruised my ego." He leaned back and attempted to stretch his leg. "My aunt left to go get some cannoli ingredients." He grunted as he shifted position looking for a comfortable one.

"Quite the band you have now. One has an injured hand, the other can't stand behind the microphone." Heather's attempt to lighten the mood wasn't working.

"I hit a curb while riding. Wasn't paying attention. I was," he stopped and took a breath, "preoccupied with it."

"It? Your head?"

"No. The voice *in* my head. It kept badgering me. Wouldn't shut up." Cole's eyes were moist. "I can't concentrate. I feel like each day another piece of me breaks off and drifts away."

"Cole, I know you're suffering. Is there anything positive the voice whispers to you? I know my voice—or you can call it my instinct—urges me on at times. Sometimes it's the only cheerleader I have."

"Cheerleader? Are you kidding me? My voice is a relentless self-appointed inner critic. The same tape keeps playing over and over in my head. It hurts." He paused and exhaled. "It hurts."

"Maybe it's time to let go; be still. We're all broken. And if we embrace that we know the light will come in—if we let it."

"Let go of what?" Cole slammed the end of one crutch into the floor. "Don't you think I would if I could? It's not that easy. I don't like this. And I can tell you, I'm not going to figure this out in a sweet four-and-one-half-minute segment like on your show." His eyes were wide, and his voice grew louder, as he struggled to his feet. "If I knew what the hell to let go of, don't you think I would? Do you think I like this? I hate it. And what was that you said, 'be still'? That's the worst thing I can do. When I'm still the voice steps in and clobbers me. Hell, today I was moving and it almost killed me."

He hobbled to the kitchen and pulled the bottle of Scotch out of the cabinet. He placed it on the counter, sat on a stool, and looked at Heather as she approached.

"Cole, I don't know what you're going through. You're right about that. But what I do know is that I'm lost, freaking lost, on what to do or say to you anymore." Her voice, while not a yell, was increasing in volume. "No matter what I say, you push it away. Both Aunt Phil and I urged you to see a therapist."

"Shit on that. It won't help!"

"Oh, and that is helping," Heather said pointing at the bottle of Scotch. "You keep avoiding but from what I can see the only thing you're sidestepping is coming to grips with that demon of a voice you talk about." She leaned in, hugged his neck, and placed the bottle back in the cabinet. Big Betsy walked by and rubbed her leg on Cole's.

Heather poured Cole a glass of water.

"Cole, did you ever read the Rumi piece in which he talks of the visitors we receive every day?"

"The one that mentions darkness, shame, and malice?"

"And," Heather continued, "he tells us to 'welcome them' and 'be grateful whatever comes because each has been sent as a guide from beyond.'"

Cole lowered his head.

"You told me that you wanted to bring Suzy to a campus counselor because you saw physical bruises on her body.

Cole, just because you can't see your bruises doesn't mean they don't exist."

She got up and hugged him again. "You need a therapist. I don't know what else to do or say. Do it for you. Do it for me. Do it for us."

She squeezed his hand and left.

• • •

42

When Bartley entered the office waiting area, he saw Turkle texting on his phone.

"What's this meeting about? Seems as though we now have a standing Saturday meeting with the Senator." Bartley stood over his colleague.

"DiJohn. The bomb. Rivera." Turkle didn't look up from his phone as his thumbs pecked at the screen.

"Jesus." Bartley looked to the ceiling and pulled his thin pale fingers over his chin.

The door from the inside office opened. Wackenslong waved the two to enter. "We're glad you're here."

"We?" Bartley muttered to Turkle. "Again, it's *we*?"

"Coffee is on the credenza if you wish. It's fresh." Wackenslong closed the office door behind them. "As I said, we're glad you two could make it this morning."

Turkle and Bartley scrunched up their noses at the familiar smell. At the end of the table, with a scowl on his face, sat Ned Spano. The president and director took seats on either side of the table. The Senator sat at the end opposite Spano.

"Well, gentlemen, it looks like CCC keeps making headlines. I'm guessing you heard Heather Rivera ambush me on her two-bit radio show."

"That was incredibly unfortunate. Very, very nasty on her part. Not a nice person at all. Despicably bad." Bartley fumbled to find his footing in what he saw as enveloping moral and legal quicksand. He attempted to steady his hands as he raised the coffee cup to his lips.

"Yes, it was unfortunate." Wackenslong sounded measured, almost matter-of-fact. "Especially when she announced the news of the bombing. Gentlemen," he looked in turn at Bartley and Turkle, "was that as much of a surprise for you as it was for me?"

"Senator, I didn't know of it," Bartley sputtered. "Darla had met with the professors. She, Pat told me, was keeping incredible pressure on them." He looked at Turkle who nodded. Bartley continued, "We thought our plan was progressing. Bombing wasn't on the table. Not in our wildest thoughts. Not sure who ordered that."

"My thoughts exactly," said Wackenslong with no attempt to disguise his sarcasm. "Who does such an amazingly, bizarrely, unthinkable act? Incredible. Hugely incredible."

Bartley looked back and forth from Turkle to Wackenslong, eyes wide. A little coffee spilled from his cup.

"Mr. Spano," Wackenslong looked the length of the table at the slouching co-conspirator. "Tell us what you know about the bombing. And please sit up straight when you talk. You don't want to appear rude. That might piss someone off."

Spano sat up and extended his arms in front of him, fingers tapping the table. "I done it."

"Huh? You did what?" asked a stammering Bartley.

"I done it. I put the package on that swishy-ass professor's porch."

"And who told you to do that?" Turkle asked.

"No one. Well, you did," Spano said pointing at Turkle.

Turkle squinted. "What are you talking about?"

"Remember that night you told me I had to make a speech to those big shots in the room at the college? I said I didn't wanna. You grabbed me by the collar and said we all have to be flexible." Spano looked at the Senator. "And that's what I did. I was flexible like he said. I thought it all up myself. Listen, sometimes a person has to take things into his own hands."

"What the hell? No one asked you to think. We don't kill people! Incredibly extraordinarily dumb on your part." Bartley wiped his face with a napkin. "Incredibly dumb."

"Don't call me *dumb*. I'm doing your dirty work. I'm the one who could get arrested. You sit back in your fancy office, safe. We're partners, so treat me like one. Give me the respect I deserve. I've talked to those fancy-assed people at the meeting. I planted the drugs. I was flexible and planted the bomb. I thought you'd be happy." Looking at Wackenslong, he said, "You told me to wait for instructions. Well, he gave me the instructions."

"You planted the drugs in the wrong professor's office. You almost killed another professor with a terrorist-type action. And you thought we'd be happy?" Turkle's blue eyes blazed as he looked at the hoodlum.

"Gentlemen," Wackenslong stood and walked to the other end of the table, "I think this will all work out well for everyone." Spano's body language shifted from aggressive to apprehensive. "Mr. Spano, we appreciate your initiative and your ambition."

Wackenslong leaned in from behind Spano and spoke into his ear. "Here's what you're going to do, *partner*. You're going to go home and stay there until I or one of my associates calls you. Do not call anyone. Do not text anyone. Go home and take the day off. You deserve it. Any questions?"

Spano felt Wackenslong's breath on his cheek. "No, sir."

"Good. Now you can go. And remember partner. You didn't see us today. Understand?"

Spano nodded again, pushed back his chair, and walked out of the room glad he hadn't received another head pounding.

Wackenslong walked to his closet, pulled out a can of air freshener, and spritzed it toward the ceiling fan.

"This is very, very bad." Bartley looked at Wackenslong and Turkle for some kind of assurance. A strategy. Something.

"It is and it isn't. But I have a plan, Mr. President." Wackenslong retook his seat. "When numbnuts decided to place that package on the doorstep, he didn't consider that he might be caught on at least one surveillance camera from a neighbor's home. My contacts in the sheriff's office, though, tell me there wasn't one camera."

Bartley looked like he would cry. Turkle stiffened his lip.

"There were *four*. From different angles. They all caught our 'partner' in the act."

"Incredibly unbelievably good luck. Right?" Bartley was grasping for something positive.

"Yes, incredibly so," Wackenslong said.

"The sheriff's office has already been in touch with Spano's probation officer. He's been serving a two-year probation for a previous drug conviction. I don't think we'll see or hear from him for quite some time."

"What happens when he inevitably tells the judge and probation officer about us? That will look exceedingly bad, awfully bad for us."

"No one will believe him," Turkle said. "I reported the pass card he used to get in and plant the drugs as stolen one hour before he entered the professor's office. That covers us there. The cameras will do the work for the bomb. We can show he was one of many students we gave a chance to with financial aid, but he chose not to take advantage of that opportunity. He's a low-life."

"And Darla has both DiJohn and Fitzgerald dangling with uncertainty," the Senator said. "She has scared them with potential legal consequences. They are not watching the other hand as we get ready for the next steps. They will be focused on themselves."

"Incredibly extraordinary. Never expected to be saved by front door cameras. Who would have thought?"

"In this day and age, none of us can expect privacy when we're in a public space. But Spano is a fuse short of a live bomb. Idiot set himself up." With that Wackenslong stood up, ended the meeting and the three departed the building.

Across the street, someone stood behind a tree.

Click! Click! Click!

As Wackenslong had said, no one could expect privacy in a public space.

• • •

43

The car rolled up to the curb in front of a tidy but age-worn clapboard house. Like the others in the neighborhood, it had a shotgun floor plan. Simple and functional. It sat on the precarious edge of urban progress. Two blocks south, flippers purchased similar structures, gutted and then sold them to the young professionals who had become the faces of gentrification. A few boutiques and cafés had opened their doors to bring a modern vibe to the area.

To the north a few blocks, houses begged for a coat of paint. Some with boarded-up windows had signs warning NO TRESPASSING. Crime rates, while not out of control, gave residents pause once the sun set behind the downtown skyscrapers.

"That's where Johnny V got his start." Turkle pointed to an asphalt basketball court on the corner. The rusted backboards at either end sported bent hoops without nets. The court with its cracks and weeds looked more like an obstacle course.

"Similar story for so many other athletes who've risen from these circumstances," Peroni said. "That's why it's easy to get them on board. And his backstory will resonate with the public. Which helps us."

"Johnny V knows he's got talent. He also worships his mother. She works two jobs and has been the moral compass for him since his father died about fifteen years ago. Even though Johnny can sign a contract, we need to show respect as well."

Peroni nodded in agreement.

"And he holds Coach Gil in high esteem. Like a second father. Ricky, follow my lead in there," Turkle said as he opened his door. "We can't officially sign him for six months, but let's see what we can do to have them commit now."

They exited the car and walked up the creaking steps. Before they could knock, Johnny V opened the door.

"I was beginning to think you changed your mind once you saw the neighborhood." With a smile, he stepped to the side. "Come on in. Mom made some iced tea and chocolate chip cookies for you." Turkle and his associate followed Johnny to the first room on the left. Mrs. Valentine stood to greet them.

"Welcome to our home. Thank you for taking an interest in my Johnny."

"Mrs. Valentine, thank you for raising such a gentleman. He brightens a room anytime he enters. And when that room is a basketball court, well, he brings the house down as they say."

Turkle tenderly shook her hand and slightly bowed from the waist. She smiled with pride. Turkle saw his mother in her eyes. A single mother proud of an only son.

"Allow me to introduce you to Ricky Peroni, the owner of PTM, Peroni Talent Management."

"My pleasure to meet you, Mrs. Valentine. Thank you for your time."

She smiled, nodded, and pointed to the sofa, two mismatched chairs, and the snacks on a small scratched, but polished, wooden dropleaf coffee table. "Make yourselves comfortable and please enjoy the refreshments."

"Mrs. Valentine," Peroni began, "as you probably know, your governor signed a law that allows student-athletes like Johnny to earn money while they play ball at the college." He paused and nibbled on a cookie.

"I know a little bit about it. I've done some reading. You know, Johnny does earn money. He works part-time bagging groceries."

"That's great. I think that work ethic has gone a long way to help Johnny become the young man he is. If I may, what do you earn in a week?" He directed the question to Johnny.

"Oh, minimum wage plus some tips. Not a lot, but not bad money."

"Well, you might be doing better than I thought," Peroni said without a hint of the sarcasm in his thoughts. "You see, I am talking about thousands of dollars—and all you have to do is keep playing basketball at the highest level you can. Thousands. Of. Dollars. For doing what you do best."

"How?" Mrs. Valentine sounded skeptical.

"In the past," Peroni continued, "Colleges—even ones in smaller conferences like CCC—would get money from athletic clothing companies if the teams bought their uniforms or laced up their sneakers. The kids did the work on the court, and the school got all the money. For extra money, players had to work on the weekends or at night. Just like Johnny does."

"But the school gives him free tuition and pays for his books. I've always thought that was a great deal for Johnny, for us. I could never afford to pay even as low as the prices are for this college."

"And he can continue to get that free schooling and make thousands of dollars on top of it. It's a winning situation for everyone."

"What does Coach Gil think about this?" She turned to her son.

"Mom, Coach told the team about the new law. He said he was still learning about it from Dr. Turkle." He nodded toward the director.

"This is new for everyone," Turkle interjected. "The coach is learning. I'm learning. Johnny and you are learning. And we're fortunate to have Mr. Peroni come to town and help us learn some more."

"You see, ma'am," the agent sat on the edge of his chair and placed his iced tea on the table coaster, "not many students will have this opportunity. Only the true stars." Again, he nodded toward Johnny. "And, more than likely, only in a few sports like football and basketball. At least to start. At a school like CCC, Johnny may well be the only athlete on the team to be offered the opportunity to endorse a product line.

This opportunity isn't for everyone." He pulled an envelope from his inner coat pocket. "I would like to sign Johnny, to an exclusive contract to represent him. I brought a copy of the contract so you can see it and ask questions before Johnny signs it."

"A contract. Sounds legal. Do we have to do it right now? Is there a rush?"

"Yes and no. But here's something to think about. Let's say you take a few weeks to consider the offer and during that time, Johnny injures himself and can't play. It happens." Peroni looked at Turkle. "I've known athletes in basketball to injure themselves in a game and never play again. No play. No pay. If he's under contract, though, well, there's pay at least for a little while. Kind of like an insurance policy. And I'm prepared to offer Johnny a signing bonus. My company will give him ten thousand dollars just for signing the contract. That's before we start getting any endorsements. All we need is his signature."

Mrs. Valentine sat back in her chair. "Wow. We could use the money. I know we should jump at this. I still wish the coach were here with you two today."

"Mrs. Valentine, I understand. Coach Gil has my highest respect." Peroni sipped his iced tea. "His first concern is always the well-being of his players. All I can say is that this is complicated."

He turned and looked Johnny in the eye. "You are a gift to the CCC basketball program. These endorsements are not for every player. They're for the star players like you.

And consider this. While you have a social media presence, once you have an endorsement, your following will increase. That gives you more name recognition beyond CCC. And that catches the attention of pro scouts."

"Pro scouts? Like the NBA?" Johnny asked.

"Johnny, you don't yet understand just how good you are!" Peroni leaned in. "There are people out there jealous of your success last year and what, I'm sure, your team will accomplish this year. Coach has a lot on his mind. He doesn't need to be distracted by this. I can tell you he wants this type of agreement as much as we do."

Johnny looked at his mother who looked at the two visitors in her living room.

"May we have a few days to consider this?"

"Well, I think that—" the agent began his rebuttal when Turkle interrupted.

"That'll be fine. This is a big decision. We want you and Johnny totally on board and comfortable. Call me if you have any questions." He handed her his college business card. "We're here for you." Then turning to Peroni, "Ricky, we've taken up enough of their valuable time."

"We do appreciate your time," Peroni said as he folded and slid the contract back into his coat pocket. "Johnny, I hope we get the opportunity to work together."

With that Turkle and the agent stood, shook hands, and Mrs. Valentine showed them to the door.

"Thank you, again," she said, "for taking an interest in my son. I'm grateful. There's a lot to digest here."

She closed the door and walked to her son and hugged him. Then holding him at arms' length she smiled. "Your father would have been so proud of you. I am. I know it hasn't always been easy for you. You continue to be my rock." A happy tear fell from her eye and she hugged him again. "Now," she said regaining her composure, "we have homework to do. In addition to Coach Gil, who else can help us understand all of this?"

Johnny snapped his fingers. "Professor Fitzgerald. I bet he could help, and I have his office phone number from when I was in his class. Let me see if he's in."

He punched in Cole's CCC number, got a voicemail greeting, and left a message.

"Mom, how about we celebrate? I'll even buy the pizza tonight!"

"And we'll toast the star of the CCC basketball team!"

Outside, still curbside with the car idling, Turkle and Peroni were debriefing.

"Do you think she'll agree and let Johnny sign?"

"Not sure. She's a strong mama bear. You gave her a few days. I say, wait four or five days. And then we'll call her if we don't hear. Don't want her to feel like we're strong-arming her. We have to be delicate with this. Let me get you to the airport, Ricky. I appreciate you coming to town. We get this contract signed and that opens the door for the other colleges we've contacted."

"Which then gets more commitments for the clothing and shoe company."

"Exactly. We need to focus on the snowball effect. The athletes win, the schools win, and we win," Cole said. "When that law officially goes into effect, we'll be far ahead of the other schools. And more money for us. Glad you are along for the ride. We couldn't make that money when I was playing. We'll make up for it now."

"Anything for The Young Turk!"

From across the street, the men couldn't hear the sound of the camera shutter.

● ● ●

44

He carried his kayak to the water's edge, walked it in past the first breaker, slid into the seat, and began paddling toward the horizon. A dolphin pod appeared a few feet to the right. Off to the left, a lonely shrimp trawler dragged its net for the day's catch. A paddle boarder skimmed the water. In twenty minutes the sunrise would splash colors across the water and bounce off the stratus clouds. This was the best time of the day. Peace. Solitude. No one judging him.

Today, he paddled out beyond the first small breaker, about twenty or thirty yards offshore with the outgoing tide. He then placed the paddle across his lap, opened the cover to the storage compartment in the bow of the kayak, and pulled out a zip-lock baggie. Inside was an envelope addressed to "Teagan Cross, Channel 13." He opened and read the words one more time.

"It's sunrise on the water. I have always found peace at this hour and on this water. No one is here to question my actions or motives. No one to cast aspersions. I can always be myself. This has been where I draw my energy to face the day. It has helped me

dodge the pettiness and meanness of Central City College. These early morning paddles used to get me through the day. Recently, they haven't been enough to sustain me. I no longer have the energy to keep fighting. I'm beyond tired. I'm done. I've lost the will to paddle.

"I'm thankful for so many people who have been my support. Too many to name all. Professor Benny DiJohn, thank you. You have always been there for me, even when you didn't understand what I felt or needed. You did your best to be a shoulder. I am sorry for all you face, mostly alone, from the college administration. You were always my crutch. Unfortunately, I feel I was your weight. I love you like family.

"Professor Polonia. Thank you. You understood my fears better than anyone on campus. You pushed me further than I would have gone on my own. I wish I had your strength.

"Dr. Turkle, I've blamed you often. But now I forgive you. You can't help yourself. I feel sorry for you. Maybe you don't have friends like I have in Benny and Cole. Or anyone who can guide you. Sadly, though, your actions have ruined many lives. I wish I'd been stronger to prevent it or thwart you. I feel though, in short order, you'll be held accountable. Thank God.

"My beautiful wife, Debbie, and precious daughter, Marie. I'm sorry I have been a disappointment. I love you. And I'm sorry for the grief my lack of strength has brought upon you.

"Every sunrise brings with it new opportunities. New chances for better choices. Chances to write a better next chapter. My choice today, though, is to close my book."

Professor Cliff Singer.

He folded the letter back into the envelope, zipped it inside the baggie, and then placed it inside the compartment with its corner sticking out from the cover.

He picked up the paddle and continued his southerly route. The breeze ruffled his rash guard shirt as he paddled by the bungalows and condos. Off the bow, a dolphin broke the water's surface. As the nature preserve came into view, the kayak slowed, the water lapping against the sides. Cliff looked at the trees as he drifted farther south. Tears filled his eyes.

Then, the kayak rocked forcefully from side to side.

• • •

Later that morning.

The bumper sticker always brought a smile to Cole's heart. "Make Love Not War." Psychedelic colors surrounded a yellow sunflower. The old hippie in Benny had never died. It probably kept him moving forward through all the chaos around him.

Cole pulled the coffee caddie and bag of bagels from the passenger seat and went around to the back patio where he knew Benny would be sitting. Surrounded by oak trees and palms, the deck provided shade and serenity. Benny often used the space for his daily meditation practice.

"'Bout time you got here. I've already had to drink two cups of my rot-gut coffee."

"Good things are worth the wait." Cole put the bag on the table and handed Benny a cup of coffee from Nico's. They toasted one another.

"Ah, a slice of heaven. I appreciate you bringing it."

"How was your first night back in the Benny castle? Navigating OK with the bandaged paw?"

"Did fine. A little clumsy in the bathroom if you know what I mean, but otherwise going as expected. Cliff got me settled in after he dropped me off. He even made a run to the grocery store for me. And I had a surprise visitor." He nodded his head toward the inside of the house. "My 83-year-old aunt showed up on the front porch after Cliff left. Said she was here to take care of 'Little Benjamin' and there was nothing I could do about it. She's sleeping in the guest bedroom."

"Maybe your aunt and mine ought to start a homecare business. And *Little Benjamin*?" Cole batted his eyes just like Benny often did to tease him.

"Don't start with me, Dr. Fitz."

"I'm thinking we should rename the band *Little Benjamin and the Hog Ties*," Cole said.

"Bite me!" Benny bit into a bagel.

"On a more serious note. Cliff. How's he doing?"

"I'm worried. He's crawled into a hole, and I fear he's going to bury himself." Benny put his cup on the table and adjusted part of the bandage on his hand. "He thinks someone will kill him."

Cole's phone rang. "It's Heather," he said, "Let me get this."

"Hey, Hon. What's... Ah, I'm at Benny's; just got here. Why? Oh. OK." He ended the call.

"Heather said to turn on the TV. Channel 13. Something we need to see."

Benny led them through the kitchen to the living room. Cole pointed to a backpack and duffle bag on the couch. "Guest luggage? Your 83-year-old Aunt travels like a Millennial."

"She prides herself on staying and looking young," Benny said as he clicked the remote. Up popped Teagan Cross doing a live remote from the beach.

"Isn't that where you usually drop in your kayak?"

"It is."

"And once again, breaking news." Cross faced the camera as a man in a wetsuit walked toward the ocean. "That was the captain of the Marina Norte Lifeguard and Rescue Crew. About an hour ago, two fishermen found this kayak floating in the ocean. No one on it or near it. The only thing left was this letter." Cross held up an envelope in a zip-locked baggie.

"Shit. Damn it! That's Cliff's kayak."

"Maybe someone stole it from him." Cole felt his stomach tighten.

Cross continued. "We're not at liberty to divulge the contents of the letter, but we can confirm it had been signed by Central City College Professor Clifford Singer."

Benny and Cole stared at the TV. Eyes wide, and breath shallow.

"We're not sure what happened or if any harm has come to Professor Singer. One thing we do know is just after sunrise this morning a kayak—we think this one here," Cross pointed to Cliff's kayak on the beach, "was caught on a few of the beachfront condo surveillance cameras. A person— whom we could not make out in the videos—was paddling southward toward the nature preserve. The ocean rescue team told me that the current more than likely pulled the kayak back to this part of the beach. Stay tuned for more information as we get it. Signing off for now, this is Teagan Cross, The Channel 13 News."

Cole and Benny sat in silence as they switched from one newscast to another.

"Benny, is there anything I can do for you?"

"Finding Cliff alive would be a good start."

Cole and Benny hugged and wiped away tears.

"Heather wants to stop by and see you. How about we bring you dinner tonight?"

"I'd like that, Cole. But I'll pass. My aunt wants to cook for me." He nodded toward the closed bedroom door.

Cole turned toward the front door and Benny called to him. "Make sure you come back and visit. I don't need another friend to leave me for good."

"We'll be here to see you tomorrow. I need you more than you know."

Benny locked the door behind Cole and moved toward the guest bedroom. He gently knocked. "He's gone."

• • •

As the sun set behind him, Cole walked to the ocean's edge with a solitary carnation.

"Cliff, I'm sorry." As tears streamed down his cheeks, he tossed the flower into the outgoing tide, bowed his head, and prayed.

What now? Crossroads? Or the end of the road?

Cole noticed a movement out of the corner of his eye. A tiny sea turtle hatchling barely longer than Cole's thumb clawed its way through the sand.

"It must have gotten separated from its nest," Cole thought.

He knelt on the sand and watched it as it moved toward the pounding surf. He realized instinct drew the hatchling to the sea. Still, watching such a small being take on such an immense challenge made him shake his head in disbelief and appreciation.

When it first hit the water's edge, the hatchling got pushed back and turned around by the incoming waves. It didn't quit. It didn't return to its starting point. It reoriented and continued toward its goal. Determined, the little creature made it into the water. A hoped-for future in an overwhelming environment.

Something so small didn't let a force bigger than itself stop it. Why do some move forward despite what seem to be overwhelming odds, while others shrug and give up?

As Cole looked at where the hatchling had entered the water, he thought it's not always about how big you are. Forward movement depends on determination, motivation, desire, and discipline. And, connections with and help from others. Cole could not remember feeling more isolated than he did at this moment.

The chance that little hatchling survives is slim to none. But that didn't stop it. What's stopping you?

Cole stood, the waves lapping at his feet.

"No more under the radar. No more invisibility. No more avoidance. Time for action. And time for me to seek help."

He turned and walked to his car.

• • •

45

Cole felt trepidation as he pulled on the heavy glass doors and entered the lobby. Hands sweaty and pulse racing, he still was not sure this was what he needed to do.

Really, Cole? Do you think talking to a stranger is going to silence me? You should know me better than that. There ain't no way around me.

Cole stood by the elevator looking for the name on the office locator board.

"There he is," Cole said to himself. "Dr. James May, Suite 600." He hesitated for a moment.

Go ahead. Give it a shot. Deal with me here. But I'll always be the voice in your ear.

Cole entered the elevator with a slow deliberate gait. The door closed and he pushed "6" on the button pad. His thoughts raced from his mother, father, and Ian to Turkle, Bartley, and the senator to his colleagues and students. And Heather and Aunt Phil. He closed his eyes and took a deep breath as the elevator stopped and the doors opened. Directly in front of him was the office of "May and Associates, Psychotherapists."

"Good afternoon, sir."

"I have an appointment with Dr. May," Cole said almost in a whisper. "My name is Cole Fitzgerald." He looked around as if expecting an eavesdropper to be lurking.

The receptionist gave him a clipboard with some papers to sign. "Dr. Jim will be with you shortly. Have a seat and help yourself to a cup of coffee." She pointed to a coffee pod machine in the corner. Fifteen minutes later, Cole was escorted into one of the interior offices.

"Dr. Fitzgerald, welcome. I'm Dr. James May. Most people call me 'Dr. Jim.' Whatever you're comfortable with. May I call you Cole?" He stood with a warm smile, shook Cole's hand, and pointed to a cushioned chair with arms.

"Yes. Cole. Thank you."

"Please, have a seat."

With the look of an intimidated first-semester student, Cole sat and gripped the chair's arms. Dr. Jim sat back, crossed his legs, and asked a few non-threatening questions about where, what, and who Cole taught. He had a relaxed face and lively hazel eyes. Cole began to settle into the chair and released his grip.

"What brings you here today? I saw on your paperwork that you suffer from anxiety attacks. Tell me a little bit about that."

"Well, I'm not sure checking the box *Anxiety Attacks* was the best way for me to explain my problem. But your form did not have a box to check that said *Silence the Voice in My Ear*." Cole offered a weak smile, rolled his eyes, and exhaled.

"Ah, that little person sitting right here," Dr. Jim said as he pointed to his shoulder. "Tell me about this voice," Dr. Jim said as he sipped water from his mug.

For the next twenty minutes, Cole touched on several topics from his family to college politics and finally to the common thread of the dreaded voice.

"And the kick in the shins was when the kayak of one of my faculty colleagues washed up on the shore. He was in a terrible place emotionally and he remains missing at sea. The voice keeps reminding me that I let him down."

"How long has the voice been with you?"

"Since my childhood. I always thought it was just my self-doubts speaking. A way to deal with the shitstorm in my family dynamics. Over the last few years, it has grown more intense and badgering."

"What does this voice say to you?"

"Mostly that I'm weak, not good enough, or not to trust anyone."

"How does that make you feel?" Dr. Jim asked.

"Vulnerable, less than, a fake, not good enough. Overall Doc, I'm not sure who I am any longer. I question—or should I say *it* questions—almost everything I do. And at the same time, I am pushed to be a faculty leader, a union organizer, and the voice to stand up to the administration."

"Interesting," Dr. Jim noted. "You are bothered by a voice in your ear, and at the same time, your colleagues want you to be the public voice for them."

Cole tilted his head and looked away for a moment. "I never thought of that. Does that mean something?"

"I don't know. Perhaps." Dr. Jim let the silence sit for a moment before he continued. "Why now, Dr. Fitzgerald? Tell me why you decided to meet with me now."

"Well, like I said, this—the voice, the anxiety, the trying-to-be-all-things-to-all-people person in the room—finally got to me."

"Yes, I heard that. But why *now*? Why is this your time to step forward and confront the voice? Or at least I think that's what you want to do."

Dr. Jim's words caught Cole's attention. *Now…is…your time.* He thought of all the times he had his students write those words and ponder them. It was his turn.

"Two women," Cole said.

Dr. Jim sat back and raised his eyebrows. "Continue, please."

"My significant other, Heather, and my second mother, Aunt Philomena. Two strong women who, when working in concert, become an inescapable force. They have been doing what I can only call an ongoing sort of intervention. Here I am."

Cole related how Heather and Aunt Philomena made him confront his alcohol abuse, his rage, and his overall lack of self-care. Dr. Jim asked more questions to get Cole to dig deeper.

"We have a few minutes left, Dr. Fitzgerald." Dr. Jim glanced at the wall clock behind Cole's chair. "Before our next visit, I'd like you to consider a few things. Consider it homework for the teacher." Dr. Jim paused. "First, please read Pablo Neruda's poem 'We are Many.' He writes of the many sub-personalities we all confront from time to time. From what you have shared today, you seem to have a *Critic* and a *Worrier*. And they appear to be on your shoulder speaking into your ear."

"Two voices?"

"Possibly. Or one voice that can take on the sound of as many internal demons as necessary to protect you."

"Hell of a way to *protect* me," Cole said. "More like rattle and scare the shit out of me."

"Perhaps. We will explore that next session. Next, I'd like you to consider your *boundaries* and *limits*. Again, from what you have told me today, those seemed to be blurred. It seems to gain respect, status, or standing, you're willing to deny who you are and what you need. That, as you have found out, is unsustainable."

Cole's eyes widened. "Sounds like I might be feeding the voice rather than standing up to it."

"Perhaps. We'll consider that more next session. Think about it, please."

"I will. Yes, I will."

• • •

46

1 PM. Thursday

On his way up to the Board meeting, Cole's thoughts bounced back and forth between Benny, Cliff, his students, and Ian. Of all people, Ian kept reappearing in Cole's thoughts. Cole stared at himself in the mirrored door and thought of his conversation with Dr. Jim.

"What the hell has happened to me? Mr. Smug Ass. I knew it all. Wouldn't let anyone push me around. So I said. What did I do? Yeah, I challenged the dean in faculty meetings. Big freaking deal. I encouraged my students to write letters to the campus newspaper and the local community newspaper. I took the safe road. I told myself I was their coach. But I didn't get on the field with them. I looked the other way. I graded. I guided. I pontificated. But what did I do? I took the easy way out. Benny gets injured by a bomb. Cliff, a psychological wreck, gets arrested, and then...God only knows. Students still need a safe place to find themselves. A corrupt Senator is the puppet master of the administration. Johnny V has more balls than I do. You know what? It stops now. All of it. I'm tired and must do something. Now."

About time, Cole!

He exited the elevator and walked toward the Board room. In fifteen minutes the gavel would sound the meeting to order. Like the circus a few weeks ago when Spano accused Benny, the lobby was packed and loud. Three TV crews interviewed Board members, staff, and administrators at different parts of the lobby. Conspicuously absent from interviews: faculty. They were present but the administrative gag order prohibiting them from speaking directly to the press still stood.

Cole shouldered his way through the lobby, picked up an agenda from a stack on a table, and squeezed into the meeting room hoping to find a place to stand.

"Cole! Over here!" Dominic Panagrossa waved his meaty hand from the center of the room and mouthed, "I got you a seat." Cole moved through the bodies toward Dominic. He felt a hand on his shoulder and turned. It was Turkle.

"I'm sorry, Cole, about Cliff. Have you heard any new developments? I don't understand it. He had a wife and a daughter. He couldn't just disappear. I wish I would have seen something like this coming."

Cole clenched his fists at his side, took a breath, and looked at Turkle. "Pat, how could you not have seen what he was going through? He was set up on those drug charges. You know that. But why for God's sake? Tell me that, Pat."

Turkle showed no reaction.

"And all you did, Pat, was continue to put pressure on him. Yeah, we all wish you would have seen something at some time that was worth something." Cole made his way to his seat. Turkle made his way to the front row of the audience.

"I see you were personally greeted by the *mamaluke!*" Dominic paused. "Cliff, God rest his soul. If he's dead, it's because of him. I spit on him. And them, too." Dominic pointed to the Board members entering from the side door and taking their seats on the dais. "If he turns up alive by some strange act of God, I still spit on them."

"Odd," Cole thought as he scanned the room with his eyes, "that the vice president of the college is not in the room for this meeting."

Bartley took his customary seat to the Chairwoman's right. She hammered the gavel and called the meeting to order. After the Pledge of Allegiance, she spoke.

"Ladies and gentlemen. Thank you for coming today." She held out her arms to include all sitting to either side of her. "We want your input. Central City College has been hit with one challenge after another. In addition to our budgetary struggles, we have the recent bombing at Professor DiJohn's home, multiple investigations by the state attorney's office, union organization, and less than twenty-four hours ago, we have, it appears, a faculty colleague, Professor Cliff Singer, missing at sea.

"This is not the college all of us up here know. We need to do something. It's our job—the Board's job—to do that. This community needs CCC. I want to hear from you. We don't need politics and drama. We want to hear considered and deliberative input. You don't have to fill out a speaking card today. Just stand in line. And faculty, I especially want to hear from you. Dr. Bartley told me just before we entered that he encourages faculty to stand up and speak their minds without fear of recrimination. Isn't that right Mr. President?"

"Yes, definitely so, Madam Chair. We have an incredibly extraordinary faculty. I want to hear their wonderfully great ideas and thoughts about these distressingly concerning events." He rolled his shoulders back and forth, while his eyes darted from one side of the room to the other. "And I thank our wonderfully phenomenal press core for being here today. We're all about open communication."

"Jesus, Mary, and Joseph. He makes morons look intelligent. Does he even listen to himself?" Dominic looked at Cole and shook his head. "That's the best we could do when hiring a president? In a way, Benny's fortunate he's banned from campus. He doesn't have to listen to this."

"Again, I'm asking faculty, in particular, to step up and begin the dialogue." The chairwoman waited.

No one moved. Silence engulfed the room.

Do you want to be visible? Want to make a difference? This is your time.

Cole made his way to the podium and a murmur rippled through the audience.

"Madam Chair, Board members, President Bartley, and most importantly, my faculty and staff colleagues, I'm Professor Cole Fitzgerald. Thank you for having this meeting and allowing us to speak freely." Cole looked Bartley in the eye.

Bartley moved his neck back and forth while he forced a smile and nodded his head.

Cole continued, "It's not so much what we need to do—it's what the Board and the administration need to do. You have abandoned us. This administration is more interested in numbers, data points, and 'on-point messaging' for the press. When was the last time any of you visited a classroom? Same for the administration. President Bartley talks a great story, but he has no idea what we do or how we do it. He and his cabinet wouldn't know a classroom if they had to find one."

Stifled laughter came from the audience. The Chair sounded the gavel and reminded everyone of the expected decorum.

"Ma'am, I've wanted to come before you for the past year, but like the gambler who rolls one bad bet after another, I thought things would take a turn for the better. Unfortunately, they didn't.

"Our college has wandered off course. Once focused on building relationships, we have deteriorated into lose-lose contests focused on, ironically, winning at all costs. We need leadership more than ever.

"The college faculty—as well as the college's middle management—is subjected to a daily diet of manipulative micromanagement. An atmosphere of mistrust and disrespect has been fostered at a terrible price to all involved."

Cole paused, gripped the platform, and continued. His voice echoed through the silence.

"I can tell you, the faculty members are not playing the victim and most assuredly we're not cowards. And we are not creating the drama or playing politics. This administration has devolved to having faculty arrested and banned from campus, the rest of us gagged so we cannot speak to the press, and now," Cole stepped back to compose himself. "Now, we may have lost a colleague who had been strong-armed by this administration.

"For too long, we've experienced a display of organizational power simply because it could be done. Fragile egos rely on bullying as their method of choice.

"Leadership is followership. When the followers stop following, then the leaders are no longer leading, they are, at best, managing. The result is management that has lost respect and cannot effectively enforce its position through punishment or buy it with rewards. It cannot maintain legitimacy if it loses authority, regardless of the amount of power it holds.

"You, the Board of Trustees, are the stewards of this college. I ask that you speak up for our faculty and our students. We need a change in leadership. Heck, we need leadership. What we have now, to borrow a phrase, is anything but incredibly extraordinary. It fails on so many levels."

Faculty jumped to their feet. Turkle remained seated, ramrod straight, and looked at Bartley who leaned toward the Chairperson to say something. She held her hand to silence him. As Cole returned to his seat, he noticed Senator Wackenslong standing in the back of the room. He motioned to the Chair with a slight wave and pointed to his chest.

"Dr. Fitzgerald," the Chair said, "thank you for those words. We, too, all of us up here, want leadership. The community deserves it."

She motioned to the back of the room. "I recognize one of our community leaders who has just joined us. Senator Wilbur Wackenslong. Would you like to address the Board and the gathered guests today?"

As the senator made his way to the speaker's podium, Bartley looked uncomfortable. His eyes did not match the smile on his lips as he bounced his head twice from right shoulder to left shoulder.

"Madam Chair, thank you for convening this timely and critical meeting." Wackenslong pulled an index card from his inner jacket pocket, placed it on the podium, and looked at each board member. "I came today for two reasons. One, to listen to what the faculty have to say about our great CCC. They, as they tell us, are on the front lines. They work with students each day. And, according to them, have to deal with a manipulative and micro-managing leadership at this college."

Dominic leaned toward Cole and said, "*As they tell us?* Get ready for the return fire."

"Madam Chair and ladies and gentlemen in the audience today, our college has not wandered off course. Yes, there have been a few hiccups. But anyone who has ever been a leader knows that will happen. Leaders take chances. The current administrative leadership at Central City College has taken on challenges that few would want. I realize that

Professor Fitzgerald is held in high regard by his colleagues. Well, most of his colleagues. But while he is determining which student to call on next, our administration has been finding creative ways to grow this college, serve more students, and, frankly, keep faculty on the payroll. They fight for quicker ways to gain tenure and fewer office hours. They may know their subject matter, but when it comes to running a college, they are misguided."

The Senator took a sip from his bottle of water and let his words settle over the room like an uncomfortable wet blanket. He continued.

"What was it that the professor just said? That the faculty are subjected to a daily diet of manipulative micromanagement. That an atmosphere of mistrust and disrespect has been fostered at a terrible price to all involved."

Cole looked directly at the Senator. Wackenslong continued his well-rehearsed tirade.

"How would you like it if day after day the people you lead continually disrespect you? I can only imagine what the faculty say and do when students attempt to challenge them."

A low buzz rose from the gathered faculty. Teagan Cross didn't look up from his notepad as he wrote and flipped page after page.

"You all know how much my family thinks of this institution. Just across the parking lot," the Senator pointed to his right, "is the *Wackenslong Center for Performing Arts*. This year we donated computers so the faculty could better connect with their students. That's not micro-management. That's leadership!" He tapped his fist on the podium. "I can't speak for the charges brought against Dr. Bartley. Perhaps they're spurious. Maybe not. That is something for you to decide— and the state attorney's office."

Bartley blinked and looked toward Turkle for support. Turkle stared at the senator.

"I know every one of you up there on the dais. We have worked together in other venues to grow Marina Norte. My family's new industrial complex—that, by the way, Professor Fitzgerald thought appropriate to disparage on TV, even though he never contacted me or anyone on my staff or in my family to discuss his concerns. He complains and points fingers yet he doesn't do his fact-checking. I would think he expects more from his students."

Wackenslong turned his body and looked directly at Cole. "Professor, when you attack what you do not under-stand, *you* create a no-win situation. Don't blame this Board or the college administration." And then looking back at the Chair, Wackenslong said, "Madam Chair, I urge you to investigate Dr. Bartley and do what you need to do to make sure our college continues growing and is not debilitated by complainers, naysayers, and lawbreakers. Let's put this behind us and move forward. Thank you for your time and your continued leadership."

Wackenslong placed the index card in his jacket pocket. He looked at Turkle with a glance that said, "That's how you do it. You crucify the bastards." He walked out of the room with Teagan Cross following to get a soundbite for the evening news. Cole and Dominic looked at each other with confused expressions.

"Hear that sound?" Dominic asked. "I think it's the bus bouncing over Bartley."

"Thank you, Senator." And then looking toward the sound booth, the Chair said, "If you would, tech crew please lower the lights. I have some slides I'd like you to see. Would Professor Eulonia Polonia come to the speaker's podium? I believe you have some information you'd like to share with the Board.

• • •

47

1:30 p.m. the same day in the Vice President's office.
You're a talented woman. You deserve this opportunity.
Don't let anyone stand in your way. You can do this!

Darla adjusted her red bodycon as she looked into the mirror on the back of her office door. Her new ankle-strap pumps provided an eye-catching accent.

You've always been known for your stunning posture!

She smiled as she heard her secretary enter the office.

"Dr. Merlot. Are you ready for Dr. Edwards?"

"Yes, please." Darla made her way to the conference table as her colleague entered.

"Richard! Thanks for making time. A lot is going down today. Please, have a seat," she pointed to the chair at the other end of the table. Edwards nodded as he sat. He placed a file folder on the table in front of him.

"Thank you for the text. I stopped in the Board room. It was standing room only. Did you know about the meeting?" Edwards was a member of the president's cabinet but his question sounded like someone who had no understanding of the inner workings of the college leadership team. "Doyle looked pained. Shouldn't we be in there with him?"

"As I said, Richard, a lot is happening. We're where we need to be, right here. As for Doyle, he'll have to deal with whatever the meeting delivers." She flipped through some papers in front of her. "Are you ready? Any questions?"

Edwards opened his folder. "I'm a little confused. Dr. Craig has an unblemished personnel record. She is highly respected by the faculty. I've not heard of any complaints from staff. And she, if I may be blunt, is the lone African-American in the president's cabinet. So, why are we doing this?"

Merlot looked at Edwards for an uncomfortable few seconds. Adjusting his butt in his chair, he moved his shoulders up and down.

"Poor bastard," Merlot thought.

A knock on the door. "Dr. Craig is here. Shall I show her in?"

"Richard," Merlot said in clipped tones, "follow my lead." Turning to the secretary, "We're ready."

The diminutive Lori Craig entered with an armful of file folders and her ever-present smile. Merlot directed her to the seat at the middle of the table and offered a bottle of water.

"Thank you, Darla. I'll take you up on that. I've been running all morning. Had a great meeting with the curriculum committee," she raised and lowered the file folders showing evidence of her meeting. "Real progress on the new student success course. Long overdue." She sipped from the bottle. "I was on my way to the special Board meeting when I got your text to come here immediately. What's up?"

Merlot adjusted her body and crossed her legs as she leaned over her papers. She let go a low sigh. "Lori, you know how much I respect what you've been able to do with our student success initiatives at this college. Especially now with the large influx of new students. We need to help them navigate this new journey."

"Well, true enough about the navigation part," Craig interrupted, "but not so accurate about the influx of new students. My faculty contacts have told me they see high absentee rates. That's concerning on several levels."

"Your *faculty* contacts?" Merlot raised an eyebrow. "What are your *administrative* contacts telling you?"

"That all is A-OK. The absentees will level off. It's to be expected with the population we serve. I keep hearing to look at the data points. Focus on the increased enrollment."

"And that's a problem?"

"It can be," Craig said. "For one, if those students don't attend, then they generate 'Fs' and GPAs that will be difficult to rebound from when they do start attending. That's setting them up for failure. And, looking down the road for the college," she opened one of her files, "my research tells me that enrollment numbers now if the trend of absenteeism continues, will lead to disturbing retention and graduation numbers. As in so low they could affect future funding."

Edwards looked wide-eyed at Merlot as if he'd never thought of such ramifications. Like he never connected enrollment with retention statistics and graduation rates. Merlot ignored him.

"That's one of the reasons we need to talk," Merlot swiveled her chair to face Craig. "We fear you're not on board with the messaging President Bartley has been publicly conveying."

Craig's head pushed back and her eyes narrowed. "Who are *we*? And what messaging? I'm not raising any speculation that faculty haven't already been talking about. This triumvirate of absenteeism, retention numbers, and graduation percentages needs to be part of everyone's messaging. How do you have a viable student success emphasis if those numbers spiral out of control?"

"That's what we are talking about. Your negative concentration on what might happen as opposed to what is happening. But that's not the only thing we need to discuss. There is a bigger issue." Merlot reached behind her and pulled a folder from her desk. "We've received a complaint about you."

"About me? A complaint about me? From whom and about what?"

"I'm not at liberty to divulge who as we're currently investigating."

"Investigating?"

As the two women ratcheted up the level of the conversation, Edwards squeezed his arms into his body as he clasped his hands in front of him on his lap. He looked straight at Merlot.

"Human Resources has received a complaint of," Merlot appeared to read from the paper in front of her, "conduct unbecoming of a Central City College administrator."

"What?" Craig turned and looked at Edwards. "Do you have anything to offer on this?" All he did was point toward Merlot. Turning back to Merlot, Craig asked, "What are you talking about?"

"The complaint alleges that you can no longer conduct yourself in an unbiased manner regarding faculty relations."

"That's bull, Darla. You know I have a better working relationship with our faculty than anyone in the administration. That's a fact. Proven over and over again."

"That doesn't give you license to undermine the president's cabinet."

Stunned silence.

Merlot continued, "Of course, you have the right to associate with whomever you want, but once that association transitions into a cabal to help faculty unionize, then your objectivity, as well as professionalism, are called into question. And hence, this complaint."

"I'm at a loss. A total loss. A 'cabal to help faculty unionize?'" She repeated the words to grasp their elusive meaning.

Merlot flipped to another page in her folder. "There is also an allegation that you have used your administrative position to clandestinely connect faculty with members of the press. Which, as you know, is a violation of the gag order."

"Clandestinely? What? I would never consider it, let alone do that. I call BS! I demand to know who's casting these false accusations?"

"I cannot tell you that at this point in the investigation. In the meantime, you are hereby immediately placed on administrative leave effective the end of the workday today as we determine whether or not you should be terminated."

Edwards summoned the courage to interject, "Please give all your files about the student success initiatives to Professor Savannah O'Rourke. She'll be stepping into your position on an interim basis while we sort this out. And there you have it." He never took his eyes off the paper from which he was reading.

"And be advised," Merlot continued, "starting tomorrow, you are not to come on the college property or have contact with any faculty member. Any contact will be orchestrated through either Dr. Edwards or me. Further, I would advise you to stay away from all faculty off campus as well. Especially, Dr. Cole Fitzgerald."

"Cole? What does *he* have to do with this?"

"Dr. Fitzgerald is the faculty member with whom you have been accused of connecting to the press to undermine our administrative team. And as I'm sure you know, he has been accused of assaulting the college's Director of Human Resources. The MNSO will soon be investigating that as well."

• • •

48

1:45 p.m. same day back at the Board Meeting
What in the hell is going on? Wackenslong threw you under the bus. How did you let this happen? You're the president. Take charge!

"Madam Chair. I'd like to say a few words." With each word, Bartley's voice escalated to almost a squeal. "I'm incredibly excited to see the good Senator here today. And the fact that you've called this meeting and all these phenomenally wonderful faculty have shown up, well, it's just extraordinary." He stopped, searching for the next string of adverbs.

"Thank you, Mr. President. We're a fortunate institution in a challenging time. We all have questions. Perhaps today we can move toward the answers." Then turning to the projection booth, she said, "Please start the projector."

The lights dimmed as the first slide of the PowerPoint presentation came into focus.

"I received this from one of our senior faculty, Dr. Eulonia Polonia. Would you approach the podium please, Professor?"

"Thank you, ma'am." Eulonia stood at the podium and looked at each Board member. She held her gaze on the member texting on her phone. When she saw Eulonia's glare, she put the phone aside and sat up in her chair. The Professor began.

"I've been examining, as have some of my faculty colleagues, the numbers from the campus enrollment office. As we dug deeper we found that the 25% increase in student enrollment mirrors another 25% increase—an increase in the number of no-shows."

"No-shows?" the Chair asked.

"As in, these students have not shown up for class. They are absent. They do not attend class."

"Ah, yes absenteeism. Many of us up here did hear about that a few days ago. Unfortunately, we learned about that from a radio show rather than our college administration." She looked at Bartley and Turkle. "And, Professor, you know this how?"

"Simple. Check the roll for each class."

"Isn't it possible that the matching 25% numbers are just a coincidence?" asked the Chair.

Bartley jumped so quickly to support the Chair he almost knocked his front teeth out on the microphone. "Yes, madam Chair. You exquisitely nailed it. An astonishingly accurate coincidence."

Eulonia bit her lower lip and scrunched up her nose. "Mr. President, there is no astonishing coincidence for the improbable number of student no-shows. Rather than an upsurge in our student population, we've raided the cemetery."

The crowd buzzed. Even for Eulonia, this was a bizarre statement.

"Cemetery?" The Chair displayed confusion in her voice and on her face.

"Plain and simple. Many of the 25% don't exist."

"What?" the Chair exclaimed.

"Their names are made up. Others are real names, but of people who died years ago. You'll find their names in the cemetery."

"And you can prove this?" asked the Chair.

"Yes, I can. I have here photographs of a few of the cemetery markers with the same names as the supposed students on our rolls." Eulonia waved a stack of papers in her hand. "How's that for an incredible coincidence?" The crowd buzzed. "Look at the screen."

Eulonia clicked through a half-dozen slides of grave markers—photos that Suzy had taken for her. Eulonia held up a pile of papers again and said, "You will find those names on classroom rolls. And, ma'am, the Board has to ask itself if these people don't exist, where is *their* financial aid going?"

The Board members looked at one another. "Go on," the Chair instructed.

"I have seen how some student names have been changed by a letter or two. So that it looks like a real student, but again, it isn't."

"Explain please."

"Ma'am," Eulonia said as she pointed toward the president, "it would be like placing *Doyle Bartley* on my class list but spelling the last name as *B-a-r-t-l-e-e*. Again, I have proof." She held up another batch of papers.

"Also, from what I can ascertain—and what someone with inside knowledge of our finance department here has told me—there seems to be an overseas account."

Turkle had been keeping Wackenslong up-to-date with quick texts. The senator responded, "Don't worry about it."

"Dr. Bartley, what do you say about these accusations?" The Chair and the entire Board looked at the president.

"This is utterly preposterous! Why do you believe that person? She is a known union sympathizer and will do anything to make us look bad." The veins in his neck stood out, his eyes widened, and looked as though if he didn't take a breath he would pass out.

"Yes, it sounds preposterous to us as well. But do you have facts that will refute what the professor has just presented to the Board?"

"Why are you believing that union sympathizer?" Bartley waved his index finger toward the Professor.

"I'll take that as a no you do not have evidence to present. Is that correct?"

"Madam Chair, may I address the Board again?" Cole stood up holding something in his hand. The chair waved him to the podium. Eulonia stepped aside but remained with Cole as he spoke.

"You want evidence. I have evidence. Like Professor Polonia, I received an anonymous tip from within the CCC Financial Aid Department." Cole held up his hand. "This

USB drive holds evidence supporting what my colleague has just shared with you."

"This is insanely outrageous! The faculty don't even take roll. They don't know who shows up or not. They're lying!" Bartley pointed at the two professors standing side by side.

Eulonia addressed the Chair. "Ma'am, there are elephants in those string beans!"

"Madam Chairperson, I have told you that this is nothing more than an incredibly disgruntled faculty. Especially those two." Bartley, again, pointed and sneered at the professors. "Extraordinarily disgruntled. They want *everything* without doing *anything*. The Senator said the same thing."

A soft *boo* arose from the audience. Someone made a farting sound. The Chair banged the meeting back to order.

Bartley patted his head with his handkerchief, cracked his neck a few times, drew a deep breath, and continued. "And, as you probably heard on the unbelievably biased media, one week ago the state attorney's office subpoenaed me to testify about this ludicrously outrageous charge of financial malfeasance. I did not and will not honor them with my presence."

"Mr. President, that was not a wise move," the college attorney interrupted.

"I agree," added the Chair as she looked at Bartley. "You don't ignore subpoenas, especially as a representative of CCC."

"I disagreeably disagree! What they have maliciously presented is fiction, lies, and innuendo. No one will force Doyle Bartley to do anything!"

"Unless it's Turkle, Merlot, or Wackenslong," Cole thought.

"Madam Chair, if I may," Eulonia stepped back to the podium.

The Chair nodded her permission.

"Professor Fitzgerald has gathered evidence from several sources—students, citizens, and college employees. My research corroborates and adds to everything he has brought forward proving malfeasance."

As Eulonia spoke, two men in black suits, white shirts, and thin black neckties entered and stood quietly in the back of the room. Their hands by their sides, they focused on Bartley.

"And this goes deeper and further," Eulonia continued. "Professors have been targeted and manipulated to do the bidding of a corrupt administration. Heck, Professor DiJohn, has been banned from teaching his classes. For what? He was almost killed by a package bomb planted at his house. And Professor Singer, he's still missing."

"Incredible nonsense, Madam Chair," Bartley yelled into his microphone. "She has nothing on me. And she is crazy. Always talking about pachyderms and vegetables. Incredibly eccentric. You. Have. Nothing. On. Me!" He tapped his index finger on the dais accentuating each word.

You idiot. You didn't see this coming? Your so-called team set you up.

"Madam Chair this is outrageous. A terrible injustice!" Bartley looked for someone to pay attention to him.

No one is listening to you. No. One.

"But we have someone who does, Mr. President, have *something* on you," Cole said, as the two black-suited men made their way to the podium. "Madam Chair this is Agent Little and that is Agent Fish. They are with our States Attorney's Office." Cole made way for Agent Little.

"Ma'am, if I may."

"Yes. What is your business here today, sir." The Chair sat ramrod straight. Every Board member followed suit.

"Dr. Doyle Bartley, in accordance with Florida Statute we have a warrant for your arrest for contempt of court for your failure to appear as required by a subpoena concerning a felony." As he spoke, his partner, Agent Fish, made his way up the stairs to the back of the dais.

"Dr. Doyle Bartley, you are hereby under arrest. Please stand. You have the right to remain silent."

Bartley looked like a kid caught by his parents skipping school. He stood and put his hands behind his back as his rights were read. Agent Little joined them as they came down from the dais. They each held one of Bartley's arms and walked him down the center aisle and out of the Board room. As the door opened, flashes and commotion came from the lobby. The media had been made aware of the spectacle and was there in full force.

"Well played, Professor," Eulonia said to Cole.

"Just what I was going to say to you, Professor. Incredibly well played."

• • •

49

Cole finished tuning his guitar on the darkened stage. He began fingering chords and humming to himself.

"Good evening, rock star!" Benny walked up on stage and sat on the stool next to Cole. "I might not be able to play tonight, but I can at least support my favorite band. And make sure you don't give my spot away to the stand-in bassist."

"Oh, I was thinking of giving your spot to Bartley as he'll be looking for a new job soon."

"You mean when he gets out of prison," Benny said. "I saw the evening news. Dip wad. Ignoring a subpoena."

"And then there is the added intrigue of the administration investigating Lori. They're looking to terminate her contract."

"Any updates about Cliff's disappearance?" Benny asked.

"Still considered an open investigation. According to what the dean has heard, there was some surveillance video from a few of the beachside condos. They can see a kayaker paddling south toward the nature preserve. Appears to be

Cliff's kayak, but as the local news continues to maintain, it cannot be determined definitively it's him paddling."

"Possible he could be alive?"

"Possible."

A glimmer of hope.

Joe handed Heather a glass of wine as she made her way toward the stage. She hugged Benny and Cole. "Quite the day on campus. I heard that Wackenslong called you out and chastised the entire faculty. What am I missing? You're good Cole, but not so good that these idiots focus this much energy on you. It seems excessive even for them. How does this help the administration at all?"

Cole placed his guitar on the stand. "From what I have pieced together, Bartley and his crew gave up on getting me on their team. They decided to destroy me and anyone in what they considered my circle of influence." He drew out the words, paused, and continued. "Accusing me of both conspiracy to create a faculty uprising and assault on a college administrator, casts doubt on my integrity and by extension the ethics and character of the entire faculty. Merlot told Lori today, the college will also come after me for violating the gag order."

"Sounds like they're running scared and playing any card they think will catch attention," Heather said. "Interesting development about the gag order. It just so happened that exactly at the time Eulonia was addressing the board, someone dropped off copies of the cemetery photos at the station's lobby desk."

"Who," Benny asked?

"Not sure. The front desk worker said she saw the envelope on the desk when she returned from the restroom. All she could see was the back of a young woman walking out the door to the parking lot."

Cole smiled and looked at Heather. "By the way. Thanks for the camera you gave to my student. She told me she is getting used to it."

"No way. She took those photos?"

"I didn't say that. Did I?" Cole smiled.

Joe brought Benny a beer and Cole a tonic and lime.

"None of it will stand up to a fact check but it gives them time. It distracts the public with the dirt of another breaking news alert, and confuses the Board, while Turkle, Merlot, and Wackenslong move on with their scheme. Not sure, in total, what it is, but it's getting uglier." Cole held his glass up. "To the States Attorney's Office."

"Bartley is a stooge," Cole continued, "he has been made to look like he's in charge. Reality sees Turkle, with Merlot in close tow, directing the moves. Bartley is toast. Do you think it was a coincidence Merlot and Edwards were away from the Board meeting? Merlot does the sinister dirty work behind the scenes. She and Turkle don't trust Edwards in front of a questioning audience. He'd break in no time."

"Dick Ed!" Benny said. "A weak-kneed spinless puke."

The drummer flashed the stage lights. Joe turned off the house music. Heather hugged Cole and then looked him in the eye.

"How you doing?"

"Better."

"I like your new drink."

"I'm coming to grips with my demons. Speaking with Dr. Jim has opened my eyes. Or at least I've begun to open my eyes." Cole reached in and hugged Heather. "Thank you for helping me find my heart, again."

"We, you and I, will get through this. I have no doubt." She kissed his cheek and joined Benny at her table.

You really don't deserve to have someone like her in your corner.

"Probably, but she's there and I'm not letting go," Cole said to himself as he counted down the first song.

• • •

"Ladies and gentlemen, you've been the best audience *The Silver Fox* has seen in weeks. The band thanks you. Don't forget to take care of your servers and your bartender, Joe." The crowd cheered. "We're going to finish with a new song. This is for anyone who has felt the burden of that doubting inner critic. And, honestly, who amongst us hasn't had such chattering visitors? We call this 'The Voice in Your Ear.'"

Billy B played a haunting introduction and then Cole sang.

Voice in your ear
Hand on your shoulder

Sometimes quiet
Sometimes bolder.
A whisper, protector, or speaker of fame
And then nothing but a ball and chain.
That Voice in your ear
I know you've heard it
Before the dawn
In the hour of the wolf
On the edges of the night
You wake, turn, no escape in sight.
You can run
You cannot hide
You better be ready
For a long, long ride
I know you can hear
I'm the Voice in your ear.
You can't deny me.
I'm louder than a horn
Calling you, begging you
Please remove the thorn.
Deal with me here. Deal with the fear.
I'm the voice in your ear.
Come on confront me
You can't have peace
If you don't understand me.
Ain't no way around me
I'm the voice…in your ear.
You can run

You cannot hide
You better be ready
For a long, long ride
I know you can hear the
Voice in your ear.

The stage lights went dark and the band congratulated each other on a good night. As Cole unstrapped his guitar, he saw Suzy walk through the door. She was by herself. She looked directly at Cole as she approached the stage with a steady gait and a determined look.

• • •

The late-night waitress at Nico's placed three glasses of water on the table and handed Heather and Cole menus. Another was placed where Suzy would be sitting when she returned from the restroom. Cole adjusted the window blinds to block out a flickering light bulb on the outside sign.

"One more will be joining us in a few minutes. You'll recognize him. The old guy with the bandaged hand." Cole smiled at Heather as the waitress went to get coffee.

"Cole, be good," Heather giggled.

"I didn't anticipate Suzy coming in tonight and asking to speak with us," Cole said.

"She told me last week that Spano had threatened her. We met for coffee. At the time she was so scared of him that she wouldn't even walk in the park with me. I mostly listened. I pushed her to see Ms. Robertson, the counselor. She's frightened for herself and her daughter. Wait, here she comes." Heather nodded toward the restrooms.

Heather slid to the inside part of the booth seat. They both sat facing Cole.

"Ms. Rivera. I mean, Heather, I didn't know what to do or who to turn to. Ned has always been hotheaded but even more so now. He seems to be under a lot of pressure. Thank you for pushing me to see Ms. Robertson. I have and she is helping me see what I can no longer avoid."

Cole thought of his conversations with Dr. Jim.

"And he's dangerous," Heather added.

"I've been doing some homework," Suzy smiled at Cole, "But not for your class, Professor."

Cole raised his cup to her. "You probably have learned more doing what you're doing. Consider it homeschooling."

"Heather, I've been using the camera you gave me. I followed Ned and, well, did some photojournalism. At least I think you might call it that."

"Following him was a dangerous move."

"Had to do it and glad I did."

Cole briefly looked at Heather and said, "And her photojournalism showed up at the Board meeting today." Then looking at Suzy, "Professor Polonia tells me you made a trip to the cemetery."

"And to my station?" Heather added.

Suzy gave a shy smile. "And a few other places. Let me tell you what I saw."

Suzy's recollection of where she'd been and what she'd seen sounded like the itinerary of an undercover operative. From her backpack, she pulled an envelope, opened it, and spread photos on the table.

"That's Wackenslong's office!" Heather said.

"And that looks like Spano." Cole pulled a photo for a closer look. "Before or after the bombing?"

"Not sure what happened but that was how he looked the night he came to my Aintin's apartment and threatened me. Looked like someone had hit him in the face. Had bruises on his neck as well."

"And that's Bartley and Turkle. Bartley looks piqued." Cole fingered the photos.

"These I took at the CCC gymnasium," Suzy continued sliding a few more photos to the middle of the table.

"That's Merlot getting in her car. That photo shows Turkle." Cole picked it up and studied the photo. He didn't know the two men with him.

"Well, see that guy there," Suzy pointed to the photo with Turkle and the two men outside the gym. "Here he is again."

"That's Turkle's car he's in. Where are they?" Cole asked.

"That's near my area of town. Johnny Valentine lives there."

Cole sat straight up, looking like he was just seeing the light for the first time. "That's an agent," he said pointing to the photo. "A sports agent. Or at least I think it is. Johnny V called me after they left. Turkle brought an agent to meet him and his mother and talk about endorsements. They offered him a large sum of money to sign a contract now even though the *Pay for the Name* law does not take effect for a few months."

"And perhaps a violation of the law the governor signed," Heather added. "A law that Wackenslong shepherded through the legislature. It needs to be investigated, at the least."

Cole sat back in his booth. "While we've all been focusing on the enrollment and financial aid numbers, perhaps a sports scandal has been in the wings, too. Hmm."

"I have one more photo to share. I took this early one evening outside the senator's office." A photo of Merlot and Wackenslong showed them both leaving an office building. Merlot was carrying her stilettoes in her hand.

Heather tilted her head and said, "This is getting...."

"You dumb bitch! What are you doing here? And with them?" Spano had walked in with another woman when he spied Suzy. He stood at the end of their table. "I asked you a question!"

Spano's eyes were bloodshot, his nose running, and his head still held the evidence of Wackenslong's table pounding. And now he also sported a fresh set of scratches, almost claw-like, along the left side of his face. The blood was fresh.

"You get too fresh for your whore?" Suzy felt emboldened as she pointed to the scratch marks.

Spano stepped back from the tabletop and moved his untucked shirt to the side revealing a gun stuck in the waist of his pants. Heather leaned back. Suzy expected the move. Cole smiled.

"What are you smiling at, Teach?" Spano angled to face Cole directly. "How about we go outside and I pop your...."

A gagging sound completed the sentence. Spano's head snapped back and he fell to the floor.

"That's twice, nimrod—and I did it with a bad hand." Benny stood over him with a server's table cleaning towel in his hands. "You couldn't even carry out a package bomb without screwing it up."

He then looked over his shoulder to a cop coming into the diner. "Officer, this young man just threatened these two ladies and this old man," Benny pointed at Cole, "with a gun. Your timing is impeccable."

Handcuffing Spano, the officer said, "You can thank Six Gun Charlie here for the timing. We had been tailing him after an alert was sent in about a B&E at the Skyview Condos."

Heather and Benny looked at Cole.

"It appears he entered one condo," the cop continued, "but there was a guard cat or something that ran him right out of the place. Caught it all on the surveillance camera."

Heather, Benny, and Cole all smiled.

"And there is also a warrant for his arrest for violating probation." The cop walked Spano to the waiting squad car.

• • •

50

3:30 a.m. the next morning.

People, especially that boss of yours, have no idea how good you are. Not a clue.

Turkle stared at the ceiling. Across the room, a mister rhythmically changed from one primary color to the next as it belched a lavender fragrance into the air. To his left, Darla slept in a fetal position hugging a pillow, her naked back to him.

You didn't deserve the hand you were dealt. Injury, separation, death. You will not be invisible any longer.

He took a long slow breath, held it, and then slowly exhaled. His cell phone lit up on the bedside table. Mrs. Hobart's name flashed on the screen.

"Hello. Mrs. Hobart, what's wrong?"

"Your mom, Dr. Turkle. She's had a stroke. The ambulance just left with her for the hospital."

"I'm on my way."

"It doesn't look good. I have passed along her end-of-life directives to the hospital."

Sitting up Darla looked at him. "Your mother?"

"Yes. Stroke. I need to go to the hospital. I'll be in touch."

"After the announcement, if you're not back, I'll text you. Let me know when you get to the hospital."

Turkle threw on his clothes as she spoke, half listening.

"Tell Wackenslong not to worry. Everything will be OK." He kissed her, tucked his phone in his pocket, grabbed the keys from the dresser, and left the apartment.

• • •

Except for the occasional trailer truck, the dark two-lane state road belonged to Turkle. And the voice.

This is a blessing. Your mother will find peace, which means you will find peace.

"How do you figure that? She's the only person I've ever been able to count on. Always in my corner. Believed in me. Pushed me. Loved me. Even when I knew she was disappointed in me, she didn't judge me. How am I to find peace? I have no one!"

You have Darla and Wilbur. Soon you'll have the college.

"Not sure it's been worth it. I've hurt people and to carry all this to its end, more people will be hurt."

Hurt or be hurt. Who looked out for you when you broke your kneecap? As your daughter lie dying, who understood your anguish?

Turkle blinked his eyes.

That is why you have to do what you have to do. They will now notice who you are. No way around it.

"I don't want to be invisible. Plain and simple."
You won't if you listen.

• • •

"What time is it?"

"4 a.m.," Bartley barked. "Where the hell is Pat? I've been trying to reach him." Out on bail, Bartley had to appear before the college board later this afternoon. He was making a last-ditch—and futile—effort to maintain his job.

"His mother was rushed to the hospital. Doesn't look good."

"When will he be back? Today's big. I need him. He needs to be there!"

"We know. I'll be there for you. So will Pat." Darla could hear the stress in Bartley's breathing. "No worries."

"Easy for you to say." He disconnected as he swore out loud.

Darla hit speed dial. "I just heard from Doyle. He's a basket case. How're you doing?"

"Going over my notes for the big meeting."

"Do you need any help? I could be there in thirty minutes if you'd like."

"What about The Young Turk?"

"He had a family matter to deal with."

"Meet me at my office in an hour."

"See you then, Senator."

She disconnected and smiled.

• • •

Turkle entered the darkened room. A nurse had just completed checking vital signs and the IV drips. His mother had been intubated and placed on a ventilator. A low repetitive *thump, thump,* followed by a sucking noise filled the room.

"You must be her son?" the nurse asked. "She asked for you right before we sedated her."

Turkle looked down on his last connection to life as he knew it. He cupped his hand over hers and sighed.

"Can she hear us?"

"Yes. She won't respond, but she can hear your voice. I'll let you two have time. Press the call button if I can help her or you." The nurse pulled the curtain around the bed to give them privacy and exited the room.

"Mom, I'm here. I love you. Thank you." He pulled the chair close to the bed and began their last night together.

• • •

"Dr. Turkle, I am so sorry for your loss. I know those words can never convey or come close to what you feel now. In her short time at Timber Estates, she made friends and she will be missed."

"Thank you, Mrs. Hobart. Will someone contact me about her possessions and what I need to do?"

"Yes. I'll call you in a few days."

He disconnected from the call and walked out the hospital's front door to the parking lot. The sun had broken through the pine trees. Turkle flipped through his texts. His secretary had left a message to call Bartley.

"Doyle, this is Pat. Sorry to just be getting back. I had a family emergency."

"Well, we've got a hell of an emergency right here at CCC. It's incredibly horrible! I'm out on bail and I have to testify before a grand jury about irregularities in our financial aid department. That's next week. Today I need your help with the Board. They want to fire me. Horribly extraordinary. What're we going to do?"

"Have you called Wackenslong or Darla?"

"Left a message for him. She hasn't come to her office yet. Get here as soon as you expeditiously can." He disconnected.

Turkle smiled to himself.

Told you!

• • •

51

"Incredible. Where the hell is everybody?" Bartley slammed the receiver of his desk phone. "Is this a holiday or something?"

He turned to his email. Nothing incoming. Looked at his cell phone. No texts or voicemails.

Face it. You're all alone. No help. You're a hot mess in a hotter mess.

"Dr. Bartley," his secretary's voice over the intercom refocused his attention. "I reached Senator Wackenslong on the phone. Would you like me to put him through?"

Bartley lunged for the phone and punched the line with the flashing light. "Wilbur! I need your help! This is getting terribly out of hand. The Board Chair wants answers and I have none. At least, none that she'll like. What can I do? The meeting is today."

Bartley could hear Wackenslong, with his hand over the phone, speaking to someone in his office. Then turning his attention to the president, he said, "Doyle, there's nothing I can do with this. It's in the hands of the state's attorney.

Financial aid fraud or some such thing. And your failure to obey a subpoena. I'm sure you've got something that can give you deniability. Right?"

"Deniability? You know me better than that. You were in on the plan from the beginning. Offer aid so people can come to our school. Increase enrollment. That would lead to more tuition dollars for us. More students lead to investment from the community's donor class. That was the plan."

"Whoa, Doyle, slow down. Yes, we talked about increasing enrollment. Every college wants to do that to increase its revenue stream. I did support that. But it looks like, at least from the little I heard on the morning news today—."

"The morning news! Horribly inexplicable chaos."

"It looks like whoever directed the student population increase didn't vet the students well. Looks like the money was given to anyone who showed a need for money with or without a desire or qualification for college. Like that asshole Ned Spano. Dumb shit barely got out of middle school."

"Preposterous. Impossible."

"Doyle, you've been set up. From what I've gathered, financial aid, also, was given in the name of people who don't exist. Those dollars went into an overseas account. Played by your people. Maybe Pat? Maybe people further down the food chain in your building. If you haven't done it already. I suggest you lawyer up. I gotta go."

The call went dead. Bartley looked at the clock. He turned his chair and looked out the window at what was to be his empire. He was to be a big deal in the community.

Now he was on the news for fraud and ignoring the State's Attorney's Office.

You're screwed.

• • •

Campus security had been called in to control the overflow crowd. The news crews interviewed anyone who would stop on their way through the lobby to the Board Room, including faculty.

"Wish we could get a turnout of faculty like this for one of our meetings," Panagrossa said as he got off the elevator with Cole and Benny. "Hey, you two gonna get me in trouble for being with you?" he asked with a grin.

"Look over there," Benny pointed to a camera crew interviewing Eulonia. "All of a sudden, they want faculty to speak their minds. This might be the beginning of the final reckoning for the weasels and ferrets. I think I'm the least of their concerns right now. Hell, even the security Sgt. waved us through."

By the time they muscled their way through the crowded doorway, every seat was occupied.

"Over there," Cole pointed to the back wall. "A straight-on view of the debacle."

From where they stood, they scanned the room. Edwards sat in the front row on the edge of his seat like he expected to hear a fire alarm and run for the door. His head swiveled scanning the room as if he lost his date at a funeral. Finally, he stood and waved to the back of the room. Through the door, just to the right of Cole, Merlot and Turkle entered. They both wore smiles that belied the purpose of the meeting. They sat next to Edwards.

The Board members entered and took their seats on the dais. Bartley occupied his usual seat next to the Chair. Holding a piece of paper with one hand, he tugged at his tie with the other and rolled his shoulders frontward and backward a few times.

"I know it's cliché," Benny said, "but that is a deer in headlights."

"No," Dominic said, "I'd say that's a great imitation of a crackhead looking to score a line to relieve him of his misery. I almost feel sorry for the dopey bastard. Almost."

The gavel came down. "Ladies and gentlemen. We are here today to discuss the termination of President Bartley's contract with CCC. Unless specifically called for by the Chair, we will not take comments from the public today."

Then turning to Bartley, "Mr. President what do you have for us? Since we last met, we have been informed that you will be testifying before the grand jury that is considering the charge of financial malfeasance." She looked at a paper in front of her. "I believe the amount of money in question is somewhere around ten million dollars."

A gasp arose from the audience.

"Madam Chair, this is a lynch job." He awkwardly moved his arm toward the audience. "And out there is your mob."

Someone in the audience booed the president.

"We will have order or I'll have security clear the room," the Chair said. "Dr. Bartley, this is not a lynch job or a mob. We, the Board members, your staff, and the faculty, want to believe you and want this matter to be clarified and put behind us. Please give us something credible and verifiable."

"This entire show here today is amazingly unbelievable," Bartley continued wiggling his shoulders, pawing at his necktie, and moving side to side in his chair. "I have been a loyal servant of this body since I've been here. If I have done such a bad job, then why did you extend my contract and give me a pay raise last year? You are for whatever reason, tilting at windmills. And we all know that windmills do terrible, horrible damage to our environment. If there are problems it's because of the way our mail system malfunctions in this beautifully desolate community. You see, Madam Chair, the financial aid ended up, in some cases, going to the wrong people. Yes, that's right. That's where the postman delivered the mail. That's a fact. A horrible fact, but a fact. I have become a victim of mail carriers. They don't like me. Never have."

The audience murmured.

"I am totally stranded on a desert island in the middle of the city. With nothing but coyotes around me. You know that coyotes when they are hungry, do dastardly things that they would not normally do. That's the problem, coyotes. They are everywhere!"

"Dr. Bartley are you OK?" the Chair asked. "Windmills, postmen, and coyotes? I'm lost."

Bartley paused and looked out at the audience as if he just noticed they were there but had no idea who they were. Kind of like George Bailey lost in his *It's a Wonderful Life* dream.

He took a drink of water and continued as the Board Chair gave him a wide berth. Turkle had sat back in his chair steepling his fingers to his chin. Merlot was busy texting.

"Have you been to the hospital?" Bartley resumed his stream of consciousness ramble through the thickets of his mind. "They need help. I'm bringing them that help by expanding our nursing program. Do you want your mother taken care of by untrained staff? Do you want a janitor messing with your bedpan at night? That takes financial aid, damn it!" He pounded the desktop. The audience was silent. The news cameras rolling.

He continued. "Athletes thank me for getting the governor to sign that *Pay for the Name* law that makes getting agents legal. Hell, that takes basketballs to do!" He laughed out loud at his turn on words. For the first time, Turkle looked a bit uncomfortable. Merlot's fingers continued to bang on her phone screen. Edwards smiled and nodded every so often as if he understood what his president was blabbering about. Perhaps he did. But few others seemed to be following. The Chair was about to speak when Bartley raised his voice.

"Mark my words! What I have done here and plan to see through to its fitting end, the world has never seen and will never see again. I have done more for college students than anyone. Before my exceptionally well-delivered tenure here at CCC, people were conspiring to destroy this college. I stopped them! That's an incredible factoid!"

The college's attorney, who sat at the end of the dais for every meeting, raised her hand. The Chair nodded.

"Through the Chair to the President, if I may?"

"You may."

"Dr. Bartley. I know the entire Board is thankful for your comments this afternoon. You have given us a great deal to consider. At this point, I urge that you relinquish the floor and end your comments. Please, sir." She looked sadder than an elementary school child who lost a puppy.

Bartley looked at the attorney, the audience, and then the Chair. His ashen face, devoid of any expression, poured sweat. He nodded his ascent to the Chair and sat back staring at his hands.

"Madam Chair," said the Board member to her left. "I move that, effective immediately, we place Dr. Bartley on administrative leave without pay until the grand jury concludes its investigation."

The motion was seconded and unanimously approved.

"And I would like to move," the Board member continued, "that we appoint Dr. Patrick Turkle, Director of Human Resources, as the interim president until such time that Dr. Bartley is reinstated or removed for cause."

That, too, was seconded and unanimously passed.

"Huh?" Benny asked turning to Dominic and Cole. "Wonder why Merlot, the current VP, is not interim? This gets stranger."

The Chair motioned to the sergeant of security to come forward. She leaned over the dais and said in a soft voice, "I want your men and women to keep the press from moving to the front of the room when I end the meeting. I would like to give Dr. Bartley a moment to exit." The Sergeant nodded her understanding and motioned to her officers to get in place. The Chair gaveled the meeting to an end.

The college attorney walked to Bartley and whispered something in his ear. He smiled, got up, and walked out of the room with her.

• • •

"Ladies and gentlemen. Citizens of our great community and state. It is with humility, pride, and a sense of duty that I announce to you today my intent to run for the office of governor of this great state."

On cue, "We Are the Champions" blared from the speaker system as campaign operatives waved *Wackenslong for Governor* signs.

Wackenslong raised his arms for silence and continued his remarks. "I am running on a platform of accountability for public officials, providing access to a quality standard of living, and improving higher education opportunities for everyone, not just the fortunate ones who have been born into money. As you know, my family has built a small street-corner shoe store into a thriving nationally franchised apparel business. Soon it will help provide hundreds of jobs for Marina Norte citizens in our new downtown industrial complex. There is no reason every household with desire and determination out here in our community cannot do the same."

Applause and more sign waving. A one-word sign stood out from the rest in the middle of the crowd. *STRUNZ!*

"You need to move along, ma'am," one of the Senator's staff said.

"Officers! This man is sexually harassing me!"

The staffer ran toward the back of the crowd. Philomena smiled and continued to wave the sign.

Wackenslong pointed to the building behind him and said, "That is why I have chosen to hold this news conference outside the administration building of Central City College and in front of *The Wackenslong Center for Performing Arts*. In there, the CCC Board is making a tough but needed decision to review its college leadership and make the necessary adjustments to ensure integrity and accountability. I've just been informed that Dr. Doyle Bartley has been placed on an indefinite leave of absence while the unfortunate charges leveled against him are investigated. Would you please welcome—and I offer my wholehearted support to—Dr. Patrick Turkle, the new Interim President for Central City College."

Turkle bounded up to the stage, shook Wackenslong's hand, pointed and smiled at the crowd, and returned to the ground-level side of the stage.

The *STRUNZ* sign bobbed up and down in the crowd.

"And," the candidate continued, "please give the loudest cheer of the day for my campaign manager, Dr. Darla Merlot!"

While signs waved and "We Are the Champions" blared for the umpteenth time, Merlot ascended the stage stairs in shimmering gold bodycon. Her new black stilettos had matching gold speckles. She and her candidate stood side by side, raising their fingers in victory. Today was her first official day as campaign manager. And also, the day she resigned as Vice President of Central City College.

• • •

52

After morning classes, most students had either left campus for their day jobs or headed to the campus library. With the classroom floor quiet, Cole often used the time to grade papers, plan lessons, or prep himself for another mind-numbing committee meeting.

Today, he sat at his desk, exhausted. He clicked on his streaming music app and scrolled to the smooth jazz channel. The eucalyptus-scented candle he lit filled the office with an aura of calm. A sad smile came to his face as he looked at his brother's photo on the wall.

After the past few weeks of witnessing and enduring escalating chaos, trauma, injury, and worse, he had to be still. He had confronted and weathered, better than he could have imagined, the politics of CCC, his inner voice, and his alcohol dependence. "Thank God for Dr, Jim, Aunt Phil, and Heather," he thought.

Despite Bartley's demise, Cole still had questions and suspicions. As he shared with the Board, he had evidence, but still, there were loose ends that needed connecting.

The buzz of his cell phone shifted his attention to the name on the screen.

"Hey, Debbie. How are you and little Marie doing?"

"OK, Cole, thank you. We're hanging in there."

"The investigation remains open. They'll find Cliff." Cole did his best to sound reassuring despite his doubts.

Just then a knock came at Cole's office door. Panagrossa pointed to his watch and motioned for him to follow.

"Hold on for a second, will you?" He held the phone away from his mouth. "I'll be there in a few minutes. Need to handle this right now."

"OK. But make it quick. This is our final organizational meeting before the union vote. We need you." Panagrossa readjusted the files lost between his arms and solid belly and walked with his determined waddle to the meeting.

"OK, Debbie, I'm back." Cole pulled a piece of paper closer and wrote as Debbie spoke.

• • •

Faculty filed into the classroom for the union update. The hard-nosed Panagrossa had a reason for optimism.

"We've not won a thing yet but where the union stands today compared to just a month ago, well, no comparison." He looked at the packed room in front of him. "Our polling with faculty shows we have about 60% on board. We could gain or lose a few percentage points, but we're in a good place, in my humble opinion. I thank you for your commitment to this cause."

The door opened and Cole walked to the back of the room and sat. He looked preoccupied.

"My friend," Dominic said looking at Cole, "do you want to say anything? This hasn't been an easy semester for you."

Cole let out a long exhale. "Semester? It's been a long few years. I'm tired as I know so many of you are. The new faculty, thank you for the courage to step up for the union vote. The senior faculty, thank you for not taking the easy way to retirement." He paused. "We have to fight this administration as they'll take no prisoners. They will kill us—literally."

No need for him to elaborate, those in the room had followed, if not lived, the unfolding chaos. "Ironically, I think what has happened with Bartley helped us win over a few more adherents. Once again, it will be the faculty who help guide this college through the rocks and waves.

"There is more to our movement than the union. There are a lot of dots to connect. And I think we are getting closer to a resolution."

Cole's voice had a slight tremolo to it. Regaining composure, he continued. "As many of you know, Benny and Cliff were kayaking buddies. The ocean was their safe place. Benny told me how, at the end of a paddle, they liked to catch and ride a wave to shore. Sometimes they got flipped and dinged up. That never stopped them from going for another wave. They'd climb back into their boats and paddle harder. And it was always worth it. They both believed if you don't get into the water, you can't ride the wave. And if you don't ride the wave, you will never experience the exhilaration and view from the crest.

"Friends, we have been battered by wave after wave but you all have continued to pull yourselves back in the boat. We're about to ride the crest."

The door opened and Eulonia Polonia entered.

"Dominic," Cole said "thank you for all you've done. I know it hasn't been easy for you. And I believe, Eulonia has more to share."

She nodded and walked to the front of the room. "The time has come for us to blow the elephants out of the string beans. As you probably know, Professor Fitzgerald and I shared evidence with the Board that corroborates what a student—a student!—has discovered about the enrollment. Another student helped verify that information with photos." She looked at Cole. "It is much more than no-shows and has everything to do with financial fraud."

Once again, she shared her findings of the money, bank account, and no-shows.

"This is big!" she said. "The community needs to know what we're up against here. Not from a 'poor-faculty' standpoint, but from an 'abusive-administration-that-has-run-the-college-into-the-ground-while-lining-their-pockets-at-the-expense-of-our-students' standpoint."

Cole raised his phone. "Heather Rivera just texted me and would be happy to have Dominic and Eulonia on her show in the morning."

He didn't say it, but Cliff's wife, Debbie, would also be a guest.

Dominic adjourned the meeting and Cole returned to his office to make some phone calls. His final call was to Heather to confirm they would attend Wackenslong's kickoff rally and fundraiser that night.

"I think the dots are connecting," he said.

• • •

53

As with all events like this, it drew people who wanted to be seen. As if being in the same room with judges, business owners, or politicians conveyed a sought-after level of respect and status that couldn't otherwise be earned. Insecure people seek security one handshake and selfie at a time. To be seen with Wackenslong in the room added a special touch of gravitas.

Tonight, his backers brought in a diverse group including well-heeled donors, a veritable who's who of politicians, the inner city ministers' coalition, and student-athletes. CCC was unofficially represented by Turkle as he could not use his college position to endorse a candidate. He sat at a front-row table to the center-left of the head table with other notables from the city power structure. He looked at Merlot sitting next to the senator. They smiled at one another. Her resignation from the college, rather than a surprise, was part of a well-orchestrated plan to get the senator elected and favorable treatment for the college in the next year's budget cycle.

Four generations of Wackenslongs had left their mark on Marina Norte. Their story had grown into a legend about the tiny back alley cobbling shop that had spawned a regional empire of top-end athletic shoes and clothing. Their factory had become a major employer. Along the way, they became civic leaders, philanthropists, and opinion shapers. When they spoke, people listened. That allowed them to influence major appointments to city offices, bless who would run for office, and make significant donations to political candidates and causes. While his father, grandfather, and great-grandfather preferred to control the stage from behind the curtains, Wilbur gravitated to the footlights of political showmanship. He inherited the cunningness of his family but lacked their circumspection. That would become apparent tonight like a badly stitched shoe. The shine and gloss would not be able to hide the structural deficiencies.

Cole and Heather exited the elevator and headed to the restrooms. "I'll be quick," she said, "Wouldn't want to miss the candidate's speech."

As Cole entered the Men's Room, Wackenslong exited wiping his hands with a paper towel. They stared at one another like a bull and a matador. The senator stepped back, held the door for the professor, and then headed for the celebration.

Ding. Ding. Ding.

The Mayor of Marina Norte, as Merlot had promised, served as the host for the "Wackenslong for Governor Kickoff Rally and Fundraiser." And as the mayor had assured, a table of big donors sat directly in front of the head table. He tapped the side of his water glass with a spoon again.

"Good evening and welcome to the beginning of the campaign to elect the person who stands up to bullies while standing up for you."

Applause and cheers erupted. Political operatives off to the side of the head table waved signs.

"Wilbur Wackenslong has built a solid reputation as a person—THE person—who will fight for you. Born and raised here in Marina Norte, Senator Wackenslong understands what it means to work. His core value has always been discipline. His heart aches when he sees how many of the residents of our city and our state struggle to make a decent living for themselves and their families. Well with this election, with this man—our fellow citizen—we have the opportunity to bring the greatness to this state that it deserves. Ladies and gentlemen, I give you the next governor of our great state, Senator Wilbur Wackenslong!"

Predictably, a band entered from the hallway and marched down the center aisle to the head table playing "God Bless America." The campaign operatives marched around the room's perimeter and up and down the aisles holding their signs high. People stood, whistled, yelled, and clapped their hands.

Wackenslong approached the microphone and waited for the noise to subside. When it did, he announced, "Thank you. I am Wilbur Wackenslong. I'm running for governor. And I'm asking for your vote." More orchestrated bedlam.

He held up his hands for quiet and then recited a few talking points about the coming campaign. "Mostly, tonight, we need you to sign our volunteer list, take a yard sign or two with you, host a neighborhood coffee session, or start a social media campaign group. We could use your donations as well. Whatever you can spare, we will humbly accept and put it to good use. Thank you for coming tonight. I need you. We need each other." He returned to his seat as the audience gave him a standing ovation.

"The senator has agreed to take a few questions from the audience," the mayor announced. "Raise your hand and use one of the microphones that are stationed about the room."

A young woman raised her hand and made her way to the microphone in the center aisle.

"My name is Suzy McDonald. I'm a first-year student at Central City College. Senator, can you tell us why you've been conducting business with a convicted drug dealer on the CCC campus?"

"What did she say?" one of the guests whispered to her table.

"Ma'am, I have no idea what you are talking about."

"The same man who falsely accused a professor of assault. A professor who was protecting me from that drug dealer. Why are you working with that person?"

"You see what happens, folks?" Wackenslong ignored Suzy and directed his comments to the audience. "As soon as a candidate declares for office, all manner of scurrilous accusations are made. I won't be distracted. I'm here to represent you."

The audience applauded their candidate while, at the same time, another person approached with a question.

"An interesting non-denial denial, Senator." Benny had made his way to the microphone to the right of the room. "I'm the professor this young woman mentioned. I did step in and did what any thinking person would do in such a circumstance. Unfortunately, Central City College decided to form a relationship with that drug dealer against me. A bomb was left at my front door." Benny held up his bandaged hand. "And you supported it. But I'm not here to address that. I'd like you to tell the crowd what you know about the missing and possibly dead Professor Cliff Singer. Tell us how you knew that the then Director of Human Resources of CCC, Dr. Patrick Turkle, strong-armed him and forced him to set up money transfers to an off-shore account. If Professor Singer didn't oblige, he would lose his job. That sounds like blackmail, doesn't it, Senator?"

A hush enveloped the crowd. The press waited expectantly.

"Sir. Are you asking a question or telling an answer? Is that how you teach? I cannot tell you what the college administrators do. As you are fully aware, there has been a recent realignment of leadership with the temporary removal of Dr. Bartley."

"Assuming what you say is true, that you don't know what's going on with the administrators, why did you offer such a full-throated endorsement of Dr. Turkle for Interim President?" Benny was playing Wackenslong better than he could play his guitar.

"I was just following the recommendation of the Board Chair. Other than that, I have to put my trust in the college to run itself. I am sorry for your professor but, again, I cannot speak for your administrators."

"Well, I can help your recollection, Senator," Suzy said still at the center microphone and holding up an envelope. "Would you like to see photos?"

"Perhaps this will help your memory." Cole stepped to the microphone on the left side of the room holding another envelope. "Tell us how you came to be involved in the siphoning of money from sports agents into an off-shore account as well as an email scam that tapped into fraudulent financial aid distributions. Or do you deny being involved with Doctors Turkle and Merlot to divert money from CCC to you?"

"This is preposterous! You have nothing on me."

"But I do." All eyes turned to the slightly-built young man with a Mohawk haircut. Kerwin Lucas approached the center microphone where Suzy stood. "I am a student worker and have found evidence of what Professor Fitzgerald mentioned. I have names, email addresses, and letters that announced financial aid awards that never made it to the students. Unless, of course, those students are living on an island off the coast of Belize."

"And, the initials PTM that are associated with the account," Cole said, "I understand now that they stand for Peroni Talent Management—the agency you and Dr. Turkle have conspired with to sign college athletes to endorsements early—and illegally."

Turkle remained ramrod straight at the table.

The fine-tuned attack continued to pepper the senator. The news media pushed closer to each speaker.

"Senator! You. Should. Be. Ashamed!" Eulonia pointed at the senator from the microphone where Cole stood. Then she faced the audience and delivered her motto. "Ladies and gentlemen, there are elephants in the string beans!"

Two hundred forks clanked against the plates.

"I provided evidence to the Board Chair about inflated and fictitious enrollment numbers that have been accompanied by financial aid grants given to non-students. Where did all that money go? Senator?"

"Ma'am, you will need to ask Interim President Turkle about that. One more time, that is a college issue."

"And you don't know me but, I understand, you have used your influence and pressure to take money that was meant for our basketball program and athletes," Johnny Valentine cut an impressive image. Three students standing side by side in the center of the room. "He," Johnny turned and faced Turkle, "even came to my house with a sports agent. Was that the intent of your *Pay for the Name* law? Pressure athletes and their mothers to sign a contract illegally before the law took effect?"

"Son, you said it for me. I wasn't there, Dr. Turkle was."

"But you stood to benefit, didn't you, Senator?" Cole took to the mic again. "Isn't it true that once CCC athletes start making endorsements they would be for the Wackenslong apparel brand? You and your co-conspirators at the college were creating a tidy monopoly before any other companies had a chance to cash in on the opportunities. An opportunity that would give your company a head start with other colleges in the region. Or we could say, you were doing what you could to make the family business great again."

From the back of the room, a man walked up behind Benny. He was rubbing his head, holding his eyeglasses in one hand. Benny smiled, patted him on the back, and stepped to the side.

"Let me shed some light on my supposed death. I'm Professor Cliff Singer."

The news cameras rolled and flashes exploded. "That person," Cliff turned and pointed at Turkle, "threatened my family. If I did not create an off-shore account, or if I told anyone that I did, he would see to it my family would be hurt. I have proof and so does the state's attorney's office."

Wackenslong and Turkle looked at one another. Cole broke the silence.

"Senator, you and your co-conspirators have injured a great many people. Why? Because you have the power? Partly. But what you have encouraged, or at least looked the other way on, was the premeditated assault on good people and their families. When I found out about the tragic death of both your daughter and your young grandchild some 25 years ago, my heart ached. I can only imagine the loss. Dr. Turkle is more than a business associate, isn't he? He's your former son-in-law who became your henchman. And Dr. Merlot, whom you first met years ago as a campaign intern, became his able assistant and your mistress." Then turning to the crowd and the reporters. "This is not fake news. The Marina Norte Shariff's Office and state attorney's office have all the evidence."

With that, Agents Little and Fish approached from the back of the room and handcuffed Wackenslong and Merlot while a third escorted Turkle from the room.

• • •

54

Joe filled the last champagne flute. Cole waved the group toward the bar and they each grabbed a glass. A lot had transpired in the week since the campaign rally confrontation.

"This is to you for all you had to endure. This is to you for your courage, fortitude, and resilience." He raised his tonic water-filled glass. "To you."

"Here, here!" And they toasted.

"And to you, Cole," Benny said, "you are the leader our faculty needed. Invisible no more!"

"Here, here!"

"Ah, that tastes so good." Benny smacked his lips. "Joe, another bottle of champagne. We need to toast the state's attorney's office and sheriff's office for moving quickly on this and arresting Bartley for ignoring the subpoena. Turkle, Merlot, and Wackenslong will face embezzlement, financial aid fraud, tampering with student-athlete endorsements, and who knows what else will turn up. I understand the Vice President for Finance has turned state's witness. And who knows what Bartley will say and do now."

Joe uncorked another bottle. "Oh, put that bottle on Professor Fitzgerald's tab," Benny suggested.

Everyone in the circle laughed for the first time in a long time.

Dominic Panagrossa had shepherded a winning vote for faculty unionization. A close vote, but a victory that just a month ago seemed implausible. "We still have a lot of work to do," he said, "but at least we will be able to slow the *mamalukes* down and make them accountable." He finished his champagne and placed the glass on the bar. "If you will excuse me, I have a date tonight. A table awaits at Gambardella's." He winked at Cole who raised his glass and toasted, "Who's better than us?"

The Board Chair tapped Lori Craig to be the Interim President and asked Eulonia to lead the presidential search committee. The Chair's charge to Eulonia, fittingly, ended with, "Professor Polonia, we trust under your guidance this committee will strain all the elephants from the string beans."

Benny's hand was healing toward a full recovery and he was back on campus doing what he loved best—teaching and connecting with his students.

Heather found out yesterday that the State Association of Broadcasters had nominated her to receive this year's Excellence in Broadcasting Award for her tenacious coverage of the college scandal.

She stepped forward. "I'm in awe of how you all stood up to the overwhelming odds against you. I don't know where to begin but since he stands in front of me, I'll start with you, Cliff."

Debbie hugged her husband's arm and pulled him close. She shuddered when she thought about how she might have lost him forever.

"After your 'suicide,'" Heather said, "you helped build and gather evidence against the quadrivium of evil. Not bad for a dead guy. I've never seen such courage."

"Debbie deserves the credit," Cliff said looking at his wife, "She kept me strong and focused. She's the one with courage."

"Well, I did have help." She looked with a sheepish grin toward Benny. "I couldn't have made it through this without you. Here's to Little Benjamin!"

Cole's head snapped back. "Little Benjamin?"

"Meet my 83-year-old Aunt," Benny laughed.

"Debbie was in the guest room that day I visited you?"

"Not really."

"I was." Cliff did a small wave of his hand. "And I was so glad you didn't want to meet the old lady."

"Wait." Heather pointed at Benny with one hand and Cliff with the other. "You two concocted Cliff's disappearance?"

"Had to. It was the only thing I could think of. Cliff was scaring the crap out of me. So that day when they found Cliff's kayak I was out there, too. Well, not on the water but waiting in the nature preserve."

"But the kayak was found back up the beach where you put in for the paddle." Cole was confused.

"Yeah, we planned that, too," Cliff said as he pushed up his glasses on his nose. "I hopped out to the south, at the preserve. The current runs to the north and it pulled the kayak back."

"Where it was found, reported to the police and press," Debbie added.

"I'm surprised you didn't figure that out sooner, Professor!" Benny said. Cole shook his head.

"It was the only thing I could think of," Benny continued, "to save Cliff from Turkle. And himself."

"Great plan but what about the police? They might not be pleased with this hide-and-seek," Lori added as she entered the room and joined the circle of celebration.

"Taken care of. You remember Roxie the drug-sniffing dog? We called her detective. And as a side note," Benny added, "might I mention that Roxie has more personality than her partner? Anyway, when Cliff explained, and showed evidence, about the off-shore account and explained how Turkle was threatening him, the humorless human proved most helpful."

"Benny saved my life. No doubt about it." Cliff sniffled and blinked his eyes. Debbie kissed his cheek.

They all raised their refilled glasses, clinked them together, and drank.

"And one more group," Cole said, "without whom, I'm not sure we could have had the results we did."

"The students!" they all said in unison.

"I wish they could have been here with us to celebrate," Lori said.

"They are!" Heather held up her phone. "I've brought the three of them in on a video call."

They all gathered to see Suzy, Kerwin, and Johnny V. They, too, were holding up a toast—coffee cups as they sat in Nico's Diner.

Lori squeezed to the front of the circle so the students could see her. "We have not met. I'm Lori Craig the Interim President of your college for the next few months. You three represent the hope of higher education, our college, and our community. Because of your bravery, you will be awarded a key to the city by the mayor at a ceremony in the near future. I will be in touch."

The three students howled from their booth and high-fived each other.

"Professor Fitzgerald, do you remember that first time you and I met in your office? Do you remember the four words you told me to write down?"

"Yes, I do, Suzy," Cole said with a wide smile as he, also, thought of his first meeting with Dr. Jim.

"Well, because of the faith you've shown in me—all of you have shown in me—for the first time in my life I can say 'Now is my time!' and know it's true. Thank you."

Heather squeezed Cole's hand and said, "This story, for me started when the three of you agreed to come on *The Facts and Fiction Hour.* I think you should do a return visit. My producer will be in touch."

The rest of the group shared their gratitude with the students and Heather disconnected.

"And one more announcement," Cole said. "At the end of this semester, I'm taking a sabbatical." He turned to Lori and said, "Thanks to the support of our new president."

"Interim President," Lori added with a smile.

"Like all of us standing here, this ordeal has brought me face-to-face with who I am and who I am not. I had lost contact with the guy I see in the mirror. I've come to realize that nothing on the outside will make me happy. That has to come from the inside.

"I'm sorry for dragging you along in my torment. The anger, mistrust, and lack of respect that I've projected on the administration, I'm coming to see, may well reflect my lack of trust in myself. To paraphrase a dear friend and mentor," Cole nodded to Lori, "I've spent too much time watching my back and now need to concentrate on following my heart."

Cole paused and looked at the friends standing in front of him.

"All of this has taught me that much of what I thought was important was window dressing. I've come to learn that the packaging is not important. What's inside the wrapping matters more."

Heads nodded in agreement.

"Eulonia and I have been meeting with some of the inner city community leaders. People who know what the residents—and therefore many of our students—need to move toward and embrace better and happier lives. My heart has been in the right spot. Eulonia will help to get my head there, too. She sends her best to everyone."

"I'm glad we have her to help keep the elephants out of the room!" Lori tipped her glass toward Cole.

"I still love teaching but, I need to get reacquainted with myself and where I want to go on the second half of this life journey. This semester, along with your friendship and patience, has helped me start that renewal process. I have a long way to go and will need more guidance."

He raised his glass. "And I love every one of you. I promise when I return from the sabbatical I'll be a better person to myself and you. Thank you all for believing in me. For enduring me. But more so, for seeing me."

"Does this mean I get to lead the band in your absence?" Benny slapped his good hand on the bar top and raised his eyebrows.

"I'm taking a sabbatical from the college, not the band, old man! Anyway, someone has to be around to make sure you don't go hog-tying any more customers."

"I love you, brother man," Benny said as he raised his glass.

Cole acknowledged Benny with a smile and nod of his head.

The group applauded and toasted one more time.

"As someone often said," Benny smiled, "this is incredibly extraordinary!"

Cole hugged Heather. "Yes, it is."

• • •

2:45 a.m. the following morning.

Cole slid out of bed without awakening Heather. He walked to the kitchen for a glass of water. He stood in the quiet of the condo and listened.

Silence.

Would it last?
Cole slid back to bed, smiling, and hopeful.

• • •

Acknowledgments

The quote attributed to John Severson can be found in *Surfer Magazine*, volume 1, issue 1, 1960.

The lyrics and music for "Weasels and Ferrets" are by Steve Piscitelli and appear on his CD *Same Tune, Different Song* (©2007).

The lyrics and music for "Voice in Your Ear" were written by Steve Piscitelli (©2020).

The words by the 13th-century poet Rumi can be found in "The Guest House."

About the Author

Hi, I'm Steve. Thank you for taking the time to read my latest book. While I have written fourteen previous books, *The Voice in Your Ear* is my first novel. To say this has been a learning experience is an understated cliché. Thank you for "taking a chance" on a first-time novelist. I appreciate your faith and support.

I retired from classroom teaching in 2015. My thirty-three years in the classroom saw me working and growing with middle school, high school, and college students. In addition, I was fortunate to work with audiences across the United States and Canada when I facilitated workshops and delivered keynote presentations.

I experienced how effective teachers, staff, and leaders connected with students and colleagues. These people helped me grow as a teacher and a person. The ineffective ones left their mark as well.

I live in Atlantic Beach, Florida, with my wife of forty-eight years, Laurie. I love where I live, with whom I live, and what I choose to do.

You can find more about me, my books, blog, videos, podcasts, and music at www.stevepiscitelli.com.

Grateful.